The Wheel

Farley Dunn

THREE SKILLET

THE WHEEL, Dunn, Farley L

First Edition

 THREE SKILLET

www.ThreeSkilletPublishing.com

ISBN 978-1-943189-00-7

For Levi . . . the real one.

Chapter 1

THE MAN awoke to water and mud.

He sat and spat, clawing his way to air, the iron of blood bleeding from his lips.

He leaped to his feet, forcing his legs into a run. He was tall, and with big hands. One held a gun, an old-fashioned gun. A slugthrower.

A bright blue light flashed in front of his eyes, hitting him in the chest, and he stumbled. The pain was real, and then it was gone. This war was red and black, filled with yellow flashes of pain and death. Not the blue of another world.

A horse galloped by, the sound that of gurgling flesh, a man's last grasp at life. Then another. Black, with muddied armor. A flag, long and pointed, flew from a tall pole.

He raised his hand, signaling. These were his men, and his horse lay dead, killed by exhaustion, enemy fire, or worse. His helmet, missing. Would his men know him?

It was the fifth or eighth or tenth man that stopped, he wasn't sure. It was there, and it stopped, and the horse turned in the mud, and the man saluted.

"Sir." The man threw out his hand.

He reached for it, to pull himself aboard. The moment of contact, skin-to-skin, took his breath away. It was like holding an electric dynamo, and it burned into him, filling his head with an inrush of knowledge. Soldiers killed. His field promotion to general. The military objective they must fulfill. And there was so much more. The man's name—Levi—they carried a shared past that went to West Point and beyond. His own name, though. He searched, certain he would find it, and it wasn't there.

Then the battle crashed around him once again, and he gasped with indrawn breath at the knowledge that was now his.

"Aboard, old friend. They never told us it was like this at the academy." Green eyes flashed against pale hair forming a halo under a metal helmet.

"They never do." He yelled his reply, pulling hard and swinging aboard, his weapon held high. The big animal jumped, leaping forward, and he wrapped an arm around the man's waist.

"They have machine guns. We didn't expect that." Levi had one hand on his helmet and the other on the reins. He nodded, looking to the back of the animal. "Took out half our men. There's an extra, sir."

"Extra?"

"In the bag." He tapped his helmet. "You're missing yours."

"Who are they?" That had not come through in the handshake. He reached to the saddlebag and pulled a helmet out, fastening it on his head, the motion of the horse fitting his body as if he and it were one.

"Ruskies, we think, sir. Fool communists." Levi spat the words. "Better we're dead than living under their foul breath."

"Don't cross your fingers." An image of a sun flashed in his mind, and a great long needle slipped soundlessly into its corona, the unheard screams of a million souls tearing at his gut. That wasn't here, though. That wasn't now. "There are worse things than being here, this day, this battle."

"Can't think what, sir, but if you say so." Levi half turned, and through the streaks of mud on his face, he grinned.

Something exploded nearby, and the horse reared. The light flashed, yellow and white, before going dark, and something fell into the mud at their feet. Neither soldier looked. The man with the big hands didn't have to. He felt the rage of the fallen comrade's death burn him inside, like a torch to his soul. He pictured a gun with a blue light, and it lanced into him from an unknown source a mile away. He shook his head. That wasn't real. This was real, the blood and the death, and the shells flying overhead.

The animal leaped a low wall and into a shallow stream. It smelled of the darkness from beyond which no man could return, and its color was more black than red. It roiled with death, and soon it would carry more.

A rattle of a distant gun, and the man just in front of them screamed. The man's mount stumbled, and with a twist of its head, it lay still.

"The stars above!" The tall soldier gasped. His stomach wrenched him sideways, the two deaths double the fire.

"Can you make it, sir?" Levi spurred the horse. "We'll be safe in another hundred feet."

"Sure." The noise surrounding them was deafening, and he leaned and yelled, "My name. What's my name?"

He didn't get his answer. It was the next shell that took them down. It whistled, calling, and he knew it had his number. The wheel was turning once again, and his time had come.

It was mud at first. All mud, and the stench of sulfur. And horse dung, the odor of death mixed with life. Then came the white light, blinding him to all else. White and red and blue. Not the blue from before, but the blue from now, from this world, from this existence. It was the blue of a sky overhead that knew no war, no flying machines, no satellites, and no death raining down from silver needles; no black beetles and no unseen enemies worse than the tales from men's imaginations.

And last of all, it was black. The noise of his impending death exploded in his ears. He had one last thought, that he wished he'd learned his name.

Finally, it reached deep into his soul, and with the wrench of an uncaring fist, it twisted his life from him, leaving him motionless in the mud.

Chapter 2

"THIS is him. Ser!" The soldier, fresh with his deacon's stripes, knelt in the mud, turning over the dead body wearing the general's uniform. "The markings on the collar. I'm sure this is him."

He wiped it clean, and sure enough, there were two stars.

"Check the arm." Another man in a crisper uniform touting a bishop's oak leaf stepped to his side. His tall boots were spattered with mud and blood, but his clothes were unmarked. Off to the side stood four blank-eyed soldiers, perhaps men, and perhaps something else. When the uniform moved, the blankeyes watched him, as if they were under his control.

"A minute, ser." The soldier pulled out a tool with a mean edge, and he flicked a switch. A blue light flickered along the business edge, and it cut through the wool uniform like butter. The soldier yanked the material away, exposing an arm bruised and shredded in a number of places. On the forearm was a tattoo of a wheel. "This is it, ser."

The crisp uniform knelt and traced the design with an outstretched finger, the whorls of steel and springs; dreams and starlight; spiderwebs and dust. And pain. Always the pain.

"Can you read it, ser?"

"Here. It's different than last time." He pointed to one spoke that swirled off to a constellation of points. "Perhaps . . ." He appeared thoughtful. "Did you find the transfer capsule?"

"One minute." The soldier dug through the man's uniform, locating something in an inside pocket. "Here, ser. He had it with him all the time." He held up a silver stick, slender, with a gleam that seemed to wink before going dark.

"Never got to use it. Pity. We might have found him and stopped this, then." The crisp uniform took the stick, wrapping it in his hand protectively.

"Shall I?" The first man held up the cutter.

"Take the skin." The uniform nodded. "We'll need it for our report."

The blue light flashed, and the deed was done.

Chapter 3

DREAMS had been dreamed, and the omens had rung true. The dreamer's dream was contained.

A table as large as a room glowed with red light, and in the center, all the possibilities of creation swirled with multicolored patterns.

A voice screeched, "The dreams are changing. Call the dreamers to attend! The dreamer becomes undreamed!"

And the table was touched, and the possibilities swirled within.

Chapter 4

BLACK and oil extended the breadth of the cosmos and beyond. Beneath its glittering surface, a metallic gleam flashed for a moment and disappeared, consumed by liquid night once again.

In the distance, something moved. A shift, bare and small, as if forgotten. Never there, except in someone's dreams.

Stardust sprinkled across the cosmos, a spiderweb of faint light, with little more than the memory of dust for its underpinnings. A thousand races died, and in their places, a thousand more were born.

A giant finger the width of a star system stretched forth, and a pointed nail touched the night just where the spiderweb of light had left the faintest trail of stardust.

The oil moved, sluggish against the fabric of time, and then it settled into the black of the night once again.

Chapter 5

A DARKNESS as wide as the universe collapsed in on itself, and the man's eyes opened. Someone breathed at his side. He turned, and a name formed in his mind. Sundra. And with the name, he knew their two children, the flitter parked on the roof, the time he'd stolen her kiss at the university, and the way she'd moved against him the night before their son was born.

He was a mystery, though. He didn't know himself at all. A blank slate. Unknown and unnamed. A cipher in the void of space and time.

He remembered the noise, though. And the mud flavored with blood.

He took a deep breath, wishing the smells and the sounds away. He wanted what he had this night, not that world so far away. He wanted to be next to his woman, greet his children in the morning, and feel their arms around his neck.

He also wanted to know his name.

He closed his eyes, certain the rest would come. The rest would always come.

He turned to Sundra, wrapping a strong arm across her firm waist, and against the gentle rise and fall of her back, he fell asleep once again.

"DADDY!" The door crashed open, and brilliant sunlight flooded the room.

In that one word, a hundred images fell into his brain, each neatly clicking into its assigned slot. Levi and Caitlan, bike rides in the park, a third birthday party with candles that refused to go out, and a long boat ride up the river, holding his sleeping daughter the entire way back.

He didn't need a memory to know what happened next.

Four pajama-clad feet leaped onto the bed, mischievousness filling two pairs of eyes. The girl was light, boasting blue eyes and golden hair. The boy, taller, was nearly a twin, with white hair and green eyes.

"So, that's how it's going to be. I'm home one day, and I'm already under attack!" One day. How did he know that? He laughed, grabbing at the boy. "And how old are you, Levi?"

His son's age. Why was that important?

"Eleven!" The boy squealed as fingers dug into his ribs. "No, Daddy! Stop!"

"I can't stop." He upped the ante, bringing louder peals from the boy, as he glanced at Sundra. She had a pillow bunched in her arms, for protection, he figured. In that moment, he saw small feet kicking, and he knew they'd done this before. "Afraid, Sundra?" He grinned.

"It's always like this the morning you get back." She leaned in and gave him a quick peck on the cheek. "Thank you for coming early."

"Early?" He frowned, but Caitlan wanted some of what Levi had, and he had to tuck her under his arm. He was lucky she was smaller. She was easier to control.

"For Levi's birthday."

He was hit with a cacophony of memories, forced into his brain like a deluge down a drain pipe. In that moment he saw three missed birthdays, a flood of tears, and angry words with Sundra on the link. He also knew she hadn't spoken with him for three days the last time, and that he was trading three weekends on the station for this one day home. That was not cool at all.

"Daddy! Come see!" Levi rolled off the bed, taking much of the bedding with him, and he grabbed his father's arm. "Come, Daddy! Come see!"

"What?" He glanced at his wife. "Sundra?"

"Don't look at me." She smiled, an expression of true pleasure.

"It's all Levi's doing. I didn't even have to help much. Just go." She pushed on his arm.

"Can I go too, Mommy?" That was Caitlan. She had her arms around Sundra's neck, and she was twisted in what remained of the bedding.

"In a moment, baby. It's Levi's birthday."

"I want a birthday." Her face screwed up, and her eyes turned red.

"You'll get one. It's just not your time." Sundra looked at the man with pleading in her eyes.

He grabbed Levi in his arms, and he pulled him back on the bed. He was that soft and hard that made up eleven-year-olds, the stomach and the knees and the ribs and the fingers. And he smelled good, like a fresh puppy just from a bath. The man leaned into Sundra, and he whispered, "First, tell me my name."

"Daddy!" Caitlan sang the word out. "That's your name."

"Daddy doesn't know his name." Levi barely got the words out, before he squealed in delight once more, his mock agony at being shaken no more than part of the special day.

"Go on." Sundra laughed, bumping her forehead against his. "It hasn't changed."

"Humor me." He gave her a kiss, catching the side of her mouth, and letting the boy slip away from him. "Just say it to me."

"Slate. Slate Knalb, of course. What else would it be?"

The storm drain opened wider, and the world fell into his head. The shuttle, the rebreather that had cut out on him two years ago, and the six weeks in the tank, just to regrow one lung. And Bren. Could anything worse happen! Bren, when they were eighteen, killed in the Packing Wars, the pointless, pointless Packing Wars. And there was so much more, and, and—

He knew his name.

Slate. Always Slate.

And always, always losing everything in the end.

He shook it off. That wasn't now, and it was now he had to live. "You!" He pointed to Levi, who was leaning in and motioning him through the door, tempting Slate with giggles and a gleam in his eye. "You wait, you little trickster."

"Can't catch me," Levi yelled, and he was gone.

"Can't catch him, Slate." Sundra leaned in and gave him a kiss. "But you'd better try." She laughed, pushing him away. "Today belongs to your son."

"It does, does it?" He leaped up, grabbing a pair of heavy, belted pants draped across the back of a chair, and he hopped into one leg as he stumbled out the door. He blinked, his breath taken away, as he exited the room. The hallway was glass, wall, floor, and ceiling, the reason for the brightness. It brought on a crippling vertigo that was there and gone before he could catch his breath. Outside was nothing. Truly nothing. He looked back. "What . . . what floor?"

"203rd. Slate, we've lived here for three years."

"Three years?" He laughed, pulling his second leg on and glancing back outside. "Maybe we should move higher. Where is here?"

"Don't start. You're the one who chose St. Louis Tower." She lay back, her nightgown gaping at the front, apparently aware of what she was doing. "And you know why we're stuck on this floor."

And he did. Not before, but in her words, it hit him like an elevator turned loose from its moorings. The investments lost in the Crash, the savings wiped out, even Levi's private schooling gone. It was why he worked the station. Then, the cost of the third child they'd hoped to have. The permit. For the price of one child permit you could move up another hundred floors.

"Any chance of Trey?" He snapped the belt shut.

"Are we about to PowerBall?"

"Daddy?" The call filtered hard against the glass.

"Go!" She threw a pillow at him. "One day. Don't waste it." She pulled her daughter up under her arm.

"Coming!" He yelled it. "This better be good." He looked back at Sundra, then pointed to Caitlan. "You, lady, mind your mother." He laughed when she stuck her tongue out at him. Then he was off and running.

Chapter 6

IT WAS the third time around the air suspension part of the track that caused the crash.

"You are dead, Levi!" Slate leaped out of his remote beam and fell into the secondary beam with his son. Of course, with two drivers, the beam fragmented, and Levi's arc car skittered into a sun, collapsing into a flaming ball of light.

"Daddy! No!" But by that time, the boy was in Slate's hands, and the game was shot anyway.

"Gotcha, Levi." He rolled onto the sofa with the boy, pressing his face into his neck to blow just below his ear. He hadn't known to do that, but as soon as he did, he remembered how it made Levi wet his pants. He used to do it to him just to make him scream.

"No! Not that!" Levi twisted loose, just as the game holo faded away, slipping into the shadows, and the living room and the view through the wall of glass returned. "Daddy! Anything but that!"

Slate pulled the boy up under him, one hand under his head, the hair damp with sweat, and he whispered in his ear, "You're mine, Levi. I can do anything I want." As he bent to blow on his neck a second time, the building shivered, and they froze.

"Daddy?" Levi, warm and perspiring from the game, pulled Slate's arms around him tighter, twisting up into his father's embrace. "It never did that before."

18

"Shush for a minute. Let me listen." He caught Sundra coming in off the glass hallway. She held Caitlan in her arms.

"Slate—"

He pulled one hand from under Levi and held it out. "I need to listen." He whispered the words.

And there it was. A grinding sound, low, like stone on steel, with just a hint of a whine to give it an edge. Like Bren the night before he died, said he heard sounds, and no one listened.

"Slate?" echoed by Caitlan's, "Daddy?" Both were whispered, and still, the sound was harsh in the silence of the room.

"Stay, Levi." Slate disentangled his body from the boy's, pressing on his chest to hold him on the sofa. "Don't move."

"Where are you going, Daddy?" Concern flashed in the boy's eyes.

"Don't you worry. Eleven-year-olds don't have to worry on their birthdays. That's the one day their daddies take special care of them." Slate smiled, and he made sure it was warm and reassuring. "I love you, son."

"I love you too, Daddy."

The boy's breath was warm on Slate's face, and that frightened him. Bren's breath had been like that. Bren. Slate's big hands felt the boy's small ribs, and he leaned to kiss him on the forehead. Then he stepped away.

"Sundra, away from the windows." He took her arm, gave his daughter a kiss, and watched them walk to sit by Levi. He was pleased to see his son take his wife's hand. She was a good woman and a wonderful mother. She would take care of his children. He didn't know why he thought that, but he knew it was important. She would. She would have to.

He stepped into the hallway, looking down. Covering the face of the building, other hallways snaked across the surface of the structure, some clear, more in jewel tones, others patterned in pulsing lights. Some showed people walking, most clothed, some not. Privacy was by mutual consent, not by mutual exclusion. If you didn't want to look, then don't. Otherwise . . .

That wasn't what he searched for.

The ground. It was there, barely, the morning mists from the river sweeping across the landscape. There was no city. In that look, that sweeping look, he knew the hundred stories underground where the shopping malls stretched into the virgin bedrock, and even deeper where the machines fabricated air and water and reprocessed nutrients to grow food in vast underground caverns. It was a hundred kays before there was another scraper like this one, three hundred fifty stories of life and heat and love and families and all the things that make up a person's existence.

The world, green as far as the eyes could see. The hundred-kay greenbelts, humanity's gift to the future. Let the world heal, and humanity would heal, also.

Except the stations. And the Packing Wars. And Bren.

By all that was good, the stations were worse than death. But then, the Crash had been the same, and he would work in a sour pit, just so that his family didn't have to live there. He'd made that decision long ago, and he'd sworn never to regret it. Mostly he didn't. Mostly.

Today? Yeah, he regretted it. Levi, sweat-damp hair, and building that game just to play with his daddy. And Caitlan. More than anything, he missed Caitlan when he was gone, never mind how much he missed Sundra. Sweet, sweet Sundra, sweet even when she yelled at him and made him sleep on the sofa. He loved that woman more than, than, than what he gave up working on the station. His life. Yeah, that's what he gave up, the weeks and months he was away from his family.

The building shook again. He placed his hand against the glass, feeling it vibrate.

"Sundra, get the kids dressed. We're going out for the day." He kept his hand on the glass. The grinding wasn't louder, but it shouldn't be there at all.

"Okay."

Her voice was very bright, and he looked at her. Her voice was too bright, and that was when he knew she understood. Bad things were happening. Very bad things.

"Levi?" Slate stepped to the boy and swept him up in his arms. Eleven was big. Big to hold very long. "How 'bout some clothes? Warm, too. Might go to the Falls." He set him down, patting him on the rear. "Go, now. I want to leave yesterday." He watched him scramble away, no sound, no voice, no agreement. Just going. Slate took a deep breath.

"The Falls? It'll be cold." Sundra put her hand to the side of his face.

"Dress warm. Caitlan, especially. I'll get food."

"Food? You don't think . . ."

"A picnic. That's all." He smiled. He could see it in her eyes,

20

though. He wasn't fooling anyone. "A picnic, Catie? Would you like that?" He kissed her cheek, blowing a raspberry. She brushed his face away.

"Can it be my birthday, too?"

"Of course it can, sweetie. It can be your birthday, too." Sundra kissed her on the temple on the way out of the room. "It can be your birthday every day of the year."

Slate's stomach was a rock. He wanted to smash his fist into the day, make it back to what it was supposed to be. Instead, what did he do? Grabbed a satchel and began dropping in all the food he could find. He wasn't exactly sure why, but he wasn't leaving anything edible behind.

That's what Slate did, hoping his world wouldn't fall apart.

GETTING to the flitter was more work than it should have been. More nightmare, perhaps, was a better way to say it.

It was a straight shot to the parking levels, express from the 203 Station. Every floor had an express, even if you had to sometimes wait on it because another floor had commandeered the core track. Still, the wait was never long, not with the inertia dampers and MagThrust. This time, Slate didn't think they were the only ones headed out. That caused backup. It didn't cause the electrics to wobble, though, the lights blinking just enough to know they blinked.

That was something else.

"Slate? Are we going to make it?" Sundra had a backpack on, and Caitlan rode one hip. Sundra's tweedies were lined with llama, one of the few breeds that did well enough in the wild to harvest, and then, just their fleece. It was a good choice. Her top? Full false down, the kind that was flat enough to be a shirt, but warm enough to bake you if you stayed inside too long. Better choice.

"Hope so." Slate looked at Levi, glued to him like a third leg, the boy's arms around him. He caught his wife's eyes, and he changed his answer. "Yeah. We're heading on a picnic, right, Levi?" He rumpled the boy's hair, the texture soft like Sundra's.

"I wanna see the waterfall." Caitlan had her head on Sundra's shoulder, and she buried her face in her mother's hair.

"It'll be the best day ever." Slate would have taken her, just to hug her in his arms, but he had a backpack of his own, and a duffle besides. "Think so, pal?" He bumped Levi with his hip.

Best as Slate could remember, that was the first of the real hiccups. The lights blinked, really fast, like they were as scared as Slate was, and they came back on as fast. He might not have noticed if he weren't in step-up mode already. He looked at Sundra to see if she'd caught it. Yeah, she was already looking at him, a question in her eyes.

"It'll be fine," he mouthed to her, his words invisible. Then the car jerked, faltered, more like, and began to pick up speed again. He took a deep breath and pulled Levi closer. If that were possible.

There were eight levels of parking. Not enough for the whole building, of course, but that wasn't part of the design. Most people didn't keep a private flitter; didn't have one or only leased a share. Out one day a week, you only needed one-seventh interest. It was a practical solution to a practical problem.

Slate needed one on a regular basis, the only good thing about the station. They paid the lease. It was the company's on the station, but his when he was home. Thank God.

"In." He tossed his duffle in the undercompartment, reaching for Sundra's backpack before tossing in his own. "Now, Catie."

"Do as your father says." It wasn't cold in the garage, but Sundra pulled her collar tighter. It looked like she shivered.

"Thanks, Levi." Slate took a slim package from the boy, cringing to see it was a wrapped present. He hadn't even gotten to open it. He slipped it in with the bags.

"For the Falls, right, Dad?" Levi smiled tentatively. "We can open it there."

"You got it." He nodded. "In the back, please. Now."

Other people were loading up, all across Level 5, and he wanted to be gone. The urgency? Something thrummed in the back of his head, and Bren kept knocking in his brain. Knock, knock. Slate? It's me, Bren, and I'm coming home.

Whatever that meant.

The floor shivered. He climbed in and palmed the screen. It glowed green, and when he released it, the green turned into a nebula, then coalesced into the StiRik logo, a feathered loop around a stylized letter R. He'd been told it looked a bit like a DNA strand caught in a tornado. The systems began to come online, air and lights, with the gentle beat of a muted rezband in the background. The seats self-adjusted, and the windows cleared, transparent in the muted lights of the garage.

"Welcome, Slate. I see you are initiating travel today." A carefully modulated voice spoke. "This is not an official day of work.

22

Where shall I plan your destination?"

"The Falls. Right?" Sundra.

"Is the Falls an acceptable destination, Slate? I can integrate Sundra's prompts into my permissions file for the day. Travel time is one hour forty-three minutes, with a seven-minute delay. The egress ramps are already backed up. This seems to be a popular excursion day."

"Integrate and negotiate. I want out quicker." Slate looked at Sundra, only to have her bite her lip and turn away. It was the redness in her eyes that told how she felt.

"Negotiations may require credit disbursement. How much—"

"Just do it, any level."

"Negotiations commenced. Egress slot confirmed. Cost—"

"Unimportant. How long?" He glanced back at the kids, the internal ESyst already up and attempting to entertain them. Caitlan was tossing a virtual ball back and forth in her hands. Levi was holding a lemur, all nanodust and lumens made real, and it was licking his face. He laughed and looked like the rush to board was forgotten.

"Thirteen seconds. Initiating electrics now with turbines coming online." The flitter began to move, and quite rapidly, although the buildup of speed was so smooth it was hardly noticed. They were still, and then they were jettisoned toward the egress ramp, internal inertia dampers doing just that, and slotting in with computer efficiency, shooting from the building exactly thirteen seconds later.

Sunlight slashed through the flitter, and immediately, the canopy silvered, cutting the glare. The whine of the turbines bled through, with just a hint of oil and hot metal, then the sound rose out of the audible range, and things were silent.

"Just a trip to the Falls, right?" Sundra reached for his hand. "For Levi's birthday."

"Mine, too." That was Caitlan.

"Right, Slate?" Sundra reached to his face, stroking his cheek on one side. "For both of them?"

He swiveled his seat and grabbed Caitlan's ball. "Right, Catie, if you can convince your brother to share." He tossed the ball to her, reaching to pet Levi's lemur. "Nice, job, Levi. When did you create this one?"

"Just now. Want to hold it?" He held the creature out.

"I told you he's good." Sundra nodded. "Real good."

The flitter vibrated, and Slate looked up, past the ball, the lemur, and the inside of the flitter. He looked for their residence. St. Louis Tower should still be visible, what with the clear day. Ground fog didn't affect nearly a kay up.

Also. The system hadn't put out a turbulence warning. The vehicle shouldn't have done that.

He felt his stomach churn, then something hit him, like a sledge-hammer in his gut. He took a deep breath and held it, but the pain didn't fade. It was like . . . Bren. Like Bren, all over again.

The dash dinged, and a private ear popped up from its recess. It sat cupped in an orange ring of light. Slate took it and slipped it into his ear.

"Tell me." Sundra looked at him hard. "I want to know."

Slate nodded and put his finger to his lips, listening. He kept the ear low, always, with the kids. Anything that came in over the private channel was something they didn't need to hear. He suspected this wasn't good. Too many omens today.

He depressed the orange ring, and the tiny voice in his ear started up.

"Flitter SLT682. Flight Plan 473.6 St. Louis Tower, destination Niagara Falls, validated and in progress. NorAm Logistics and Routing will be redirecting your return trip to Chicago Tower. Temporary housing is under negotiation. Confirmation expected shortly." The voice went quiet, leaving a dull buzz in Slate's ear.

Slate held his finger in the orange depression until the ear beeped. "Explanation?"

"St. Louis Tower unresponsive. Reason unknown. Confirmation received Chicago Tower."

He sighed, his finger still in the orange. "Cost?" Chicago Tower was very toney. It would eat up a lot of credit reserves very quickly. Anything decent, anyway. Anything affordable would be a bunker unit at worst; an atrium climber at best. Neither would offer a view of outside, and that was not acceptable.

"St. Louis Tower malfunction necessitates mandatory redirection, and all costs are reimbursable per insurance contract Provision 144.b, courtesy of State Tower Insurance Company, Policy Number 213-4HH-246-04."

"Slate?" Sundra pushed on his leg.

He released the orange button for a moment. "We're redirected to Chicago tonight. Insurance is covering it."

"That's good, right? Free lodging?" She smiled and looked more at ease. "Our insurance dollars at work?"

He laughed. "If they'll give us an outside unit."

"I don't think purgatory plans to freeze over by the time we get there. But, you never know."

He smiled and pushed the orange light again. "Negotiate. Outside room, State Tower Policy whatever you said a minute ago." He looked at Sundra and chuckled.

"Lodging confirmed. Outside room 96F."

"No higher?" He hated low floors. Sometimes acid rain etched the glass, and that obscured the views.

"Floors 76-99 are surcharge free within your contract, Provision 144.e. Would you care to renegotiate?"

"No. 96F will be fine. Oh, how many baths?"

"One private within unit, one communal for Level 96, shared by keycode chip broadcast, Level 96 only."

"Satisfactory. Initiate contract. Stock supplies within Provision 144.e limits."

"Contract published and filed, per Chicago Tower and NorAm Public Housing Authority."

"Logging off." He waited for the response. It was impolite to log off before the system cleared you from contact. And he suspected they recorded each impolite disconnect.

"Thank you, Flitter SLT682. Enjoy your day at the Falls."

He released the circle, looking at Sundra.

"I heard enough. Thank you for requesting supplies. I'll be too tired to fill out a requisition tonight." She smiled. "It'll be a vacation for the kids. Time off from school. They've needed that."

He smiled back. *He* needed a vacation. It was the thousand needles in his stomach that worried him, though. It had happened before, when Bren died. He'd known, even before the reports came in. Like a fist to his solar plexus, the kind that makes you want to roll over and vomit.

That's what he wanted to do now, a thousand times over.

Something really bad was going on. He just didn't know what.

Chapter 7

THE SPRAY lashed Slate's face, and it *was* cold. But then, at the Falls, it was never really warm, not anymore. It was too far north, too near the new permafrost layers that had driven the old Canadian monarchy into coalescing with the States and OldMex to form the NorAm Union. He hadn't known that before stepping into the spray, but he knew it now, as surely as if he'd known it all his life.

At least inside the Falls Tube he'd be dry.

"C'mon, Catie!" He laughed as she batted at the spray, even as she tried to bury her face against his neck. "You always love this!" He swung her around, only to cause her to grab him more tightly.

"Want inside." Her muffled voice seeped out.

"Yeah, Dad. Let's go faster!" Levi grabbed his arm, his orange wetsuit, little more than a slicker, really, and very old fashioned, hanging loose at the waist. Levi had a wet streak down his shirt and pants, because he refused to snap the buckles. "I want to look for fish."

Sometimes they saw them, too, caught in eddies that formed where the Tube nestled against the rock surface. Then the force of the water would scoop them out, and they'd shoot away. They still had a holo of one that had stayed almost five minutes, gaping at them as they laughed and pointed, its too-intelligent eyes telling of a self-awareness that hadn't been there before the Sino-EcoDisaster that had forced the world to retreat into its massive city towers.

Sundra ran past them, the rented slicker in her hands rather than on her shoulders.

"I'll take one of those!" Slate yelled after her, his arm raised to flag her down.

"One of what?" She tucked under a canopy at the entrance to the Tube, shaking water off the slicker. "It's colder than I remember. I should have put this on."

"You have a coat, Daddy." Caitlan. "You can't wear two." She'd begun to rock with her mother's appearance. "Want down, Daddy."

He let her slide out of his arms, as Sundra called to him, laughing. "You didn't answer me." She held the slicker to him. "This?"

"You." He was close enough he leaped to her and wrapped her in a hug, his arms around her, enjoying the wetness of her hair, and remembering the last time they'd showered together. "Right now." His lips found her neck, only to feel her push him away.

"Birthday. Kids." She whispered the words in his ear.

"So?" It was this moment, and he wanted to soak it up. Like it was the last time for everything.

"That's how they got here, remember? And we've got them for another fifteen years."

"You mean I have to wait fifteen years?"

"Wait for what, Daddy?" That was Caitlan.

"To kiss. You're such a baby." Levi put her in her place, as he sloughed his own slicker off. "Mommy and Daddy like to do that."

"Don't want to watch." She shivered.

"That's right, and you shouldn't want to watch. Thank goodness." Sundra cupped the girl's face in her hand. "That's a mommy and daddy thing. For private."

Another group came down the walk, four people, one walking backward and laughing, motioning with his hands, the others with heads ducked and peering out of their slickers.

Slate gestured. "They could take a lesson from you. A little water never hurt anyone." He dropped his own slicker as they pressed under the canopy, pulling Levi in as the group crowded through the doors.

"Sorry, guy." The laughing man bumped into Slate, clapping him on the shoulder as he caught himself, and pushing away with an apologetic smile. "Women. Don't want to get wet. I should come to the Tube with three women."

"No bother. My kids." He pointed with a grin, making that connection, how they were the same. "Glad to have 'em with me."

"You're lucky." The man was at the door, the last one of the group to step through. "Hey, kids, enjoy your vacation. See you later." He waved and was gone.

Sundra helped Caitlan out of her wetsuit, folding the slicker into itself for use when they came out the other end. "You know him?" She looked at Slate and nodded at the door.

"Why?" His own folded, he put a hand to Levi's suit. "Too many people, too small a space. Friendly enough, though."

"Careless, if you ask me." She stood, taking Levi's slicker. "The logo, here. Did you notice?" She indicated her collarbone.

Slate turned to the door, but naturally, they were long gone. Caitlan was chattering, and of course, Levi had begun to pull Sundra forward. Slate shrugged. It was just a bump, and things like that happened. An apology had been exchanged, no offense was taken, and the other group was gone. He'd thought nothing of it.

"It was Chicago Tower. The logo. And why'd he call this a vacation?" The kids ran ahead, the Tube cutting directly under the Falls. Farther in, and there was a switchback leading to the underground shopping kiosks and eating arenas, but that was a good twenty-minute walk. They wouldn't get lost, not in here. Besides, there was a gaming display that Levi was never able to pass up. If nowhere else, he would land there.

"It's the Falls. Of course it's a vacation. You recognized his logo? You are sharp." He laughed, but he also tried to think what the Chicago Tower logo was, and for a moment he was mystified. Today, the information he'd needed had just been there. And he'd accepted it. Why not this?

"We met there, remember? My parents . . ."

She didn't finish, but with those words, his mind filled up with warm and welcoming people, a two-story top-floor unit—only in Chicago Tower!—and the embarrassment of thinking Sundra was another girl he'd met, and introducing himself to her parents with a false identity. He'd told the other girl he was lead in a rezband—SpikedHornedLizards, the most outrageous name he could come up with on the spot—because he desperately wanted to suck up to her father, head of MLabel Recording. He'd even had his hair painted with luminescent rezfoil. Sundra's father? BioMetric Chip Enhancement. For weeks after, he was forced to produce a rezguitar when he visited. He hadn't known Sundra had a much younger brother who thought the rez scene was the only one on the planet.

And he'd worn the rezfoil the whole time.

They'd even attended a rez concert together at the pinnacle of the Tower, 40,000 preteens jumping up and down to the flashing lights, olfactory scents, and throbbing gyrations of performers painted bright pink and gold underneath the glittering sparkles of a laser cloudshow. Slate didn't remember seeing another adult in the whole window-roofed hall.

"And they were—" He remembered this part, too, as it came crashing in with the rest.

"I don't want to cry." Sundra reached to her eyes. "Not on Levi's birthday." She nodded toward the kids far ahead of them, their voices muted, obviously involved in the games. Just having a good time. Jackal Cry. That was one of Levi's favorites.

Sundra's parents. Young, still, for healthy adults in this day and age. It had been flitter burn. It was a quick way to go. Quick and painful. It wasn't so infrequent as to be unusual, and it never happened in the lower latitudes, but this close to the frozen wastes that made up the old Canadian heartland, winter sometimes had a catastrophic effect. Static charges in the cold of winter's extremely dry air and a thousand meters in elevation meant nature didn't have to take no for an answer. Flitter burn was just that, a static discharge from the flitter to a cloud, and often right back, cloud to flitter. Only thing was, at that height, the static discharge was invariably deadly. If you got flitter burn, you roasted.

"You're right. Not on Levi's birthday." He put his arm across her shoulders and pulled her tight. His other hand went into his pocket, coming out with a slender silver stick. He held it up, looking at it. The Falls Tube was self-lighted—engineered bioluminescent lifeforms installed on the outside of the transparent walls—and the light was shadowy due to the crash of the water tumbling over and all around them. It would be darker in the dead of winter. When the Falls froze, the lifeforms barely glowed, and the Tube was a romantic destination for lovers. Now, the light was a dappled blue green. The silver stick winked, as if imbued with an internal power source.

"Holo stick?" Sundra reached for it, turning it over in her hand. It sparkled once, then went quiet.

"Don't know." And he really didn't.

"Come, now. It was in your pocket. For Levi?" She smiled. "We left his present in the flitter, you know."

He reached in his jacket, pulling out the wrapped box. "Nope. But that," and he pointed with the box to the silver stick, "is a total mystery to me."

"So," and she glanced back to the entrance, now no longer visible. "That man. Not a pickpocket, I guess. Maybe a putpocket?"

"Dunno." He grinned, taking the stick. They were at the games area, and he slipped it back into his pocket. He saw Levi finishing up a game, and as he jumped out of the remote beam, the boy hooted and pumped a fist in the air.

"Did you see that, Dad?" He yelled it across the room. His voice echoed against the unfinished bedrock ceiling.

"Do you see this?" Slate held the present overhead and yelled back. "Someone has a birthday, and I want to see what's inside." He acted as if he were looking under the wrappings and would tear it apart within moments.

Sundra smiled.

"Can I open it, Daddy?" Caitlan, bringing a laugh from the two adults.

"No, baby. It's your brother's." Sundra grabbed her hand.

Levi was more emphatic. "No, Dad! Don't! I want to open it!"

"Finders keepers! Nine-tenths says I get to pop the package!"

Just before Levi reached to grab it, Slate tucked it in his jacket and took off running, a game of chase on, his legs outpacing his son's, two to one.

He did get taken down, though. He got distracted, and that was the precise moment Levi gave the chase all he had. The culprit? The man and three women from the Falls earlier, walking along the Tube, three heads in deep conversation and one up and laughing.

The odd thing was, they weren't admiring the Falls. Not even looking at them. Now, their actions were practiced; mechanical and rehearsed; with flesh for bodies, and computers for brains. Like the man was a laughing automaton, and the women were discussing the next day's agenda. Rather like the Falls were old news to them, so they weren't important, instead of one of the biggest vacation attractions in a hundred kays.

Now, what made him think that? Whatever it was, it caused Levi to take down his father, and he grabbed his arm and sat on him.

"Got ya', Dad!" Levi grabbed at his coat, and the silver stick clattered to the floor. The boy reached for it. "What's this?"

"Don't know. Let me have it." Slate went for it also, but Levi was quicker.

"Trade." Levi leaped up, holding it over his head. "Stick for present. Give it up." He danced with excitement. Caitlan had reached them, and she began dancing also, leaping for the silver stick.

"Okay! Okay!" Slate pulled the gift from his jacket and held it up. "You win."

It did seem that the stick glimmered at him as he reached for it, just a wink of light. Slate glanced around to find something bright enough to reflect off the stick. There was nothing. As Levi tore the package open, Sundra leaned in to whisper, "I saw it, too."

Then Levi leaped and yelled, "I got it! A holo imager! Just what I wanted!" He held the flat device over his head, waving it back and forth.

"Us?" Slate stood and pulled Sundra close. "Take one."

"All you do—" Sundra started.

"I know, Mom. I'm eleven. Say cheese."

For the rest of the day, holo images of everything they saw followed the family through the Tube. Of course, they weren't really holos, more like nanodust woven together by interactive nanolumens. The holo imager, a simplified and portable version of the ESyst unit in the flitter, had evolved from the simple hologram, and the name, although now woefully inadequate, had stuck.

Even fish swam along after them, lighted by the imager, small creatures that would remain alive until the activated nanolumens faded into the night.

Chapter 8

"NAH! I don't think we should look at it. It's nothing, I bet."
Slate held the silver trinket in his hand, watching the glow from the
flitter's dim interior lights gleam along its surface. The kids were
asleep in their compartment, sectioned off from the front of the
cabin.

"What do you mean, nothing? Here, let me." Sundra took it,
laughing, and she opened the holo viewer. "I've never seen a holo
emitter this shape before, but I'm sure that doesn't matter."

"It doesn't. It's the compatibility matrix that's important." Slate
pushed her hand away. He wasn't sure he wanted to see.

It had become a joke between them. The mysterious stranger,
bringing secret news of St. Louis Tower; or Publisher's Marketing
Network's latest drawing, the winner delivered in a new and
unusual manner. They could be rich, in theory.

Slate leaned back in the seat, pulling his wife's hand into his.
The canopy was clear in the cold night air.

"Think of all the stars out there." It was a distraction from the
little cylinder, and he knew it. "You know, humanity has never
reached a one. Not in the thousands of years we've been here.
We've never made a home for us out there."

"Why would we want to?" Sundra laid the stick on the console
between them. The intake diaphragm, not accessed, had already

irised closed. "No air. No life. What would be the point?"

"How do you know?" He rubbed the skin on the back of her hand absently. The mother of his children. His lifelong companion, even if there were big gaps he couldn't remember. That didn't bother him much, though. Just because there were holes didn't mean he hadn't lived those holes. They just hadn't come to him, yet.

And he couldn't miss what he didn't remember. Could he? He didn't even *know* to miss those lost parts of his life.

"What about that ship?" She looked up at the stars, answering his question, her eyes partially closed, and her irises big under dark lashes. "You remember. The Cassiopeia."

In that word, he did, the thirteen years of construction, planting the fusion thruster inside a nickel-iron asteroid, and an entire station to service the construction teams. His station. The Reagan NavSat IV. There were twelve, all named for world leaders from the distant past. Distant past meant any time before the EcoDisaster. The Sino-EcoDisaster had changed the world, and the Cassiopeia was going to change mankind. Keep the human race alive. If the planet Earth ever died, there would be a backup plan.

She was so far out now that the signals could be coming from a dead ship for the next century, and they'd never know. Even Pulse-Laser com signals were no faster than a light wave could travel. Man could invent near-light travel but couldn't find a way to keep in touch with it. However long the ship was gone, it took nearly that long for the com pulses to get back home.

A second ship hadn't been built. Never would be, either. That was Slate's take on the matter.

"The Cassiopeia," he mused. "Whole families lost to the stars."

"Ours lost to stardust and dreams." Sundra smiled, triggering the holoviewer feed of the children. A true hologram, it was no more than a ghostly image, dark blue in the dim light, reflecting the darkness of the children's compartment. Levi was twisted up, wearing nothing more than shorts, with a thin blanket covering one leg and part of his torso. Caitlan had on Slate's shirt. Both had exited the Tube without their slickers, and they had been soaked.

Slate was shirtless, also. He had another, warmer, but the flitter was advanced enough to warm him to cabin neutral, even without his shirt, and he hadn't bothered.

Sundra's false down was at her feet, and she wore only the silk from underneath.

"Stardust and dreams." Slate repeated the words, imagining what it would be like out there, if there really were places filled with something so ephemeral as stardust and dreams. At least he could touch the silver stick. He looked at Sundra. "It's warm. Have you noticed that?"

"We're lucky to have it." She squeezed his hand, leaning back into her seat and caressing the padded seating surface at her side.

"Lucky?" Unsure what she meant, he picked up the silver trinket. It seemed alive to him. Somehow, in some way, alive. That didn't make sense, but there it was. Warm and alive. Speaking to him. Calling to him.

"With your work. You know. You have to have it, and we get to use it when you're home." She turned her face to him. "Like today and going to the Falls. Not many people get to do that."

"Not without taking the MagBus." That was the bi-monthly shuttle that serviced OutTower travel. For those without personal flitter access, anyway. "You're talking about the flitter."

He'd meant the trinket he held.

"Certainly." She laughed. "We didn't have this before." Before the Crash, she meant.

"Always the silver lining."

He ran his hand up her arm, continuing to hold the stick in his other hand. He knew what she said without her having to say it. Then they'd maintained a two-day lease. Two days a week, sharing it with another two-day and three one-days. It'd been expensive, but a good lease-share, too, with flexible shareholders that didn't mind shifting schedules to accommodate special requests. Except the Furgesons from Level 321. Tuesday was theirs, and they'd never consented to shift, no matter how important the emergency. More than once he and Sundra had paid the exorbitant MagCab rates for a single transport. Especially when Sundra's parents were still alive.

At least they'd been able to afford it then.

"I'm not talking about the flitter. This." He turned the gleaming needle over in his hand, watching it catch the light.

She laughed at him and leaned his direction, placing one hand on his exposed torso. Her fingers just touched a tattoo that reached to her from his ribcage.

He wrapped the silver device in his fist. "It's very warm." Calling him, his name. *Slate, Slate.*

"Only because I warmed it for you. It wasn't warm to me."

"Give me your hand." He held his out, palm open. When she didn't move, he reached for it. "Come on. You need to feel this." He didn't mention it calling his name. Low-level telepathic fields were illegal except in specially licensed children's toys—for psychiatric purposes—and some limited uses in the treatment of mental illness. He'd never had one used on him that he knew of, but he didn't think this was it.

"Sure. But I feel silly."

"You'll sense it. The warmth. Wait a minute." Slate put his palm over hers, the metal stick between their hands. He felt the thing warm. "Do you feel it?"

"Now. What did you do? It wasn't warm before, and now it's hot."

He shrugged, scooping it out of her palm and into his grip. As he moved it over the area of the holo diaphragm, an image flashed above the viewer, then disappeared when his hand was past.

"That's weird." Sundra reached to the viewer. "The iris is closed. Let me see that." She triggered the iris, and she held the metal tube over it. Nothing. She put it in the viewer field, and she spun it like an old-fashioned compass needle, the way you did on viewers without auto-detect. It triggered the machine to initiate playback mode. The needle twirled rapidly into a blur, then spun down, resting a centimeter over the diaphragm, silently waiting.

"The flitter works, just not the stick. Don't guess it carries a holo after all. We're not getting rich tonight." Slate yawned. He could see Chicago Tower in the distance, and it had been a long day.

"But it did it for you. You saw." She pressed the silver object into his hand, wrapping his fingers around it. "Do your stuff, little thing."

He *had* seen it, and that was the problem. It had shown his face. He didn't intend to try it, either, but it seemed the gleaming fragment of *something* had plans of its own. As soon as Slate's fingers were wrapped around the shaft, it began to warm. The viewer kicked on, even without the needle in the interface, and a hazy image appeared. A face. Then the face solidified into his own and smiled.

"Oh, there you are, Slate. Just in case you haven't learned it yet, that's your name. Slate." There was a pause, as if the holo-Slate were having a conversation, and he was listening to someone they couldn't hear. "Well, ah, the last name. Not everything lines up. Usually enough, but not always, and that makes it harder. But that's beside the point. The point is that you're Slate, and if you haven't heard it before, then you just downloaded a whole washtub of info into your brain as I said that."

"Is this a joke?" Sundra frowned. The holo-Slate was listening again, his face going through several expressions, and she prodded real-Slate. "If so, I'm not laughing yet."

"That's right, you don't know what a washtub is. How could I have forgotten?" The holo-Slate ran his hand through his hair, interrupting real-Slate before he could answer. He slapped himself on the forehead. "How do I explain a washtub? That puts me in a bit of a quandary, because in some realities—"

"What was that?" Real-Slate dropped the needle to the floor, and the holo winked out. He rubbed his hand. Where the needle had been, it was hot like fire, like it had pulled its energy directly from him, right through his flesh.

"I get it." Sundra laughed. "A practical joke. You know Gunther, Level 189? He did this, I bet." She leaned down to pick up the needle.

"Don't. It's hot." Slate grabbed her arm. "You'll burn yourself."

"No, I won't." She took his hand off, and she held the silver trinket up. "Cold. Well, not cold. No temperature, really."

Slate took her hand and pressed her fingers against his palm. "There. Feel?" It was where the needle had rested.

"Slate!" She put her fingers against her tongue to wet them, then pressed them against the spot in his hand. "It's burning up."

"You're telling me."

A chime in the cabin went off, and the lights around the floor came up, giving off a soft glow. A voice whispered, "Entering Chicago Tower airspace. Flitter SLT682 negotiating Chicago Tower for unrestricted approach. Ingress validated for temporary rental, Unit 96F, State Tower Policy Number 213-4HH-246-04. Your confirmation code is ASHI-VUI45C. NorAm Logistics and Routing wishes to thank you for making Chicago Tower part of your travel plans."

"Guess we're there." Sundra still held the needle. Individual housing units could be seen covering the Tower. There were no walkways on the outside of Chicago Tower. Rather, the units were separate blisters, all assembled with the internal hallways tucked away, invisible to approaching visitors. It looked rather like a tower of soap bubbles, ready to come crashing down at any time. Lights were on in some, and others were blanked with varying degrees of opacity.

"Mom?" That was Levi, and he irised the divider out of the way.

"We're staying here? Cool." He pulled out his birthday gift and held it up to the canopy. Moments later, nanodust blisters lighted by nanolumens floated around the cabin. Some were opaque, but those that were clear had miniature people still walking, eating, and playing holo games in their temporary little worlds. He began to gather them up, holding them in his hand and studying everything going on inside.

"Anything else on the ear?" Sundra reached to take Slate's hand. "I've managed not to think about it much, but this morning worries me."

"Later." He shook his head, motioning to Levi, as he dropped the silver tube inside his pants pocket.

"Sure." She rubbed his arm as the flitter braked too sharply for any rational person not to flinch.

Slate winced. He always did. Levi? He loved it. But then, boys would. It was the thrill of near-death, the adrenalin-fueled heartbeat of youth. As usual, the inertia dampers dissipated the excess energy, storing it in the fuel cells, and they were inside, making their way to 96F's flitter stall.

The fun part for Levi was the elevator. Slate had forgotten. Sundra's father had explained it all. Rather than disrupt the design with an internal shaft, eating a quarter of the available living space, the outside of Chicago Tower was littered with lift blisters. Each was equipped with military-grade inertia dampers and variable-direction MagThrusters. Each clear lift blister crawled around the housing blisters at lightning speed, skipping from one to another with computer dexterity and efficiency. The lift walls could be blanked for the faint of heart.

For the less faint of heart, fleeting glimpses could be caught of people at dinner, or shaving in front of a mirror, or occasionally changing into evening clothes or pajamas. For those on the inside of Chicago Tower? They didn't pay attention to this particular elevator at all, one filled with a bare-chested man, a boy wearing only shorts, a girl nestled in her mother's arms, wearing only her father's shirt, and a pretty woman dressed too warmly to be inside a public con-veyance.

If they had, they might have noticed the father holding the boy upside down, with the mother's hand covering her mouth, and the boy red-faced with laughter, that was if they'd bothered to look. They might have even commented on how cute the little girl was, if they'd been able to see her.

However, only a holo imager could catch the interior of an express elevator in action. If it were coordinated with the Tower mainframe, and set to grab a shot just as the elevator bounced by, then for a time, nanodust might dance upside down, laughing as more nanodust, lighted by nanolumens, grinned at a birthday boy having the time of his life.

But then, unless it was a very, very good imager, it might catch nothing at all, just stardust shimmering in the night sky, the lonely dreams of nothing at all.

Chapter 9

CHILDREN deserve their own beds. Not a bed, but their own beds.

Now, Sundra was with Caitlan in their bed, and Slate had Levi wrapped around him. Tight. Like if the boy let space get between them, his daddy would disappear into thin air.

Slate was on his back, with the bedroom blister clear, and he watched the night sky. Levi, half across his chest, moved against him, turning his head to rest it in the crook of Slate's shoulder. His hair, soft in that small motion, made Slate smile. He listened to the boy's breathing, the soft, quick breaths followed by long moments of stillness, then more quick breaths. It was the way Levi breathed in his sleep, in this unusual fashion, and Slate enjoyed it, the small body, not so small at eleven, but still thin, and too warm at night. Already he'd had to throw the blanket off, leaving the two of them exposed to the sky and the millions of stars overhead. Where their skin touched, father and son, was damp with the slickness of Levi's sleep.

Slate smiled. His son, Levi. He pulled him closer, his hand resting lightly on the boy's back. Yeah, this one was his, and he loved him with all his heart. As much as Sundra? That made him smile wider. Yeah. Differently, but yeah, as much as Sundra.

He blinked his eyes clear, and he watched through the blister.

Millions of stars, and not another one that knew the footprint of man. The Cassiopeia, but that was a pipedream. Nothing more. Space? Nah. Earth was man's. That was as far as he would ever get. The Cassiopeia was a lost hope, evaporated in dreams and starlight.

He held up the silver stick, gently and loosely, afraid of it warming in his fist. It shouldn't have done that in the flitter, engaging the holo without being in the field.

It glistened in the starlight. *Slate, Slate . . .*

In a quick motion, he grasped the needle in his fist, squeezing it tightly, taking a deep breath as it warmed, then grew hot. He squeezed it tighter, willing it to burn a hole in his hand. He'd hold it all night to keep that face pressed inside. He didn't want to see what it tried to tell him. A joke? He didn't think so. Sundra hadn't seen the women, the ones that were no more than extensions of the laughing man.

He was about to drop the needle and let his palm cool when a face leaped into the air over his tightly gripped hand. The face . . . the same, and yet, not quite the same. A different angle, perhaps. It seemed to be looking around, then holo-Slate's eyes found him.

"Ah, there you are." Holo-Slate smiled. "Yeah, I'm you." The image paused, waiting for a time, and then he started up again. "So, you're going to just lie there. I wish I knew where to start." As before, the holo-Slate ran his hand through his hair, making a face and looking off to the side as if coming up with what to say next.

What bothered Slate was that he remembered doing that exact thing himself at times when he was unsure what to say. This was freaky-eerie.

"Not freaky-eerie," holo-Slate started, still looking off to the side. "More like, well," and he looked at Slate, "when you have a dream, and you know it's real, and then you wake up." He grinned. "I'm your dream. Well, not really. It's that I'm you, just not the you you. I'm the you you were, or, depending on how you look at it, I'm the you that you will be at some point in the future, which is really the present, unless you count," and the holo-Slate grimaced, "backwards." The holo stopped talking for several minutes while the holo-Slate looked like he was attempting—unsuccessfully—to interrupt someone Slate couldn't see. Then he burst into speech again. "I—I—am so sorry. I knew you wouldn't understand. I had to try, though. You see, it really all comes down to that tattoo on your back—"

Slate released the stick, watching it fall in slow motion to the sleeping pad at his side. It hit and bounced, the light shimmering off its unbroken surface, brighter than could be accounted for by the limited starlight.

His tattoo.

Caitlan had come in earlier, crawling in with Levi and him for a time, before Sundra had come in to carry her back to the other bed. She and Levi had traced the designs on the tattoo, not so much on his back, but where it wrapped around one side.

After he and Levi were alone, they'd talked, father and son stuff about nothing and everything, and Levi kept messing with one part of his tattoo.

"Enough, son," he'd finally said, pulling the boy up under one arm. "It's not going to be different just because you mess with it over and over." He'd chuckled, rumpling the boy's hair, and finally reaching to Levi's side and making him laugh until he kicked the blanket off to the floor. He'd also thought of the shirt he wore most nights for Sundra.

"It's different, Dad." Levi had his arm across Slate's chest, and his head was just under his chin. "I promise. One of the wheels is different." The boy looked in his father's eyes. "Promise. Part of it is missing."

"And you are a silly, silly boy, and I love you very much." Slate kissed him on the forehead. "Tattoos don't change, and they don't break off." He chuckled. "You, though, have you had a fun day?"

"Yeah, Dad." His arm pressed against Slate's chest, pulling himself closer, and he wrapped his leg around his father's. "When do we get to go home?"

"Me. You. Mommy. Catie. Sounds like we are home, son. The important parts, anyway." Slate hoped that sufficed. Those were the important parts to him. The rest? There was still no news, and Slate hated to think what that might mean. He'd just known to get away. The reason? He couldn't have said.

"Thanks, Dad."

"What for?" He squeezed Levi as he asked it. He didn't really care what for. Just the fact that Levi had said it was enough.

"For being my dad."

Slate couldn't reply to that. The lump in his throat was too big. He rubbed Levi's back in reply, and when he heard his breathing even into his "asleep" pattern, he kissed him on the forehead again.

Then he watched the stars for a very long time.

41

"LEVI, look at this." Slate leaned over the bed and shook his son's shoulder. "This is incredible."

"What?" The boy rolled over and rubbed his eyes.

"Snow and ice everywhere."

It was, too, as far as the eye could see. But then, this was Chicago, only a few hundred kays from the Canadian wastelands, and it was not summer. Not by any stretch. It was cold. Very cold. Within the bubble, the panoramic scene wrapped the horizon, with not another city or sign of human habitation as far as the eye could see. Off in the distance was the flat sheen of Lake Michigan. It was frozen nearly half the year now. Scientists predicted the glaciers pressing down from the old Hudson Bay across the remains of defunct Ontario would one day reshape the iconic body of water, but not this year. Not this century, most rational people believed. That was good enough for Slate.

"Can we go out and play?" Levi was sitting up by then, his white hair and light skin a ghost against the scene outside. His arms were on the bed lip, just where the bubble disappeared into the floor. He reached out and pressed his hand against the transparent barrier. "It's not cold." He turned to his father.

"No." Slate stepped onto the bed and knelt, wrapping his arms around his son, and resting his chin on the boy's head. He put his hand on the glass, also. "It wouldn't be."

"But, it's freezing out there." The boy's body shivered under Slate's hand. "How come this is warm?" He put his hand beside Slate's.

"Active biopolymers." The answer was just there. Slate smiled. He hadn't known that, but as soon as he said it, he knew he'd studied biopolymers in university. He wasn't an expert, but he applied the technology at the station. It was how they balanced the heat loads in the various torus rings.

"Bio. That means alive, right?" Levi had his hands on Slate's arms by then, holding them to his chest.

"Of course." Slate nodded, Levi's hair moving under his chin.

Levi reached and tapped the surface. "So, it's alive."

"At some level. It doesn't think, if that's what you mean. It, how can I say it," and he chuckled, remembering the holo from the night before, "it's like the window dreams it's alive, but it can never wake up. Like you, Levi, all snores and squirms, keeping me awake at night, and you don't even remember, do you?" He twisted the boy around, pulling him to the bed, and he sat on him, with his knees to either side. "What did you dream last night, Levi? Huh? Tell me that." He kept touching him, all over and rapidly, and every time he did, Levi let out a wail of mock despair.

However, laughter told the story otherwise.

"I don't know, Dad. Mom!" Then, a burst of laughter drowned his pleas for help. He kicked his feet, but Slate had him pinned.

"So, this is what the commotion is all about." Sundra was at the door, and she yawned. "I need up, anyway. Good morning, boys."

"Mom!" Levi stretched out an arm, pleading.

"Not in your dreams!" Slate grabbed the arm and flipped the boy onto his stomach, reseating himself on his buttocks. "You're mine."

That was when Caitlan came tearing in, pushing past Sundra, and leaping onto the bed. "Let him go." She hung on one of Slate's arms.

"So, this is the way it is? Another enemy?" Slate pulled her to him, planting a raspberry on the back of her neck. "I know how to defeat little girls," which gave Levi just enough squirm room to wriggle out and leap off the bed.

"Nah, nah. Can't get me!" and the boy, so filled with life and energy, was gone out the door.

"Happy, Catie?" Slate bundled her up in his arms. "Your brother escaped. You want to escape?" He held his hand like he intended to tickle her.

"No, Daddy!" She balled up in his arms, a turtle in Slate's shell.

"Then, I guess I'll keep you. Did you see the snow outside?" He adjusted her to look at the view.

"Where did it come from?" Unlike Levi, she made no attempt to touch the clear barrier.

"Why, is the question. It came for you."

"For me?" She giggled. "The snow came for me?"

"Sure enough, little girl." He kissed the top of her head. "It knew we were coming last night, and it got all white just for you."

"I love you, Daddy." She twisted around and put her arms around him.

"I love you, too, baby." And he did. More than she would ever know.

Chapter 10

"SLATE, about home."

He looked at his wife. He had been expecting this question. They were in the Chicago EPlex, the kids were in rented suits, and Levi was at the top of a waterslide. He yelled, and Slate raised one arm high in the air.

"Slate . . ." Sundra reached to rest her hand on his arm.

"I haven't heard anything. I'm sorry." That was what worried him. Nothing. No calls. No news. Just that one redirection from NorAm. There was nothing on the feeds. Blank, like the whole of St. Louis had sunk into a hole in the ground, taking the city and all its three million inhabitants with it. Make that minus four, because they'd gotten out. Still . . .

"Janette." That was Sundra's close friend. She lived in the unit just below them. "I tried to face with her earlier. Then voice. Nothing."

"Link?" Links used less bandwidth. If the repeaters were out, that should get through, anyway.

"That, too." She had a worried expression on her face. "And it's not just Janette. The kids are missing school. I should have been linked by their teachers by now."

"Did you try to—"

"Of course, I did." Her eyes were red, and her words were sharp.

"Oh, I don't mean it like that." She looked away, finding Levi and waving. "Watch for Catie!" She yelled the words, turning back to Slate. "Do you think . . . with the flitter . . ."

"Sure." The answer left a rock in his stomach. Yesterday, he'd been *driven* away. Today, she wanted him to go back.

"And Slate?"

"Yes, Sundra?" He dreaded this. Discussing yesterday morning, his driving *coercion* to get away, was unpleasant, at best.

"How did that man know we were on vacation?" She looked at him. "You remember, at the Falls?"

"It was the Falls. People vacation there." He'd wondered the same thing, though. And the holo device? It smacked of something, even if he wasn't sure just what.

"You will go home, just to check? I need to know everything's still standing."

He looked at her sharply. Still standing? It seemed they were on the same page, after all. That had been his thoughts, exactly. He picked up the two S-Units on the table before him. He thumbed an icon on one, and both lighted up. "Levi? Find your sister. Time to go."

Levi's image appeared on the device. "Dad. We just got here."

"Four hours ago. Pack it up, buddy. I'll meet you in the changing rooms. Tell Catie to look for your mother."

"Okay, Dad." He wiped water from his face, and the screen went dark.

Slate grabbed two bags from the floor—they contained the kids' clothes—and dropped the S-Units in the top one.

"You don't mind, do you?" Sundra linked arms with him. "About St. Louis?" She rested her head on his shoulder, leaning in from the side.

"It's less than an hour from Chicago." It wasn't the answer she wanted. He knew that. It was probably nicer than she expected.

"Two, there and back. Bring Caitlan's packie. The purple one. It has her travel toys in it."

"Sure." He knew the request for what it was. It wasn't the toys, although they would come in handy, once the novelty of this place wore off. It was the pretense the bag would be there to bring back. That made home all right. In one piece. Whole. Undamaged.

Slate didn't think so.

He would go see, though. Find out, and come back to be the bearer of the news. Good? Harumph. That remained to be seen.

"Here." He held out the bag with Caitlan's things inside. "See you in a bit."

"Make sure he rinses. Levi tries to avoid it." In a normal tone, like they were home and this was every day.

"He'll rinse." He smiled and gave her a quick kiss, and he pushed through the door. "Levi?"

"Here, Dad."

Slate looked around the corner to see knees behind a short wall. Swimwear slipped down one leg, then the other. Levi held it out for him to take.

"My clothes, Dad?" He looked over the low wall, his hair plastered, and water still beading on his skin. A drop turned loose and ran down his face, dangling from his chin.

"Your shower?" Slate gave him a mock knuckle sandwich, and he watched the droplet fall to the floor, shattering in a slow-motion explosion. It wasn't slow motion. It was . . . it was thinking about St. Louis and heading back that direction. It was . . . not knowing what he would find.

"Dad! I showered last night."

"I told your mom . . ." Slate nodded the direction of the showers. "No clothes until you do."

"Okay." He dug his fist into the towel at his side, and he picked it up. "Do I have to soap?"

"You'll rinse? Even without soap?"

Levi nodded.

"Hair, too?"

"Dad!"

"Do I need to watch?" He wanted to laugh at the expression on his son's face.

"*Dad!*"

"I'm turning your suit in. Here are your clothes when you're finished." He set the sack on the bench. "Be good." He ran his hand over Levi's hair, and it came away wet. He shook it and laughed as the boy trotted away. Oh, to be eleven, again!

At least he had eleven in his hand. Well, in his bed last night. That was the best he could do. The rest? He had to take life the way it came.

Even if that meant St. Louis Tower and whatever he found there.

THE SILVER tube glimmered beneath the brilliant midday sun. The sleep bubble was awash with light, overseen by a brilliantly blue sky. A perfect day for Chicago Tower. The shiny tube lay where Slate had dropped it during the night.

Waking, Caitan and Levi had taken Slate's attention. The holo device had gone unremembered.

It was not forgotten. It was never forgotten.

It shifted position, rolling slightly to one side. Then it began to spin, sensing, looking. When it determined there were no nearby active pheromones, electrical activity, or organic DNA matching its bonded human, it spun down, gently resting on the floor once again.

Waiting.

It could tell, however. Slate was still on Earth, and very much alive.

The tube gleamed in the light, more brightly than could be accounted for by the ambient sunshine.

And it was warm. Very warm, as it continued to search.

Chapter 11

SLATE pulled his hand away to see the StiRik logo coalesce on the screen.

"Welcome, Slate. I see you are traveling alone today. What is your planned destination?"

"Home." That was programmed in. Even from the station, he never had to say more than that. But before he could push back in his seat to get comfortable, the flitter's voice responded.

"Please clarify. Preset home destination is not compatible with known destination coordinates."

"Say that again." He sat up, putting the two items he held in the seat next to him.

"Please clarify. Preset home destination is not compatible with known destination coordinates. What is your planned destination?" The voice was polite and warm, but it was stuck on this.

"Um, display an updated NorAm map." It pulled up on the screen immediately, with all current city Towers marked in red. He reached to tap St. Louis Tower and let his hand fall away. "Where is St. Louis Tower?"

"May I suggest Indianapolis Tower? The high today is 18 Celsius, 64 Fahrenheit, with clear skies. Travel time is approximately 43 minutes, plus or minus 3 minutes due to variable wind conditions."

"No. I want St. Louis Tower."

"Destination unknown. What is your planned destination? Des Moines is experiencing light snow—"

"Give me NorAm Routing." Slate felt his jaw tense. The system was telling him St. Louis was not there? That was impossible.

"NorAm Logistics and Routing. AI Kendra, IBMFlashMatrix DataSystemsClone speaking. How may I help you?"

"Kendra? My flitter doesn't recognize St. Louis Tower. Can you update the system for me?"

"Thank you for your request, ser. Let me check your vehicle. I have it, ser. Our records indicate Flitter CT682 received the most current update available at 12:01 A.M. local time last night. Is there anything else I can help you with?"

"Are you sure?" Then it hit him. "Kendra?" He waited on a response. Being polite to an AI was a hot-button issue right now, as they had only recently received full citizenship status. Besides, it showed breeding and good manners. Slate had both, or at least he liked to think he did. Working on the stations? That had nothing to do with breeding. That was pragmatism. Financial pragmatism.

"Yes, Flitter CT682?"

"This is Flitter SLT682. Can you verify you are speaking with the right person? Slate Knalb, Flitter SLT682, registered to NASA-Sun Systems EAU. Repeat, Slate Knalb, Flitter SLT682, registered to NASASun Systems EAU." He picked up the ribbon Caitlan had given him, and he fingered it nervously. Something was very much not right here.

"I am sorry, ser. Our latest system updates verify your transponder signal as Flitter CT682, NASASun EAU OffWorld Station, currently assigned to Mssr Slate Knalb, Chicago Tower 96F. May I be of any further help?"

"Thank you, Kendra." He glanced at the map, figuring. "Yes. You can do something for me. Can you get me a high-altitude drop directly to Little Rock Tower?" That should take him to within seventy kays of St. Louis. He was qualified for manual control. There were a dozen systems he could override, claiming mech-failure and dropping out of routing control.

"Negotiating with Little Rock Tower. Route confirmed. Your expected travel time is one hour, thirty-nine minutes. Thank you for flying with NorAm Logistics and Routing. Have a nice trip."

"Thank you, Kendra." He felt the turbines coming online as the flitter started to move, and in less than a minute, he was airborne, his canopy shimmering into muted shade even as the sun flashed across its surface. He set a cabin reminder for forty-five minutes.

Slate held the ribbon, but Levi had gone to a little more trouble with his present for his dad. He picked up the glass EMarble from the seat and held it to the light. He laughed. It was what he expected. His son had given him himself. Deep in the glass was an image of Levi laughing as he rolled and roughhoused with someone Slate couldn't see. He knew who it was, too. It was him. Or it soon would be. This was a DreamMarble with a double interactive recording matrix, automatically backed up online for safety and preservation, just in case the worst happened. Daredevils used these to record their most adrenalin-pumping feats. The automatic backup was in case the original didn't survive. Sometimes the unthinkable happened, and the only thing left was the uploaded record of the person's untimely demise. Some people enjoyed those types of dreams.

Levi's recording had already been overlaid in the matrix, probably last week while Slate was on station. When Slate played it back, his interactions with his son's recordings would be interwoven with the original layer, creating a final dream sequence, replayable over and over in a home ESyst module.

Slate tossed the marble in his hand, and he caught it. He chuckled. How many chores had Levi traded off for this? Each marble was quite expensive. He'd thought Levi's contribution had been the holo game back at St. Louis Tower. Then, just before he'd boarded the flitter, Sundra had handed him this, telling him that this was what his son wanted more than anything for his birthday. A DreamMarble of him and his dad spending the day together.

Now it was Slate's turn to record his half. Well, he had over forty minutes. That'd make a good dent. He slipped it into the ESyst iris, and he said aloud, "Record mode, matrix layer two." He watched as his son coalesced in the back of the flitter, slowly becoming opaque. He was in his pajamas, and Slate laughed. The figure was frozen until it was totally solid, and then Levi turned to him.

"Hey, Dad. Wanna play?" His green eyes twinkled, and he grinned, showing perfect white teeth against smooth skin. He reached and poked Slate on the arm. The illusion was very real, with touch, smell, and vocal perception filters. Whatever the holo did would seem and feel very real, even if Levi wasn't actually in the flitter. Of course, the holo couldn't fly the flitter or pick up

50

anything. What it could do was interact with Slate's sensory perceptions, and as long as Slate accepted it, it would feel very real.

"Hey, you little brat. Get up here." Slate twisted his seat around and grabbed the boy under the arms, setting him beside him in the seat. "I think I would like to start off with a story."

"A real story?"

"Hey! All my stories are real."

"No. I mean a station story." Levi put his hand on his dad's chest, tapping his fingers. "Real stuff, what you really do."

"Oh, you want the black spiders from the dark galaxy, and the twin sisters that suck the air from the airlocks."

"Yeah, Dad. Those." Levi's eyes were bright, and his excitement was palpable. "And the one about One-Eyed Jack that got lost in the meteor storm."

"One-Eyed Jack, huh?" Slate leaned back, pulling Levi under his arm. "Well, One-Eyed Jack was born with two eyes, right in St. Louis Tower. It wasn't a Tower then, because people lived on the dirt. Every day they walked on the dirt under the open air, and they even dug in the dirt with their hands—"

"They did not, Dad. Nobody digs in the dirt with their hands. That's so gross." The Levi holo made a face, as if disgusted by the very idea.

"Did, too. Promise." Slate teased the boy, and he began to tickle him as he talked. He wanted laughter in the dream, too. Dream-Marbles carried emotions especially well. The words he said? On awakening, most were forgotten. The emotions? They never faded away.

Before he could finish the story of One-Eyed Jack, he had Levi wrapped in his arms, kicking to get free, and laughing so hard tears were in his eyes.

"And then, Jack said, 'Arrgh!' And he leaped onto the lander's ramp—" and all the while, Slate poked and prodded his son in all the secret places that made him wail with laughter.

"Dad!" Levi huffed with exhaustion, pulling at his dad's arms. "Just tell the story. Stop! Stop! Tell the story!"

"So," and Slate poked him in yet another secret place, bringing another round of laughter, "do you want me to stop or start? I can't do both, son." And he jabbed him again, this time under the back of the knees.

"Not there, Daddy. Please! I'll wet my pants!" Levi arched his back and screamed with laughter.

"Holos can't wet their pants." Slate whispered the words in Levi's ear just before he grabbed him on the top of his leg, and he let his fingers dance, causing the boy to twist away, his legs jerking in exquisite agony.

"Please, Daddy!" This time Levi managed to get his arms around Slate's neck and his legs around his waist. "Just a story, Daddy. Finish One-Eyed Jack." He held Slate tightly. "Please?"

Slate wrapped his arms around his son and laughed. "One-Eyed Jack. I can do him. It was the blast of a laser that took out Jack's eye. Right into his head." Levi shivered against him. "What?"

"Did it hurt One-Eyed Jack?" He leaned back, cupping his hands around his father's neck. "Did he cry?"

"Nah! One-Eyed Jack never cried. He stood and called out, 'Is that all ya' got, ya' ragged fiends? I've still got one eye, and as long as I have an eye, I'm coming after ya'!' "

"And next?" Levi was snuggled against him again, warm, and as real as a real boy. "What happened next, Daddy?"

Slate went on, Levi's voice continually whispering in his ear, *What's next, Daddy?*

That was just it. He didn't know what was next. For all he knew, home was no longer there. And if it was, why was it no longer on the map? Even as he held his son, that worried him. Thank God for Levi and his DreamMarble. At least Levi was with him, even if he was really five hundred kays away in a city that wasn't really home.

The flitter's voice came up softly, "Reminder, Slate. You are forty-five minutes into your journey. Enjoy the rest of your trip."

"Sorry, Levi. We have to continue this dream later. Daddy has things to do."

"Sure, Dad. Don't forget me." The Levi holo put his hands on both sides of Slate's face, patted twice, then grabbed him in a big hug. "I love you, Daddy."

"I love you, too. I won't forget." He reached to the ESyst controls, punched the iris, and Levi froze, slowly fading from around him.

"Now, let's see what's happened to St. Louis Tower." Slate pulled his seat up to the manual control console, and he engaged the landing gear, canopy lock, and emergency harness restraints at the same time. None would actually trip, as this was designed into all NASASun flitters for access to manual maneuvering in emergency situations. It was a custom, aftermarket, and very proprietary system designed for NASASun's sole use. Emergency situations were pretty much the norm in the depths of space.

"Flitter CT682. This is NorAm Logistics and Routing. You have multiple system failures. Do you need assistance?"

It was a standard message sent out by non-AI communique. Slate called out, "Negative. Manual Control Initiation Permit 47B NASASun. Please negotiate." The building cloud cover was perfect, too. It would impede satellite observation. He could truly claim a mechfailure.

"Negotiations started. Mechfailure confirmed. Permission granted. Flitter CT682 now under sole control of independent operator, Manual Control Initiation Permit 47B NASASun. You have one-half minute to log in before NorAm control reinstates. Commencing now. Twenty-nine. Twenty-eight . . ."

Slate's fingers flew over the controls, logging in with his station override. This required manual input, as voice could be copied, and prints could be hijacked. All three? Not likely.

"Slate Knalb initiating manual override." He placed his hand on the screen. It turned red then faded back to green.

"Manual override completed. Voice systems now offline." The system went silent.

Slate was now completely alone in the flitter with not even a map to give him directions. But this was what he was good at. It was his job.

And one more thing. It had his adrenalin pumping. He wanted to know what had happened to his home, and he was going to find out.

He hit the flitter turbine feed, and he heard the fans whine as they gulped massive quantities of air. The flitter angled west, thin clouds flipping past the canopy, the inertia dampers holding Slate firmly in his seat, as the speed soon began to approach 1,500 kays per hour, faster than any flitter was legally allowed to fly. Well, taking manual control by tripping factory-installed safeties wasn't exactly legal, either. So what? Maybe he should record this for Levi, too. He touched the iris. "Record mode, matrix layer two, reinitiated." He looked behind him to see Levi reappear in the back seat.

"Hey, Dad. What's going on?" It was that high-pitched ten-year-old voice, cycling through the second of what were probably ten individual introductions on the marble.

"Wanna come watch?" He grinned. "Daddy's flying on manual."

"Really? Cool!" Levi, still in his pajamas, flung himself towards Slate, his head and shoulders forced between the forward seats.

"Can I sit up front?"

"Come on." Slate held out a hand to help him climb over. "You get Mommy's seat."

"How fast are we going?"

Slate looked. "Oh, about 1,480 kays."

"Really?" Levi was breathless, and he climbed on his knees. "I've never been this fast. Nobody'll believe me when I tell 'em. Cool, Dad!" His smile was ear-to-ear.

"Can't tell, Levi. Secret. Not even your mother can know I'm letting you dream this." Slate was very pleased, though. He reached and placed his hand on the back of his son's neck. "You're a good kid, Levi."

"Thanks, Dad. You're a fun dad."

"Ha." Slate laughed. "I bet you say that to all your dads." He let go to make an adjustment on the console. At this speed, St. Louis would show up pretty quickly, although it was all by dead reckoning from here on in. The clouds had thickened, and he reached to engage the radar system.

"Dad!" Levi hit him on the leg, and hard.

"Hey! What was that for?" He looked at him with a laugh.

"I don't have another dad. I don't want another one, either."

"Good answer, son. Now, get ready. We're coming up on our Tower."

And Slate really expected that's what would happen. It was what he didn't see that surprised him.

There was no St. Louis Tower visible.

What rose in front of him was a billowing cloud of flame. The flitter jerked sideways, buffeted by an outflow of superheated air.

"Daddy!" Levi looked terrified.

"Look away, Levi." Slate fought with the controls. He wished he could reach the ESyst iris. This didn't belong on the DreamMarble. No way. And once recorded, it couldn't be wiped clean. The Marble and its online backup would have to be destroyed. More than anything, he hated that.

He forced the flitter down as something came at him out of the maelstrom, barely ducking underneath. It looked like a military-upgraded flitter. That meant weapons. Very uncomfortable weapons.

He had an epiphany, one of those things where you put all the facts together at once. St. Louis Tower. Military flitter. Big ball of flame.

This was really bad.

"Son, maybe we should stop the recording." Now he dodged flaming chunks of ejecta. He suspected overriding NorAm Logistics hadn't been a good idea. And he couldn't contact Sundra with the voice systems offline. Could it get any worse?

That was when he cleared a wall of black smoke, only to find himself heading directly at what was left of St. Louis Tower.

"Hold on, son!" He threw his arm out instinctively to catch the young holo, his movement as unconscious as it was ineffectual. The craft's built-in collision avoidance system flipped the turbines into full reverse, the screeching whine filling the cabin, as Levi passed through Slate's arm, his image flickering before solidifying again, leaving him huddled under the dash, crying.

"Make it stop, Daddy."

"Brace yourself," was all Slate had time to say, when they slammed into what was left of a windowwall, tipping sideways, and spinning around as they hit the remains of interior wall after interior wall. It was the central core of the building that finally stopped them.

The Levi holo flickered once, then remained steady.

The smell of smoke and burned plastics filled the cabin. The canopy was cracked, and the turbines wound down, the whine dropping to a low-pitched hum before coughing to a stop.

"Craft malfunction. Systems in manual mode and inoperable at this time. Notification will be sent to NorAm Logistics and Routing when reconnected to NorAm Control for full automatic operation."

The voice went silent.

"Levi, I'm disengaging the recorder. Okay?" The boy was just a hologram, built out of nanodust and lighted by self-powered nano-lumens, but the recording was running. He had to keep this as emotionally low key as possible.

"Okay, Dad. I'm scared." Tears glistened in the holo's eyes.

"When I bring you back online, everything will be all right. Don't you worry, son. You're still safe and secure in Chicago, and I'll be home before long." He hoped. He climbed over the canted seat, and he reached to the ESyst iris. He punched it, watching Levi. He blinked back tears at having to see him go.

"Dad?"

Slate frowned. He punched the iris again.

"Daddy, I want there with you."

"Come here, son." He reached forward and pulled the boy to

him, to have the ten-year-old wrap his arms around his neck. His real son might be eleven now, but this hologram was only ten, and that age difference seemed important to Slate, as if the boy were more vulnerable in this very precarious situation. "It's not disengaging."

And Slate couldn't remove the marble manually.

"The button doesn't work?" By then, Levi's legs were wrapped around Slate's waist.

"I guess we're getting out together." At least as far as the broadcast allowed. The range was quite limited on consumer units, restricted to a hundred meters. However, Slate's flitter belonged to NASASun, and it had a commercial grade broadcaster for use from station to station. As long as the ESyst unit had power, it would be difficult to get out of range. Whew! Getting out of here might cause some nightmares. But leaving the holo behind would be even worse, embedding the DreamMarble with feelings of abandonment and isolation.

Slate guessed it could get worse. A lot worse. And the Dream-Marble was being backed up. Automatically. Short of ripping the console out of the flitter, and that was tantamount to murdering the holo, Levi was with him to witness whatever he found here.

Might as well get going.

Slate palmed the panel to open the hatch, only to have it whine, move half an inch, and the override click in. The acrid smell of burning wiring billowed through the gap.

"Dad. Make it open." Levi's cheeks were wet.

"I'm trying, son." The boy was hot in his arms. Slate kicked at the door, relieved to see it move a small amount. He kicked again and heard the motor whine for a moment, then the override clicked once more. "Open, you sucker, you." He hit it hard with the heel of his boot, relieved when it swung out until it bumped the remains of a twisted steel column. The motor whined for a moment, the hatch banging the column and rocking the flitter, before it clicked off for a third time.

"We'll be safe, now, right, Dad?"

"You bet." Bright and cheerful. He shifted to stand, wishing the holo perception filters weren't quite so complete. Ten-year-olds were heavy, even if he was carrying nothing at all. His mind thought he was, and that was what counted. Heavy or not, the boy *felt* heavy.

He ducked under the partially opened door, stepping carefully to the concrete floor beneath him. Where the flitter had torn through had left a pale gray track showing its erratic path through the labyrinth of interior walls. Everywhere else was blackened. Off to one side, there was no floor. Worse, it seemed there was no building. If they hadn't been stopped by the building's central column, they would have gone off the other side.

Slate walked up to the express shaft, not daring to hope. It was as familiar as yesterday morning, although smoke-blackened. He placed his hand on the panel beside the door, surprised to hear a familiar ding and see the panel light up.

"It works, Daddy." Levi had his head on Slate's shoulder, and he smiled. "Will it take us home?"

"Maybe. Wait and see. We'll get you home, one way or another." He poked him gently in the side, biting on his ear; and he laughed when Levi jerked his head away.

He smiled, relieved, when the doors began to open. After all, the central core of the building was the escape route for three million people in a worst-case scenario, and it was built to be indestructible. It even ran on an independent backup power supply. When the doors slid back, his smile faded. There was no car, and he could see clear through the other side.

"Is it broken?"

"I think so, son. We have to find another way down."

That worried him. Was this the thirtieth floor, or the three hundredth? He tried to remember his altitude when he took manual control, although it was his height when he hit the building that counted. If the smoke cleared, he might have some idea how bad their situation was.

He rubbed Levi's back, his ribs sharp beneath his pajamas. If only the flitter's power would fail, then the boy wouldn't have this memory. Truly, he hated this. He knew adrenalin junkies loved to rent DreamMarbles just for this very thing, hoping someone would die, and they got to live it in perfect safety. Not eleven-year-olds. Eleven-year-olds shouldn't have to live their own deaths.

He looked back at the craft, wondering if there was anything inside he needed before heading out. Then, wrapping his son in his embrace, he hiked him up around his waist, working his arms under him, and said in his most cheerful voice, "Are you up for an adventure?"

"Will it be fun?"

"Always. When you and I are together, it's always fun. Right, kiddo?"

"Right. It's always fun."

It was those bright green eyes that told Slate the truth. His holo-boy wasn't having fun at all, and for that, he hugged him a little tighter.

Then he began to look for a way out.

Chapter 12

THEY had been lucky. If they'd hit the building on the two-hundredth floor, they would have never made it down. Of course, if they'd been even higher, there might have been no building in their way to hit. Who knew? Then, at that height, the firestorm that had thrown them sideways might have cooked them like chickens in a can.

Not a fun way to go.

As it was, they'd been able to make it down thirteen floors of devastation, until they reached levels that were actually intact. And it wasn't much better.

Popping echoed down a corridor, and Slate and Levi pressed themselves into a doorway. Slugthrowers. The messy kind that traveled through doors and walls, taking out anyone hiding inside.

Why was this happening?

He was making this like a game for Levi. *Get ready, run, Levi!* But it was no game. People had survived. Doors were being kicked in, and shots were being fired. Just who were these people? And who were they looking for?

Or did they intend to take out everyone they found?

Two floors up, they'd tried an express. The corridor looked completely undamaged. The flooring was polished, and the lights burned brightly. The air was even clear. Slate had palmed the door, and they'd waited. Luckily, someone had warned them, yelling at them to run. They had, but almost too late. They rounded the corner just as a dozen armed blankeyes trotted out, lining up in formation, followed by a suited officer in full dress.

"It moves, it dies. Go."

And the blankeyes did.

Slate stood, his legs shaking. He was no soldier. He was a father, and a husband, and he held his son in his arms. If he died, his son watched him die, and he would dream it over and over, never letting it go.

Not acceptable.

He pulled Levi tight and turned to run, trying each door along the way. Finally, one opened, only to be caught by an old-fashioned chain. He heard a voice inside, "No! Stay out!" Slate forced his shoulder into the door and sent the chain flying. Inside, an elderly couple huddled on the couch, holding each other.

Slate slammed the door shut. "I'm sorry. My son . . . is there a way out? A downstairs?" Lower floors were less desirable, and people often converted two units into one. He could only hope.

"Don't hurt us." It was the woman that spoke.

"Please." Slate knelt before them, cupping Levi's face in his hand. "My son, Levi. Help us."

"A stair." The old man. "There." He pointed down a hallway.

"Thank you." Slate stood. "Come with us." He looked back at the door, imagining it bursting open at any time.

"This is our home." The old woman's voice broke, and her husband hugged her and nodded.

Slate pulled Levi tight and ran, taking the stairs two at a time. On the floor below, they'd found another two-level, this one unlocked, and made it down yet another floor.

This time they found a bank of windows that let them see outside. Tops of trees brushed the glass. Only a few more floors, and . . . something. At least they could get outdoors.

The building began to groan. Dust seeped from the ceiling, and one of the panes cracked with a sharp sound.

"Daddy?"

"I'm scared, too."

"You promised safe."

"I know, and I am so very sorry." Slate pulled Levi to him, sheltering him. "I want you to be safe so very, very much."

"I'm scared."

"You and me, buddy."

The cracked window shattered, and the room filled with dust. Then, another window shattered, and with a great train wreck of a sound, darkness fell all around them.

"DADDY?"

Slate felt Levi's hands on his face. Then they shook one of his shoulders.

"Daddy, wake up."

"Yes, son?" His head hurt, and he couldn't feel his legs. This was worse than bad. And his back. That infernal tattoo itched like nobody's business. At least there was light streaming in through the broken rubble over their heads. And they had air. The flitter must still be functioning. He had Levi with him. Still recording. He chuckled at that and coughed.

"You were asleep a long time. What happened?" Levi's voice shook.

"I think the building fell. Are you okay?" Of course, he was. He wasn't even dirty. He couldn't get dirty. He wasn't even real.

"I watched it move." Levi crawled over Slate, and that was when Slate realized he was on his side, and Levi had been behind him the entire time.

"What moved, son?"

"The wheel. Your shirt, it got torn, and I was touching the wheel, and it moved."

"It always moves. Your mother hates it." He tried to roll onto his back, and he couldn't. He reached for Levi, only to see him flicker once. "Son, quick, come here." He grimaced when fire shot through his back. He wondered if it was broken.

"Daddy, what?" The boy clambered his way. Of course, no dust stirred. The boy was only nanodust and lumens, held together by the flitter's broadcast unit. And a very strong perception filter.

"I love you." He put his hand behind the boy's neck and massaged the muscle and skin. He had to say this before the flitter lost power and killed the recording. "I love you more than anything, Levi. I love your mother, too, and Catie. I love you all." He stopped to cough.

"Daddy, why are you saying that? Get up. We have to get out." Tears ran down the holo's cheeks. The boy pulled at Slate's arm, but of course, he couldn't move it. He flickered again and stabilized once more.

"Hug your daddy. I need to have you hug me." He pulled the holo to him. "Now, quickly."

"I love you, Daddy." The pajama-clad boy snuggled next to Slate as best he could, his hand alongside his father's face. He flickered again, and he was gone.

Slate lay in the rubble unable to move for a very long time, with his eyes moist, and powerless to see more than what he had just lost. After a time, he jerked awake. He could no longer feel the pain, and it was darker. Was it darker, or was his vision going? He had no way to know. He took a shallow breath, and his world went black again.

Later, minutes or hours, he didn't know which, he awoke to voices.

"He was still uploading when the building came down. He has to be here."

Who does? Slate questioned. Did Levi wander off? He tried to call for him, but his mouth wouldn't work. Here, he called. I'm here. He searched for the voices, but he discovered he could no longer see. The voices faded first, then he no longer wondered about the voices.

He wondered about nothing at all.

Chapter 13

THE MASSIVE crane strained at the beam, lifting it centimeters, then half a meter. The crew had been at it for hours, attempting to reach one particular location. They simply had to get there.

"Can we pull him out?" The speaker was dressed in a crisp uniform with an oak leaf, and he wore a military-style cap. The men working around him were efficient and blank-eyed, more machine than human, with one small stripe, the mark of simple laity.

"Let me review the recording, ser." A second man, obviously military also, although his deacon stripes told he was not as high a rank, looked inside a box where a hologram played. He adjusted a control, and the images speeded up, almost a blur, before stopping. He touched the controls again, and the images reversed. "Here, ser. This is where the building began to collapse. If you watch here . . ." What he meant was that it was his superior's responsibility, and he didn't want to take the heat if someone misread the information. Recovery of the body was essential.

"We have the boy touching the wheel. Is that proof enough?" The uniform asked the question, but not loudly.

"Your call, ser. If you think we can predict from what we got. Remember, we're getting a ten-year-old's view. It's how he interprets it."

The uniform took a deep breath and held it awhile before releasing it. "Let's see what you've got."

After running the hologram back and forth several times, the uniform made a decision. He pointed to the crane operator and instructed, "This, left one meter, then pull straight up." To the other three blankeyes, he motioned. "I need powerjacks. And winches. Stabilize this first." He patted the end of a twisted steel beam. "Let's get this man out of here."

The crane whined, and the cable buzzed with tension. The two uniforms, one lesser and one greater, stepped back to let the blankeyes at the scene of carnage. Many people had died, but this was the only one that mattered.

To these people, at least.

IT WAS long past dark, and floodlights washed the remains of St. Louis Tower. At least they washed this one particular spot. Slate's body had finally been forced free, and the four blankeyes strained to lift him from within his crippled sarcophagus. Once outside, they dumped him unceremoniously onto the rubble.

"He's filthy." The crisp uniform with his oak leaf turned up his nose. "Show me the tattoo."

"Flip him over." His underling spoke to the blanks, indicating his instructions with a rolling motion of his hand. When they were finished, he called, "Water!"

"How did the family get out?" The uniform pressed his boot against Slate's shoulder, rocking the body. He brushed his sole along his back, but the skin was too dirty to reveal much more than that there was *something* etched into its surface.

"We don't know. Family vacation? They show up at Niagara, then in Chicago. Should we pull them in?"

The uniform looked thoughtful, then shook his head. "Not if we have this. Not if it's successful. Clean it so I can see."

The man reached to the bucket now at his side, and with a torn piece of Slate's shirt, he scrubbed the residue of the building's demise from his back. Under the harsh lights, the tattoo stood out against the pale skin like burnished metal on alabaster.

The uniform studied it, touching it with his boot, then knelt to brush one part with his outstretched finger, just where a smooth circular line intersected a jagged loop of toothed gears. "There. That's where we go next."

"Are you sure, ser?" The kneeling man touched the spot, rubbing his fingers over the tattoo.

"Of course, I'm sure. Transfer capsule. Does he have it on him?"

"Not that we know of, ser. Now that he's out, I can check his clothing." Hands ran along the body, delving into pockets, and pinching loose seams. The man sat back. "Not here, ser. I don't think he ever got to use it."

"That presents a problem."

"Yes, ser." He slipped his tool from his jacket, and he thumbed it on. The end shimmered with blue light. "Shall I?"

The uniform snorted, and he smiled. "You know the routine." He turned and began to walk away.

The blue light glowed, the man's hand moved, and he stood, holding the prize out to one of the blankeyes. Without looking back, he followed the uniform, stepping carefully through the rubble.

LEVI lay face down, sleeping, this time truly eleven years old. The sky through the bubble was dark, and Caitlan was curled up on the opposite side of the bed. She had a stuffed bunny wrapped in her arm. The bedding was rumpled, and toys scattered the room, as if they had played a game before drifting off to sleep.

On the floor at Levi's side rested a silver charm of metal, dropped and forgotten. Even in the darkness it glowed. Then it began to spin, faster and faster, until it was no more than a blur. In a flash of light, it was gone.

Levi lifted his head for a moment, and not seeing anything, he wrapped his arm around his pillow and closed his eyes. Soon he was asleep once again, blanketed by darkness, under the light of a million stars.

Chapter 14

THE METAL bauble glowed, skimmed from all that had been dreamed, and they could not work it.

"It is the same as the dreamer's. It is proof that he dreams."

The grand table, reflecting the void—the whole of creation—drew in on itself, star systems becoming mere clusters of lights, tracking a dream that might be a different dream.

Another had come, and another must be found.

"Find him."

"Find him."

"Find him."

The image shifted endlessly, and there was no one there. It seemed the one they searched for would not so easily be found.

Chapter 15

INTERLOCKING cogs, blackened with star soot and weary with time, engaged once more. The giant timepiece, each gear encompassing entire galaxies, moved like a lumbering giant. Its footsteps echoed among the stars.

Time, that great equalizer, shifted, and things that had been were suddenly no more.

Stardust, great swaths of ancient behemoths burned out eons before, drifted free, and shooting stars littered the skies of a million worlds.

It was an omen, saying, Beware! Tomorrow is slipping through your fingers, and the rising sun may never come.

A finger touched the oil that lubricated the stars, and in the blackness of the eternal night, suns imploded, and galaxies winked out as if they had never been. The agony of a million races screamed into the void with indescribable terror, only to be snuffed without a second thought.

Bigger things were in play this day.

Spidersilk glimmered, stretching from world to world, the web of a hundred million possibilities, forming a harp capable of playing music of unimaginable beauty. Each note was a life—born, lived, and died—and each song was a race of beings, blooming from simple amino acids to one day fly among the stars, then coming to an end, old, weary, and worn.

Sometimes the races survived the turning of the wheel. More often, they did not.

Yet another cog connected, blackened oil moving against blackened oil, and the web shifted, changed once again, threads released with a throbbing backlash through time and space. A hundred thousand suns went nova, and with them, a hundred billion notes of the song became no more than silence in the night.

The finger shifted and withdrew, and in flowing concentric rings, the black oil of time and space began to smooth.

The universe surged forward once again.

Chapter 16

A TREE floated overhead, distant in the glow of glaring twin suns. Green tufts at each end anchored the massive trunk, and on the dark side, the glow of a thousand lights revealed the city that encircled the midpoint.

Kartye Tree.

The thought was just there, hard and cold, as well as the hundred thousand souls that called the city home.

"Let's go, ser." A hand clapped him on the shoulder. Other hands clipped a line on a harness running between his legs and over his shoulders. The hand pulled on the harness. "Taut. All clips firm. Not losing anyone this trip."

Pictures flashed through his mind, a woman's face, solemn panic in her eyes as she floated toward one of those twin suns. A tether drifted her direction, but it was beyond her opened palm. There was nothing to be done. Hours, perhaps, she had to exist, before she reached the edge of the Torus. Her breather would provide her oxygen from the thin atmosphere, then the air would thin, she would leave the Torus, and her life would be gone. Yet, even as she floated away, she was already dead. Ship's fuel was long exhausted, and there was no recourse for anything lost to the vile fingers of the two suns.

Life was hard aboard the Trees of Turbulence. The name was

there, and in that flash of insight, he also remembered the Great Exodus. One hundred million people on massive vessels designed for a quarter that amount. Four pairs of feet taking up floor space meant for one. Four mouths crying out for each bite of food.

The pressure to survive had torn the ships apart, socially and physically, and the Trees had been born. Now, Kartye Tree, untethered and without power, was lost forever, if her reciprocal compression engine couldn't be restarted.

He turned and looked behind him. Towering a hundred forty meters into the air against the dark sky and half a kay long stood the compression spring that would soon enable the tree's engine to push the tufts apart, releasing the energy of ten thousand ratcheted gears, recharging the tree's energy reserves, and using the inertia of the ensuing momentum to keep it from falling into one of the Torus' massive stars.

The trees had been the salvation of the Great Exodus. Each had been constructed from metal stripped out of the original ships, nickel-iron asteroids picked up along the way, and the sweat of a million people. Hydroponic gardens had been reengineered to grow underneath the unfiltered light of distant suns and then replanted on the outside of the ships. The pièce de résistance was the massive spring-driven Gessimer Engine that powered each tree. Every step taken aboard the ship ratcheted the two ends of the tree closer and closer, winding the nuclear-bonded SunSteel spring tighter and tighter, until the built-up energy was released in a reverse gravity thrust that drove the ship forward.

Kartye Tree had never worked properly, though, barely producing enough momentum to keep the tree from falling into Death and Destruction's gravity well, the aptly named stars that refused to release her to rejoin her brethren trees.

Now she did not work at all, and the planetoid that had been captured as a factory for building a new spring was emptied of its useful components, and the spring was ready to install.

One hundred fifty years of labor and untold lives had been sacrificed, all for this one moment in time: the survival of a world, one in the shape of an old-fashioned plant no one alive remembered in its original form.

Kartye Tree was being given new life.

EACH thing the man touched, he understood, as if he had worked with it before. The usage, its construction, even the end goal of what it was to accomplish was simply *there.*

Himself? For that he had nothing. No self-awareness that told of a history and a future that might be open to him. He was a blank slate, a holo-blank, ready for the stylus of life to write its purposes upon his soul.

If he had a soul.

He wasn't even sure of that. One thing he was sure of was the thruster that would fling him toward Kartye Tree, the spiderline that he carried affixed to his back, and the disaster that a missed attempt would be for the desperate people that might die if the tree went unrepaired.

He also knew this was his third attempt.

Each previous attempt had seen the tree farther and farther away. Soon, the Factory would be lost for another handful of years before drawing close enough to Kartye Tree to once again attempt tethering. By then, the tree would have succumbed to Death and Destruction, and the massive stars would have feasted once again.

"Hook me up!" He yelled the words, to see a dozen men in black, the shadows of Death and Destruction at their feet, scramble in place. The rumble of oversized wheels on metal tracks told of equipment being moved, of a wheel manually turned, a spring that would never leave the Factory being tightened. His spring. The thruster spring.

Once tethering was complete, the hundred-forty-meter-tall spring would make the trip first. It was the most important thing. The men? Without the spring, they were forfeit, anyway. The spring was all that counted. Once the spring was delivered, the men would use zip-line thrusters to make their way across, one at a time, as preparations were made to install the spring.

Without the spring . . . a more immediate inrush of understanding surged through him. Weeks . . . weeks only in the latest estimates before life support began failing, slowly at first, but with greater rapidity as more and more resources were shifted to resisting Death and Destruction's inexorable pull. One hundred thousand voices, lost to stardust and dreams, snuffed out in the blazing devastation of Destruction's nuclear furnaces. Or had they passed perihelion to be pulled into Death's embrace, instead?

He shook the thoughts away. He had to focus on the tree. And Katerine.

He staggered.

Katerine . . . over a dozen years they had been apart. The sacrifice had almost been too much. The spring was failing, had been failing for over a century, but by the time he left the tree, the scientists had pinned a final date. Two decades, maybe two and a half, and the repairs—half measures at their best—would fail. The new spring must be in place.

He had volunteered. And Katerine's tears had fallen like rain.

Whatever rain was. Just words. But the emotions had been very real. The world was coming to an end, either then for them or in twenty years for the world.

He had chosen then. Katerine had opted for twenty years.

Now, after thirteen years, he wasn't sure her way wouldn't have been the better choice; even the twenty years had been an optimistic gamble, forcing them into this mad try for success.

Arms grabbed his shoulders and slammed his back against the thruster. The Fist, the metallic thruster arm that mated to his harness, twisted with a jerk and locked on. The spiderline was looped onto the guide drum, and a green light flashed through the sky. Far, far away, it burned against the trunk of Kartye Tree, a beacon for his homecoming.

"Targeting locked. Aiming." The words came from behind him. "Building release thrust, pressure at three hundred . . . three ten . . . three eighteen . . . three twenty and holding. Ready." The mechanisms of the Factory hummed, the emotional tension more brittle than coiled SunSteel in a vacuum. A hundred twenty men held a hundred twenty breaths, afraid to jinx what could be their final chance at redemption.

A hand clasped his shoulder, and a voice spoke in his ear, as hands affixed goggles and a short-range breather to his face.

"Final attempt. They're going to try to catch you. You've got to be there a thousand percent."

He nodded. It was all he could do. His throat was choked with the memory of Katerine . . . Katerine. What had he done all those years ago?

"Seven gees is gonna hurt. Good luck, Slate."

The thruster released, punching Slate into the air, his breath torn from his body, and his vision blurring with the pain.

He didn't notice, though. Another type of pain hit him even harder. Green eyes. A boy's voice. And falling. Everything falling, tumbling around him, and unable to keep the boy safe. And a love lost . . . not Katerine . . . it ripped him apart! He had loved her so much . . . and she was gone from him forever.

And a daughter he could never hold again.

The pictures tore through his thoughts like a series of windows into a life he might have had, the images moving faster and faster, a runaway rocket falling into the sun.

And there was more: Kartye Tree, a mother, a father killed making repairs to the spring, and the repair failing anyway. Friends, Jell, and Kan, and Roni, his first love at thirteen, and the beating he'd gotten from her father. His scars reminded him of what might have been.

And minister! He held a job, an important job!

He was Minister of Tree Security . . . had been Minister of Tree Security. That was the reason for Katerine's tears. Not him, not the loss of his companionship. She had cried for her loss of position.

However, the tree was far, and his knowledge was instantaneous. This was no slow infusion in bursts and stops. Knowledge that was his was simply there, known when he needed it, or waiting until he did.

Slate knew what he had to do when he reached the tree, the grapples that were extended, the spiderline that stretched in every direction. He had set it all up thirteen years before. It was his masterpiece.

And it would work. Third try. It would work.

That mantra kept him focused as the tree grew in his vision, soon becoming his world, a continued home to one hundred thousand people.

If he could stick his landing and win this once and for all.

Chapter 17

THE EXTENDED spiderline caught him, but barely. He could tell he was going to miss, and he wrestled frantically to get his hundred-meter grapple unwound. Clipping it to his harness, he waited until he was at the apex of his trajectory, and he tossed the hook. It was spring loaded—always the springs!—to react when it made contact, wrapping around whatever it touched. For the tree's sake, he hoped it was the spiderline.

The problem was, throw it too hard, and the mass of the grapple would send his mass the opposite direction. Good old Newton, whoever she was. Thank God for Newton's lessons, learned as a kid. Slate didn't want to fly off in space. Being pulled in by the Factory a third time was a death sentence.

For all of them.

The spiderline would have acted as a trampoline, if he'd impacted squarely. Hit, let it absorb the excess momentum, and he would have come to a gentle rest in the arms of the tree. That was what he'd hoped for. The grapple? Ho, ho. His one second of acceleration at seven gees had pushed him to two-fifty kays. Stopping from that speed all at once, and on a grapple latched to his harness . . . as soon as he threw the grapple, he knew it was going to hurt.

"Gos—*arrrgh!*" He yelled out the broken curse, his neck

whipping sideways, and his harness cutting deeply into his leg. He'd show a bruise there. He grabbed his side. At least one rib, either bruised or broken. He'd swear to that. He hung at the end of the grapple's hundred meters for a few moments, catching his breath. "I gave up thirteen years for this?" He reached a gloved hand and began to pull himself in.

He had caught on the terminator line, just where the tree was half in light and half in darkness. Windows blinked above him, and far towards the end of the tree, just catching Death's light, the Plexan covering one of the tree's tufts sparkled against the blazing furnace. In a macabre sort of way, it was quite beautiful. In a realistic sort of way, it was the tree's death dance with the blazing behemoth. Fight or die, riding a blazing tree into the night.

Boy, did life's choices twist the world into a mess!

By that time, black-suited figures were out on the web, throwing grapples, flinging themselves into space, and arcing back to the web. It was an orchestrated dance of mad fleas, all coming right for him. And for the spiderline attached to his back. They were welcome to it.

He waved, and one of the black-suited fleas waved back.

"Minister Knalb!" A feminine voice called through the tenuous air.

"Ex-minister," he called back, pulling his breather aside, and letting it float at the end of its tether. He could breathe, although the air was thin. These people were Outers, used to being outside. Their red blood counts probably topped the charts.

"Not anymore. Listra, at your service." She pulled back a face covering as she bounced up to him, calling out in greeting. With ease, she wrapped the web's spiderline around one of her feet, remaining perfectly still. She handed him a silver canister. "Air?"

He shook his head. "I need inside. Help me up."

With her name he had immediately known a deeper story, the congenial nature that made her a favorite among the Outers and an envied target of the Huggers, those who rarely stepped outside the tree's safe and secure walls. It was as if an old-fashioned book had fallen open, and Listra Bonaparte's story was laid out in captioned storyboard form. There was more there, pages and pages, and he could peruse it at his leisure when he was ready. Now, though, he held out his hand, as the web flexed with the movements of the other fleas removing the line from his back and hauling it towards the tree.

"Don't lose your grip!" Slate laughed, his mood buoyed with the success of his trip.

"Star-forged!" A masculine voice called to him, one hand held high, the line wrapped securely in the man's grip.

Slate understood the response. Star-forged was as strong as anything could get, and all spiderline was star-forged. He turned to his companion. "What do you mean, Listra, not anymore?" He let her help him remove the harness, handing it off to her once he was free. It would slowly drift towards the tree if released, but it would be a waste of time for someone to come retrieve it.

"We have not shared everything with the Factory." Her motions were very compact, with little excess movement. Gravitational attraction to the tree was very weak even this close. It wouldn't do to leap too hard out. Slate's concern with the grapple was everyone's concern outside of the tree, unless one were tethered. "The Godders have gained new strength, infiltrating the Cabinet with their filth."

"Ah! A chance to wrest back what we've lost. What do they claim, now?" He laughed, invigorated. It was why he'd become minister in the first place. His hand-over-hand up the web became faster.

"If it is God's will . . ." She grinned, as she continued to hand-over-hand past him.

"It is never God's will." Slate had always liked this in Listra. "You do know you'll never be a Hugger favorite with that attitude."

"I revel in my role as Hugger fodder." Mirth crinkled her eyes.

"Good girl. Now, what's God's will for the tree this century?" It had been increased protein crops at one time, then releasing caps on reproductive rates. Slate remembered the days of "God viewing" when Destruction had undergone twenty years of erratic sunspot activity. There were still a number of blind Godders roaming the ship. Religious nuts never listened to good sense.

"The same old. If God wished for us to rejoin the Exodus, he would have provided a fuel source."

"And *that* is what?" He motioned to the Factory, just visible in Death's corona.

"I belong to the choir, ser." Listra held up a hand.

"What would they have us do? Fall into the grip of Death and Destruction, casually waiting to die?"

"I think that's the idea. I'm glad to have you back as minister. The door, ser. I'll leave you now." Listra gave a casual, militaristic salute, twirling the wheel that released the seal, and allowing the door to pull back and slide sideways. "Within hours, we should have the spiderline affixed to the retrieval drum."

"Volunteers?" How many, he meant. The drum would have to be spun manually.

"Enough, willing or otherwise." She grinned, pulling her face covering back down and lifting her grapple from her waist.

Slate watched her leap into the thin atmosphere of the Torus, and flinging the grapple out with practiced ease, once again she became a flea against the spiderline web. When she was no more than a dot among the black fleas, he turned to step inside, wondering if Katerine had rebounded since their breakup over a decade ago. He wanted her to be happy. He really did. Happy with him would be better, but that he could do nothing about.

Chapter 18

"AH, YOU are so clever!" Slate grabbed the man's shoulders walking just in front of him, then slapped them both at the same time, before releasing his hands and spinning around, clapping his hands together. "Oh, this is wonderful!"

"It's only what we had to do, ser." The technician had a broad smile on his face, though.

"How did you think of this?" He strode enthusiastically to one wall to run his hands along a set of steel brackets bordering each side of a seam. The seam was new. A massive pin was thrust through the brackets. There were pairs of similar brackets running full length down the side of the curved wall.

They were in the spring chamber, that kilometer-long, double-walled tube that slowly ratcheted forward, tighter and tighter, compressing the ship's spring, only to release it to fling the massive ship forward. It also provided power for water and waste processing, as well as lighting and atmospheric conditioning.

It was stilled now, and that was an ominous sign.

The opening for installing the new spring was ingenious, however. It had not been there just over a decade ago.

"Tell me how it works." This innovation Slate was interested in. Very interested in. Thirteen years of his life were invested in this one project, and he wanted the ship to live. This was its salvation. It had to be its salvation, because there was no other answer. "Where did you get the metal for the pins? And these brackets? They are massive! How many are there, did you say?"

"Seventeen hundred and three," a voice from off to the side called out. It echoed, every sound loud in the vast chamber. "That's just on this side."

"The metal? This is a lot."

"Have you seen our spring, ser?" There was amusement in the question.

"Not yet. I did just get back aboard. Shall we have a look now?" He expected it would be a nightmare of repairs and stopgap measures. It had been when he left, and it had to be worse now, as it seemed to be stilled entirely. It would also have to be removed before the new one could be installed.

"This way." The technician had a smile on his face.

"What's so funny?" Slate looked at the man's badge. "Larstrun, is it? Larstrun, what's so funny?"

"Larstrun Gilbreath. Of the North Latitudes Gilbreaths. My great gram was schoolmates with your great gram, but of course you wouldn't know that."

"That doesn't explain what's funny, Larstrun of the North Latitudes Gilbreaths." They had reached a much smaller door, one that Slate did remember. He understood the man's reference. They had a connection. This was no friend of the Godders, else he wouldn't have interconnected their history that way. This was more. "By the way, glad to meet you, Larstrun of the North Latitude Gilbreaths."

"And you, ser." Larstrun nodded, his body making a slight bow.

So, there was a connection, but it was not equal to equal. Perhaps their classes were equal now, but they had not been in their great grams' time. This man would be a good one to have around, if the Godders did cause trouble.

The door opened with a loud clang, the metal seal one of endurance, not that of ease and soft touches. During a normal decade, it was designed to be opened perhaps twice a year for maintenance, and rarely more. Longevity was the key here.

Inside, banks of lights flickered, some turning on immediately, the majority requiring several seconds to power up. Some were bright white, with others in duller hues. That reflected repairs done over the centuries. It was colder, also. This was the spring chamber, sandwiched between the inner and outer walls of the ship. Atmosphere in here was residual leakage from imperfect seals. Air was too precious to waste on utility chambers.

The ship was totally extended at this point. With a broken spring, how could it be otherwise? That left a full kay of massive ratcheting gears exposed, the grabber arms like great claws ready to rip away the well-oiled metal tracks. Small release springs attached to each grabber arm were extended to their maximum length. When the arms ratcheted forward, the springs would slowly tighten over the kilometer crawl. Only at the end would the release mechanism trigger, and the springs would quickly expand to power the Gessimer engines, enabling the ship to leap forward once again.

It was a marvel of engineering brought on by desperation. It was also broken.

"The . . . spring. Is it coiled?" Slate had done maintenance on it over the years. He knew this room. Where was it?

"You saw the brackets?" Larstrun smiled.

"Yes—"

"And the pins?" His smile grew wider.

"I'm not sure I follow you."

"Well, there you go." He laughed and slapped the exterior wall. Another set of brackets and pins mirrored those on the inside. "We have both these walls done, but only the interior on the opposite side will be cut. We're working inside the spring chamber round the clock. Listen."

There was a dull grumble of complaining metal, and the hull vibrated under their feet.

"Torch?" Slate referred to an ion-plasma torch. However, without the spring to power the plasma generators, that seemed unlikely.

"WaterPic. We run the compression off a manual spring. A team of ten powers the winder, and two men handle the Pic. It works. It's just slow."

"Have you paid attention to Death and Destruction?" Slate had. He'd paid close attention. But he also knew it had probably taken the best part of the last decade to cut these massive doors in the hull. "Without that new spring in here—" And that's when it hit him. His eyes leaped from bracket to bracket, a smile growing on his face.

"You noticed?" Larstrun laughed.

"Those brackets?" It was indeed a brilliant solution.

"The spring didn't do them *all,* but it made a really big dent." Larstrun grimaced. "We had to cannibalize a few residential floors for the rest."

"Now, that couldn't have been good." Complaints must have

besieged the Cabinet chambers from misplaced residents. Slate cringed at that.

By that time they had moved back into the big chamber, and several people were headed their way. One was dressed in flowing robes, and most wore large ornamental necklaces. They appeared heavy, and the men walked like they were.

"I didn't expect this. Sorry, ser." Larstrun murmured the words. "Godders."

"Ser Gilbreath." The leader of the group nodded his head at Larstrun.

"Speaker Craigs-Toy." Larstrun was terse.

"Minister Knalb." He nodded again.

"Speaker." Slate nodded his head, the man's purpose flooding his thoughts with his name. Craigs-Toy was Leopold Craigs-Toy, head echelon and top executive of the Godders Walk of Faith United Peoples, representing the Godders faction of worshipers in the tree.

They wanted Kartye Tree to fall into the suns.

They claimed a revelation from the spiritual realm that God's chosen would be reborn in a cataclysm of fire, and they would come out the other side, ready to take their rightful place at their God's side, wherever that may be.

They had also sabotaged the spring on more than one occasion.

Listra's comment made sense to him now. *Infiltrated the Cabinet with their filth.* He recalled the mounted campaigns for votes over the years. They were a nuisance most of the time, or at least they had been thirteen years earlier. It seemed they had become more, in his absence.

"We are glad to see your return has been successful." Craigs-Toy murmured his sentiments with his head bowed and his eyes on the floor. "I am honored to speak with you in the presence of Sage Dom-Cronian. He has ascended to Prime in this Glorious Decade of our Coming Cataclysm."

Slate could hear the capital letters in the man's speech with his emphasis on the words he considered important. The man actually thought Kartye Tree would be allowed to sink to its death with one hundred thousand souls aboard? Better that ten thousand Godders take leave of the city, jumping into the void to be swept in by the grasp of the twin suns' gravitational pull. It would leave more space for sensible people, in his opinion.

"You are aware, I am certain, of our successes at the Factory?"

81

"Your perceived successes, yes." Craigs-Toy nodded.

His Prime stood mute.

"Perceived?" Slate almost smiled. "I am proof that repairs are underway. The spiderline is being readied as we speak."

"Elections are days away. Then a Cabinet vote will be held on the matter of this—" and he motioned around the cavern with his hand "—atrocity. The installation will not be completed before then. After the vote, the work will be of no matter, in any case." Craigs-Toy smiled ingratiatingly. "Your attempts, however misguided, will not go unnoticed by God, I am sure."

"You think not?" Slate had about used up his quota of diplo-speak. He had just arrived back after a thirteen-year absence, he had no idea what had happened to his successor, and he was determined the spring was going in. Who did this man think he was? God, himself? "Perhaps his Prime Sage will be pleased to speak with us at a later date. I have only arrived, and I need to review current policies and events before speaking further about this matter."

Craigs-Toy looked to the Sage, and after a moment the hooded figure nodded. Craigs-Toy turned back to Slate. "As you wish. Our one regret is the wasted man-hours that could be put to the service of the Congregation." He nodded, and the group turned and walked briskly away.

"Well done, ser." The compliment was Larstrun's.

"The man is a fool, as are all of them." Slate glowered for a few minutes, and then he stood tall as he felt his backbone stiffen within him. "Steppen was minister in my stead. A good man, I remember. What happened to him?"

"Thirteen years happened. Thirteen years and one misguided religion." Larstrun's words were dry; very matter-of-fact.

"He quit?" That didn't sound like Steppen, not the Steppen Slate had known.

"Involuntarily." Larstrun cleared his throat and pointed at the far wall over a hundred meters away. "That's why this isn't finished. The minister had requisitioned extra bodies to speed up the work. Then he went missing. He was found yesterday."

"Found?" That sounded ominous.

"Parts of him, ser." Larstrun turned away for a minute, his face pale, before he continued. "The Godders really do not want the work to continue, at any cost."

"Then we will have to make the cost acceptable, I suppose. I think it's time I took charge." He grinned and looked at Larstrun.

"Yes, ser!" Larstrun seemed renewed. "I am really glad to have you back, ser."

The curved metal wall nearly a hundred forty meters distant began to hum. Then, close to the top, a powerful stream of water broke through, spitting metal shards and water to the floor below.

"Time to go, ser. This gets messy at this stage in the process, and you will not want to stay. Your old quarters have been readied for your residence. May I show you the way?"

Slate thought he could probably find his way without any problem, but he had gathered the situation. Larstrun was more than a functionary, and more than a guide. He now had a bodyguard, a vassal, so to speak, and he would be at his side every moment Slate walked the tree.

He wondered what Larstrun expected from the relationship. Or if maybe the tables were somehow turned, and Slate was the vassal. If so, the question was still the same. What would Larstrun expect? A step up the social ladder? Power? Position? Whatever it was, Kartye Tree had changed, and Slate wasn't sure it was for the better.

And Katerina. Where had she disappeared to? That was a question he had a vested interest in answering. He really wanted to know.

And his side. It had begun to ache. Severely. He'd have to get to a medic before long. What he had given up for the tree! Ach, but he hoped it was worth it.

Chapter 19

SLATE looked into the sky to see two suns blazing low on the horizon. Up where the Torus faded from cobalt to black hung the Factory, suspended by the finest of spiderwire lines, the original strand tautly glistening where it caught the suns' light and reflected it back to Kartye Tree.

He smiled, very pleased. More than pleased, in fact. He made a fist and pumped it in excitement. His enthusiasm was palpable, and for good reason. A celebratory crowd stood on an observation platform mounted where the massive coil would soon be drawn into the tree's hull and installed to power her once again, and they had gathered to rejoice in the future that was unfolding right before their eyes.

The glittering metallic ovoid, Kartye Tree's new spring, was suspended halfway between Kartye Tree and the Factory. Three more weeks would pass before it reached Kartye Tree, but its visible presence encompassed a century and a half of construction that would undo a millennium of failure.

Kartye Tree would travel space once again, no longer trapped in Death and Destruction's gas torus, doomed to eternally fight the fingers of gravity that were determined to pull her in. A world somewhere would be found, and her people would be allowed to live unfettered by the restrictions of space and food and unending labor required aboard Kartye Tree to achieve the most menial of tasks.

Springloaded Fists had vaulted fleas out to the spring, conveying long spiderlines—stabilizing threads, now attached—and she was making her way in.

God save the Queen!

Slate turned to the small crowd at his side, and he raised a fist in the air, calling out, "God save the Queen!"

The chant was returned, "God save the Queen!"

"What does that mean?" Larstrun leaned in to whisper the question.

Slate shrugged. "But isn't it magnificent? Our children, and their children, will live again, and under the sun of a real world." He lifted an arm and punched the sky.

"Barring a Cabinet vote," Larstrun muttered.

The Godders had taken another seat, but Slate didn't intend to let anyone take down this success. "Think positively, my friend. Their god may be sending them to a fiery purgatory, but mine is carrying me to the stars."

Only a small fraction of the tree's inhabitants could be present, but their successes were being broadcast to the entire tree. The Godders' campaign for noninterference, otherwise known as self-destruction, had gained more of a toehold than Slate liked. Previous Godder terrorism had not been forgotten, especially by those given responsibility for the security of the tree. That meant Slate. He'd been determined that this celebratory party encompass represen-tatives from each section of the tree, even from the Godder quadrant.

The tree turned from night into Deathlight as the party con-tinued. The collar to which the spring was attached circled the cir-cumference of the trunk, resting on massive ball bearings created just for this purpose. In a century and a half, they'd had plenty of time to prepare.

This gathering had been equally long in the making, and the mood was one of anticipation. The gases in the Torus tended to concentrate around objects in their midst, and although there were breathers available, those closest to the ship didn't need them. Food was out: harvested fruits and vegetables from the tree tufts, and cheeses from the animal farms deeper within the tree. Elongated bottles of Flamewine, from reds to greens, rested in racks, to serve as refills for glasses up and down the esplanade.

Even live music played, although the instruments were simple string devices, with just a few operated by blown air.

Sunrise would occur several times for the celebration before the festivities ended, as the tree ship spun on its axis. Three sunrises and three sunsets for those who retired early, and four or more if the drinks lasted long enough. Of course, counting both Death and Destruction, the number was twice that high. It was the Godder representatives that seemed most interesting. Their faces carried less excitement and more anticipation. Each time the suns rolled into view, they spent that half hour gazing into the twin furnaces, their eyes unprotected, and their lips moving in prayer.

They didn't dampen all of Slate's enjoyment. Nothing could do that. He did watch them carefully, though, and he was glad he'd invited them. He'd learned long ago that success lies in keeping your friends close and your enemies closer.

He wanted the Godders as close to him as possible.

No matter the reason, that could really spoil a day!

MINISTRY quarters were quite generous, more so than any one man needed.

However, after thirteen years on the Factory, Slate didn't begrudge himself even one of its creature comforts. He deserved each perk that came with the office.

Water was what he'd missed most while on the Factory.

And heat? With a hundred thousand human bodies on board Kartye Tree, steam pipes running along the outer hull bled excess heat, keeping the interior of the ship cool.

There was hot water in excess, for whatever purpose one desired.

This night, Slate desired a shower, and heated water jetted from multiple heads, filling the enclosure with steam. Soap-making facilities aboard the tree were less abundant; good quality soaps came at a very high price. A cloth, scrubbed briskly, he had found, was often sufficient to clean most grime away.

Tonight he sat in the torrent, his skin red with the heat, and he traced the design on his leg. It had always been there, for as long as he remembered. Yet, somehow, he didn't remember the day he had the tattoo done. The design, a circular pattern, wrapped his thigh, almost touching at the back. It was quite beautiful, filled with loops and whorls, gears connected to gears, and explosions that could only be interpreted as stardust and dreams. At least that's the way he thought of it.

On the outside of his leg, a series of interlocking gears flexed and shifted each time he changed positions. Katerina used to say she liked to watch them move. He'd always thought she meant the muscles under the skin, but more and more, since returning from the Factory, he'd begun to wonder.

Then, on the inside of his leg, there were coiled springs, interwoven with tiny lines that seemed to leap off his skin. They often looked alive, as if they moved when he wasn't looking. Yet, they were always where they were supposed to be when he brushed them with his hand.

This night, it was the stardust that had his attention. He guessed it was the spring and the celebration. Much of the tree was in a celebratory mood, for the world was changing for one hundred thousand people. For generations, as long as anyone could remember, all they had done on their little world was vainly fight against Death and Destruction's gravity well, hoping that this day was not the day they would be pulled into that very visible purgatory.

They had prayed for deliverance for their children and their children's children. This time, this year, this lifetime was their salvation. And he, Slate Knalb, was alive at this moment in time, to see this success come to his people, and they would be free!

Yet, here he sat, the unending torrent of heated water beating against his body, as he toyed with this wheel he'd carried for as long as he remembered. What did it mean?

"Nothing." He said the word aloud. He brushed the beaded water from the tattoo with the flat of his hand, only to have the jetted spray cover it once again. He laughed. "It means nothing. It's just a tattoo, and I've used far and enough water."

Standing, he twisted the cutoffs, watching for a moment as the water swirled around his feet and into the grating. Steam surrounded him, and he shook his arms and legs to disperse the remaining water. Finally, he brushed himself off with his hands. Pausing at the tattoo, he laughed softly.

"What are you there for, funny design? Why would I have such a thing etched into my skin? I must have been blasted out of my mind."

One perk of the minister's quarters was outside windows, and another was a balcony high up the tuft wall. He stepped to the balcony and stood under Death's light, his skin still wet, and his shadow moving as he watched. Sunrise every hour of every day. It wasn't a bonus, and there were many people who preferred interior quarters. A human wasn't designed for hour-long days. Work-sleep cycles aboard Kartye Tree were based on a standard twenty-five hour day. Sunrise and sunset? Mere decoration to be shut out or enjoyed.

It was officially night, so the tuft was empty, except for a few night owls working far overhead, planting flowers in a landscaping bed while suspended in harnesses. There were fruit trees near Slate's balcony, but none within reach. Being so far up the tuft wall meant he looked out on the upper branches of the trees. Upside down. Trees could be genetically modified to grow hanging from a grassy ceiling, but humans needed to walk on a floor.

Anyway, even if he could reach the trees, ministers couldn't strip the tuft's fruits at will. The harvest belonged to the tree.

He was surprised to hear a knock from the other room, and he turned from the bucolic scene.

"Coming!" He grabbed a towel and wrapped it around his waist, walking rapidly down a long corridor and crossing a generous living space. Passing a table, he lifted a two-way, and he pressed the send switch. "Larstrun? Is that you?"

"Minister, ser?" The reply was immediate, suggesting the paired instrument had been waiting in the man's hand.

"How's Godder activity tonight?" There had been concerns with the celebration, but nothing had come of it.

"Surprisingly uneventful, ser. May I ask why?"

"I have a visitor at my door. Not you, I assume." He triggered a lever and glanced into a monitor beside the door. "Two, actually. One male, light-colored, young. The second, female, medium tones, with severely cut hair. Are you picking them up?" The male was looking directly at the camera with distinctive green eyes.

"One moment." There was a pause. "I am now. I'm running the visuals. No match to any known Godder terrorist in the system. The female is a follower. Shall I send security?"

During Larstrun's speech, the male had reached into his jacket. Slate's heart jumped. "Larstrun—" It was what the youth pulled out that stopped him. He raised an open palm to the camera, and inside was a silver tube about ten centimeters long. It filled the screen.

"Ser? I can have them there in thirty seconds."

"Hold." There was something oddly familiar about the male. He tried to place him, and he couldn't. Yet, that cylinder. That had his name written all over it, even if he couldn't decide just why.

Then the boy closed his hand in a fist, and after a moment, a figure appeared above his closed hand. Slate froze.

"I'm inviting these two in. Be prepared if I call."

"Yes, ser. I'll notify security, just in case."

"Certainly."

In the display the youth lowered his hand, and he reached to knock once again. The woman spoke to him before turning to look back down the corridor. Slate reached for the door, and he triggered the release.

"Ser." The green-eyed youth looked surprised to see Slate at the door. "I mean, Minister." He cleared his throat and looked away, clearly ill at ease.

"Minister Knalb." The woman was more articulate. "My apologies. I am Elder Alaina Bellows, a lay counselor with the Walk of Faith United Peoples. I am sure you have heard of us."

"Yes." He held his hand on the two-way, prepared to press the send button. He glanced at the youth. There was something about this boy. Even more, there was that cylinder he'd held in his hand. He made sure Elder Bellows could see the two-way he held. "It's late."

"Certainly, ser. I tried to contact you earlier, but with the celebration." She shrugged. "My young friend is insistent he see you, and he did not have permissions to be in this level of the ship. So, he begged me for my assistance. You will want to see what he wishes to show you."

"The cylinder?"

"You saw it?" The youth was breathless with excitement, and he grinned, his face lighting up.

"Let me, Levin." Elder Bellows placed her hand on his arm for just a moment before pulling it away and turning back to Slate. "He is young, and I apologize. There is friction between the Peoples and the changes brought about by your success on the Factory, and I am aware of that. As are you, I am sure." She smiled apologetically. "I have not come to create problems. Nor would I, in any case. My only purpose is to assist young Levin. May we come in?"

"I'm hardly dressed, Elder." Slate laughed. "But something tells me I can trust our young friend, and your words? You are a credit to your religion."

"You mean," the youth looked at Slate, his expression one of astonishment, and he glanced back to the woman, "we get . . . to go in?" He grinned again. "Wow! This is so cool." He looked past

89

Slate, as if he'd never seen in a minister's quarters before.

"Let me notify my security team." Larstrun was hardly a team, but he was the next best thing. He spoke into the unit, "I'm good." After a moment, he answered, "Yes, I'm inviting them in." He made a face. "If you insist, I'll check." He asked, "Any weapons?"

The woman smiled and shook her head.

"Only this. It's not a weapon." The youth opened his hand, showing the tube.

"Will it explode?" Slate smiled. He thought not.

"No!" The youth looked horrified. "It's just got pictures. Of you." He glanced at the woman, again clearly unsure of himself.

"Go on, Levin. You have shown me. Tell him."

"And pictures of me." Levin's look was clear-eyed and earnest, with no deception.

"We're clean, Larstrun." Slate motioned them in, putting the two-way aside on a low table. That look had said something about the boy. This was important to him, and he believed what was on that cylinder. That alone had Slate's interest. The cylinder first, and with his oddly felt connection to the boy?

This he couldn't pass up.

Chapter 20

"HOW long have you two known each other?" Slate sat in the expansive living room on a sofa, and his guests were in matching chairs across from him. He still wore his towel. At first he'd thought better of leaving the pair unattended while he dressed, but now he was too fascinated to care.

"We don't—" Levin started, and he cut his words off. "I mean, we do, but . . ." His voice trailed away, and he took a deep breath.

"Only this one day." Elder Bellows smiled. "He came to me during the televised festivities, and he was most insistent that he be allowed to see you—"

"I had to." Levin interrupted her, sitting on the edge of his chair. "I'd never seen you before. Then, on the viewer, it was you." He laughed, looking away. "I mean, I didn't think you were real, at first, and that was how I knew you. Then I saw it was the celebration." He stopped, grinning broadly, as if he didn't know what else to say.

"You didn't think I was real?" Slate was enjoying this youth, even if he wasn't making sense.

"My mom, well, my foster mom, likes old vids. You know, the ones that claim to be from *before*. I thought that's what was playing, and that's why you were on this." He held the silver tube up. "I mean, anyone from *before* couldn't be alive now, so of course . . ."

He shrugged.

"From before, you mean pre-Exodus." The way the boy stressed the word, it was clearly an age-specific shortcut.

"Yeah, pre-Exodus, I guess." He grinned, as if he'd never thought of it that way. "Sure, pre-Exodus. That sounds cool. I like that."

"Tell the minister of your silver toy." The elder smiled, as if she considered what he would say next as something close to fantasy.

"Right." Levin had sat back, and he moved to the front of the chair and leaned forward, his green eyes animated, and his voice shaking with excitement. He held out the tube. "I've had this ever since I can remember."

Slate watched him rub his finger along the cylinder, thinking, *as with my tattoo.* However, this was the boy's story, not his. He nodded agreeably.

"I don't know how it does what it does, but it talks to me."

"Sure," Slate said. "Like a two-way."

Levin laughed. "Not really, ser." He glanced at the elder.

"Show him, boy."

He licked his lips. "You want to see?" He was flushed with anticipation.

"Can I hold it?"

"Sure." The youth shrugged. "It won't do anything, though."

"But it does for you?" Slate reached and took it from the boy. "How does it work?"

"I hold it in my fist." He balled his hand. "Like this. Let me show you."

"No." Slate held up his hand. "In a moment." He grasped it in his fist, and it began to warm. Quickly. And thoughts filled his head. Memories of a woman, and a girl, and a boy—this boy!—flooded his mind. This silver stick, and his face talking to him from nothing at all. Dazed, he flung his hand open and watched the small tube vault into the air and tumble to the floor in silence, a slow-motion dance, as it hit and bounced, coming to rest at the youth's feet, slowly spinning to a stop.

Yet, it had done nothing except warm in his hand.

"Did it burn you?" The youth was kneeling and had the cylinder in his hand before it stopped spinning. He seemed oddly pleased.

"Are you all right, Minister?" That was the elder speaking.

Slate took a deep breath before answering. "Yes, Elder, just surprised at how the tube felt in my hand."

"Your leg." Levin still knelt, and he moved closer to Slate. He looked in Slate's eyes, then back to his leg. A small amount of the tattoo was exposed. "You . . . your tattoo. Where . . . I mean—" He could barely speak. "—where did you get that?" He seemed as if he wanted to touch it and could hardly keep his hand away. "Please, ser. May I see it?"

"My apologies, ser." Elder Bellows stood. "Levin, this man is a minister, and you are being forward. Ser, I will take him away now."

"No, Elder. Wait." Slate looked in the boy's eyes. "I know you. I don't, and yet, when I held that *thing* of yours, I saw you. Not grown, but small. How did that happen?"

"Your tattoo. I can draw it for you, if you wish."

"In that desk, Elder, if you will." Slate was certain the boy could. Yet, he'd never met this young man. Katerina? Perhaps, although any children she had after he left wouldn't be the age of this one.

Levin took the paper and pencil and made a wide arc, and then, talking the entire time, he began to fill in toothed gears, whirls, and stardust. One edge was ragged, falling away unfinished.

"It's the same as you wear. It's like a giant wheel." Levin glanced up at Slate expectantly, his pencil still poised, his eyes intense. "Since I was a boy, I've drawn it. When I first drew it, my foster parents tried to take my tube away, and I had to hide it from them. After that, I told no one. It was mine, and it never worked for anyone else."

"What do you mean?" Slate remembered outside the door, the boy holding the cylinder up to the camera. "What does it do for you that it does for no one else?"

"You saw." He continued to draw. "I never knew it was you. I mean, I knew who you were, your name, you being on the Factory, then back as minister, but I'd never seen you, not until today."

"Why's that edge not finished?" Slate pointed to the ragged section. The rest was exactly like the tattoo on his leg.

"You never show me that part." The youth put the pencil down and turned the paper a quarter turn. He ran his hand over the design lovingly.

"I never show it to you? I've never seen you before." Slate's pulse vibrated in his temples. In that vision, he'd seen this boy a thousand times. He'd watched him grow up. If he believed what he'd seen, he'd been a father to him.

"I've seen *you*." Levin held out the tube. "Here."

93

"Elder, you've seen this?"

"Yes, Minister. It is as he says."

"Show me." Slate motioned to the boy. "I want to see the 'me' in this thing."

"Here." Levin was still on his knees, and he held out his hand with the tube in his fist. He smiled expectantly. After a moment, something began to coalesce in the air above the young man's fist.

It was a face. Slate's face. It smiled, and it looked around and said, "Oh, there you are, Slate—"

Levin opened his hand, and the face disappeared.

"How did you do that?" Slate watched the youth take the silver tube out of his hand and rub the spot where it had been.

"It just does it." He grinned. "It's different every time, although they repeat after a certain point. Want to see another one?"

Slate motioned. The boy balled the cylinder in his fist, and the same face appeared. Again, it turned until it found Slate's face.

"Ah, there you are." The image smiled. "Yeah, I'm you—"

The boy released it, rubbing his palm again.

"Let me see that." Slate held out his hand, and Levin gave him the cylinder.

"It only does it for me." He grinned.

"How did you get my image in this? And it talks. How does that happen?" He was certain now there was a portable image player concealed somewhere, either in the youth's clothes or with the elder. "You say you saw my tattoo on this?" He still hadn't shown his leg. What surprised him was that the tattoo the boy drew matched, and exactly, all except for that one unfinished edge.

Slate didn't get his answer. Alarms went off, the sounds piercing his ears, and before he could sit up, the room was jarred sideways. Levin fell to the floor, and the cylinder slipped from Slate's hand. The two-way crackled to life.

"Minister! Pick up, Minister!"

Slate looked from the youth to the woman, and he grimaced. Striding to the two-way, he picked it up and clicked it on.

"Slate, here."

"Ser, we've had an attack on the spring. The line's separated."

"How bad is it?" He turned to the two people in his quarters to see them looking back at him.

"Catastrophic, ser. You must have felt it."

"Spell it out, Larstrun." Slate drew in a deep breath. He wanted to close his eyes. Not a good idea, not with his unknown visitors.

"Godders, ser. The spring is free." Rising panic filled Larstrun's voice.

"That impact. We were hit?"

"Not just hit, ser. Holed."

"The Cabinet?"

"Don't know, ser. Surely gathering, at least before long."

"Meet me here. Five minutes. I'll be ready." He set the device down, walking to stand before Elder Bellows. "Your people may have just doomed us. You are not to leave these quarters."

The youth looked frightened. He was back in his chair, his face pale. Slate knew he should restrict him, as well, but curse that little tube. Those visions. He'd seen them as clear as real life. He *knew* this kid he'd never seen. And he trusted him. Why? Crazy if he knew, but he'd trust him with his life.

"You. Levin, right? You're with me. Don't move from my side." Slate headed for clothes, walking briskly. As he passed the boy, he clapped him firmly on the shoulder. "Up, boy. Like I said, don't leave my side."

And blast it, if the boy didn't try to hide a smile when he told him not to move from his side. What did the boy think this was, a father-son outing? This was war. If those Godders wanted a fight, he'd give it to them, because he refused to let anyone on this ship die, simply because of a few deluded, crazy old men.

Even if they claimed to have heard from their god.

Chapter 21

SLATE ran down the corridor, Larstrun at his side, and the green-eyed boy trailing close behind. Four security tailed them.

"Ser," the boy called.

"Yes, Levin?" Slate motioned for him to move closer. He also caught Larstrun's frown.

"We . . . there is air, you know, in the Torus. Holed . . . that isn't serious, is it?"

"Only if we wish to rejoin our people." Larstrun spat the words. "Your people wish otherwise."

"Me?"

"Him?" Slate pointed. "What did he do?"

"He was with that Godders woman. Why is he with us, ser?"

"I am not—"

"Because I like him." Slate laughed and clasped the boy on the shoulder, releasing him immediately. What he didn't say was what he'd seen when he'd held that tube. How that was possible was another matter. And that wheel. He did know the wheel. He'd drawn it exactly, and that was impossible.

Slate wanted impossible at his side.

He noticed the boy flush with pleasure when he said that.

"You like him, ser." Larstrun didn't sound so welcoming.

"Green eyes. Who has green eyes like that, and a magic cylinder?"

"You, ser, the green eyes. Look in a mirror." Larstrun snorted. "Eyes don't prove honesty." They came to a stop, damage now littering the corridor in front of them.

"This time they do. Besides, I like anyone who has a magic cylinder." Slate nodded at the boy to reassure him.

"Minister." A number of men were helping people out of damaged areas. One who seemed familiar stepped up to him. "Gungan, ser. Travid Gungan. We were together for some time on the Factory. We're glad you're here. This whole bank of quarters, fifteen in all, is crushed. Five on this level, one above, and the rest below. The worst is here. Two died." True enough, a man and a woman carried a covered body out just in front of where they stood.

The man's name, though. With it had come an inrush of memories: knowledge, quarters shared, and private jokes told in the middle of the night. He also knew the man had one foot. The other had been lost to a Factory locking pin that had sheared, releasing a section of the coiled spring. The results had been the loss of the man's leg. It was why he left the Factory.

This was a friend, of sorts.

"What do you need, Travid?" As Minister of Tree Security, this was Slate's job, to make sure this area was secure.

"To capture the Godders that did this. Toss them out." The man's words were venom.

"Yeah," another man called. "Let them roast in that fiery blast furnace out there." He pointed to the ragged hole in the far side of the damaged quarters where the twin suns were just rising.

"The spring. What about the spring?" Slate meant, was it lost or damaged beyond repair? If they'd lost the Factory, then repair was impossible. Their equipment was there, not on Kartye Tree.

"The stabilizer lines are holding it, ser." Larstrun had been on his two-way. "Three held. One snapped when the main line was severed. The impact." He shrugged. "That's what saved it. It absorbed the momentum before the remaining lines could snap."

"That's good, right?" Levin grabbed Slate's arm. "I mean, if we have the spring, we can get the ship working. Right?"

"Perhaps." He looked into the boy's eyes. There was something there. "What do you know?"

"This is here." He held out his fist, opening it to show the silver tube. It glistened in the light.

"What's here?" Larstrun reached for the tube, only to have the boy's hand close on it.

"You saw it." Levin's eyes were red. "Always, I've listened to the voice carry on unknown conversations. For the first time, they make sense. The tube talks to you. The man is talking to you."

"What does it say?" A wife, a daughter, a son? A death? "Does it predict the future?"

"No, of course not. At least I don't think so, but one of the images, it's this. You talk about a spring. I never understood before, but it has to be this."

"If he knows anything about this, ser—" Larstrun motioned for the security.

"What would I know? I'm sixteen. All I know is that you're here—" He held up the cylinder. "—and it's just now making sense." His eyes glistened, and his face was flushed with emotion, with red patches splotched across his neck.

"Can you show me?" The noise around them was loud, metal being moved and people calling to one another, but Slate had a feeling about this, and for good reason. This cylinder, this boy, and he were connected, tied together in some way.

"Sometimes I can get certain ones to appear." Levin wiped his nose on the back of his hand. "Not always, just sometimes. I can try."

Larstrun's hand shot out, and he grabbed the tube. "This? It's an explosive device, of that I'm now certain." He indicated the damage. "This is a Godder device. Security—"

"No, it's mine." Levin lunged for it.

"Hold, boy." Slate caught him, gripping his arm. One of the security already held the device. "If I may." He held his hand out.

"Ser?" The security glanced to Larstrun.

"Minister, I don't recommend trusting this boy. The Godders are a terrorist organization. See the damage they've already caused?" His eyes glanced to the broken walls and back to Slate's face. "This boy. They'll use anyone."

"*I* trust this boy. You are trustworthy, are you not, Levin?" He smiled.

"Yes, ser. I wouldn't do anything. I just wanted you to see—" He made as if to lunge for the tube again, and Slate restrained him once more.

"And I will. Security? May I?"

Larstrun nodded.

"Thank you." The cylinder was placed in his hand, and he

wrapped it in his fist. It was almost as if the little cylinder wanted to be held by him. Odd. It warmed. "Now, young man. How does it work?"

"You've seen it. I showed you . . ." He could barely keep his eyes from Slate's hand.

"I saw you hold it, and I saw an image. That's all. Now show me the technology that operates it."

"It's just my hand." Desperation edged his voice. "I just hold it, and it does that."

It was growing hot, and Slate held his fist to the boy. "If I give it to you, you'll make it work?"

Levin didn't have to. Just above Slate's fist an image appeared. It turned, looking, as if searching for someone or something, first focusing on the damage and frowning, and next, catching Levin's face and breaking into a bright smile.

"Levi!"

"He always calls me that." Levin grinned, his eyes lighting up as he glanced at Slate. "Or at least I think he's talking to me. It feels like it."

"Finished, now?" The face smiled, as if amused.

"It does that, too." Levin was breathless. "I never knew why. It's like it's really alive."

"I mean, really, Levi. I need you to be finished."

The boy just grinned.

"Now, about that spring—" The image had turned toward Slate.

"See? I told you."

"I mean, really, Levi. You have to just stop. Now." The face in the image was no longer smiling.

Levin was, though, from ear to ear.

"Now, Slate—" The man in the image raised his eyebrows and took a deep breath. "If you didn't know your name before, I bet you do now. Anyway, you are in a pickle. The whole lot of you. You still have time to make this right, but just."

"Make what right?" The face—his!—seemed to be talking right to them, but make what right?

"How could I have forgotten?" The small figure hit himself on the forehead, the first time his hand had come into view. "You don't know, yet. How could you? The second explosion hasn't happened. You," the hand pointed to Gungan, standing behind Larstrun and watching, "there, yes, you, Level 4, hidden behind a girl's play-house."

"What?" Gungan pointed to himself. "Is he speaking to me?"

"Not very bright, is he? The second bomb. This one goes off, and you lose the spring completely." His eyes were back on Gungan. "And I am very sorry."

"Sorry for what?" Gungan, again.

"You won't make it, but your daughter will tell your story, and you will never be forgotten. Not in a thousand years. Everyone will know what you do today."

"My daughter?" He looked aghast, and he turned to Slate. "I don't have a daughter."

"Ah," the face said. "I shouldn't have said that. You don't know that either, but, um, that woman does."

"Woman?"

The image nodded. "Go, now, or you won't make it. Remember, behind the playhouse. Go!"

"It's worth checking out." Slate nodded.

Larstrun motioned to the security team, and two of them took off with Gungan, running. Slate released the tube with a gasp, dumping it into his other hand, and shaking out the pain in his fist. "Hot! Does it always do that?"

"Get hot? Yeah." Levin took Slate's hand, and he felt of the palm. "You shouldn't have been able to do that."

"What?"

"Make it work." He looked into Slate's face, studying it. "He's you. I never thought he was real before. How'd you do it?"

"I held it?" He watched the kid, well aware of the worshipful look on his face. Then he laughed, looking away. "That was fantastic, you have to admit. I was there, talking to myself, and you, making me tell you to shut up. How did you do that?"

"No, you don't understand. He wasn't having a real conversation. He always says that, every time. It's not real, at least not anything we're part of."

"But he knew—"

"No, not really. You see, he always says, 'The spring,' and he always tells Levi to stop talking. I just like to pretend he's talking to me."

"And to me," said softly to himself. "I didn't pretend that." Slate held the tube out to the boy. "However this works, it's yours."

The boy took it, looking at it in amazement. He started to say something, then a muffled explosion rocked the corridor. One of the women clearing the debris leaned into the long interior hallway.

"Sers, you want to come see this." She jerked her head sideways.

When Levin didn't move, Slate threw his hand around his neck. "You, too, boy."

"Yes, ser." Levin pulled the hand from his neck, but he was smiling, and he clapped Slate on the shoulder.

They took off, running through the doorway to discover what new thing had happened to further devastate the night.

Out past the missing wall, debris shot out from the tree, blasted into bits too small to make out from a distance.

"Just like you said, ser." Levin's voice was small.

"I can see." He, the flesh-and-blood he, had said no such thing, but Slate had no better response to offer. He did believe in one thing, now. This kid? Him? They were connected, even if he didn't know in just what way.

Chapter 22

THE SPRING was saved.

Gungan became a hero, just as the image of the man had predicted. The daughter? That wasn't quite clear yet, but then, a lot of things weren't quite clear. Gungan's good deed? He had found the bomb, just as the face had said. Only just enough time? A counter had been running, and the worker had pulled it free and run into the corridor, only to find the exit hatch sealed. When the bomb blew, it took the hatch, Gungan, and one of the security with it.

However, the ship was spared.

The hundred-forty-meter-tall spring now rested in its chamber. Walls had been removed, and walls had been replaced. Slate had watched men wrestle with tools as tall as they were in order to fit the spring into its housing.

"This is something." Levin's enthusiasm flashed from his green eyes. "I mean, Kartye is about to move again. Who would have thought . . ." He was looking everywhere, still awe-struck. "When I was a kid, we thought it had always been broken. Now we have a future."

"Because of you." Slate tapped him on the chest with his knuckles. "You saved us."

"Nah." Levin reached to one of the pins that continued to hold the hull together. It would be removed once the seam was fused. For now, the boy ran his hands over it, studying it. "Well, maybe." He turned to Slate and beamed. "Yeah, I did, didn't I?"

"You did, kid." He nodded at him. He'd taken the kid under his wing, felt sorry for him, and given him a portion of his quarters. Foster kid, never feeling like he belonged. No kid deserved that. And, like he'd said to Larstrun the first day he'd returned, the place was too big for one man. However, it fit one man and one boy just about right.

They hadn't looked at the cylinder again. Slate didn't want to know what it said. It had already spoken too much truth. It had been Gungan—the remains of him—they'd seen ejected from the tree that day. Slate had no doubt of a child. Gungan hadn't been celibate, even on the Factory.

They did have one thing of Gungan's, though. That missing foot? The prosthetic had been SunSteel, direct from the Factory. It had eventually floated in, was found on the trunk's exterior, and had been memorialized in a Plexan display in the shopping tuft. Plans were in effect to rotate it between the shopping tuft and the business tuft.

It was the Godders that had claimed responsibility, and they had announced plans to continue with their efforts. Kartye Tree would not be allowed to restart her engines, even if she had to be blown apart to keep her here.

Security were at every door anywhere near the engines.

"Want to go up?" Slate pointed to where the top of the spring disappeared into the hull of the ship. "The ratcheting mechanism is being hooked up today. You only get to see this once in a thousand years. It's the final step, then the ship begins to move." He smiled. "Might be your last chance. Your hand doing the honors."

"Can we?" Levin's eyes were all over the top of the chamber.

"Put this on." It was a helmet with a strap for under the chin. "And this." He also held out a tool pouch. The kid didn't know it, but he was being put to work today.

"You going, too?" Levin looked up from the buckle on the pouch. "I want you to go, too."

"Sure." Slate ran a hand over the kid's hair, somehow the motion feeling right. He hadn't intended to go up, but what the heck? He could keep an eye on him better than anyone else could. He'd like that. "Over in that chest. Hand me a helmet. And don't forget to put yours on."

"Minister, you going up with him?" Larstrun approached them.

"We've secured this area, but—" He shrugged. "Safety first."

"How many have died so far?" Slate took the helmet from Levin and slipped it on his head.

"Four, ser." Larstrun frowned.

"How long until the spring is ready to engage?" He pulled his own tool pouch on. Again, he hadn't intended to work, but he had done spring maintenance in the past, and the skills needed were not unfamiliar. Besides, it might be enjoyable to do manual labor, rather than spend the day worrying about who was going to blow up whom.

"Six days, ser." He grinned. "Sooner, if you get that bolt ratcheted in."

"Then make sure no one blows anything up before we get completed." He slapped Levin on the arm. The boy beamed.

"Yes, ser. You have a productive day, ser, and I'll keep an eye on the Godders." He bowed slightly, and he turned and strode rapidly away.

Slate called over a gloved worker, the one, he supposed, assigned to accompany the boy. "I'm taking him up."

"You sure? Have you ever?" He thumbed up with a question in his eyes. "I can follow along, if you'd like."

"Not necessary. It's been thirteen years, but the training is still there." He tapped his temple.

"Your call, ser." The man tipped his hat. "Any help needed, and I'm right here."

"I appreciate it." He pulled a pair of gloves from the pouch and held them up to the boy. "Ready? These, first. We have quite a climb ahead of us."

"Sure." Levin grinned and fumbled in his pouch, finally pulling out one glove, then after digging, finding the other. He put them on. "Ready."

Slate grabbed the railing on a vertical ladder, and he motioned. "You, first."

"So cool!" Levin leaped to the third step, and he took them three at a time.

"Slow down!" I'm not sixteen, he wanted to call to the kid. However, he didn't want the kid to have to slow for a . . . and he frowned. How old was he, anyway? Thirty-five? Forty? Forty-five? He realized he had no idea. Birthday parties. He remembered those, but candles on a cake, or words on a card? Was there anything that told him his age?

It wasn't important, just really, really odd. Like every other bizarre thing he didn't know about his life, things he never thought to ask himself. They just become "known" when something triggered the memories.

He could keep up with a kid, though, whether he was thirty-five or forty-five.

"You're amazing, you know that?" He yelled the words. He laughed when several of the technicians in the chamber waved and yelled back their thanks. He clarified, "You, Levin!"

"No, it's just that you can't keep up." Laughter was there, and the boy was about to curve out of sight. "What's amazing about that?" He waved and disappeared, light against the shadows overhead.

"You think can't keep up." Slate leaped, and he put his arms into it. He'd catch that kid, and when he did, he'd let him know who was boss. Even if he had to wire him to the spring to slow him down.

SLATE sat in a bosun's chair, suspended from a gantry crane. His feet were braced against metal scaffolding, and he strained with an outsized two-armed wrench twice as long as he was tall.

Levin stood on a metal catwalk, with a loose harness and a tether looped around his waist. He pulled on the opposite end of the wrench.

The SunSteel metal band they were anchoring to the ship was two meters thick. The single bolt was nearly as big around. The wrench, a double-action leverage wrench, worked on the same principle as the ship's drive. Ratchet up an internal spring, and when it released, the resulting force was a culmination of all the small forces ratcheted into it.

So, Slate pushed, Levin pulled, and the wrench clicked. Then they did it again. Every hundred pulls, the wrench reacted, and the giant bolt made a quarter turn. It was backbreaking, but it was what would hold the spring in place for a thousand years.

"A tour? Right." Levin, covered with sweat, called out to his partner. He laughed, his arms resting on one of the curved jaws of the wrench. "I'm glad to be done."

"You're earning your keep, that's all."

The boy had done well, though, and Slate thoroughly approved. He hooked his end of the wrench onto a restraining cable attached to a separate gantry crane and pulled himself onto one of the catwalks, catching his leg with his elbow to rub it. His tattoo itched.

"Hooked up over there?" Slate was as tired as the boy looked, and probably sweatier. It was good to work his muscles for a change. He'd done this daily at the Factory, and he never thought he'd miss it. Truth was, he did.

He also missed the job being completed.

"Ready."

"Push it loose, but go easy. Don't overcompensate."

"Hey, I'm so tired, I can hardly compensate at all." The boy pushed his hair from his face with his shoulder and smiled.

"Can't keep up? Did I hear those words earlier?" Slate razzed him. "Huh, little boy? Who's amazing, now?"

The boy's smile turned into a laugh. "You are, but I'm catching up. Just you wait."

"How long? The rest of your life?" Slate pushed, and the wrench shifted off the bolt, hanging free in the air. "Grab that—"

That was as far as he got before the catwalk shifted violently under his feet. He looked up at Levin to see him hanging on for all he was worth.

"What—" Levin yelled as the outer skin of the tree began to ripple around them.

The explosion rocked the tree.

This was no little bomb attached to an exterior wall, designed to release an attachment footing for an anchor line. This was an attempt to split the tree in half. It very nearly worked, too.

The blast from the explosion rolled over them, the concussion lifting them from their feet, and sending Slate against a structural beam. His tether yanked at his harness, knocking the breath out of him. Somewhere, he knew, the massive wrench was swinging free, and he had to get out of its way. And Levin. Where was Levin? He shook his head and gasped, drawing in air, and panting in relief to find himself in one piece.

"Levin, are you injured?" He could see where the wrench had broken free, ripping a gaping hole in the skin of the tree. Beyond the ragged edges blistered the light of Death and Destruction, raw fingers drawing all life in.

"Levin!" He pushed off, the gravity fading as the tree slowed to a stop. There'd be trouble in the tree tonight, if someone didn't get that back up.

"Levin!" Then he saw the boy's tether. It fed through the ragged hole. He was outside the tree!

"Levin!" Slate threw himself that direction, his own tether keeping him short of the opening. He unclicked the buckle and threw it wide, grabbing Levin's tether and pulling it inside. It was easy, too easy, and his stomach crawled in dread.

The ragged end told the tale.

"Levin!" He grabbed the metal's flayed edge and pulled himself to look out. He saw the wrench, spinning end over end, along with other debris. The ship was dark. All power was out.

"Levin!" Then, there, a limp form, arms and legs extended, spinning away from the tree, his torn tether trailing behind.

"No! Levin!" Slate aimed and leaped, his legs springboards. He sailed through the air after the trailing line rather than the boy. He could never hit something so precise as the boy. The line? It extended for a dozen meters. That he could intercept. It was when he was half there that he knew his aim was high, and they would miss.

"No!"

He clawed through his pouch, desperately looking for an answer, anything. What he found was a roll of spiderline, a hand light, and a plumb bob. What he pictured was a bolo. Crafting quick knots to each end of the line, he looped it into a long T. He grabbed the tail and let the bolo fly, only to have it hit the boy's foot and skip off. Worse was the Newton thing. He was more off course than before.

Coiling the line, he lobbed a second toss, this time relieved to see it loop firmly around one leg. Slate tightened the line gently, bracing himself as it jerked, then began reeling his young friend in.

Or, reeling himself out.

"Levin." He patted the boy's face, feeling for warmth. For life. His chest moved, which meant he was breathing, although raggedly. Wrapping the bolo line around them both, and tying them together, he glanced back to the ship. He would have to get a line to the ship or find an object with sufficient mass to let him spring back that direction. And it had better happen soon. There was gravity, but it was minimal, and the farther they drifted, the harder it would be to overcome their momentum.

"Levin." He patted his face again.

"Oh, my head. What happened?" He blinked his eyes, looking frantically around.

"We're outside the ship."

"Outside?" He struggled to sit, shifting them both.

"Hold still. Please. I need line from your pouch." His tattoo had

107

started to really itch, and he could barely keep from reaching to it. What else could go wrong before all this was done?

"It hurts, bad. Here." He touched his side, holding his breath for a minute, and then relaxing. "More than death, that hurts." He coughed, and pain twisted his features.

"A rib, maybe." Slate pulled the line out and looked for the tail of his own. "I have to untie us. Can you hold my belt?"

"My hand works. Sure." He reached blindly. "I can't find it."

Slate looked at him. His eyes, green and glistening, were open. "What do you see?"

"Nothing. It's darkside, isn't it?"

"Yeah. It's darkside. Here." He took the boy's hand and slipped it inside his belt. "Hold to that."

"Gotcha." Levin grinned. "You. Me. I finally understand."

"What do you understand?" Slate had the knots tied, but the distance from the ship had begun to worry him. The damage looked very minor from this angle. Just a small, ragged hole. Was anyone even looking?

And the itching! It had become very distracting.

"This." He pulled the silver trinket from his pocket. "I always wanted to be that person the man was talking to. Now I am." He laughed and coughed, grabbing his side. "What you need is on this—" His words cut off as another round of coughing racked his body.

"What I need?"

"Everything I've done my entire life has been about this moment, and I never knew. I wanted to be Levi, and the man in this to be my father, and the whole time it was you." He laughed again, coughing roughly, this time spitting up blood. "Funny. This had to happen. I see it now. It always did, every time."

The boy went quiet just as Slate felt a fist thrust into his gut, and he doubled over, barely able to contain the pain. Had he been injured, too? Internally, maybe, although he'd felt no indication earlier. Now, though, he was certain. When the pain eased, he looked up.

"What had to happen?" Slate realized the boy had let his belt go, and he grabbed his shirt, pulling him back. Blood seeped from his mouth, and his eyes stared ahead. Slate patted his cheek only to realize he was gone, this boy who had saved the tree and become a friend to him. His death—unfair and unwarranted—made Slate rage with the need for revenge. Yet here, in this moment, there was little he could do. He pulled him close and wrapped his arms around him, giving him his last wish.

"Levin," he said. "You can be Levi, and I will be your father. You were magnificent, do you know that? Absolutely magnificent."

He caught sight of a reflective object drifting by, and he trapped it in his hand. The silver tube. The boy's most prized possession. He held it tightly, refusing to let it get away. If the boy was dead, he should at least have this with him.

He felt for a pocket in the boy's clothing in which to place the silver tube. It was when he prepared to open his fist that he realized how hot it was. His face appeared above his closed fist, just as it had once before, and the eyes looked down to something Slate couldn't see. Tears flowed down moist cheeks, and the face whispered, "Levi. You can be Levi, and I am your father."

Slate released it before it could continue.

"You knew, and you chose this anyway." He wiped at his face, his eyes blurring. "You are a fool." He knew what he meant. He was the fool, because he hadn't seen what this boy had wanted all along. The boy had wanted him.

But he wasn't going to live if he didn't get back to the tree. He could make it, just, with the boy's help.

"Forgive me, Levin. I have to leave you behind. I'm so sorry."

Tying the line around his waist, he took aim, guessing he wouldn't have a second chance, and he lobbed the bolo hard the direction of the tree. The boy would give just enough additional stationary inertia that he hoped the bolo would reach the tree in time.

Just as it left his hand, a shadow passed overhead. Slate looked to see the wrench coming his direction. An image of Katerine flashed through his mind, and he regretted what might have been. Then, the wrench grabbed the line and yanked him sideways, entangling the line around the boy's leg, twisting, pulling them tighter with every pass, until there was no more room, and Slate could no longer breathe.

Soon, he floated, forever tethered to the boy, their bodies bound together by the eternal strength of spiderline, as they stared into Death and Destruction, their blind eyes seeing neither.

THE TREE WAS SAVED by accident more than design. This was the first time in a thousand years that the spring was being tensioned. Enormous bars a kay long, built and installed just for this purpose, stretched the length of the spring chamber, tying the two ends of the tree together. However, the tensioning bars served a dual purpose. They also strengthened the central trunk while the spring was installed. After all, three of the ship's four support walls had been removed. Something had to hold the two tree tufts together.

Removal of the tensioning bars was to have commenced the previous day. A glitch in personnel scheduling had created a shortage of manpower, and the removal was delayed twenty-five hours.

The tree would live, even if everyone couldn't be saved.

Chapter 23

"THIS is the place?"

The massive black ship had materialized out of nothing, coming to rest in a gas torus surrounding two bitterly hot suns. Its surface gleamed with an oily light, as suited men belched from its orifices.

They had the map. The next to current one, anyway.

"Search." The command was flung across the ether.

There was some floating debris, widely scattered: sheared metal, indicating an advanced race had passed through; organic material, evidence of non-indigenous life; and a silver cylinder, also known as a transfer capsule.

"Ser. He is here." A gloved hand held up the cylinder, and it glittered in the light of the suns.

"He only needs to be found. Scan the system. We must have his map." The speaker, erect and perhaps more crisply attired, if that were possible in a spacesuit, turned and made his way inside, leaving the work to the myriad suits wearing blank eyes.

"Team 6, insystem. Team 7, outsystem. Teams 1 through 5, begin concentric looping with ship as home, 10-kay increments. Stat."

The teams started moving immediately with purposeful efficiency. Rather more like machines than like men, but then that was to be expected.

It took longer than they'd hoped. It was a very large gas torus, and indeed, the tree's engine had engaged just fine, set off by the very explosion designed to break her in two. The reverse gravity thrust did exactly what it was designed to do. It reversed gravity, and the debris field from the explosion was directly in its path. Finding the silver cylinder? That was luck. Finding the map? They earned that.

And Levi?

He was a surprise they hadn't expected, and it didn't set well with them at all.

Chapter 24

A DOZEN dreamers stood over a vast glowing table, from time to time leaning in, pointing at one location and then another. To say dreamers, though, was like calling Michelangelo a water colorist, Houdini a quick-change artist, or Vanzetti a dime store merchant. Occasionally one would speak to another, the sound more a screech than a voice, and the surface of the table would shift, the patterns within changing, the same, yet never the same.

The table was a map, a map of time and space. A map of stardust and possibilities. The story of what had been, and what was to come.

Dreams. Maybe what was to come. Perhaps, if they were lucky.

They tracked a man, although the path was unclear, and they could only guess, perhaps guess. And others tracked him, too, others who were sharp-witted and quick. So very quick.

The patterns shifted again, the guesses coming from smaller patterns that were similar, yet never the same.

"Here." A screech, and an arm reached over the maelstrom and jabbed at stardust. The display revolved as the arm dropped, centered on where the hand pointed. The scene exploded into individual galaxies, then star systems, then nothing.

Eyes looked up.

"He is here," the arm repeated.

"There is nothing there." Screeches, still. The space was empty, no planets, just twin suns surrounded by a vast, elongated gas torus.

The voice screeched, "He is here, but only for a brief time. He will soon be eaten by the gravity of the suns."

"And we will start over." The speaker was unseen, but the effects were not.

"We cannot . . ."

"He is necessary . . ."

"We are so close . . ."

"Then we must be diligent, and the search must begin."

However, it was already too late, even before the pursuit could get underway.

Chapter 25

SPACE churned, and time danced.

It was not a dance of joy, but of commanded coercion. Time was being twisted, forced to be what it wasn't meant to be, to surrender its reign over all that was and to allow it to become that which might be.

Time had become a dream, one of fierce battles won, the grand designs of war realized, and fists of victory raised high in exultation.

Time had also become crushing defeat, the lover lost, the end of hope, and eternal damnation in the face of inescapable despair.

The wheel began to turn. Its blackened metal shifted within the oil of space and time, its vast cogs of stardust and dreams wheeling to new possibilities. As cog met cog, civilizations flowered, spread through the stars, and as quickly withered, the cogs moving on to yet more possibilities. Whole races were snuffed out, the ash of their desires and hopes littering the oil of time like winter's scattered leaves, soon sinking beneath its surface to be seen no more.

The words of a poem whispered in the darkness, carried aloft by stardust, and drifting across the night to slip softy through the skies of a billion worlds, causing the dreams of a million billion creatures of all shapes and sizes to tremble, although none knew why.

Life is to life;
Twelve days to reign.
Death is to death;
No man can tame.

Reach out to one;
Gift all your pain.
Be true to truth;
Death comes again.

Darkness swallows;
Taking our name.
Breath gives new life;
To love is vain.

Then the whispers were silenced, succumbing to the night, eaten by the hungry stars. Despair rose up in triumph, as a thousand million suns winked out.

And the giant finger touched the oil, and time moved forward once again.

Chapter 26

A METAL world. Heat. Fire.

A word came to him . . . purgatory. Then, hellfire and brimstone.

In the distance, a lake burned. A lake of fire. He was finally here, cursed to purgatory and a lake of fire. All he needed was a pitchfork.

All on a metal world.

He laughed, and in that laugh, he knew. It wasn't the world that was made of metal. It was him. He reached forward, and a metal hand forced metal fingers into rock, shattering the ground. He squeezed his fingers, and coal became diamond. He turned, and mountains crumbled to dust.

"Unit Three Lima Niner. Coastal region depletion wrapping up in twelve days. We have you set to cycle offworld at end of current duty rotation. Acknowledge."

"Acknowledged. Transferring load."

"We'll keep the Pit open. Bring it in, Lima Niner."

"Acknowledged. Will do."

It was a standard announcement to someone at the end of his nine-month duty rotation. However, with that one word, *offworld*, he was thrust back into the cold of space, floating, running out of air, before he yanked himself back to the real world.

He took a deep breath, and his head spun.

He was Unit Three Lima Niner, and this was Purgatoria. Like a pent-up volcano, a picture of this world flooded into his head, burning into him.

Purgatoria was a prison.

Well, not a true prison, but it might as well be. This was a mining camp, and he was a miner. A metal miner—encased in metal; made of metal; mining for metal. He laughed again. A metal world, indeed. How fantastic was that?

His reply had been the same, standard, what he was expected to say. Still, the exchange let him know the jig was about up. Made sure he acknowledged it so that he could be booted out for a cheaper replacement. It was always about the bottom line. Time on the rock brought experience, but it also brought pay adjustments. The company would rather pay for injuries than for skill.

In that acknowledgement, just as he'd known about his job, he also knew the next step on his job. His hands held one hundred tons of lithium-laced basalt, and he was to transport it to Refining Nodule Six Charlie. He had seven kays to go and one encrusted lava river to cross. He could normally cross the river without concern, but the extra hundred tons was a different matter. Short periods of immersion were survivable, but he was responsible for repairs. He didn't want repairs. He wanted all the money from this hellish existence.

He turned, and his vision blurred, flickered, and reset to a blank field of blue with a slowly spinning circle in the center. Scrolling words popped up underneath, accompanied by a pleasantly modulated voice. "Sensory input overload. Recalibrating. Vision returning in four, three, two." The voice stopped, and his eyes flashed bright white, before settling into a pixilated scene. He waited, and after a minute it cleared enough to make out the world outside.

"What was that," he muttered.

"Unmarked thermal vent. Position now noted for future reference. Three-percent-damage tag assigned to Unit Three Lima Niner. Internal report to Tanon Base Nine logged and transmitted."

"Idiot. Couldn't you wait to log the report?" It was a machine, so of course it was an idiot. He could have swapped out damaged parts from a chop shop cheaper. He'd done it before, but now that they'd installed these autolog systems, miners couldn't get away with much of anything, anymore.

"Report logging is automatic. Thermal vent now noted on all mapping schematics. Logging bonus, one-point-three percent nominal gross, Nodule Six Charlie; point-seven percent leased access."

"Point seven? You have got to be kidding. Point nine. Renegotiate."

"Renegotiation commenced. Terms accepted."

Whoo-hoo! He would have punched his fist into the sky, but for the hundred tons of rock in his hands. That bonus would more than cover damages, and it was retroactive to the total time he'd been onworld.

It hit him. How long *had* he been onworld? One duty rotation, three, ten? He had no idea. He didn't even know his name. Unit Three Lima Niner? He didn't think so.

He knew himself well enough to understand his pragmatic nature. Right now, he had a lava river to cross, and two fistfuls of black basalt to deliver, and it wasn't going to walk itself to the Nodule.

HE WASN'T the only metal man in town. Another miner, fists full, lumbered along in the distance, and in that glance, he knew what he looked like.

Dang, he was ugly!

After reaching Refining Nodule Six Charlie, he made his way to the Pit.

"Hold, Lima Niner. Repositioning intake. Ninety-second delay on my mark. Mark."

In front of him, the landscape began to shift. The ground rumbled under his feet, vibrating his vision, the image shaking, pixelating in one corner, then clearing.

"Initiate load dump."

"Dump initiated." He opened his hands, and the ground shook as the tonnage impacted the interior of the pit and began to tumble out of sight.

"Hit the showers, Lima Niner. Section shutdown in thirty-two. No sense in going back out."

"Pay compensation?" If he wasn't going back out, he'd be shorted without it.

"Oh, you guys! You're breaking the company's back. Give us some leeway."

"You give me pay compensation." That was in the contract. He didn't know what the contract was, but he knew he had to be given compensation if he were asked not to go out. He had to request it, but they couldn't refuse.

"Logged." The voice sighed. "Thirty-two credited at two percent per. Happy?"

"Very." That was a nice chunk of change, and all for taking what he expected to be a very hot shower. "Which shower units are available?"

"Let me check. Two seven, behind the Kiln. It's yours till full shutdown. Enjoy."

He turned and moved away, his vision sliding sideways, recalibrating, and adjusting again with each step. There. The Kiln, a vast building with belching smoke pouring from overhead stacks. He chuckled. Let's heat up Purgatoria some more. He rounded the building to enormous open hangars, with multiple jetted sprayers attached to numerous robotic arms. He stepped on a platform.

"Three Lima Niner, initiating shower sequence now. You are scheduled for sensor repair in Repair Bay Thirteen. Costs can be billed or deducted from future earnings. Do you have a preference?"

"Future." It something bad happened, he might not have to pay it. He chuckled about that. If something bad happened, he wouldn't need his pay, either.

By then the platform had rotated him into position, and magnetic clamps had his arms immobilized at his side. The sprayers kicked in, just as his vision faded to an advertisement for a virtual simulation that could be billed in three convenient installments, discreetly listed as Excel Entertainment Services.

The ad was the price he paid to get the shower for free.

After two more ads, one for com service to any three systems for one low price, and the second for discount upgrades for sensor inputs, his vision returned for the rinse portion of the shower. He caught the sprayers' jets flushing his vision sensors, then a blast of air whisked the remaining water away. In the heat, it would dry fast enough, but there was spotting to deal with, too. Good work demanded clear vision. Clear vision demanded the blast of air.

Backing into the sleep port was his most looked forward to part of each day. He wasn't the first in, but it was close. That was nice. He'd have the recreation areas to himself for a time, and he wouldn't mind that at all.

Chapter 27

HE FLOATED unsupported in the zero gee room, stretching his back. Music played, the subharmonics just at the edge of hearing, although he knew he could strengthen his hearing module, if he wished. He didn't wish. He wished to be alone, but that wasn't going to happen. The company was too tight to provide individual environments for the miners. It was something he just *knew*. Like when he'd docked his unit, he'd *known* to transfer in, just as he'd *known* to initiate the full biopack replenishment and full flush option, even at the inflated cost. Anywhere else it would be half that, but here? They were a captive audience, and when you've only got one dealer, that's where you get your goods. At any price.

The lighting changed, becoming a throbbing purple, and he glanced around to see a slender woman push off into the room.

"Leatha." As soon as he called her name, his history with her flooded his thoughts. They'd transported in together. He also knew that Leatha was male, late eighties, heavyset, and a career miner, one of the best. If he was lucky, he had another half century of productive work ahead of him.

The thing was, Leatha preferred being female. That was okay. Nothing wrong with being female. Especially a pretty one.

Him? He preferred being him.

"Saw a unit parked. Yours?" She winked. "*Three Lima Niner.*"

"Not going there, girl." He knew she'd appreciate that. The girl part. "Against the rules to admit to unit IDs in virtual."

"Never hurts to try." She wore a silky kimono, and it hugged her like water drops gracing a flower petal.

He noticed she smelled about as nice, too. But then, in virtual, smell was a matter of choice, not of body chemistry. "Second shift should be headed out." He closed his eyes, tuning out the purple lights. "Beautiful out there."

"Like purgatory." She made it sound like a curse.

"This is purgatory, although we call it Purgatoria. However, this part's not too bad." He opened his eyes to see her at his side, the kimono revealing more than she knew. Or, rather, revealing more than she ought. He winked at her, letting his eyes travel farther south than he probably ought. He closed his eyes again, this time with a smile. His body was back in his unit having a good time about then, even if the insensate fool didn't know it.

"Purgatoria and like purgatory. You're right, though. Who'd ever thought we could visit purgatory and go home again, and that some of us would prefer purgatory to real life?"

"You can be what you want to be on Purgatoria." Not in purgatory. There was a difference.

"Oh, you're no fun." Someone else was coming in, and she swam that way, something only possible in a virtual environment. The person she sidled up to may have been human, but he or she looked more like a cross between a lion and a bear.

"Reynalt." He called to the incoming miner. The name was there, in his head, and as soon as he said it, he knew as much about the man as anyone at the station knew. A loner, he kept to himself, but he liked company on his off time. Willing company, male or female. He wasn't a friend. Reynalt's only friends were those he could get something from. He teased him. "That's a fantastic VR body. You'll never collect a wife like that, though."

"He doesn't want a wife." Leatha sidled up to him, rubbing the fur on one arm. "Do you, Rennie?"

"Rennie?" That was a first.

"Leatha can call me any name she wants." The response was growled as much as spoken, underscored by a feline rumble that continued long after he'd finished speaking.

Reynalt's image flickered and became grainy. Leatha's kimono changed from bright red to a ruddy orange, then green for the barest instant, before reverting to its original color. The zero gee room pixilated briefly, then solidified once more into a believable environment punctuated with pulsing purple lights.

"What the . . ." Reynalt's growl spat the words.

"Deterioration in the hard lines between Six Charlie and Seven Alfa. Heat cracks in the encasement shielding. Main banks for virtual servers are in Seven." Three new people walked in, a butch tattooed woman alongside twin Adonises. They were instantly recognizable. They were a team that rotated their appearances daily. It was the tattooed woman that had spoken. "Every few decades it has to be dug out and rerouted."

"Who does the digging?" That was Leatha. "I'm paid for prime-field ore removal, not maintenance duty."

"Check your contract." Lima Niner chuckled. "It's in there." Besides, it guaranteed an eight-percent bonus for time-in-suit, paid out on average ore yield during logged duty hours. Individual ore yield. His was higher than he'd ever managed, and that meant he could possibly take home as much for one "maintenance" duty as he'd earned on his entire assignment.

He wanted this job.

More miners filtered in. Other virtuals began to open up, from a space battle scenario in which the aliens were apparently green tentacled squids, to one in which a steamy cave was the backdrop, and the participants' clothing was optional.

"You thinking of going out, Slate?" A miner called to him, clapping him on the shoulder.

Slate. Wildfire whipped through Lima Niner, and in that one word he felt himself turn inside out. It was a gut-wrenching lurch, a hot wind swirling around him, sucking him into a vortex of burning imagery, like dry tinder in a brushfire. He knew why he was on Purgatoria. In purgatory was also appropriate. His world had been stolen from him. Literally.

He had run to Purgatoria. Long and hard, he had run.

The Contract had controlled everything. Not this one here. The Contract there, with a capital C. On Lacy's Veil Prime. He'd reclaimed those swamp lands, built his farm out of the mud and silt of a dozen rivers, and started his family there.

Daughter. An image swam in front of him. Had *had* a daughter. Wife? A bloody form. Raider's revenge for refusing to surrender his seed stock.

Son, stolen away. His life gone.

His head reeled with the black night of space. Cold death, his son in his arms.

No! His son had not died. He had been carried away, screaming, lost. Lost forever.

Slate. The name . . . there was something missing . . .

"He be in a fugue again." A tall woman with leopard skin laughed. "Let him be. He come out of it. He always do."

He jerked awake, rolling to his feet, the zero gee slipping away with the movement. "Anybody else volunteering for maintenance duty?"

He was. He had to be away. *Slate . . . Slate . . .* It was like he was being summoned . . . by something.

"No one's called for duty volunteers." Two men laughed from a virtual sea that was contained just around them. It was the Adonises, and they raised glasses filled with flame. "To private time!"

"Like this is private!" A woman walked in from the cave scene, and as she crossed the threshold between the two environments, a flowing robe appeared around her. The water glitched, blinking out for a moment, the men blinking with it. The woman nodded sagely. "See that? They'll call, and you'll have no choice. Volunteer now for the best slots."

"Thank you." That came from the butch woman, but the words carried more grumble than gratitude.

Slate, consumed with the need to be away, raised one hand and called to the crowd, "See a new area? Head out to the Crevasse? Gorgeous country. Anybody go with me?" As he said it, he knew he'd done this before. And it was. Beautiful. Wonderfully beautiful, deep within the Iron Mountains, underneath a burning sky. "Come see! All of you! You won't regret it!"

The purple lights began flashing in a one-off, two-on pattern, and an alarm shrilled in the background. A spoken voice overrode all other entertainment, and the holographic environment blinked out, leaving them standing in a neutral gray fog.

"Virtual environment has become unstable." Everyone in the room pixilated before returning to solid form, emphasizing the announcement. "Returning all miners to units. Payment compensation point two percent. Unrestricted access to Neuret, DataCast, and Excel Entertainment at no charge."

"Yes! Excel! It's gonna be a great night tonight!" Leatha jumped upward in a very masculine manner. She looked around sheepishly, clearing her throat, and murmuring, "Anyone care to come on over?"

"Like we could," Reynalt snorted. "That's what I planned on *here*."

A voice from where the cave had once been yelled, "Point two? This is *my* time. This is my *vacation*. It's worth at least point four. Renegotiate."

"Renegotiation commenced. Counter proposal offered. Payment compensation point two seven eight. Accept or reject?"

"Take it." The demand was hissed. Only the original negotiator could accept or reject, even though it applied to the entire group. More voices joined in with versions of, "It's a good price," and, "It's all gravy, anyway. It's more than we'd get staying in here."

"Accepted." The answer was yelled.

"Terms amended." The room erupted in cheers, and two of the miners immediately flickered out. The speaker wasn't finished, though. "Volunteers are being taken for hard line repair duty, Niger Cut, under full contract enumeration provisions. Please notify Tanon Base Nine by oh six hundred if you wish to accept."

There were only groans for that one. Niger Cut was indeed along a ridgeline that edged the Iron Mountains, just above the Burning Crevasse. Few places on Purgatoria were more beautiful. Or more dangerous.

The rest of the miners began flickering out one at a time.

Reynalt didn't cheer, though. Rather, he was looking at Slate, with a hard expression on his face. He nodded once, then he winked out, also.

Did that mean the man was volunteering? It was outside the "safe" zones surrounding the Refining Nodules. That was the reason for the eight percent. It was dangerous.

Very dangerous.

Chapter 28

SLATE triggered his vision receptors. The image shifted sideways. He waited. At first startup, it always took a moment to warm.

To warm. Must be sixty Celsius out there.

However, his vision mechanisms were buried deep inside the unit with him. The cooling systems in the suit kept the interior at a balmy twenty-eight, with regulators to adjust that as needed.

He lifted his arm and winced. He *hurt* and not just his arm. Every muscle in his body ached. The electro-massagers had been especially thorough. Every other work cycle he received a full electrical workout. Without the electro-massagers, nine months in a unit could cause a vegetable to emerge. It was important to keep up muscle mass.

Vision was online by then, and he adjusted the spectrum to damp out the red. Red made Purgatoria look too much like purgatory, and after nine months—nearly nine, as he was out in eleven days—the place started to feel like purgatory. He didn't need anything to reinforce that.

His arm was still raised halfway, and he closed his fingers. They resembled shovels more than fingers, but with his accumulated time-in-suit, he could use them as nimbly as his own. Mining for ore, even better. Today they would be replaced with more manipulative digits, ones specifically designed for replacing the hard line.

Running through his checklist, and after testing each part of the unit's systems, he sent the signal to disconnect the biofeeds, and he disengaged from the sleeping dock. He rolled forward on his feet to get his balance adjusted, and with one foot thrown forward, he stepped from the cavernous bay and into the red light of Purgatoria's dwarf sun.

His first stop was the outfitting hangar.

"Unit Three Lima Niner scheduled for hard line repair. Arm upgrade requested per contract provisions." Having arms upgraded was normally a personal choice. Some designs worked better in some strata. However, that was the driver's decision, so the company wouldn't cover the outlay. Occasionally, chop shops had good arms for a fraction of factory prices, if a miner was willing to take the risk of used equipment in a life-or-death situation, and on Purgatoria, every day and every decision was always a life-or-death situation.

This, however, was volunteer work, and contract stipulations must be adhered to. They would pay. The company just needed to be reminded of its obligations from time to time.

"Bay Six is already set up for you, Lima Niner. You'll have company from Nodule Six Charlie out there with you today. Unit Two Echo Five was just in, same upgrade." Something whirred over the line, and for a moment there was static coming through. Then it cleared. "Sorry about that, Lima Niner. We're skimming the Horsehead Meteor Cluster later this week, and I think it's already begun. Weather Systems never gets it right. Nothing to worry about, though. We may experience some disruption in the upper ionosphere, but the atmosphere's too heavy to allow anything solid through. Might be a pretty lightshow for those with their eyes peeled." The voice chuckled.

Two Echo Five. Reynalt? Who knew, and Two Echo Five wouldn't tell if he asked, so he wouldn't ask.

"Who's our third?" Outside of established safe zones, safety regulations always required teams of three. Slate knew there wasn't a shadow of a possibility that he and Two Echo Five were going out alone. Where'd they get the third? Seven Alfa? They had the servers. Bet no one there cared.

"I hoped you wouldn't ask." The man sounded apologetic, if that were possible, for a relay man who never saw the inside of a unit. "A first out, from Two Gamma."

"Two Gamma?" Nodule Two Gamma was the other side of Death Pass. Anyone from Two Gamma would have to ride a HoverLift to get to Niger Cut, either that or they'd been walking since the night before. Walking meant they'd be tired. Tired meant dangerous.

"Nobody wants Niger. You know that. Well, except you and Two Echo Five." Laughter. "Local daredevils, you guys. Enjoy."

And a first out from Two Gamma. Didn't that beat all? A firstie. On Purgatoria. Along Niger Cut. Well, if someone was dying today, it sure wasn't going to be Slate . . . and the last name wouldn't come. Slate what? That was a blank spot he didn't need. Slate Three Lima Niner?

Like he'd said before, he didn't think so.

He was in Bay Six by that time, and he stepped up to the robotics array that would remove and replace his arms. The lower halves, anyway, from the elbows down. He slid his arms into circular clamps eighteen meters in diameter, with openings nearly twelve, and felt the magnetic clasps secure his hands to the platform.

"Lock mining unit and withdraw arm functions now," the voice reminded him.

He locked all joints on his unit. "Unit locked. Arm function withdrawal in progress." He triggered all arm functions off and withdrew the contact plates into his upper arms. "Arm function withdrawal complete."

"Removal initiated. Mining unit must remain locked until exchange is complete. Acknowledge."

"Acknowledged."

The clamps tightened, and then spun with blinding speed, disengaging the lower arms from his body. An icon on each side of his display flashed red to indicate a problem with his arms. Yeah, he thought. They're missing. Think I don't know that? Still, they would let him know that the new arms were mated properly when they went off. Gravy, gravy.

Enormous forty-meter hydraulic pistons retracted, the movement computer-fast, as the robotics lifted the old arms and shunted them out of the way. Equally fast, new arms fell into place, were mated to his upper arms, and the clamps spun with their blinding speed. The red lights in his display turned orange, then blinked, indicating the presence of arms but the lack of function.

"Arm attachment complete. Initiate arm functions and report."

128

The circular clamps released his forearms.

Tripping switches and gears, his contact plates slid into place, and the orange blinking lights turned steady green.

"All green."

"Upgraded arms qualify as temporary loan Nodule Six Charlie to Unit Three Lima Niner. Damage incurred during assigned duties is the responsibility of Tanon Base Nine, and will in no case be charged back to operator. Any and all other damage is the responsibility of Unit Three Lima Niner, and operator accepts all charges for repairs. Do you accept?"

"I accept." What else could he say? No?

"Agreement logged. You may unlock and exit. Have a nice day."

He backed out of the seventy-meter-tall bay and lumbered into the yard, where he noted the units still jacked into the sleep ports. In each of them, somewhere, was a human body encased in biogel that would never see the light of day on this world. It wouldn't see the light of anything, not for its entire rotation onworld, except through its sensor jack in the back of its neck.

Then, on Purgatoria, human eyes weren't exactly fair game. Ten minutes outside of a unit were all you got before hyperthermia set in. Nobody, and that meant *nobody* on Purgatoria wanted to walk around outside of a very cozy and comfortable mining unit.

Even if the unit did insist on subjecting him to a full-body, electrically-charged workout every other day. He couldn't express how much that hurt, but he was pretty certain it was worse than fire and brimstone.

And that was pretty bad, if he did say so himself.

Chapter 29

THE IRON MOUNTAINS glowed with heat, and it was beautiful. It was said they were riddled with caverns, but so far, they were unexplored. Far in the distance the Three Sisters belched orange smoke, and their sides ran with sinuous snakes of red. This world raged against her interlopers.

The volcanoes looked to Slate like he could reach out and touch them. He was quite safe, though. Distances were hard to judge when you were thirty meters tall unloaded, nearly twenty-nine with all compression springs compacted.

A blue light blinked in the extreme left of his screen, warning him to toggle peripheral vision sensors. He acknowledged it and watched his display shift a quarter turn. Another unit just like him was lumbering into place, stopping two hundred meters away. Painted, stamped, or in full bas-relief in various places on its surface was Two Echo Five. Every detachable part, as well as those that were not, was permanently overlaid with those numbers. If a miner was caught in the most heinous of circumstances—and it did happen—the company wanted the parts to be identifiable. It helped them assign damages so they knew whose pay to dock.

"Echo Five." Slate keyed the com. "Pretty day to go for a walk."

"Says the man who has no friends." The words weren't hostile, and they didn't indicate gender. Out on Purgatoria, it was a standard benediction before heading into new and uncharted territory.

"Except the one at his side." Slate gave the expected reply.

One of the massive arms raised in greeting, twelve-meter pistons extending on one side, and correlating ones on the opposite side compressing. A brilliant light burned on one side of the head, indicating Echo Five was looking his direction. The head itself was little more than a bump centered on shoulders fifteen meters wide, and it could not rotate. Neither did it need to. Within were the core life support and communications systems, as fully protected from possible damage as technologically possible. Vision was strictly by sensor input. Fly-by-wire, to quote an old aviation term. Reynalt—if Echo Five were the man—would be found behind the unit's chest area. His bio unit was inserted through the back, a fully operational escape pod in case the unthinkable happened. Since mining started on Purgatoria nearly three centuries ago, only seven deaths were recorded, and scores of units were out there, decimated, lost, abandoned, or cannibalized by the chop shops for spare parts.

No One Dies Today. It was the mining company's slogan and also the reason for the three-out rule. It might be about the company's bottom line, but if people died, that cut into profits. Even if two were down, the third could trigger the releases and bring the bio units home.

"Two Echo Five requesting confirmation supplies are in place, Niger Cut repair duty. Two Echo Five and Three Lima Niner shined up and ready to go. Acknowledge confirmation."

"HoverDrop at oh four hundred confirmed. You are locked and ready to go."

"The firstie from Two Gamma—" Slate began.

"Firstie!" Echo Five snarled his interjection. "Sending a firstie out to the Cut? I didn't volunteer for a suicide mission."

Slate started over again. "Can I request Two Gamma's call sign? And has he arrived, yet?" The units were always male in the coms.

"Two Gamma sends its regards along with Unit Five Zulu Three—"

"Five Zulu Three." Echo Five again. Even over the com, his voice sounded bitter. "That's old Tomik's—"

"Let it go." Slate felt himself frown, although he knew it couldn't be seen. Sometimes, after they died, news of who had occupied which units got out. Tomik had been one of the seven. His bio pod had made it in, but Tomik hadn't survived the transit.

Five Zulu Three had a reputation.

Still, Slate believed men made their choices, and not the units they operated. Five Zulu Three didn't bring teams down. Operators brought them down.

"Five Zulu Three's rating?" It wasn't the unit's rating Slate requested. It was the operator's. It might reassure his partner. Maybe not, but it was worth a try.

The answer was quick. "Three nine five on RenChik's Operational Aptitude scale, and even higher on Deere's Driver Training School finals. Finished the eight-month program in five with the highest scores in his class."

That answer had been prepared. So, no one else wanted to work with Five Zulu Three, either, as if they had a choice in the matter.

"Are we good, Echo Five?" Slate wanted to meet the fabled Five Zulu Three unit. See if it really did try to kill off its operators.

Like that was possible.

For an answer, Echo Five's piston arms and piston legs kicked in, and his oversized foot treads, nearly fifteen meters square—each—lifted and began to carry him forward.

"I'll take that for a yes. An adventure. Right, Echo Five? Today we can play God in our wonderful machines, and we get paid for it. How great is that?"

"Wouldn't mind showing off to a firstie."

"That's the way to think about it! We'll walk the ridges of the Iron Mountains, stand at the edge of Niger Cut, and look out over the Burning Crevasse. We'll be the gods Purgatoria never had, and it'll be magnificent. How's that for a day at work?"

"You make even this seem like a resort. Makes me wonder where your homeworld is." A nervous laugh filtered through in the words. "Ignore that. Somewhere besides here, and that's all I need to know."

The thing was, Slate had no idea. Would knowing his last name give him that, too? Or would that come with something else?

He thought, Move, and he felt his massive legs shift and begin to lumber forward like it took no effort at all.

That's what was fantastic. It didn't! And he had a whole world to explore for the day!

THE SKY roiled with the lightshow. Outfitting had been correct. Weather was a bunch of idiots. They were full in the Horsehead. Overhead, streaks of brilliant yellow and red danced across the heavens, with sensors occasionally picking up a dull thud echoing off the mountain ridges to the south.

One exploded near enough to blank Slate's vision, the brilliance of the detonation overriding his external light meters.

"That one will make your bolt juice come loose." Echo Five's remark bled through like burned lubrication fluid in a stressed joint.

"Ah! Come, now. It's the best light show this side of The Galleon Whorls, and there's no light show like the Galleon." It was incredible. As far as danger? Well, a bit of that, too, but a man didn't get beauty without at least a measure of risk.

"You've been there?" Echo Five spoke as he walked, his feet crushing rock and soil into a uniform pack beneath his soles.

"Well, images, the same things anyone sees." Holos and virtuals. Normal stuff. Sometimes he pictured a ship, though, as if he'd really been there. In person. A ship filled with green, and great, bulbous windows opening on the wide-open wonders of space. But that was impossible, unless he'd lived another life before this one, and nobody got that for a consolation prize.

"Look at that." Echo Five stopped and pointed, one massive arm indicating something in the distance.

It was a shadow against the reddened sky. Even Slate's dampers hadn't been able to get all the red out, and it looked nearly black, no more than a slash against the brightness. Hopefully, it was their third. They should have received transmission by now of the status of the HoverDrop.

"Zulu Three's on the way in, I see." Slate could already make out the unit's legs hanging below the HoverLift, whose six colossal blades spun at a pace that blurred them into invisibility. Compared to the mining unit it moved, the HoverLift was massive, and the mining units were no children's toys. "It's coming in fast, too."

The com began to crackle, and Slate turned it up.

"Units Two Echo Five and Three Lima Niner, acknowledge. Units Two Echo Five and Three Lima Niner, acknowledge. This is HoverLift Charlie Delta approaching Niger Cut. Confirmation to release Five Zulu Three to jobsite Niger Cut. Out."

"HoverLift Charlie Delta. Units Three Lima Niner and Two Echo Five. Approaching Niger Cut now. What took you so long?"

"Sorry for the delay. This shower's scrambling all the coms. You'll be on your own out here until it clears." The voice chuckled. Even as he spoke, more sparks spread across the sky, although none as dramatic as those a few minutes before. "If you get stranded, feel free to tap the feed off the cables. Give you something to watch while you work." It was clearly a joke.

"And get docked a quarter percent premium? No thanks." That was Two Echo Five.

"Only if Tanon finds out, and I'm not telling—" The sound crackled, scrambling the transmission, and then it returned, only having transmitted the beginning and the last few words of the message. "—here he is."

"This is Unit Five Zulu Three. How are—" The static cut in, garbling the next words.

"Tomik's call sign." Two Echo Five sent a private message.

"Leave it, Echo Five," Slate barked. "No need to go there."

"—and this is my first time out. How about you?" The new unit even sounded like a kid, appropriate for a firstie.

"Welcome aboard, Five Zulu Three!" Slate punctuated that for Echo Five's benefit. "Eleven days and I'm off planet. You have my permission to cover for me for the next nine months, Zulu Three." He laughed.

"Gotta survive, first." Two Echo Five made his jab at Tomik's old unit, still on private. By then the HoverLift was close enough to read the suit's call numbers on the outside.

"I can see you now." The arm on Five Zulu Three's suit flexed, as if waving. "You, you're Two Echo Five, and, and there's Three Lima Niner!" The enthusiasm level in his voice jumped, as if he recognized Slate's number.

"So, I'm toast?" Echo Five, brusquely. "How do you like that, Lima Niner? The firstie sees me and just rattles off my numbers. He sees you, and he's ecstatic. Maybe there's a connection, and you never told anyone?"

Only two of the com lights in Slate's display were green. The third was orange, showing a third com registering but not in the loop. The remarks had been just for him, and that was as well, because the insinuation suggested something very sensual in nature. And perhaps something very inappropriate, even though the only real restrictions anymore were violence and coercion.

However, the two miners could hardly know one another.

"Never met the kid." Slate said that to put Echo Five in his place before switching his com to include the firstie. "How's your trip out been, flying instead of walking?"

"Exciting."

"That's good, right?" Echo Five had a sneer in his voice.

"Kept thinking I didn't want the HoverLift to let me go." Zulu

Three sounded like that had been a real concern. "The guys up there kept teasing me, that if they got tired, they wouldn't be able to hold the switch any longer. I didn't expect I'd survive immersion in a lava lake."

He sounded embarrassed, as if the truth was finally obvious, and he only now saw through the joke.

It was the firstie's honesty that engaged with Slate. The miner wore his feelings, his enthusiasm, on his sleeves. If he wasn't out in eleven days, and the man wasn't just learning the skills, he'd consider pulling a transfer to Two Gamma. Or see if the firstie could make it over to Six Charlie.

And look at him! A human! Coming all the way to Purgatoria to run around in a giant suit of iron. How fantastic was that, for someone to want to come to one of the most beautiful places in the universe, even if it was also one of the deadliest?

Of course, Slate hadn't come because of Purgatoria's beauty. He'd come because everything else in the universe had conspired against him. He'd been stripped of everything valuable to him, and he hadn't wanted to see his own face anymore. Well, he'd gotten that. His face was hidden for months at a time, and no one here knew who he was.

That had seemed very satisfying to him, and for a very long time. Now, inexplicably, it wasn't. It was that firstie. He never expected to feel this way on Purgatoria, but he really wanted to show the new man the ropes.

It might even be fun.

Chapter 30

SLATE slammed his hand into the ground, and heat-stressed rock shattered. "That's how you do it!"

He drew his hand back hard, and rock and dust flew through the air. A thick cable whipped through the sky after it, snapping, showering the area with powdery debris, and surrounding him with a gauzy haze. The cable was the three-meter-thick hardline connecting Six Charlie and Seven Alfa. The outer meter was triple heat shielding and insulation, and the center of the line carried the necessary infrastructure along the surface of Purgatoria. Lava flows had buried a seventeen-kay stretch, eventually cooking through the DuraCeram insulation.

It all had to come up, every last kay, and new line run. Five Zulu Three stood off to the side, his arms immobile, and his vision indicator lights showing he was watching Slate work. Two Echo Five was farther down the line, near the edge of the Crevasse, beating away at the rock that had buried the line, in places up to forty meters deep. Here, Echo Five had already gotten the excess rock back down to the original level. Zulu Three watched because that was his job. One watched; two worked. It was the rescue thing. One survivor could carry two bio units back to base. Three damaged units meant three dead miners. And dead on Purgatoria was dead forever. There was no going back.

"You think you can do this?" Slate tossed the cable to the side. When it didn't go as far as he wanted, he caught it with his foot and kicked, laughing when it tangled, and he had to pull it off and carry it away before dropping it where he wanted. "Sometimes it doesn't work like I want, but nobody's watching." He shrugged his shoulders, which did no more than compress his arm seals by tightening the pistons on his arms, front and back at the same time.

"I'm watching."

The Two Gamma unit's words came through in a whisper, and Slate looked at the top of his display. Two lights blinked green, and one was orange. That meant the discourse excluded Two Echo Five. The words had been just for him.

"Something you need to say?" Slate scrolled his vision toward Two Gamma, pausing his unit. "I'm all ears."

"You really enjoy this. I can tell." The words were almost wistful.

"Ach, maybe not en-*joy*," drawing out the word, "but I do enjoy this!" He swept his hand out to indicate the Burning Crevasse. It bit deeply into the core of the planet, and at the bottom, molten rock surged endlessly. Day or night, the area glowed with the intensity of a world come alive.

"Maybe someday I'll feel that way."

"It takes a while for it to grow on some of us."

"Especially if someone didn't have a choice in coming."

"How long you had in the suit so far?" It wasn't exactly good manners to discuss personal matters. That way, differences that came up during personal time didn't equate to scores evened out on company time. Still, the firstie had started it.

"Couple months."

"Chatter says you're really good." His scores, anyway. Those were impressive. But a pat on the back couldn't hurt.

"Top ore yields in Two Gamma," said with pride. "Two Echo Five doesn't care for me, does he?"

"Not you. Your call numbers. We knew the guy who wore it last." Knew he died wearing it. That was a crock, for Tomik, if not for this miner.

"Oh." Two Gamma still stood off to the side. "Can I try?" He motioned toward the exposed end of the cable, his massive arm moving out, and the hand pointing as easily as flesh and blood.

"Absolutely." Slate grinned. That's what he'd wanted, for the newbie to prove himself. To *want* to prove himself. "Dig beside the cable, then yank it out fast. It'll help break up the rock down the line. The more you pull out, the faster it goes. Hit it hard." He backed up, giving the Gamma unit plenty of room.

Slate was watching Zulu Three, and that's why he didn't see the first meteor whiz by, but he saw it slam into the mountainside just on the other side of the Gamma unit. Dust and rock leaped out, splattering them with minute pieces of ejecta. Pulverized residue filled the air.

Gamma didn't see it, either. It all happened just as he slammed his fist into the rock, ripping the cable wide in a great arc. He was pelted with numerous small projectiles as he bent over.

"I did it!" Zulu Three exulted, holding the cable high, just as the next meteor, fist-sized, slammed into the back of his unit. "Hey, what's the deal?" His exterior vision indicators scrolled back and forth across the front of his head, indicating he scanned the area.

The rate of impacts picked up.

Slate ignored the question and shifted into full disaster protocol. "Meteor impact zone! This is not a drill. Defensive mode now. Repeat, this is not a drill." He made sure all three lights in the display were bright green.

"Acknowledged." Zulu Three had already started to drop his unit.

However, the protocol required an affirmative response from every unit. "Two Echo Five, do you read me? Meteor shower. This is not a drill. Defensive mode now. Repeat, this is not a drill."

Slate had already begun to lower his own unit for the least possible exposure. He had to disengage several high-pressure hydraulic lines to the upper and lower legs, and one linkage in the shoulders had to be released for the arms to come up and adequately shield his bio unit and his head. Those were the critical areas that kept the miner inside alive.

Echo Five? All he got back was static, not surprising with all the debris in the air. He hoped he had found a cave or an overhang. When the shower stopped, he wanted someone to come carry him back to base if his unit was incapacitated.

He couldn't feel the fragments of space rock hitting his metal body, but he could hear it through his sensors. He could just see Zulu Three, legs folded under his body, and the arms twisted grotesquely over his head and back. He'd done it and done it fast, though, like in the training drills.

Smart man. Very smart man.

Slate kept on the com, but there was nothing. Not from Echo Five or Zulu Three. It was all static, in the sky and on the com, as they were pelted by the rocky rain from above. Many burned up on the way down. Of those that did, from time to time, one would detonate while in midair. The concussions rocked the huge mining units.

As the barrage slowed, Slate began picking up pieces of transmissions.

". . . arm twisted . . ."

". . . never thought . . . do this often . . ."

He tried again, "Echo Five. Zulu Three. This is Three Lima Niner. Report condition."

"This is Two Echo Five. Still in defensive mode. Sensor red on right arm. Otherwise—" The com crackled, cutting off the transmission, just as a meteor slammed into the Crevasse, sending molten ejecta flying skyward.

The ground shook and slipped under Slate's feet, and after a moment, it held steady. That unsettled him. Echo Five was at the Crevasse. A quake? This area was not noted as high-risk for quakes, and that was the reason for locating the cable here. For the ground to drop? That hit had done something big. Still. Once the units were locked in, they were frozen for the duration. There was nothing to be done anytime soon.

Slate checked the time piece in his display, getting itchy. That big one had brought on an additional round of small meteors pelting the area with an erratic volley of small stones.

"Lima Niner?"

Slate checked his display. At least something was getting through. "Yes, Gamma?"

"Seriously. Does it do this all the time?" The voice quavered.

"Not *every* time we're out. Hey, I was paying attention to you earlier. You slammed your hand into that rock, and just that fast, you fell into defensive mode. By the book. You'll make a good miner, maybe even already are one." Distract him. That's what he needed to do. It was Echo Five that had his thoughts.

"Thank you. Does it?"

"Don't guess you get meteor strikes where you come from." Keep talking, kid. We'll get through this if you just keep talking.

"Shipped in from Wendy's World."

The name tore through Slate's consciousness like a volcanic explosion, consuming him. His family. In that one name, he remembered it all. Every detail. The raiders had come from that god-forsaken place, taken his family from him, and left him with nothing.

Nothing except death.

And Zulu Three was one of them.

He wanted to rage, tear his metal fingers into Zulu Three's suit, puncture the life-sustaining systems running through the head, and fling the bio unit into the Crevasse, to have this *thief* die as his family had died.

Not his son. His son hadn't died. He'd been stolen. Stolen. Dear God, was that worse or better? Ripped from his heart, with no way to know if he'd lived or died.

He hoped he died well, if that had been his fate. Fast and well. He could not . . . would not picture the alternative.

"Lima Niner?"

He couldn't answer. Not that *monster* that he'd said he admired just moments before.

"Can I just talk?" Occasional impacts still littered the ground, and the com brokenly buzzed, but this close, it was understandable. Barely. "No one asks . . ."

In Slate's display, peripheral left seemed to be gone. Echo Five's com light was blinking from orange to red. And Zulu Three wanted to talk. About what, Zulu Three? Someone on your world who needed my seed stocks more than I needed my wife and family? It was all back with him, pounding into his mind like a pile driver into soft stone: the off-worlders come to trade if you would, or to take if you wouldn't. You want to talk about that, Zulu Three? Your uncle, maybe, or your father? Were they the ones that stole my life from me?

"I'm . . . I'm . . . Lima Niner? You there?" He sounded scared. More firstie than miner.

"Here." That's all Slate could get out. Echo Five still hovered between orange and red. He'd need Zulu Three if Echo Five were in a bad way. His stomach churned. "Wendy's World, huh?" Just the name of the place was sand in his throat, and it was a grittiness he couldn't spit out.

"They didn't give me a choice coming here." The voice was quiet for a moment, then it laughed. "Yeah, I had a choice. Here or something worse. Here, maybe I can buy my freedom back. Danger pays better."

"Bravo." Dry and bitter. Who cared about him buying his freedom back? Some things never came back. Never. Wives. Children. Lives lived.

"Have you ever had a family?"

Shut up, man! Shut up!

"Lima Niner? You there?" There was laughter, again. Dry, frightened laughter. The voice of a boy. "I don't want to die without someone to talk to."

"Stop it, Zulu Three. Nobody's dying." Yet, the ground shook, once small, and again violently, giving the lie to Slate's words.

"Feel that? And Echo Five's not answering. I've been trying, and nothing."

"Base says you were top of your class. Why pick here? You could've requested any assignment, and they would've given it to you." The question that he wanted to ask was, and why with me?

"I was the best, because I had to be the best." He laughed sourly. "Then I wanted to be with the best. Where you from, Lima Niner?"

Slate didn't reply to that. The question hit too close to home. Besides, he didn't have to answer. Boundaries were boundaries. Let the fool prattle, if he wanted, but it didn't mean he got answers.

"Don't want to say, huh? Me? I don't brag, either. I shouldn't have said, earlier. It always gets a rise out of people. Who wants to be from Wendy's World? Who wants to be around anyone from Wendy's World? Not me."

"What's this place offer you?" A change of topic, he hoped.

"I thought . . . never mind. Hoping. Not anything real."

"What does that mean?"

"You know Wendy's World?"

"Thieves." He muttered it, the word erupting before he could stop it. What he almost spat out was *murderers.*

"Worse than that." There was that dry laugh, again. "Oh, much worse than that."

"Can we get on another subject?" Slate drew in a deep breath, and he forced himself to be professional. He didn't know this guy; didn't want to know him, not now. But to shut a man out here in the middle of Purgatoria? He wouldn't do that to another person, even someone from Wendy's World. Besides, this man hadn't destroyed his family. He hoped. Getting even here, on this day, wouldn't bring them back.

"I grew legumes, once." After a pause, Zulu Three chuckled. "Lima Niner, you know what legumes are?"

Great! The kid's a farmer. Now, he'll want to talk farming, and

141

all the memories that'll bring back. He sighed, giving in a little. "You mean beans."

"Beans, sure. That's all I remembered, but it got me out of the fields. I offered to grow legumes. Sorry. Beans, and I was good at it. One year, when the crops were failing, I knew what to do. It was something my father had taught me, and it got me to the green-houses. That bought me a chance for a real education."

"You're not growing beans, now. Not on Purgatoria." Slate found that amusing. He gave in some more. While they were on this job, he'd give the firstie some breathing room. Then they would go their separate ways. That was best. It hit home especially hard to him just why the miners didn't get personal.

The real problem was the memories he'd stirred. There were so many bad ones that he had to keep them buried way down deep. The man had boiled them all back to the surface.

Eleven more days, he reminded himself, and he was gone. This time he didn't think he'd be back.

"Once a slave, always a slave." Zulu Three cut in, interrupting Slate's dark slide into himself. The kid laughed, but it was bitter. "Grow beans there, mine ore here. Maybe here I can buy my way out, if I work hard enough."

"Out of what?" Gambling debts, probably.

"You know. Wendy's World. Then find my family."

"Don't we all? You're looking in the wrong place. Nobody's on Purgatoria." Slate laughed. "Nobody important."

"You didn't say if you had a family."

"Didn't want to."

"Have one or say if you have one?"

"Say. It's personal, and we don't discuss personal between miners."

"Is that why you broke the rule?" There was a ragged edge to the question.

"*I* broke the rule? You, you've been asking prying questions. *I* broke the rule?"

"Sure. You asked about where I was from, and now you don't want to talk to me. What bad thing happened to you there?"

"Never been there." Not to Wendy's World. He should've never asked that question. He was just being helpful, trying to get the kid's mind off the meteor shower. Now look what was coming out of the muck.

"Then what?"

"Your people came to me a very long time ago, and now I'm here. Good enough?"

"My people." That seemed to set him back. "You never had a family, then. I did. I had a family, once."

"Then we're the same. How's that? We're here together on this world, and we're the same. No family. We're alone. How do you like that? Can you leave it be, now?" And we might die here, but he didn't have the guts to smear that all over him. No, not even a thief from Wendy's World. No one deserved that, not here on Purgatoria, not locked down in a meteor shower.

Oh, Slate hated this! Not so much the storm. That was a part of this world. Beautiful had been a red sky, a new person to enjoy, and eleven days to offworld. Now all his memories were vomited back up. All on a world that wanted to kill you, if you relaxed your attention for a split second. He wanted beautiful back, his family back, but his life was this now, and that kind of beautiful was lost forever.

Zulu Three began to move first, the arms swinging around in a way that would be impossible for a human. Halfway through the procedure, one arm hung, tried to bump past the problem several times, then began to move once again.

"Slowly, Zulu Three." Slate cautioned the other miner. "Double check lower hydraulics and arm linkages."

Com was improving, but Echo Five was still fluttering between colors. Slate began to unfold his own unit, feeling the unit's balance readjust as the massive arms and torso rose up on its titanic legs. Standing, he could see where the edge of the Crevasse had collapsed in on itself. It had been twenty kays away before. Now, he felt he could look into the heart of the planet from right where he stood.

"Why here?" Static crackled, but Zulu Three's question came through fine.

"Look at that." Slate used the words to ignore the question. Off in the distance, the meteor shower still sprinkled the sky, but farther away now; the atmosphere glittered with their remains. It was a display of life that had been given and snuffed out once again, the small shards burned to ashes in their frenzied dance. Occasionally one hit the surface of the planet, sending dust and debris flying.

"But why here?"

Slate hadn't answered the question. He hadn't wanted to, and he still didn't. The boy could have been asking any number of things, from why did the meteor shower impact here; why was the cable placed so close to the Crevasse; or why were they here in the first place, mining on Purgatoria? He chose the easiest.

"The rock stratum was tested down to three kays."

"The cable. You're talking about the cable."

So, that hadn't been the question. "It's the reason the Crevasse stayed there." He pointed. "This ridge held it back. Can you pull up Echo Five? He's between orange and red in my display. I'm getting nothing."

"Here, either."

"We head that way next." The meteor shower had kicked up an extraordinary amount of dust, and the air glowed red. They couldn't see Echo Five's position clearly enough to distinguish between rock and machine. The poor signal concerned Slate. Not worried. Not yet. Maybe, though.

"Is it safe?"

"Sure. I've seen the survey reports." He knew what was under here. Or had known.

"It did collapse. You felt the quakes, too. What about the Hover-Lift? Would it be better to have them pull Echo Five out?"

"We can't even contact Echo Five." Slate moved his hand in front of him, and the air swirled with fine dust. He knew what the kid was asking. Was it safe to head that way to check on him? "This has killed our signal until it settles. No HoverLift rescues today."

"I'm nervous, I guess."

Slate laughed. "The first acknowledgement of a smart miner. Always be nervous on Purgatoria. It's the people who aren't scared that die out here."

"Yes, ser."

In spite of his upbeat manner, the edge of the Crevasse had Slate concerned more than he was willing to admit. That had to have been some sort of wallop to damage the bedrock and create that cave in.

"Follow me." Slate began to move, putting repeated pressure on each leg as he landed it, like a hammer drill, testing to see if the rock was stable. He saw the firstie following, trusting him. Like he believed in him, even without knowing him. That was best. His two hundred tons were going to shift the rock if anything was.

He did note that his left peripherals were still out. He'd have to get that sensor replaced as soon as he got back. That left a whole swath he couldn't see without turning his entire body. And his articulation pump in his left leg was sending him warnings. He didn't need that to fail.

Even so, they were here now, and he had Echo Five to look after. Yeah, that sensor had to take back stage for now.

Chapter 31

TWO ECHO FIVE'S arm was more than twisted.

"Can you read me, now?" Slate stood over the fallen behemoth and triggered Echo Five's com frequency. It occasionally blinked green and faded back to orange before he could make contact. He signaled the Gamma unit. "Zulu Three, I'm cutting you out, so I can boost the signal to Echo Five."

He cut it as soon as he finished talking, and he saw the unit's arm move, indicating acknowledgment. He shifted all power to the one signal, hoping it would go through. In old-fashioned space suits, astronauts had been able to touch visors, and the vibrations would allow them to speak, after a fashion. Not here. Their speech had nothing to do with sound waves, and everything to do with radio waves. Microwaves, to be precise.

He reached his hand and gently touched the outside of Echo Five's suit, careful not to shift the mining unit. The contact should act as an antenna. He saw the indicator change to green and hold for a moment, then it wavered. With this much signal loss, the problem had to be with Echo Five's receiver. With the kid here, he hoped someone wasn't dead in that suit.

"Echo Five, do you read me?"

"Ahh. Um, yeah."

"What condition are you in?" His suit, but Echo Five would

understand that. It was the suits that kept them alive. Their bodies? They stayed in the bio unit, or they didn't survive.

"I'm blind. No vision at all. How's it look from out there?"

"Tropical beach, warm sun, and beautiful women everywhere. Glad you could join us." He laughed.

"I didn't mean that earlier." The voice sounded drained.

"Didn't mean what?" Echo Five was despondent, more likely, but Slate understood. For a miner, no vision was tantamount to being a blind person walking across a floor of broken glass. There was no way you were going to miss every piece.

"That you have no friends."

"It's just something we say. No offense taken."

"You and the new guy hit it off."

"His enthusiasm undermined my independence." He laughed again.

"What independence? Out here, nobody's independent."

"From the friend at his side." Slate smiled at that.

"Yeah. Describe the damage." To the suit, but that came through very clearly.

"You took a direct hit." He didn't tell him the arm was gone, spread across the burning soil in a hundred pieces. None were big enough to read the call sign Two Echo Five etched into the metal.

"What do you mean? I took a hundred hits. How could one be any different?" He was silent for a time, and he said, "I saw that first one that hit near you. Your damage?"

"Minimal. Your vitals, can you check them?"

"Let me try." He was silent for a time before coming back online. "One arm, red. Vision shot, but you knew that. Com keeps wavering. It's only had real signal since you showed up." He stopped again, as if thinking, then asked point blank. "Direct hit. What does that mean?"

"You took a full-on impact on that arm. It's scattered over five hundred kays. They'll never find enough of it to dock your pay."

"My one bright spot."

"You need a bright spot. Another thing, we had a quake. Right here." He took a deep breath, hating this part.

"Come now, Lima Niner. I know my surveys. I've got a doctorate in planetary geology. The bedrock under us right now is geologically stable. It hasn't moved in ten thousand years."

"That last meteor hit in the Crevasse." Slate let that sit for a time.

"Cracking the basalt."

"Yeah. You're getting the picture."

"And?"

"You may be stranded for a while." It wasn't just the arm. Here, touching him, he could get a better angle. That blast that had taken his arm had decimated the side of the torso. Below? Fluid leaked out of one knee joint. If he didn't have a red light now, he would. That suit wasn't walking anywhere.

"Stranded?" Two Echo Five laughed. "Forget the cable. Provision Niner Bravo says, and I quote, 'Any miner whose unit is permanently disabled takes precedence over any assigned duty and must be immediately transported via bio unit to the nearest secure facility.' So, unplug me, and let's get going."

"Remember that meteor that hit the Crevasse?" Slate laughed sourly.

"Spit it out, Lima Niner."

"You are suspended partly over the Crevasse."

"That was twenty kays away." His words carried disbelief.

"Oh, a little meteor, one collapsed mountain, and your slide in the quake."

"You can't access the bio unit? If I can pull up the bio controls, I can release it from in here."

"You're back-down, half buried in rubble. I can't get to you. I'm sorry." He tried to glance at Zulu Three, but he was in Slate's blind spot. "When I move my hand, I'm going to lose com with you, so I'll tell you now what we're doing. Our Gamma friend is going to help me secure you so you don't slip farther down the mountain. Then we're headed to base. We'll have a HoverLift out within the day. I promise."

"Lima Niner?"

"Yes?"

"Take care of the new guy. We don't need eight and nine to happen today."

Slate laughed. "Oh, you are so right. I'll make sure he gets back safely. I'm letting go now." And he broke the contact.

Standing, he turned to Zulu Three and triggered the com. "I'll need cabling, if you can find any at the supply drop, and some way to secure Echo Five. He'll have to be picked up by HoverLift. See what you can find."

"Yes, ser."

The supply drop was about ten kays back, and together they

unearthed everything they thought might benefit them: clamps; high-impact, self-embedding anchor bolts; and a marker beacon.

"No cabling." Zulu Three held the other things in his hands. There was the replacement cable for the installation, which was seventeen kays of three-meter-thick cable. It had withstood the shower just fine, but they couldn't manipulate it to secure the injured miner.

"Then we improvise." Slate thought for a moment. "The old cable. If we strip the shielding, we can use the core. That's our plan."

The shielding was tough, but being cracked with heat and age, it was doable. Anyway, the mining units were built to dig through solid rock. Pulling out kay after kay from the rubble, together they eviscerated the core and coiled it in great loops a quarter of a kay wide. They worked it around the fallen miner's one good arm and clamped it together, then fed the rest of the cable several kays inland until they located a large rocky outcrop. That was to be their anchor.

It was tying off the cable when they realized Zulu Three's unit had more wrong with it than that glitch in the arm. It had been sticking at that same point continually, and he'd simply forced it past. However, this time was different. The Gamma unit had the cable in his hand, pulling it tight against the weight at the far end, and Slate was attaching a coupling to clamp it in a loop around the outcropping. Slate asked him to pull it tighter, and the arm jerked and slipped for a moment.

When they stepped away, Zulu Three called to him, "Ser, you might want to come see this." Fluid covered the ground where he had been standing.

"Suit vitals? Have you run diagnostics?"

"Vitals are all fine, ser. I'm running full diagnostics now."

"Something has—"

"Sorry to interrupt, ser. Diagnostics is redlining. The whole thing is going off the board. I've got systems failing all over." The longer he talked, the more rising panic colored his words.

"Let me think." He wasn't really qualified for this, although all miners had to know their units inside and out. It was what kept them alive. "Kill internal pumps, especially that arm. Shunt all nonbiological resources to your lower reservoirs first, then the remaining to your good arm. Save what you can."

"Sorry, ser. I tried that before I talked to you. Red's still coming up everywhere."

"Okay. We can do what we've done with Two Echo Five. We can shut your unit down and let the HoverLift return for you. How's that? It's what you wanted earlier." He tried to smile over the com. Clearly the man was scared out here. He was scared, himself. No telling how bad it was for a firstie.

"Sorry, ser. I can read the tell-tales. Whatever it is, it's killing the bio unit, also. It's getting warm in here."

"Turn around. I want to see that arm that's been giving you trouble." However, Slate already knew. That fluid wasn't hydraulic fluid. The cooling system had been compromised, and the unit was overheating. Whatever had been catching inside that arm had snagged something vital, and now it was broken. It would override every system, soon shutting the entire suit down.

He could see the entry point, although not the actual object that had penetrated the suit. It had hit at the shoulder rotator cuff, no doubt when the arm had been lifted after slamming the suit's hand into the rocky crust. The sudden twisting of the shoulder had been the suit's undoing.

And he had hated this miner. Now? He had no more answers to save his life.

"I'm trying base. I'm diverting all power to the emergency frequency. I'll be back in just a minute."

"Be waiting, ser." The voice was strained, yet hopeful.

He reached a metal finger and touched the unit on its metal chest. "I was wrong out there, and I apologize. You're both brave and resourceful. All this, and you've still got your head on your shoulders. You'll find that family again, someday. I'll be there to help you. I promise you that."

"Thank you, ser. I appreciate that."

Slate turned away as he reassigned all his com power to the emergency beacon. What did he think about the miner's chances? If it was getting hot in his suit now, he was going to cook. Come out? No one could survive in sixty-degree weather, not for more than a quarter hour before hyperthermia set in. And it was coming to the hottest part of the day. His readout said over eighty. This near the Crevasse, he'd expect close to ninety by the time it finished. The Gamma driver was going to die.

But he didn't have to die alone. Not even someone from Wendy's World deserved that, and especially not a firstie. Slate's choices were rotten right then. Echo Five or Zulu Three? Both needed him urgently, and he couldn't provide what either of them required.

Eleven days. Ten and a half, now. Ten and a half, and he would have been gone.

Like he said, his choices were pretty rotten right then.

Chapter 32

SLATE used his fist to punch through the mountainside where the first meteor had hit. Rock shattered, flying inward and leaving a dark hole.

Seeing where the meteor had penetrated the mountain had given him hope. Caverns. The range was pocketed with them, and they stretched back into the rock strata, deep within the world. Real pulse-echo data had long ago confirmed their existence. Their usefulness? Their exploration wasn't cost effective yet, not when so much good quality metal was just below the surface.

Besides, the mining constructs needed headroom, and a lot of it.

Slate remembered how ground temperature changed more slowly than surface temperatures, and while the air might soar to ninety, underground? He didn't think so. He was betting he would find survivable temperatures back in the Iron Mountain caverns.

He had to. Gamma was shutting down, and while the unit's bio component was designed to be self-contained for up to three days, if the driver was already hot, that told the truth of that.

Then there was Slate's suit. It was warning him he could no longer make it to base, and with meteors still littering the sky? That would continue to keep their signals from bringing help.

Water was the other issue. The suits carried some reserves. After all, the human body is seventy percent water, and even encased in tons of Ferro-carbon steel, the toughest ever manufactured, it would dry out. There were reservoirs inside. If the man kept hydrated, even outside the bio unit, it was possible he might live.

He stepped into the high-ceilinged room. The space stretched into dimness, although to the side, he could see smaller chambers opening off this one. Rubble littered the cavern floor at his feet, some from his fist, and more from the meteor. He wondered if the meteor had exploded on impact, or if the resulting meteorite was somewhere inside. It had sure taken down a chunk of the wall.

The farther he walked to the back, the cooler it got, although that was relative. Fifty-four was his best reading. That was survivable, with lots of water. Enough water might be the problem.

He stepped back outside to the Gamma unit, its joints now locked in an upright position. He noticed the foot of his unit was starting to drag, and his display was screaming at him. He'd silenced the audio, but the visual flashed red repeatedly. That could not be good under any circumstances.

He keyed the com to local. "Zulu Three?" *Wake up, man.* "Zulu Three? Don't let me down by giving up in there."

"I'm burning up." The words were slurred, and he was breathing hard. "I gotta get out. Anything. My arms, they won't move. They won't move!"

"Slow down, Zulu Three. I'm going to pull your bio unit. Can you disengage it from the main unit?"

"Disengage . . . disengage." He panted several times. "Disengage, the bio." More panting, then he said, "Done. Disengaged." His voice fell away.

"Zulu Three? Don't die on me, now. You've got a lot of life left to live. This is not your day, not here, not in this place. Stay with me, man."

All the while he was at the back of the unit, and using his massive fingers as delicately as possible, he followed procedure for bio unit removal. External readouts told him the miner had been successful—something Slate could have done from the outside, but that would have taken longer—and he grabbed the door on the back of the massive torso and flung it aside. The eight-meter-tall plate would be handled by a robotic crane in the shop, but here, it was a toy for his mining unit.

Shiny fluid gushed from inside.

It was not supposed to do that. Slate watched the liquid, light green with an oily sheen, flush across the ground. Inside was the bio unit, a six-meter sphere with a deep recess stamped into it and spanned by a handle designed to be gripped by a mining unit in the field. All he had to do was grasp the handle, twist in a counter-clockwise fashion, and the bio unit would be freed. He grabbed and twisted, and then he pulled, hard. The unit released, and it was his, a bauble in his hand, yet carrying a living being inside. It dripped with the green liquid. He knew a sinking sensation. At this point, the best he could do was hope the human inside still lived. He couldn't stay in there, not with the systems compromised. He had to come out.

His leg display now had a black X on the screaming icon, warning him of imminent shutdown to prevent permanent damage, but there was nothing he could do. He forced it to walk, as he carried the bio unit to the coolest part of the cavern. It read fifty-five. Perhaps the heat rise was the hole he'd punched in the wall. Fifty-five was survivable for Zulu Three, hopefully until rescue came.

He set the unit down and considered his options. The bio unit was designed to be carried by a fully operational mining unit, but not opened by one. Awake, Zulu Three could, again, simply release himself from the bio unit, as easily as he had released himself from the mining unit. He could just stand and walk away. The problem was, Zulu Three was not conscious. He had to have someone open his bio unit for him.

Oh, he hated what he knew had to be done! Safety protocols demanded designs that allowed any operator to exit his or her own mining unit in the case of an emergency. However, those same protocols said nothing about making it easy. It was a cumbersome process to exit the main unit. It involved climbing out a very small hatch on the chest side.

Another thing. He could not reinsert himself. That was not a field procedure. Before he made any irrevocable decisions, he had to make one more try.

"Zulu Three, I need you to be awake. You have one more job to do." Please Zulu Three, please Zulu Three, please Zulu Three. He groaned when there was no answer. Well, he'd promised. No one dies today.

He initiated defensive mode to get his unit as low to the ground as possible, disconnecting and unhooking systems as necessary. During the switchover, his leg icon finally overrode silent mode, telling him, "Leg function disabled. Repair request uplink now being sent. Please do not attempt to reanimate leg at this time."

"Thanks for the warning." Once he was out, he wouldn't be able to reinsert himself, anyway. He hoped the repair crews got here quickly.

Then the suit said, "Com unit offline. Repair request uplink will be sent when signal returns."

Sure, he thought. In this place? That's never. However, perhaps the other two units would get through. They should be sending distress signals like crazy.

He prepared himself mentally. Nearly nine months since he'd been out and touching air. This was going to be weird.

He hit the emergency disengage, and he felt the giant machine moving around him. Gears turned, life support systems disconnected, and the cooling pumps wound down. Then, around him, his bio unit hissed, and an ovoid door two meters tall appeared. He blinked, hard, and lifted a hand to his face to remove his breather. It was his first disconnection point. He began disengaging from the rest of the systems, his mind still fully integrated with his machine, until he undid the final link. He reached behind his neck, pushed the release switch, and withdrew the brain jack. All unit inputs went dead. He was no longer his mining unit.

He pushed the ovoid door forward and aside. It moved just enough to allow him access to the exterior door in the chest. With the unit in defensive mode, he should be only about ten meters above ground level. The ladder was thirteen, so he should be fine.

When his bio unit had opened, the exterior door had also triggered, as designed. The heat pouring in took his breath away. He pulled his compression cap from his head. He'd never experienced fifty-five degrees before, and it was insane. He felt the biogel already drying on his skin, as he rolled the ladder through the small hatch and climbed into the dim light of the cavern. It had seemed brighter in the unit, with its ability to see in near darkness. Near the bottom of the ladder was when he discovered what the suit's final warning had meant. The unit hadn't made it all the way to the ground before the leg function was disabled. The legs were off kilter, and his ladder stopped two meters from the floor. He took a deep breath and jumped, rolling on the ground. He got up, his thin, full-body compression suit none the worse for wear, just dirty.

Now for the firstie. He had to come out of that bio unit. Slate knelt beside it and punched in the emergency release code—something every miner knew—and stepped back to let the seals release. When the door moved forward, he yanked it and shoved it aside.

There was the miner, goopy with biogel, breather over his face, and thin, gray compressions on, unlike Slate's dark blue. Releasing that door had cut his breather, so that had to come off his face first. Slate knelt and gripped it in his hand, and he slipped it up and off the firstie's face. He was no more than a kid, like he'd sounded several times, and Slate smiled. This pale-skinned waif was as smooth-skinned as a boy. Sure, the biogel inhibited hair growth, but this kid had never shaved, not as Slate was here looking at him as a witness.

"Zulu Three, time to come awake." He patted the kid's face on one side, then the other. "We've got to get you out of there."

The kid's body was hot. Slate reached in, unbuckling his arms and legs, and working off the big straps across his stomach and chest. The inner door was a form-fitted gel cushion, but the straps were designed in as a secondary restraint system. His had automatically released when he'd triggered the door. The kid's had been opened from outside. Very different scenarios. Very different exit procedures. Just before he pulled him out, he withdrew the IVs in both arms and reached to his compression cap, pulling it loose, and spilling out a headful of white hair.

Slate rocked back as pictures flashed through his mind: holding a small baby, tossing a ball, having his son jump on the bed to wake his father up, then screaming in terror as he was carried away. His Levi. Slate looked away, knowing he was seeing something that wasn't there. The hair was similar, sure, but this was not his boy. Too many years had passed, and he had seen too many boys in that time, hoping, his hope causing him to see his own son in those tousled heads of hair. What was true was that you never got the past back. All you could do was move on. He pulled the kid forward, reaching behind his neck to release the brain jack. In that action he felt the necklace. It wrapped the kid's neck, and Slate could see where it lay pressed against his chest under his compression suit. He gently pulled it out, a silver tube of metal, a cylinder on a chain. A memento from a previous life. He slipped it back inside, patting it where it lay against the kid's chest.

"Now to get you out."

He worked his hands under the kid's legs and back, and he pulled him free, walking him to the side of the cavern farthest away from the opening. He laid him out on the rough floor, heading back to see what he could find to put under his head. Nothing. Matter-of-factly, he pulled off the top of his own compression suit and rolled it up, slipping it under the kid's head.

He stood, knowing there was water and wondering how to best get at it. His mining unit had been serviced the day before, so it should have quite a reservoir. The kid's? Proper procedure would have been to service it just before he came out on the job. His own ladder was within jumping distance, so that was certainly an option. Yet, the kid's was easier access. He chose easy access.

Once inside, he tore the interior apart, looking for the unit's water reserves. There had to be a container somewhere. He located it when he ripped the seat cushion out. There it was, form fitted between the hull and the seat. It held maybe twenty to twenty-five liters. It would have to be coaxed out with as little loss as possible. So much for retaining a water-tight seal.

His would be the same, although getting it down past that two-meter drop might be a challenge. He'd have to risk it, because by all he knew, it was hot on this world.

Chapter 33

THE KID'S eyes tracked him.

Slate didn't really mind. It was hot, they had no food, and their water was down to two liters. At least it was a little cooler at night. Forty-eight, maybe. Not much better, just better.

It had taken the kid a full day to wake. It was what had happened during that day that had unnerved him.

He'd torn a part of his shirt—from the makeshift pillow—to make a compress, keeping it wet and on the kid's forehead. He thought it might help, what with the heat. And he hoped for the rescue team. Hoped bad, for Echo Five and Zulu Three both. Come night, he maybe could walk out, but those guys? They were dead in the water.

He'd been applying a fresh compress, although it was the same one, only with fresh water, but he'd been applying it, and the cord on the trinket caught his eye. He'd worked it out and tried to see if there were any markings. Maybe, if the kid died, he'd know something about him.

There was nothing. Seamless; featureless; like it was brand new, even after being in that bio unit with the kid. Nothing stayed like that in there. Slate had learned early on that anything he kept with him inside the suit was ruined after a full tour of duty. Even the clothes he had on. Right then? He stank, and he could tell. The kid?

Not so bad. It had only been a few weeks.

He'd sat beside the kid, messing with the cylinder, noticing how it didn't have a temperature. There was something else, almost as if it called to him, like it wanted to be in his hand. It surprised him that as hot as it was outside of the suits, the cylinder was . . . nothing. Not hot, not cool. Not until he held it awhile. Then it started doing things.

Not exactly *things,* but thing. It started warming up. He sat with his eyes closed, with it in his hand. *Slate. Slate.* The longer he held it, the more he wanted to hold it, and the warmer it got. Then hot.

Then came the weird thing. The kid started talking, but when Slate realized he was awake, and he let go of the trinket to talk to him, he was still out cold. Or as cold as someone could be on Purgatoria.

Slate shivered then, and a new sense of unease ran down his back, remembering. Someone was messing with his head, either that, or he was growing delirious. He'd slipped the silver cylinder back into the kid's shirt and left it alone.

Day nine was when he woke.

"Hey, Lima Niner. It's hot in here."

Slate had been across the room, up inside his unit, seeing if there was anything useful he could cannibalize. There wasn't, but he had to look. Either that or go nuts from the heat.

"You awake?" He'd looked down, the kid small against the cavern floor, his hair white in the shadows.

"Maybe. Groggy, still."

"Good for you, Zulu Three, the awake part, anyway. I'll be right down."

"That's yours, isn't it? Three Lima Niner. It's big."

"No bigger than yours." Slate was down the ladder, and he dropped to the floor. "Ah, the miracle of an unexpected vantage point." He held a hand up toward the massive machine and extended his fingers. As tall as the unit was, it fit within the stretch of his thumb and pointer. He held them to the kid. "That tall."

Slate grinned, but he didn't look in the kid's face. Not for long. He didn't want to be reminded of who he might have had with him, had his life gone differently back on Lacy's Veil Prime.

"I've just never seen one from a human viewpoint." The kid chuckled.

"You loaded on the station, right?" He saw the kid nod. "Then shipped down?" He watched him nod again. "Firsties get that every

159

time. Like getting born. Jerked from perfection to reality."

"Then found out I got assigned a haunted unit." He laughed, and he tried to sit up. He held out a hand. "Help me, please."

"Sure, kid." Slate knelt beside him, helping him to an erect position, and pulled up the water, sloshing it around. "Thirsty?"

"You don't know. Thanks."

"Just go slow." Slate held the container while the kid gulped down more than he probably should, even with the heat. No way was he saying no.

"Where's mine?" He wiped his mouth on his sleeve and pointed to Slate's mining unit.

"Yours didn't make it inside. That's your bio unit over there, though."

"Oh. I do remember the meteors. Echo Five. Is he, um, okay?"

"If rescue gets here."

"Then, how?" He looked puzzled, and he touched himself on the chest. "I thought no one could live outside the units, and here we are." He motioned to the cave with his hand.

Slate grinned. "I saved your ugly hide, Zulu Three." He punched him on the shoulder. "Say thanks, Slate." He caught himself immediately, but he couldn't take back his name. Anyway, the kid knew what he looked like outside the mining unit, so he guessed it didn't matter much.

That was when the kid started watching him, tracking whatever he did, like there was something he'd wanted to find, and now he had. And that was when Slate first noticed the green eyes. Lots of people had green eyes, though. Lots and lots of them. But he'd started thinking of him as Levi. That had been his son's name, and he knew better, but with the kid right here, he couldn't help it.

He was smarter than to say it, though. He didn't need to go down that rabbit hole. Besides, he was now to day eight. Eight days and he was off this world.

He was getting mighty hungry, though. It was time for those rescue teams to get here. What did they think he was going to use for food? Dust and rock? He might salvage glucose from the bio units, but that wouldn't help his hunger, just keep him alive so he could starve a few more days.

He tried to laugh, but it was getting harder.

Man, he was hungry, and he knew the kid must be suffering, too. Even if he hadn't complained.

"THINK we have company, Zulu Three?" Slate had thought, *Levi*, nearly letting it slip and only cutting in with Zulu Three at the last moment. He could never, never say that to the boy.

He'd discovered Purgatoria was loud all the time. Encased in his unit, he'd never realized that. The continuing meteor showers had bombarded them for another day, with thudding resonations coming from outside the cavern before fading to a mere lightshow, glimpsed through the opening Slate had created. Sitting in Purgatoria's steaming sauna, he had plenty of opportunity to enjoy it all.

Now, the rumblings of the planet had changed to something more, a uniform sound that whined like giant fan blades.

"HoverLifts!" The kid was up and across the room. "Lima Niner, we're saved!"

His enthusiasm was catching. The kid had taken to grinning when he called him Lima Niner, like he knew a secret that he couldn't say. The grin was missing this time, but there was an issue the kid hadn't considered.

Slate had.

"They'll load Echo Five first. Don't count on a pickup just yet."

"But they have to take us. I mean, they wouldn't leave us, would they?" The kid was at the opening, watching as the sound grew louder.

"Not leave, but not prepared, either. You and me being out of those?" He pointed to his unit. "And they don't know?"

"The HoverLifts, though. They have cargo bays."

The kid was right. That was if the Lift pilots knew they were here. They couldn't just run outside to flag them down; that was a death sentence in itself. They were alive only because of this cavern.

Besides, he was really tired.

"Come on. We have to try something." The kid ran back, excited, and slapped Slate on the knee. "Your com. I bet you can get through by now."

"There are no manual controls." Enthusiasm wouldn't make the contact. The brain jack? He was pretty certain it couldn't be successfully reinserted. "When they don't see my unit with the rest—"

Slate let the next thing go unsaid. They'd assume he'd returned to base with Zulu Three's survival pod. He did stand, though. He just didn't have the kid's energy. The heat and the lack of food had taken its toll. Also, the water was gone, and he'd foregone the lion's share. He didn't regret it, either.

161

"There." The kid was back to the opening. "I can see them."

Slate joined him, and sure enough, a HoverLift beat the sky over where Echo Five had fallen. "When they come for yours, I think we can take the chance to run out and give them a wave."

Slate looked at the kid as he said that, and he wished he hadn't. The kid's face broke into a grin. It was those green eyes, and the way his mouth turned up just so. He could swear he saw his boy in that face, but then, just after he'd lost his family, he thought he'd seen his boy's face in a hundred kids. Just because he wanted it didn't make it true.

The first HoverLift rose from the edge of the Crevasse after several hours, with a mangled mining unit dangling from its under-belly, flying rapidly back towards Nodule Six Charlie.

"Hey, where are they going?" The kid was hopping at the door, trying to run out, but pushed back by the heat every time.

"Slow down." Slate grabbed the back of his neck, just below the socket for the brain jack. The skin there was still red from its installation. "There's a second. See it?" It hovered barely visible off to the side.

"Why aren't they coming?" He pulled away and ran to his bio unit. "There's got to be some way to let them know we're in here." He was digging through the wreckage left by Slate's very thorough search for water.

"You're amazing," Slate called to him, with admiration at the boy's unflagging determination.

"What?" Zulu Three stood, his hands full of stripped wiring, his resolve to do *something* written all over him.

"You, so filled with finding a way to get us rescued. Being stranded on this hellish world, I'm glad it's been with you." Slate laughed roughly, forcing himself to look away. He couldn't afford to get too attached to this boy. He watched the HoverLift. It was closer now, as if looking for something.

"Why do you say that?" The kid had stopped digging, and his voice was hollow in the vastness of the cavern. He sounded like the answer was important to him.

"You have hope, even stuck here with no food and little water. When everything is against you, you leap out there and do something, even when it doesn't make sense. If my boy were here . . ." He hunched his back, drawing into himself, and wishing he hadn't said that.

"So, you did have a family?" The kid was at his side, and he

162

grabbed him on the shoulder. "Right? I am right. I have to be."

"Why's it so important to you?" All this time, and all someone had to do was poke his memories, and everything burst to the surface once again. He turned and forced a laugh, reaching a hand to the kid's head and rumpling his hair. "What's it to you?" Forced humor was still funny, at least to the other guy.

"This." He pulled the silver cylinder from inside his shirt and held it up, grinning broadly.

Before he could finish explaining, the whine of the HoverLift increased, and both men looked outside. The huge machine, with its spinning fans and jet propulsion, rose at an angle and moved off into the sky.

"It can't be leaving." The kid fought against the wall of heat in dismay.

"It looks that way." Slate felt his heart drop, although he was more pragmatic than the kid. The pilots had seen the operator's pod removed, and his unit was nowhere to be seen. They thought they'd both gotten to safety, and he and the kid had no way to notify them differently. That pretty much summed it up. They came back, or they didn't.

"I've got to find a way." The kid ran back to his unit, grabbed a handful of wires, and threw them down. "Useless. There's nothing I can do," he yelled at Slate.

"Only a functional mining unit is enabled to broadcast." Slate's words were in way of consolation, but the kid saw them as an invitation.

"You're absolutely right!" He slapped the door of his bio unit and ran for Slate's thirty-meter mining machine.

"What are you doing?" Why he asked, he didn't know. It was obvious, and he leaped after the kid.

There was no way Slate could catch him. He was twenty years younger, better hydrated, and probably twenty kilos lighter. The kid leaped for the ladder and scrambled up at lightning speed.

"No, Levi," he yelled. "That unit's not calibrated for you." He didn't realize until afterward what had slipped out of his mouth.

The kid only grinned and climbed faster, slipping in through the hatch and out of sight very easily. By the time Slate got there, he was jacked in and in communication with the departing HoverLift. He didn't look so good, though. Slate reached in and pulled him forward, removing the brain jack and releasing the kid against the seat.

"Yours." The kid stroked the inside of the seating area. He tightened his face, looking aside for a moment and grimacing, before relaxing. A fresh sheen of sweat covered his face. "I volunteered for this. To replace the cable. I didn't have to, and I volunteered."

"Hush." Slate felt the side of the kid's neck to get a sense of his condition. "Your pulse, maybe you'll be all right. That was stupid, kid. You'll fry your head doing that."

"They're coming back." He smiled. "I know now why my unit had to be compromised. I had to be the one to get them to come back for you."

"For me?" Slate put his hand on the side of the kid's face, pulling one eye wide. Those familiar green eyes, so much the same, yet clearly not. He couldn't tell if they were responding correctly or not, but this boy could not be allowed to die here. "Can you climb down?"

"Sure." The kid smiled, but when he reached forward to pull himself up, he grabbed short of the door.

"Here." Slate grabbed his hand. "Hold to me, and I'm getting you down."

By the time they got to the bottom, Slate had the kid over his shoulder, and they landed hard when he had to drop the last two meters. But the kid did wait until they were down before he began to dry heave, with no more than phlegm to spit on the floor. As the sound of the HoverLift returned, Slate knelt by the boy, still hunched over in case of more heaves, and he put his arm across his shoulders.

"That was magnificent, you know." He laughed. "Stupid, but magnificent."

"You called me Levi." The kid looked at him, and his eyes were red.

"Did I?" It was a slip of the tongue. No more.

"Why? Do you know, yet?"

"Why do we do a lot of things? Look out there. I think our rescue is here."

"But why did you call me Levi? You have to figure it out." The kid started coughing, and then he ducked his head and retched again, wiping his mouth on his sleeve when he was finished. "Why Levi?" His eyes were on the floor.

"You look like someone I used to know."

"Your son?" As if the boy knew more than he was telling.

"I didn't say that." Slate's heart pounded, and he blinked away tears. Too many layers had been peeled back, and he couldn't go any deeper.

"Do you know what happened to him?"

There was no way to talk past the lump in his throat, so he pulled the boy up and pointed to the ramp lowering from the hovercraft seventy meters from the opening in the side of the mountain. He managed to force out one word as he squeezed the kid's shoulder.

"Run!"

The kid's arm stretched across his back, too. Slate noticed that. He decided that if he couldn't have his own kid, this one would do for the moment. He was someone's son, and he didn't think the kid's father would mind sharing him for a little while with the man who was helping save his life.

Chapter 34

RUNNING across the blistered soil to get to the HoverLift? Well, the cavern had been air-conditioned comfort in comparison.

The HoverLift was not a medical facility. The kid started to convulse once on board, and Slate grabbed a portable com unit to hold his tongue down. Two crew held the kid's arms and legs, and after a minute, he relaxed. Slate pulled his eyelids up to find his pupils totally dilated. That worried him.

"How long have you been stranded there?" One of the crew standing off to the side sorting equipment looked at Slate.

"Two, three days. I lost count." He sat by the kid, thinking of what the boy had asked him. His son? Why would he think that? What would make that connection in his brain? He had only mentioned having had a son. Once having had a son.

And called him Levi that one stupid time.

"The heat'll do that." She shook her head, glancing at the two of them and then quickly away. "Messes up internal clocks. Sorry for the delay in getting out there. First, that outrageous meteor shower kicking out half the planet's com service, and they say we're in for another round, though not as bad as the first. They assured us none of them would reach the ground *this* time." She laughed. "Then dozens and dozens of you guys stranded out there, damaged or disabled. We almost missed you two."

Slate knew why not. He just hoped the kid came through all right. He sure didn't want to lose him now. He looked at the Hover-Lift's crew. They all wore CoolSuits, with the faces uncovered while here in the ship. They hung off to the side, ready to be snapped closed with a single tap. For someone without CoolSuits? The ship was tolerable but by no means cool enough.

The retching? The kid was overheating, and that couldn't be good.

"Umm." The kid moaned, moving his head side to side, his eyes opening.

"Hey, take it easy." Slate kept one hand alongside the kid's face. It was looking into his eyes that was getting to him. He'd dreamt of eyes like these, especially in the days after losing his son. To look into them, well, memories had come flooding back, and now they hovered too close to real to be comfortable. Like he was losing his kid all over again. He wasn't. This was just some boy he didn't know. At this rate, someone he'd never know.

The Lift jumped, swerving sideways. Tools—cables, chains, and large replacement parts—shifted along the walls, and it was loud. After several minutes, it happened again. When the crew who'd talked to him earlier reappeared, Slate called to her.

"What's with the rough ride?"

The Lift jumped again just then, and hard, nearly knocking Slate off his feet, and jerking the kid sideways. The crewman grabbed a strap and held on until things settled down.

"More meteors. We thought we'd make it back before this latest round, but no. As always, Weather can't get it right." She smiled. "Don't you worry. We've got a good ship here." She stepped to look down at the kid. "Dehydration do that?"

"Brain jack."

"Poor guy," as if he wasn't going to make it. Something hit the hull hard, and the fans thumped loudly several times. A high, metallic whine caused the crew to cover her ears. It eventually settled into a discordant hum that hadn't been there before. "Like I said, more meteors." She didn't look quite as confident as she unreeled a hose from the wall, nodding to Slate before she walked away.

"Ser?"

"Yes, kid?" Sweat covered the boy's face, and his clothes were soaked. Slate expected the crew was going to be proved right. "I'm here. You just rest."

167

"This." He reached for his neck, but his hand shook too hard to make it do what he wanted.

"The pendant?" Slate put his hand on it, and he could feel it under the kid's shirt.

"Take it out, ser. It's the reason for all this."

"Sure." He worked it out like he had that day in the cavern. He wrapped it in the kid's hand, making a fist. "Here it is."

"No. Not for me. For you." He pushed his hand Slate's direction, trying to open his fist.

"It's yours. You keep it." He wouldn't have him saying good-bye. Not now, not after all he'd done to save him. And after what the kid had done to save him.

"No!" The word was little more than a quickly released breath, barely louder than a whisper, but there was no mistaking its intensity. The kid yanked with his hand, and on the third try broke the cord holding the silver cylinder. He held it out, trying to find Slate's hand.

"Why, kid?" Slate took his hand and held it. "Why for me?"

"I volunteered. I looked for you, and I volunteered." He was pale and soaked, and his words were little more than murmurs. "Slate. You said it was your name. I saw your number on the list, and I knew I'd see you again." He smiled. "It was the brain spike that made me really remember, though. Now I know why it had to happen this way."

"See me again? What do you mean, kid?" Already, suspicions ran rampant through Slate's head, but none that he was willing to believe. It couldn't be what he was thinking. Not here, not on Purgatoria. Not after all these years.

"Not kid." As pale and sweaty as he was, the boy chuckled, with a grin across his face.

"What's that?" The boy's voice had grown so faint, Slate leaned down to hear. "Tell me again."

"I'm not kid." He held his hand up, his arm shaking, to place his fingers on Slate's neck. "I'm Levi."

"Don't say that. Not . . . not after all this time." How could it be, after all he'd endured? Slate wanted to pull away, but he couldn't. Those eyes. And he wanted to believe. He whispered, "Levi's gone." Even so, he took the kid's hand and pressed it to his face, repeating, "Levi's gone."

"I finally found you. It's really me, Levi. My job is to pass on the next memory trigger. My last name is the same as yours. Levi

Knalb—"

Just like that, the name, and Slate's head reeled with a torrential wave of information flooding in faster and hotter, and in that instant, he knew everything about himself. The cylinder. It had been the cylinder all along they had wanted, not his seed stocks, and his wife and daughter had died for it. At the last minute, he'd given it to Levi for safekeeping.

And here it was. Safe. Just like his son had promised all those years ago. Why, though? He didn't remember why it was so important. How could it be worth the lives and the pain?

"After they carried me away, they gave me another name, but I remembered this one. I remembered for you, Dad. Did I do good, Dad? The pendant, it's—"

Before he could finish, he started retching again. Slate helped him turn to the side as his body shook violently. When he finished, he lay back, his eyes closed, breathing rapidly.

"You did good, Levi. In fact, you were magnificent." Slate held the silver cylinder loosely in one hand, with his other hand against Levi's face, his thumb stroking the boy's cheek. "You did so good, Levi, and no one could have done better."

He knew the moment of death. It was a knife in him that twisted until he thought he could take no more, and in the blackness of his despair, he continued to hold his hand against his boy's face as it grew cold, telling him over and over that no one could have done better.

THE RIDE in the HoverLift grew rougher.

Slate sat beside the kid. Levi. *Levi.* Wanting that to be true, and yet not wanting to have lost him yet again.

He held the cylinder loosely in his hand. Life could be so wonderful, and he tried to grab it at its best, to find what was fantastic, even in the worst of situations. To stand under the grand volcanic skies of this world; to operate, to *live* as a thirty-meter behemoth, playing in the rocky crust of this world as if it were one giant sand pile; or to fly between the stars as he had done to get here all those years ago. He reveled in it, because all the little things had been taken from him.

What could be so important about this small sliver of metal? Nothing worth someone's life, he was sure of that.

He grabbed it in his fist, angry that his son had been returned to him, only to lose him once more.

That was when the silver cylinder began to grow warm, and he remembered holding it in the cavern. It had warmed then, too, and grown hot, just like now. He was about to toss it aside when a face appeared.

"What—" he snorted, looking around.

"Ah, there you are." The eyes found him, and the face smiled.

His face smiled, because it was his face. A miniature Slate floating in the space above his hand. He knew what it was, a hologram. Yet, there was no projector he could see.

"Got it figured out, yet?"

Slate frowned. Got what figured out? He was about to toss the cylinder aside when the image made him sit up and take notice.

"Nah. Now, don't do that. You toss me aside, and I can't talk to you. And I'm really, really sorry."

"For what?" Slate responded without thinking, before realizing how silly it was. It was a hologram, and unless it was monitored with a live operator at the other end, or maintained by a computer-generated AI, it couldn't respond to him. Yet, the face did just that.

"For your son. He had to make that contact. You know, with that brain spike. I couldn't risk you dying back there."

"I don't understand. How would I have died? They would have come to retrieve the units eventually."

"Nah, not this time. I ran it several different ways, and this is the only one that worked. Levi volunteered, and I had to let him try."

"Try what?"

"To get this to you, of course. The information I'm about to give you."

"How are you talking with me?" Slate felt his frustration rising. The face—*his* face—was saying crazy things, and none of them were making sense.

"Well—" and the figure reached to scratch its head "—I'm not, really. Talking *with* you, I mean. I'm just pausing, because I know what you're going to say. Sorry. I know it's confusing—"

"You're right. It is confusing. Now, what information?"

"Well, I'm out of time, so that's as much as I can give you. I know the Lift you're in goes down in the next meteor bombardment, and I can't track you after that. You're on your own now. Try really hard to survive, and play this device. You need what it will tell you. And if your tattoo starts to itch, pay attention. And I am so sorry for what happens next. I am so sorry. Try to get out if you can."

The hologram's eyes were red as the image began to fade.

The hull of the Lift began to ring with pinging noises, then the fans began to clatter. A resounding thud at Slate's back made him jump. He tied the cord the kid had broken and slipped the cylinder around his neck before standing to look for one of the crew.

He was hardly across the cargo space, when an ear-shattering boom shook the ship. He turned, and the hull of the Lift was breached just above where the kid lay, the meteorite responsible exploding into the ship, and bursting everything nearby that was combustible into flame.

"No," Slate yelled. He only made it three steps that direction when the entire side of the ship erupted into a massive fireball. "No," he yelled again.

Then the walls of the HoverLift began to crumple around him, and Slate felt something hit him beside the head. Just for a moment, it crossed his mind to wonder what was on the little silver trinket that could be so important that someone would risk his life for it.

Then, he stepped into the pain, and his thoughts faded away.

Chapter 35

"ANOTHER failure."

"Failure, ser?" The deacon watched the blankeyes dig through the rubble of the HoverLift. "There," he called to one, "check underneath that engine cowling. Don't skip any piece of rubble."

"Even if it's here, we can be certain he didn't get it in time." The uniform, as crisp as always, and reflecting the elevated station of a bishop, turned from the scene of carnage to look across the hellish landscape.

The sky overhead rained red fire, and just visible in the distance, three volcanos belched angry tidbits of the planet's interior into the air. The ground beneath the men, damaged by the meteor hits, shook violently, and steam burst from new fissures slashed into the soil.

They seemed unconcerned.

"Ser!" One of the blankeyes stood, the one who had been near the engine cowling. He held up the curved piece of metal to expose a charred body underneath.

"Check it," the uniform commanded the deacon. "Make sure. Remember, though, with the heat, we have minutes before we must be gone."

His underling knelt at the site, and he pulled thin, membrane gloves from his side, snapping them out and putting them on. He dragged the charred body into the open and toyed with a trinket around its neck. Rubbing it, seeing the gleam of silver, he tugged at it, looking relieved when the cord split into a powdery haze of residue.

"Ser?" He held it up, then began checking the body for signs of a map. The skin was very badly burned, and bits of it flaked off in his hand as he tried to wipe the charring away.

"The map?" The uniform took the cylinder and held it in his palm.

"Here." The soldier rolled the body partially over and pointed to one buttock. Just the faintest of outlines could be seen, contorting where part of it wrapped onto the leg. A small amount of cloth remained, and he pulled it off. Underneath, a patch of vivid tattoo contrasted with reddened skin. "Is it enough to read?"

"Move aside and let me see what I can tell." He pressed a finger against the undamaged skin and snorted. "Not with just this. If the charring isn't too deep, the pigment should be detectable beneath the surface of the skin. Ship should be able to find something. Take it all."

"Yes, ser." The instrument with the blue light was already out.

The crisp uniform stepped away, tossing the cylinder into the air and catching it once again. "He's growing too strong, and the boy is now with him each time. This has to be stopped before we cannot control it."

Then, the men shimmered, and with a prismatic wink of light, they were gone, leaving Purgatoria to war once again against those who had come to despoil her.

Chapter 36

THE MAP churned within its glowing table, for everything was in flux: time and space and the very fabric of reality. No one stood near because no one dared.

"Perhaps, if we are lucky . . ."

The words, whispered, carried throughout the chamber, the space within vast, yet intimate in feel.

"Another . . . change must be made. Dream the dreams." Urgency resonated within the voice.

"Dream the dreams," from yet another.

"Dream the dreams . . ."

"We must dream the dreams . . ."

And the chant rose, until the words filled the space that contained even the stars themselves.

And still, the map churned, and no one dared step near.

Chapter 37

THE FUTURE echoed throughout all of history, its long fingers reaching out to distant worlds and even more distant stars, caressing lives and moments.

Within that echo were dreams and possibilities, painted in great canvasses of sunrises and sunsets; and war and famine; and troweled across the landscapes of life, if only one could tell which was which.

The oil that made up the void between the stars and gave life to a million races rippled, one ring of possibilities touching another, and the changes spreading from there. They moved faster and faster, until the whole of time was in transition.

Great kings raised their scepters, and as they slammed them against the floor, nations fell. Generals gave orders, and as their words rolled across the airwaves, enemies were vanquished. Politicians spoke, and in the rising of the populace, entire governments were swept away.

Time became malleable, flowing in great ribbons of light, and to touch it was to create what one wished.

Even if one should not have wished.

And the possibilities were endless.

With great anticipation, the oil was touched, and the wheels of the universe moved in a way they had never moved before.

And the stars cried for what once had been.

Chapter 38

"MAKE a wish. Any wish." Candles flickered on the cake, and the ceiling danced with shadows. It was his birthday, and he could have anything he wanted.

"I wish for—"

"Not aloud, silly. Then it won't come true."

"I know that. I wasn't going to say it aloud." Petulantly.

"Now, a real wish, not something frivolous. Ready?"

"I was ready, already."

"Don't be testy. Just do it. It's your birthday, but we're ready for cake."

"Okay." Deep breath. "I wish for . . ."

THE LIGHT shifted, and stars hung overhead. They twinkled and spun, always in new orbits, spinning, spinning.

He was the world.

Volcanoes and rivers flowed from him, and when he was hungry, he consumed whatever was at hand. The moon came within his orbit, and he grabbed at it, holding it tightly, and laughing. Then, when he tired of it, he let it go.

And always there were the stars.

One day he wished for a plaything, and grass appeared. Sheep and cows and dogs ran and played. He cried for them to be gone, and they vanished, as if they never were.

He was the world, and the world obeyed his every desire.

And still, always there were the stars.

The food of the gods was his to consume at his leisure, and he drank from fountains of milk and honey. He rumbled with vile gasses, and when he vented his frustration, everything within his sphere of influence harkened to his command.

He was a god.

And surrounding him, always there were the stars.

One day he reached out his hand, and the world became different. The stars were no longer the focal point of his days. His horizons were wider, and the vistas became windows upon other worlds, distant views of distant things that were impossible to dream.

So, he dreamed closer to home.

Of the milk of the gods. And sheep. And cows. And dogs that ran up and down and played with him as he wished to be played with.

And the stars became a part of the night.

He searched, and he found other lights in the night. He named them and called them his own, and he knew that it was good.

He spoke, and his voice was heard in distant lands, and on other worlds, in those realms to which he could not travel.

He cried out, "I wish to voyage among the stars," and a great ship carried him from his world to visit places he had not even been able to dream. In those distant places, he also found sheep, and cows, and dogs that ran up and down and played with him. Sometimes they were different, but they were always the same. He called them his own, and he knew that it was good.

When night came again, he always wished to be home, and the great ship was his passage back to the world of his dreams.

And the stars remained a part of his night.

One day he wished for new worlds to be at his side. And in that wish, other worlds gathered, but it was not as he had dreamed it. He wanted to drink of their milk and honey, and he reached for their sheep and cows and dogs, claiming them as his own. He found they dreamed of these things, too, and when they refused to let him dream all that he wished, he banished them to distant lands, never to be at his side again.

He called for milk and honey, and with his command, they appeared.

He feasted, and he called his time alone good.

And the stars remained a part of his night.

One day he stood in his domain, with his sheep and his cows and his dogs, and they rested peacefully at his side. He surveyed his world and all those worlds of which he could not dream, and he knew the frustration of one who is only a half-god, for a half-god cannot go and do as he wills; he is forced to depend upon those whose power is greater than his.

Rather, he wished to move among the worlds on his own. He wished to touch what he wished to touch, and he wished to taste what he wished to taste. His sheep and cows and goats were no longer fulfilling to him. The milk of the gods no longer satisfied his palate. Even having the stars under his dominion left him frustrated and empty.

He moved his feet, and he wandered among the many worlds of creation. He surveyed all that he had wrought, and he knew that it was good.

Each evening, when his wanderings were complete, he returned to his own little world, and when he laid his head to rest, the stars remained a part of his night.

One day, all the distant suns and the moons and worlds which he had visited from time to time came to bow before him, proclaiming his rule over all creation. They laid gifts of textiles and metals and wild creatures and all manner of foods before him, and they lavished upon him all the love he deserved.

When their presents had been weighed, judged, and accepted, they gathered before a great bonfire, and they sang their praises unto him. And the sun spoke to the little world that had become a god.

"You are one now, Slate. How does it feel?" With those words, the light shifted, and everything changed.

FOUR windows upon the world. Four places to look out, and nowhere to look out at all.

Fear filled the world.

Lightning had crashed, thunder had rolled, and now it was night.

And only four windows looked out upon the world.

The windows swung wide, and there was a screeching bird, a raptor, come to peck his eyes out. He ducked and swerved, and wrapped his arms around his head, and still the beak was there, pecking, pecking, pecking. Feet tore, and wings battered, and he was afraid.

He curled into a tight ball, bloodied, and the raptor flew away, with the promise that it would one day return.

He was alone, and only four windows looked out upon the world.

He rested and licked his wounds.

And the windows swung wide once again.

A volcano belched cruel smoke. Hot stones pelted him, and earthquakes shook the ground. His knees trembled in fear, and lava surrounded him. He burned with the agony.

After a time, the ashes cooled, and he realized the volcano was gone. He prayed for deliverance, and still, only four windows looked out upon the world.

He barricaded the windows.

A great wind came up, and it whistled around the glass, finding entry where there was no entry, and the wind reached for him, chilling him to the bone.

The wind hated him, lashing him with gales and tornadoes and hurricanes. His fingers became numb, and his ears were frozen, and he shivered in the cold. He tried to hide, and the wind found him through the cracks in the walls and the fabric of his clothes, and the wind bruised the very skin he wore.

There was no escaping the wind.

The storms raged for what seemed hours, until the winds exhausted even their fierce anger, fading into the darkness.

And only four windows looked out upon the world.

He didn't barricade the windows again. Instead, he waited, and he waited.

Finally, the windows swung wide, and God called unto him.

"If you can be a good boy, Slate, you can come out of the closet."

With those words, the light shifted, and everything changed.

THE WHISTLE blew, and they were off, two stallions, running neck to neck.

They had always run neck to neck, from the time they were two. Now they were in their prime, lean and muscular, determined to win. Any race. Every race.

They were a team.

They were fire and lightning, stamping their feet at the gate, and refusing to be held back. And those became their names.

Fire, and Lightning.

Fire pranced, and he preened for the show. His hair glistened in the sun, and his legs were long.

Lightning laughed at the pomp and circumstance, and he pawed the track, ready to be off.

Both learned their lessons well, and under their trainers' hands, they ran faster than ever before.

It came to the biggest race of all. Who would win? Fire snorted his challenges, and he was beautiful, with dark eyes and a wide mouth. Lightning laughed and pulled at the reins, uncaring of how he looked to others.

It was about winning, and nothing else mattered.

They were not the only ones racing. Everyone wanted the prize, and many were prepared to go to any length to get it. Fire and Lightning brushed it all aside and demanded more from their minds and muscles and hearts.

They were determined to win every race. Any race. *This* race.

Shoulder to shoulder, and nose to nose they ran. Lightning stumbled, and Fire held him up. Those who raced against them raced last, for in the run for the win, Fire and Lightning became one, and in becoming one, they became faster and stronger than they were alone.

Yet not everyone saw virtue in their cooperation, and they conspired to break Fire and Lightning's spirit. Some cheated. Others found advantage in chemical enhancement. Still more used whips and other abuse to gain advantage.

They attacked, and they found weaknesses to exploit.

Fire stumbled.

It was not Fire's fault, although it became Fire's downfall.

Fire had run with a true heart and an eye for the goal, and the goal was to finish first; to win. Others had wished to win by any measure, at any cost, and disregard the consequences. They had wished to defeat both Fire and Lightning, but if they could not bring down both, then they would destroy what they could.

And Fire went down, screaming in agony, Run! Run, Lightning, and win for us both!

Lightning knew anger, and he determined this, that he would achieve alone what should have been theirs, and he would make those who fought unfairly face the bitter dust of defeat.

Lightning stood by Fire's graveside, and tears filled his eyes.

"You were fire to my lightning, and you will forever be my friend. I will find a way to get even for what they did."

An arm wrapped his shoulder, and his mother's voice whispered, "You and Bren were the best of friends. I know this breaks your heart. Just never forget him, Slate." And hearing his name, the light shifted, and everything changed.

BANNERS snapped in the breeze.

Two great giants had come to do battle this day. One stood brittle with icy fury, and the second inflamed with fiery hate.

Only one would triumph, and in that triumph, the winner would rule the land.

The serfs of the realm gathered, mounded upon the hills, blue for Frost and red for Flame. Each was certain his or her champion would take the field, and they heckled and booed the opposing side.

Flame's supporters cried out chants of victory:

Red for Flame,
To burn your heart;
Our mighty fist
Will break you apart.

Then they laughed, sure their taunt would wreck their opponent's spirit. However, Frost's followers knew words, also, and in the same manner, more taunts were cast across the fields:

With an icy blast,
Your heart will freeze;
We will force you
To your knees.

The taunts were simple, and they were yelled back and forth as the two giants prepared to gather on the field. Horns were blasted, and drums were pounded, and those with foresight brought sausages to sell. This was a celebration of victory, and the battle had not yet begun.

Then, from their great houses of stone, the giants emerged. Frost bellowed his challenge, claiming the victory. Flame roared with defiance, for he would never back down. They came at each other head to head, like rams in the heat of battle.

Fists flew, legs flashed, and skin soared through the air. The battle was underway. The serfs roared, the chants growing ever louder, and the noise of the tumult rang throughout the hills.

The battle continued long after the sun was gone, with Frost and Flame stepping back to appraise their enemy's strengths and weaknesses, then attacking once again.

Fires were lighted in the darkness so that no one would miss the show.

At one point, Flame went to his knees, and many thought the battle was done. Those in Flame's red camp were silent with fear, for if their champion lost the battle, what horrors would they have to endure from the winning side? At the same time, blue cheered, the sound rising higher and higher.

Then, Flame regained his footing, panting, his limbs tired and torn. He was bloodied, but he refused to concede defeat. Frost roared, and with an icy fist, he hit the ground, and the hills shook. Those in Frost's blue camp cheered.

In that moment, Flame leaped at Frost, and for a time, no one knew who might live or die. Blue mingled with red, and they were one and the same.

The people waited breathlessly, for none could say who might be crowned victor this night. Dust rose and covered the field, and the sounds of the battle deafened the listeners' ears.

Eventually, silence fell upon the field, and with time, the dust began to clear. Flame stood tall, one foot on Frost's inert form. Cheers erupted on both sides, although the cheers from red seemed to be prouder and louder.

All the serfs ran to the field. They clapped Flame on the back, and they pulled Frost from the ground. A great party was held, with bonfires, singing, and dancing, and none were sent away hungry or empty-handed.

Two of the serfs, one in red and the other in blue, clapped each other on the back as they raised a toast, each to his own champion.

Red cried, "Ha! Vatican U. is still the best team on the planet!"

Blue snorted in mock derision, "And you, Slate Knalb, don't know a football team when you see one!"

And in those words, the light shifted, and everything changed.

THE ROCKET was more than a rocket. Just as a queen is more than a woman, and a filet mignon is more than a burger, so was the young man's rocket.

It cost enough. It should be more than a rocket.

It was fast. Oh, so fast! And red. He had ordered it red and fast and striped with a wide band of black. He wanted others to admire his rocket.

To the stars!

He leaped on his rocket, and off he went.

The wind flew through his hair, and it was glorious. He aimed his rocket this way and that, roared by his old haunts, and laughed as he rattled the windows. Then he was off to his friends, his hand in the air, his greetings unheard over the noise.

He felt a god, on his rocket of red. He would live forever, and he would fly among the stars.

Then, one day, he got a helmet, and he did just that.

All the places anyone had seen and named became his own. He donned his helmet as protection from the burning of the sun and the cold of night, and he breathed in its humid air. It was his life, and he made his rocket go faster than ever before.

He even ran from the meteors that pierced the night, and he laughed with the joy of it all.

Yet, even the time of rockets must come to an end, and a meteor is faster than a rocket can ever be. One day an especially powerful and quick meteor brought the young man and his red rocket to the ground.

It would be the last time his red rocket flew.

The red rocket slammed into a world, and the world cracked and burned. The young man also cracked and burned.

He did not die, though. Almost, but not quite.

The meteor asked the cracked and burning young man, "What gives you the right to ride this rocket from star to star, planet to planet, and moon to moon? What proof can you show that you have the right to visit all the places you've seen and named?"

"This." The young man, although broken and torn, pulled out a card. He held it up to the meteor.

"Ah," the meteor replied. "However, this is not a motorcycle license, Slate Knalb." And with the sound of his name, the light changed, and everything was different.

CYMBALS crashed, and the symphony was on.

The snare drummed the footsteps of troops marching to battle.

The tuba bellowed the call to arms.

The bass drum echoed the hearts of courageous men.

The crash of the tympani was the cannon ball flying into a wall.

The oboe told of the missiles whistling their oncoming death.

The tambourine was the bright-hot pain of exploding shells.

The tubular bells rang the fracturing of eardrums.

The piano told the tale of the last dying memories.

The French horn was the survivors' guilt.

The clarinet cried their tears.

The violin sang the funeral dirge.

The harp whispered relief.

The piccolo made them want to do it all over again.

Nothing had changed, and nothing was different, except that the little boy had become a soldier. At the ceremony to honor the heroes, they hung a medal on his chest, and they said words of honor in his name.

"Under enemy fire, you dismounted your vehicle and moved on foot to recover your team members. You left no one behind, and for your bravery, reflecting the highest traditions of our military, Slate Knalb . . ."

With those words, the light changed and everything was different.

"DID you have a happy birthday?"

"I did." Giggles. "I got what I wanted."

"What was it?"

"You said I can't tell."

"Did you already get your wish?"

"Mm-huh."

"Telling won't take it away."

"Okay. I want to grow up, like Daddy."

Laughter. "And what will you do then?"

"Be a soldier. I want to be a soldier and save the whole world from the bad people."

"Good for you. Then that's exactly what you'll be, my precious little Slate. You'll be the best soldier the universe has ever known."

"I know, Mommy. I wished for it."

Chapter 39

THE DIALS on the ship's console spun. It was one year for a fraction of a second, then the numbers blurred, and it was a hundred years in the future. They blurred again, and the Christ walked once again upon the Earth.

The dials would not remain still.

"Stabilize the draft field." The uniform stood tall, the fabric he wore crisp and smart on his lean frame. His oak leaf caught the light. "We must find him."

"I'm trying, ser." The priest—one bar only—at the console had a sheen of sweat on her face. "The sensors can't pin down his location."

"The map said he would be right here—"

"There is no here, ser." She looked at him. "We're in the middle of a slip bubble."

She was right, too. Even as she spoke, the walls of the ship became translucent just for a moment, the stars visible outside, before it solidified once again. Then an alarm went off somewhere deeper in the ship.

The uniform pressed an icon on the display at his side. "Status report."

"Ser, the engine drive field is destabilizing. If I back down the Field Vortex Intensifiers, I think we can hold it together for another hour, if we're lucky. If we want to get home again, we have to leave now."

"The MagThrusters, too? Perhaps we can use those to slingshot past the sun using the gravity of Jupiter—"

"Sorry, ser. Those were the first to go. Now the only thing we've got left is the Sagan-Armstrong Unit as backup, but I can't say for how long. Ser?"

The uniform paused, his finger still on the icon. The soldiers in the control center looked at him. Just then, the ship did its funny thing, and they could see the massive Sagan-Armstrong engine assembly far below their feet, its outline dimly visible through the ship's translucent walls.

"So, we can't follow him this time." He sounded peeved but not especially surprised.

"It would seem that way, ser."

"Then take us out, mister, and make it fast and hot. We need to burn the timeslip residue off the hull before it starts scarring the metal."

The one-bar grinned. "You got it, ser." She punched coordinates, and with a blink of light, the big ship was gone, and the skies over planet Earth were clear once again.

Chapter 40

"THE WHEEL!"

The massive table shimmered. The map that revealed all the stars in the heavens and all the events that might have been, are, and possibly will be, was in flux. It would not stand still.

"Touch it," cried one, in its screeching voice.

Yet another called out, "It is the end of all that ever was!"

Another stood to the side, and tears flowed.

Without the map, they couldn't trace the events of time and space, and if they couldn't trace the events of time and space, how could they play the role of gods?

They were mighty poor gods, indeed, if they couldn't predict what would happen next.

"The wheel must turn," one creature whispered, its high-pitched screech cracking and falling apart as it dropped to its knees.

It was very unusual. After all, if the gods themselves fail at the only thing they know how to do, who is there to answer their prayers?

It was very unusual, indeed.

Chapter 41

THE GEARS of the universe were stilled, and the wheel was frozen. The oil of space and time shook with the laughter of a creature bigger and more powerful than the gods.

Then the laughter faded away, and the oil was touched once more. Slowly at first, and then with greater speed, the wheel that made up the universe began to turn as it had once before.

Even the god of the gods must have his laughs every now and then.

Chapter 42

SEVENTEEN soldiers were lined up with packs at their sides. However, no one would have recognized them as soldiers, not from the same army.

They were dressed in very individual clothing, and many of them wore nothing resembling a military uniform. Each one had a different job to do, although some of them would deploy as teams. It was easy to tell which were which, because of the styles of their outfits. It was the new warfare, brought to humanity by the Secharri.

Of course, for centuries, no one knew about the Secharri. That hadn't stopped the Secharri from knowing about humanity. The political manipulation; the technological advances; even the financial resources that had helped man leap from star to star were not man's doing. It was the Secharri, using man, piggybacking on humanity's achievements, and stealing from his dreams.

Skimming the realities.

Humanity had taken it one step further. Create an alternate reality, and let it play itself out. Then, add in triggers for your participants that snapped the substantiative matrix of the reality—the subspace tension that held it all together—and when it "snapped," you could "skim" the best parts. Pull what you wanted from the world you had created. Medical achievements; military advancements; anything. If you could extrapolate a reality in which something could be accomplished, created, or acted out, you could skim the results out of that temporary reality.

It was simple, really.

The only problem was, the Secharri had managed to do it first, and they had the advantage.

Oh, and one other thing. Once you set your reality running, you had no control over it. It ran until one of your "triggers" snapped the substantiative matrix. If your triggers were buried too deeply, you lost that reality for a very long time.

So, seventeen soldiers were being dropped into alternate realities, with age-appropriate bodies, new identities, and individual sets of triggers. Some triggers were there for information, such as key words or images that fed the participants certain new knowledge or skills. Other triggers? The reality had to be broken, too, but not broken too easily. After all, each of the participants had a mission to accomplish while in his or her alternate reality, and the cost of building just one of these fictional realities often reached deeper into government war chests than a ships-and-lasers sort of war.

The soldiers were pulled, one team at a time, into separate reality-implantation cubicles. Each set of cubicles was grouped in a hardened dome that contained the matrix drivers for that particular reality. The necessary personalities and information were uploaded; the subspace tension was shifted just enough to put them out of phase with their current reality; and their new existence materialized with them inside.

Technicians had learned early on that anyone inside the dome translated into the new reality with the team, and with no uploaded information, they were total amnesiacs while the reality was running. No one wanted to be in the dome unexpectedly when the translation occurred.

The first four soldiers were in 18th century French military apparel. Their goal was to implant a microchip in Napoleon's head, hoping to guide the great French leader to inspire a Russian democracy that would join with the West and avoid both of the early 20th century's great wars, as well as Russia's attempted conquest of the world in the mid-21st century. The trigger to "snap" their reality was the death of Tsar Paul I of Russia in 1801. The benefits they hoped to "skim" from this reality? Cooperation between German, American, and Russian scientists, therefore bringing hyper-dimensional FTL engines to reality a hundred years earlier; and allowing humanity to advance into space before the

Secharri could gain total influence over mankind.

Three soldiers were on individual missions. One wore a 20th century space suit circa 1969, the second was in a ballerina's tutu, and the third had a pocket protector full of pencils and pens. They were headed respectively to the Kennedy Space Center, Rudolph Nureyev's dance troupe, and Harvard to meet a very young Bill Gates.

The remaining ten? They were on the way to Secharri. In 2572, the Secharri mines had opened, producing the most sought after jewels in the known galaxy. That initial contact was when humanity began to suspect the Secharri had already begun their insidious and very secretive conquest of humanity.

SEVENTEEN soldiers were lined up with packs at their sides, a new mission underway. However, no one would have recognized them as soldiers, not from the same army. Each team had a job to do specific to the clothing they wore.

The first four wore 19th century Russian military uniforms. Russia had become a constitutional monarchy, but Grigori Rasputin would infect the Russian Senate, and the Bolsheviks would revolt in 1917 anyway. He had to be removed.

One soldier still wore a 20th century space suit. Apollo 13 had landed on the moon successfully, but the moon base installed by the Americans five years later suffered a catastrophic failure. His job? To catch the saboteur before the bomb went off.

The tutu had become a domestic's smock and blouse. Nureyev's son, Alexi, needed a nanny so that Nureyev's grandson was not born when Alexi was thirteen, causing the charismatic dancer to be deported back to Russia. Nureyev's grandson would invent the precursor to an earlier and improved version of the hyper-dimensional FTL engine.

Bill Gates had joined forces with Steve Jobs and Steven Wozniak as expected, creating MicroTosh. The third soldier was rewarded with a six-month leave to visit his family on Kekion Prime, the pleasure planet.

The final ten? They were returning to Secharri. As soon as they had arrived on that world in their previous attempt, the ship's ventilation system was compromised, and all the occupants aboard died horrible deaths, causing the reality to "snap," and the ten were home before they even got started. This time? They would all die in a mine cave-in six weeks after they arrived, triggering their reality to again "snap." They best they could hope for would be to return six weeks later in that same timeline for another attempt.

SEVENTEEN soldiers were lined up with packs at their sides, ready for their third mission. However, no one would have recognized them as soldiers, not from the same army. Each team had a job to do specific to the clothing they wore.

The first four wore 22nd century NorAm Union military uniforms. Once Russia and America joined forces to defeat Germany in 1915, Great Britain was routinely excluded from the World Union due to the continued efforts of a NorAm president's dynastic family after he won a lifetime appointment to office by treachery and lies. He had to be removed before jeopardizing the first FTL flight scheduled out of St. Petersburg, Russia, by inciting terrorist activity in the British Isles.

The next three volunteered to be civilians in St. Louis Tower, the Falls Recreational Area, and Chicago Tower during the St. Louis Insurgence, in order to get an operative to safety before the building was compromised.

The last ten? Apparently Secharri technology allowed them to recognize a repeated infiltration attempt by a human contingent, and the mine collapsed once again, triggering the reality to "snap," sending all ten volunteers home.

"YES, ser!" The youthful soldier, fresh-faced, long-limbed, and well-muscled, stood at attention, his back stiff, and his eyes looking directly ahead.

"At ease, soldier." Captain Daniel Eliot, his commanding officer, sat on the edge of his desk, one leg up and one foot on the floor. "You may take a chair, if you wish."

"No thank you, ser."

"I wish, and you're making me uncomfortable."

"If you wish, ser." The soldier pulled his cap from his head and looked around for a convenient chair.

"There." The officer grabbed one at the side of his desk with his foot and slid it over. "I'll sit here." He moved to a very comfortable-looking armchair.

"Thank you, ser."

"I hear good things about you, soldier."

"Thank you, ser." The young man looked definitely ill-at-ease sitting in the presence of his commanding officer.

"What do you know about the Secharri?"

"Um," and he dropped his head, turning red along the top of his ears.

"Speak up, son."

He looked up. "I gave my girl a Secharri rosestone just before I, um, enlisted."

"Volunteered, son. We don't enlist any longer. You're a good man, doing that. What'd it cost you, about two years' wages?"

"Close, ser."

"Was it worth it?"

"Yes, ser." The soldier grinned.

"You know anything else about the Secharri?"

"The first mine was opened in about 2572 or '73, I think, and the first stone sold commercially was a sunstone."

"Yeah, all that. Anything military?"

"Military, ser?"

"Look at this, son." The officer stood and picked up a portable glass from his desk. He tapped it once and handed it to the soldier. "What do you see there?"

"Ser?" The soldier looked puzzled. "It's our arm of the galaxy with," and he paused to study it, "all the inhabited planets in red. All the star systems, anyway." He made to hand it back to the officer.

"Look again." The officer waved it away. "Those are Secharri-dominated worlds. Every one."

"Secharri? But, the Secharri, they never travel offworld, ser."

"That you know of." The officer smiled.

"I suppose, ser. But why would they? I mean, there is no species overcrowding, no pressure to expand their habitat, and their planet suits them well. If I remember my galactic species overview from the academy, they invited us to mine their world for the gemstones, even suggesting the best places to look." He shrugged. "And since we've made contact, they've built up an entire civilization. Not too bad for a backwards race of pacifists."

"I was told you'd make a good recruit for the program." The officer smiled.

"Program, ser?"

"What do you know of alternate realities?" The officer leaned forward, with his arms on his knees, and his hands clasped together. He looked right into the soldier's eyes.

"As in Stephen Baxter?" The soldier laughed. "The Xeelee

193

aren't real. That's pure science fiction."

"Was pure science fiction. We've grown up a bit since then. Let me tell you what we've learned in the past few hundred years and just why those systems are red." He took the glass and tapped it before putting it to the side.

After an hour of disbelief and proof after proof, the soldier sat back and ran his hand through his hair. "So, if I think it, these creatures can get it from my head and make dreams of it?"

"Possibly, we think, but we know for certain they use what we broadcast. You're getting a handle on this very quickly, soldier, and I don't mind telling you that I'm impressed. We have a few scientists who still don't grasp this, and that's what we pay them to do."

"So, and I understand what you're saying, that it started in the 20th century back on Earth. Radio and TV signals. We broadcast them into space, and these Secharri made their own alternate universes out of them, and they stole what they wanted? Out of these alternate universes?" He shook his head. "Just saying that sounds crazy, but it explains a lot."

"Like Secharri technology we didn't give them, and it's clearly based on human science." The officer nodded. "Nineteen twenty-six on Earth sees the first rocket launch. Forty-three years later, man walks on the moon? Then FTL in another hundred? That didn't come from us, not on a human scale of achievements."

"So, they're giving us knowledge, too? I would think they'd keep it all for themselves."

"I think, and mind you, our scientists tell me I shouldn't have an opinion on this, but in my opinion, the Secharri aren't pacifists. They just don't have an original thought in their heads. So, they need us to do their thinking for them. Now they are forcing us to think the way they want us to think, and we're finding a way to fix that."

"They must have telepathy, if they can do that. That's bizarre, because scientists tell us—"

"Soldier, look at it this way. We believe in gravity, and that's invisible. Magnetism, also invisible. Radio waves? Modern science readily accepts that our brains emit radio waves. Imagine that a million times stronger." The officer shrugged. "All I'm saying is it's possible, because it's happening."

"What am I supposed to do?"

"I'm glad you asked." The officer smiled broadly. "The Secharri can create alternate realities with their thoughts." He put up his hands in defense. "How? They sit around in a circle and hold hands, I guess. We've learned to do it with supercomputers. How would you like to take a trip?"

"I—" The soldier looked unsure. "I go back in time, ser?"

"No, it's more like you go back in reality." The officer leaned back and smiled. "Whole body, the real you. Interested?"

"You bet, ser." The soldier nodded, a smile growing on his face. "How do I return?" Of course, that was less important than the going, even if it seemed pertinent to ask.

"We give you mental triggers to pull you out. If you're willing, we're going to get to know each other really well, you, me, and the team. So, first names, if you don't mind. When we're working on the project, you call me Daniel, and I'll call you Slate. Will that do?"

And hearing his name, reality snapped, and everything changed.

"WELCOME to Raccoon Team headquarters."

Four men and two women were bundled in heavy coats with thick fur waving around their faces and hands. Introductions had been made on the way in from New Zealand, although it was mostly military talk, who'd been where, and where they hoped to be stationed if they got to pick their ultimate posting. Landing, they had walked single file through paths carved from nearly a meter and a half of snow. Before them was a low, nondescript building, topped by a crown of thick snow, and made lower by narrow windows lining the eaves. The windows gave it a human scale, although at a price. It would be dark inside.

The snow on the flat roof made the whole place look like a slice of wedding cake.

Reddened faces and mufflers kept their voices stilled. Once through the door, the banter began.

"I'm going to make sure the dinosaurs survive." Levi Castle, pale with a striking shock of blond hair, winked a green eye playfully. "Especially the T. Rex. Chomp, chomp." He snapped his hands at one of the women, also lightly colored and very petite.

"Better, we keep the pterodactyls and throw you in the nest." That was from Sundra Himura, a dark-eyed beauty, and she smiled impishly.

"They'd starve." Bren Backiel jabbed Levi in the side. Levi was tight and lean, and underneath his uniform, he was thin as a rail.

"Gotta have some fat to feed their growing babies."

They all laughed. Levi reached to tap at random controls on the wall, only to have Sundra pull his hand away.

"I want to go to Secharri." That was spoken by the tallest of the soldiers, a young man with big hands and strong legs. The other voices hushed. Just the name of their enemy took the air out of the building.

"Why there?" Bren shoved his hands into his pockets. It was something he did when he felt insecure.

"If I go way back, I can take the first Secharri egg and stomp on it. Then they'll never have been born."

"You would think of that." It was Caitlan Trotter, the woman Levi had teased earlier. "I bet you stomped the eggs in your granny's barnyard growing up."

"Might a done." He grinned in a cowboy, aw, shucks, sort of way.

"Enough talk, soldiers." The fourth man, wearing a captain's insignia, stepped to the front of the group. "We're now heading into secured territory, over a kay and a half down. Say so long to the sun."

"Except on Secharri," the tall soldier quipped. "I'll get my dose of vitamin D when I'm stomping eggs." He chuckled at his joke.

"They tell us we won't remember our alternate existences," Sundra whispered to him.

"So, if we go together, and I kiss you, I won't remember?" He made a miserable face. "What's the fun in that?"

"Oh, you!" She laughed, leaning into him for a quick touch.

"At the back, ready? Or do you soldiers need more romantic time?" The captain, Daniel Eliot, didn't smile. "The rest of us are ready to take a tour."

"No, ser. No more time needed." The tall man stood erect, and the captain turned to face an eye scanner. After a moment, he spoke into a grille, and a massive door released, swinging aside in well-oiled silence. Once everyone was through, the door swung closed, and a series of lights on the wall began turning off one at a time. As they faded away, the tall soldier caught the captain's eye.

"Ser?" It was the tall man speaking.

"Yes, soldier?"

"This takes us to the bottom of the ice pack, right, ser?"

"Down to bedrock. We're below sea level, or we will be soon." The lights were still disappearing. "Does that bother you?"

"No, ser. Just asking."

The last light faded, and the motion of the elevator whispered to a stop. It was quiet. Too quiet.

"We're there. Follow me, soldiers. This will be your home for the next nine months. What do you want to see first?"

"I want to take a ride, ser." Levi grinned.

"You do, Mr. Castle? Just where would you like to go?"

As they were talking, they had entered to where a broad set of steps led down to a wide barrier wall. A glass door was in the middle, and either side was filled with floor to ceiling, deep-green tinted glass.

"Anywhere, ser. Out there." Levi turned around, looking at every glittering thing, and the stars were in his eyes.

Still, a series of low steel posts and a gate blocked their way.

"Bren? Do the honors, please." Captain Eliot nodded. "It seems Mr. Castle would like to see the matrix drivers for the alternate reality dome. He wants to go 'out there.' The facility is live and fully operational, so keep your hands to yourself. You can feel free to ask questions of any of the employees."

"Yes, ser." Clearly, Bren was the leader in the small group. He stepped forward, keying in a code and leading the group inside.

"Cool!" Levi rubbed his hands together, winking at Sundra. "Just show me the start button."

They first looked at room assignments. Each soldier was billeted separately, with communal toilet and shower facilities at the end of the passageway. They dropped their duffels on their respective bunks and met again in the corridor.

"This is your common room—" a spacious area with comfortable seating, several tables, and a small food preparation space "—and we have a chef on staff anytime you want something special. Your freezer is packed with pizzas and chicken wings, so you can have all the midnight snacks you want." Several laughs followed, and he smiled. He waved his hand over a console, and one wall opened up. It was filled with electronics. "Games enough to keep even you guys happy."

"Swell!" Levi whistled. "A game of Solar Rider, anyone?"

"But don't expect to have much time to spend in here. Most of your time will be in the field as a team. If you haven't guessed by now, Bren is your team leader. Show your team around, Team Leader. I'm just tagging along." The captain nodded to Bren and stepped to the back of the group.

"Yes, ser. Thank you, ser." He cleared his throat and started to speak to the group, and he caught the captain's eye. "Um, Daniel, ser."

"Ignore me, Team Leader. Go on with your tour."

"Yes, ser, Daniel, ser." The young man's ears were red, though. He stepped forward and opened a door. "Acoustically soundproofed cubicles for use of musical instruments or just to let off steam."

"Or romantic encounters?" That was Levi, said with a mischievous grin, his hands drumming on everything in sight.

"Ser?" The team leader looked at the captain before answering. When the captain nodded with a twinkle in his eye, he turned to the group. "Yes, anything you do not wish to disturb the rest of the team with. Now, follow me." He moved to a glass wall that looked into a small library. Several video screens were visible, and at one end was a bank of workout equipment. "This is a communal area. You each have monitors in your quarters, and books can be downloaded to your personal glass units. Keeping in shape is expected, of course."

"Are our physical forms set?" Levi laughed with a wink at the women. "I understood we could be anything we wanted to be."

"Thor? Loki? What's your poison?" Caitlan teased him with an impish look.

"I'll take this question." Captain Eliot raised a hand for attention. "You are always you, but we can adjust your age, ethnicity, and other minor appearance parameters. So you, Levi, at eleven, will still basically be you, like you probably were at eleven."

"A menace." Sundra poked Caitlan. "Like now but worse."

"And you," the captain continued, looking at the women, "Ms. Himura and Ms. Trotter, at four or thirty-four are still the same people. You're you, just with a new set of memories and a new history, and perhaps a new hair color."

"But not better manners." Sundra looked at Levi and smirked.

"Go on, Team Leader." The captain did everything except roll his eyes. "Show them the good stuff."

They went down three flights of stairs, skirting the elevator doors at each level, and coming to a wide corridor. The space was impressive, as big as a sports stadium and filled with equipment. Men and women were scattered across the area, and computer terminals glowed, as people tapped at inputs, then moved to various locations, only to return to tap some more.

The team stepped through a two-meter-thick doorway. When

they got through, Captain Eliot did his eye thing at a security station in the wall, and a massive door closed off the corridor. He nodded to the team leader.

Levi's hands were touching everything, from the keypad to enter the glass doors, to the doors themselves, although only Caitlan seemed to notice. She had taken over for Sundra, and she continually pulled his hands away.

"We're in the alternate reality dome. It's fully hardened from any connection with the outside. There are your reality-implantation cubicles." He nodded, and there was one with each team member's name on it. The doors were open, and in each was an ovoid recliner with an octopus of mechanical equipment hanging above it. Many of them looked to be of electro-neurological origins. There were twelve reality-implantation cubicles unused.

"Are we getting company?" The tall soldier scratched his head, his eyes squinting as he looked at the empty cubicles.

"New team members?" The team leader looked at the captain for an answer, taking his cue when the captain shook his head. He continued, as if scripted, "We are a specialized team, and we will never be more than five, although other support people may be pulled in, if necessary. We hope that's not necessary."

"Six." The captain coughed the word.

"Six. My apologies, ser."

"Accepted, Team Leader." He smiled, but he shook his head as if Bren hadn't been able to figure out something very simple.

"Everyone, you will want to see this, because through those doors is what makes all this possible."

Bren started ahead, leading, and the doors were huge. He waved at a scanner on the wall, and with a resounding thud, the doors began to swing wide. Inside, a catwalk crisscrossed the vast space. It went down another third of a kay, and was at least that wide. It was filled with machinery that stretched the imagination.

"And this is the powerplant for the entire facility?" Caitlan looked over the rail. Stairs led down to various levels. Overhead was the dome arching another dozen stories above them.

"For our team, Ms. Trotter. It takes this to run the matrix drivers for our team alone." The captain smiled at that.

"Every team has one of these?" Something had finally awed her. She was slight, and her tightly clipped hair was light in color. Her expression made her seem very young.

"Your alternate reality, although created by us, is a complete universe, peopled by everyone you might possibly meet. You," and Captain Eliot's eyes found each of them individually, boring into them, "are not only in that reality mentally. This machine shifts you just enough that your physical body is in that reality. All we do is fill in the blank spaces. Your minds accept what we give you, and that becomes your world."

"And if we die in there?" The tall soldier, his eyes dark.

"Then you die in there." The captain had his lips pressed firmly together.

"I mean," and the soldier looked concerned, "do we die out here, too, or just translate back out?"

"While the reality is running, there is no 'out here' for you. We do provide triggers to exit individually without disturbing the total alternate reality. Death can be one of them. However, the triggers are not infallible. Is that what you want to know?"

"And you couldn't tell us this when you invited us to join? Ser?" Sundra's tone edged on disrespect.

Captain Eliot smiled, and it wasn't pretty. "You didn't ask. Anyone ready to go home?"

The soldiers, and they were that, soldiers, fighting a battle through the alternate realities, turned to look at each other. Sundra smiled first, and the expression leaped from team member to team member.

"I thought not." Captain Eliot continued to smile, although it now resembled a smirk. "We have our first reality set up and ready to run. Expect this: You will fail most of the time. What we expect to see is for you to make more and more progress in each scenario until your team finally reaches your goal."

"This skimming stuff. Just what are we expected to skim? That was never fully explained to us." Sundra looked at the other team members, audacious with her bold question.

"Yeah," Caitlan said, growing arrogant in Sundra's daring shadow. "What are we supposed to do?"

"Your jobs are simple." He pointed to the four lower-ranking team members. "You are to give your team leader time for that particular reality to seat in, to become totally real to him, and then you are to give him this." He held up a silver cylinder. "This contains holographic information that he needs to achieve the mission."

"Just tell him." Levi laughed. "Say, here, listen to this and get your job done."

"I understand. It doesn't work that way." The tall soldier began to speak, clearly catching on faster than the others. "Bren believes in who he is when he's in that scenario. He has to accept the cylinder and its information as part of his background, or he will reject the reality."

It was walking by a technician's keyboard when the problem started. Levi grinned, and he caught Caitlan's eye. With a laugh, he reached and typed in a random series of keystrokes before falling into line with the others.

"Levi. You're going to get us all in trouble." She narrowed her eyes at him.

"Nah. Nobody cares. Watch." He leaned to another unattended keyboard, and he repeated his prank.

The high-pitched warning buzzer stopped them in their tracks about ten minutes later. By that time they were back in the alternate reality chamber. Without warning, the massive doors at either end began to cycle closed.

Captain Eliot pulled a communication device from his pocket. "What's going on? The doors are sealing." He paused, listening, then growled, "How can a random destination have been set? No one in here's been through reality implantation. They'll be going blind." After a moment, he growled, "You think I don't know that? I don't want to go, either. My daughter has a recital this weekend. Can you stop it?" Another pause. "Not what I need to hear. How about triggers to break the reality?" His face fell.

"Captain?" The tall soldier stepped up to him. "I don't think Bren is up to this. What can I do to help?" Sure enough, the team leader was off to the side, looking very unsure of himself, with his hands crammed deep in his pockets. "But there." He glanced back at the rest of the team, to see Levi with his hands up, and a what-did-I-do expression on his face. "I think we have our culprit." He motioned that direction with the barest nod of his head.

Their physical forms were already starting to waver, the first sign that the reality shift was underway, and the captain spoke in rapid-fire agony, "The only way out is for one of us to die as soon as we get there, wherever we land. That's your job," and he glanced at the man's shirt, "Slate Knalb."

And with the sound of his name, reality snapped, and everything changed.

"WELCOME to Raccoon Team headquarters."

Four men and two women walked through the snow bundled in heavy coats. Thick fur whipped in the strong wind, beating against their faces. Introductions had been made on the way in from New Zealand, mostly where they were from and where they would like to be posted if they had their choice. They were soldiers, one and all, ready to fight a war, even if some were more ready than others.

"Where is the dome, ser?"

"Ser is fine, but I prefer Daniel." He wore a captain's insignia, though, and no one else did. That seemed to make a difference. "Caitlan, isn't it?"

"Yes, ser. I mean, Daniel, ser." She looked chagrined at herself.

"That's fine. As I said, I'll take ser. You won't see the dome. It's all two kays down, carved out of the bedrock. Let's get inside out of the wind before we answer any more questions. Anyone object to that?"

"No, ser," came several answers.

"Good. Follow me." Captain Eliot stepped to the entrance and looked into an eye scanner, then spoke his name into an indentation. After a moment, a red light turned green, and the wall irised open. Inside was a foyer with another door on the opposite side. All six stepped dutifully inside, with room to spare. The outside door closed as soon as the final person was through.

"Airlock technology, from the Station." A blond man with clear green eyes, undoubtedly of old-Earth Dutch extraction, glanced around, looking curious and not at all surprised.

"Good observation, Levi." Captain Eliot turned to the others. "What has Mr. Castle not noticed, yet?"

"We're moving, ser." This soldier had brown hair with black eyes. He grinned.

"Why do you think that, Bren?" The captain was smiling, though.

"Two things, ser. The second door. It hasn't opened, yet, and it's been several minutes."

"There's no way we're—"

"Hold on, Sundra. I want to hear this," Levi whispered with a smirk.

"Mr. Backiel is correct, so far." Captain Eliot emphasized the *so far*. "Tell us the rest."

"My ears are already clogged, ser. I had inner ear work done as a baby, and even minor changes in altitude affect me." He grinned.

"Cocky show off." Levi reached over and pushed him on the shoulder, but he looked impressed.

"Thanks. It's just a thing I can feel." Bren laughed it off. He called out louder, "We're going down, all two kays, it feels like."

"Good estimate, Mr. Backiel. Actually, however, we'll be stopping at one point seven, which is where your quarters are. The dome is below that."

"How many domes are there?" The fourth male, a couple years older than the other soldiers, tall, and with big hands, stood at the back of the group. He'd pushed his hood back off his head, and his hair was clipped close. His face was chiseled and tanned, as if he spent a lot of time outdoors. He didn't look interested in the answer, more like his question had been for the others' sake.

The far door irised open, however, just as he asked his question, and the captain held up a hand and called, "Hold all further inquiries. I need to show you around. We'll have a chance for more queue and aye afterwards. This way, gentlemen and women."

"Sexist," Caitlan muttered. "Probably calls his wife Mrs. Eliot."

"Probably." Sundra laughed. "She probably calls him O, Great One."

"Shush." The tall man leaned in to interrupt their discussion. "Keep up, ladies, and keep the remarks down."

"Who made you our boss?" Sundra turned to give him a look through narrowed eyes.

"O, Great One did, the day I volunteered for this mission. I'm Raccoon Team leader. You have a problem with that?" His response was quiet, his words were measured, and it seemed as if he were laughing at them.

"No, ser," Caitlan muttered, looking away.

"No 'ser' needed. Just yes or no. We do need to keep up, though." He nodded to the rest of the group about to disappear around a corner.

"Led by our wonderful team leader." It was one of the girls, but they both looked down their noses.

"Yes, Caitlan and Sundra. Led by your team leader." Captain Eliot motioned to the tall young man to join him. "Come up here, Raccoon Team Leader."

"Yes, ser." He began to move through the small group.

"Daniel." The captain smiled and glanced down before looking back up with his face straight.

"Yes, ser, Daniel." The young man did not smile, though. He

stood half a head taller than the captain, and the captain wasn't small.

"And our goal is?" Bren had his arms crossed over his chest and a determined look on his face.

"One step at a time, Mr. Backiel. Let's get you into a scenario or two first and let you try it out. Your first reality will be at the beginning of the 20th century. You'll be in what was called The Great War—"

"World War I, you mean." That was Bren butting in.

"Yes, Bren, we know it as World War I, but you'll find we've made a few changes."

Bren grinned at that. "Like what?"

"Oh, you are going to have fun. I can promise you that. Team leader, come over here."

"Yes, ser. Er, I mean, Daniel."

"Now, here's how we've set it up. Your team leader, Slate, is going to . . ."

And with that word, the reality snapped, and everything changed.

"WELCOME to Raccoon Team headquarters."

Four men and two women were bundled in heavy coats with thick fur waving around their faces and hands. As they passed a security point, one pale, green-eyed man lagged a bit behind the others with a vaguely guilty look on his face. The team didn't even make it to the snow-covered building before the ground shook under their feet, and they were thrown aside.

Three of them were killed instantly. When the lead man, Captain Eliot, went, the trigger snapped, the light changed, and everything was different.

"WELCOME to Raccoon Team headquarters."

Four men and two women walked across the Nevada runway underneath a brilliant sun. The heat shimmered above the scarred concrete, and the six people spoke to no one. An enormous domed building arched into the sky just ahead of them.

One man, clearly a ranking officer, looked sternly at a light-colored member of his team who wore vivid green eyes.

"No one touch anything . . ."

Chapter 43

"SER, we're back on line."

The big ship was out in the ort cloud. It had taken some time for the draft field to stabilize. They hadn't been able to go anywhere, anyway. The Sagan-Armstrong had sputtered out before they could get outsystem.

"Any luck with the MagThrusters?" The uniform was still crisp, but he looked like his crust had been broken. He chewed on his lip for a moment before straightening his mouth.

"They just came back on line, ser. Everything. We have everything, even the Sagan-Armstrong." The one-bar at the controls held her hands up and laughed. "It was like magic. They were kaput, and then they were there, fully charged and ready to go. You tell me." She shrugged.

"Can we find our man?"

"That's not going so well, ser. I'm getting a rolling series of realities, and he's in every one."

"We can't leap into one of them?"

"He's not in each one long enough." She frowned. "It's like he's falling from one directly into another. They must be getting desperate to wake him."

"We're getting desperate to stop them." The uniform took a deep breath.

"How would you like to proceed, ser?"

He sat into his chair, and he rested his chin on his rolled hand, thinking. He punched a few icons on his console, sighing once. Then he looked like he made a decision, and he raised his head with a satisfied expression on his face.

"Ser, you thinking we have a plan?"

"Just jump. You pin him down, any reality, and we just jump. We don't have a choice any longer."

"What if we initiate a reality skip?"

Several of the other crewmembers in the command center stopped what they were doing and looked the uniform's direction. That had gotten their attention.

"Some things are worth the risk."

Heard in the back, "Even if we don't all make it out," but the uniform didn't respond to that comment.

Instead, he stood and said, "I'll be in my quarters. Call me if anything comes up."

"Yes, ser."

A lot of faces refused to look his way as he exited, but a possible death sentence doesn't tend to make people especially convivial, even on a ship crewed by disciplined military types, so that wasn't surprising at all.

Chapter 44

THE TABLE, blank with glowing light, was alone. No one was in attendance.

Its surface shifted, with colors upon colors creating ever-shrinking points of light. Slowly, oh so slowly, they began to look like star systems, then clusters, then galaxies.

Alive and alone, the images told of what was, what is, and what might possibly be.

And there was no one present to control it, a universe run amok.

The dreams had begun to change once again.

Chapter 45

THE FINGER reached to the oil . . . and hesitated.

The wheel continued to turn, the black sheen of the cogs and gears and stardust and dreams apparent in the barest of ripples in the night. However, something was not as it should be.

Then, a spline shattered, one tooth abruptly shearing off, sending a spring vaulting across the fabric of space and time.

Stardust sprinkled the oil in a glittering shower of broken rhinestones as sun after sun exploded.

The finger withdrew, satisfied, having never touched the oil at all.

Chapter 46

THE MIRROR flickered in the distance, and he knew he had to take the jump. His head throbbed, though, and this didn't feel . . . somehow it didn't feel *right*. Like this wasn't his life, and yet, here he was.

Still, there was so much *stuff* in his head, and also so many *gaps* that weren't filled in. He shook his head and looked at the mirror again, just catching the reflection in his nocs. He willed himself, placing one foot forward, and he was there, just where he'd been looking, now with a different viewpoint.

He lifted a hand and motioned. A blond man with green eyes was suddenly behind him.

How'd he even know to do that? That someone was with him and would follow him through?

It was one of those things he'd come to accept, that he *knew* things, and things happened, just because he *knew* they would. Like this. Catch a mirror and step through. Catch a second, and the steps become two.

It was a mnemonic reminder. But how did he know?

He couldn't worry about that, though, because he had a whole team coming through after him. A whole *team*? He'd been alone until just before the . . . um, the shift, for lack of a better word.

Then, in that moment, he knew what he'd done. He'd translated, from one mirror to another.

"Ser."

A hand appeared on his shoulder, and the green-eyed . . . soldier? . . . associate? . . . was at his side, looking forward through the mirror and pointing.

"There, ser. Can you see it?"

He held up the nocs and looked through. A series of numbers and symbols ran up and down the side, and in one corner, different—and very impossible—images flickered past as the numbers and symbols changed. As soon as he found the mirror—and how the heck did he know he was looking for a mirror—the symbols and the image froze. He turned the nocs away, and they began scrolling again.

"What is this?" He held the instrument away from his face, turning it in his hands.

"I'm sorry, ser. You don't know yet, but you will. We picked up that back in the Zephalini Mirror. It's quite an advancement for the Zephalini. We're lucky to have found it. By the way, I'm Levi. You don't remember me yet, but you will."

"And he'll wish he hadn't." That quip came from a woman just behind them. "Sorry, ser, I'm Sundra. Caitlan's here, but you'll have to meet her later. She's slow at translation, and we couldn't get her a fresh belt when we skipped through the Corasky Mirror." She chuckled. "We might've, though, if we hadn't triggered their carbon sensors. Glad to be with you again, ser." One quick pat on the back, and she turned away.

"Ser, we have to go now before the mirror moves." Levi nodded with a squeeze of his hand. It was still on his shoulder.

He looked behind him to see perhaps twenty people, most in their twenties, one or two older, and several younger. None looked under eighteen, except one wearing a bulky pack. Each had a satchel or a case he or she carried. One was drinking from a metallic container, and a couple were sitting on large blocks of black basalt. They were all watching him.

The world was big, a vast plain with the stone blocks everywhere. The sky was vermillion, and it looked like a watercolor explosion. The sound . . . no, *feel* of a waterfall reverberated under his feet.

"I know, ser. They all feel like this, strange. Now, though, we have to go." Levi took the nocs and held them to his face, aiming at the distant mirror. "We're safe going, ser. Ragataans are canine, but they rarely attack unprovoked. This will give us time to regroup, and there are lots of mirrors in Ragata, ones easy to find. Your lead, ser."

Levi handed him the nocs, and he smiled, the acknowledgement warm, like they'd been together a long time, and they worked well off each other. Like they were more than working associates; friends, even.

Like he could be trusted.

The man nodded, and he *jumped.* Translated. Skipped. He was *there,* and the sky was no longer red-orange. It roiled with green and black clouds, and somewhere, a creature howled, ending in a sharp and repeated yipping.

"A Ragataan, ser. It irritates their aural membrane when we hit the mirror's translation circuits. Sub-strata core resonance, we think, though that's only a theory. No one volunteers to test it." He chuckled, as if there was more behind what he said, but going there required an explanation he didn't have time for. "If we come across slowly, they'll think it's the storm."

Levi had simply appeared, a breeze catching his hair and blowing it sideways. He had been adjusting his collar when he translated, and the glimmer of something metal around his neck caught the green light and then was gone.

"Oh, and you'll need my last name." He held his hand out to shake, and he fought a grin, as if he knew something he wasn't saying. "Castle. Levi Castle."

As the man grasped the proffered hand, it was a lightning strike of inrushing knowledge. He saw those green eyes and that smile at twelve, still at school together, playing pranks in the science lab. They'd messed around once with hydrogen peroxide and sulfuric acid, and for the damage to the lab, they'd been expelled for three days. Not a bad three days, though, because they'd spent those three days in the woods exploring. Then at fourteen, falling for the same girl, and the fight that followed. He knew his shoulder still ached in cold weather from where this man had dislocated it, and he also knew they'd made up, neither one ever actually dating the girl.

There was more, so much more, and all he could do was inhale and hold it, and wish his head would stop spinning. Then they separated hands, and it was like letting go of a live power line.

"Crazy, huh?" Levi—his best friend Levi—chuckled. "It always does that the first time. Wait until you find out your name."

He frowned. He knew his . . . and he tried to remember. He

211

didn't. He had no idea what his name was.

"Sorry." Levi clapped him on the shoulder again. As he did, a person materialized behind him, adjusting a pack on her back and turning to walk away. The canine howl in the distance started up again. "I'm not allowed to tell you your name. We have a job to do, first. For now, Boss will do."

"Boss, huh? And that job is?" He ran the memories of the two of them in his head, knowing his name was in there somewhere. He knew everything else. He had to know that, too. He had to.

"Archeology." The answer came from behind him, and he turned to see the woman from earlier who had identified herself as Sundra. "Doofus there is all mind games and vague insinuations. We're an archeological team from the NorAm Union, University of Terra, under the good graces of the D. Wymen Ragnost'en Endowment for the Arts."

"And we're looking for?"

She grinned. "A Secharri rosestone. The first of its kind."

With the word Secharri, his head opened up again, and a new world of information tumbled inside. The mines on Secharri; the rosestone he remembered giving to his girlfriend—Sundra? His eyes narrowed—and the manipulation of humanity's destiny by the peaceful-appearing creatures on that distant world. He knew in that instant just why their mission was so important. The fate of the human race depended on it.

One other thing? He was determined they were going to be successful, if they had to jump every mirror in this entire world to find that stone. He was determined to win.

Even if he didn't know his name.

Chapter 47

"LEVI, I know I've grown up with you. I know that in my head, but I still feel I don't really know you." The man studied his hands—unfamiliar hands, yet as second nature to him as blinking in the wind—and he noticed for the first time how big they were. Strong, muscular hands, and he wondered what he'd done before getting into archeology. They sure weren't an archeologist's hands, with narrow fingers and a delicate touch for tedious interaction with fragile antiquities.

The blond-headed man punched him on the shoulder good-naturedly and laughed. "You remember that girl we both liked? You've got to know her name."

"That's it." He reached to scratch the back of his head. "I remember that fight and everything, but I don't remember much about her. Anything, to be honest."

"She was some looker, a fourteen-year-old bombshell. Marnie." He snapped his fingers, as if he'd forgotten. "That's it. I've been trying to remember since that last jump. Remember what she did when neither of us would go out with her?"

"Why don't you tell me?" As Levi rattled on, laughing and punching on him to emphasize his most important points, the man let his thoughts wander a bit. He remembered that fight, and how his shoulder hurt when it was cold, but it hadn't hurt today. Of course, it hadn't been cold, either, but still, all he really remembered was the emotion behind the fight, and the making up afterward, him and Levi still chums.

"Wasn't that the way it was?" That was Levi, this time hitting him on the side of his knee with his fist.

"What?"

"Like I thought, off in your own world again." He laughed. "Why do I even bother talking to you? I could sit here and daydream about beautiful women and hot, sandy beaches, and you wouldn't know the difference."

"He'd know the difference." A woman's hands pushed them apart, and Sundra forced herself in between. "We're organizing camp for the night. Cheeky and Roni have set up a perimeter, and it's at 500,000 volts. They're still tweaking the amps for the Ragataans. They're tough little critters. Don't want any to get through."

"Did Caitlan make it?" Levi's question.

"Last one. She's already crashed for the night. She doesn't like these four-hour jumps. It's always a risk the mirrors might shift."

Levi snorted a laugh.

"They do. Just ask some of these guys. They've been on teams that have lost members because they couldn't make the jump."

"Then they screwed something up. As long as you keep the mirror active, it can't shift. It's psychically linked to you. You control the mirror." Levi had a smirk on his face.

"Yeah, Doofus. You go last next time."

"Besides, even if someone did get left, all they have to do is take a different route back to home base. It's simple."

"Says the man who can jump without a translation belt. Not everyone can do this with their eyes closed and in their sleep."

"Well, if everyone was perfect, then they'd all be me, wouldn't they?" Levi stretched his legs out and leaned back on his elbows. He closed his eyes and laid his head back. "Thank you, God, for making me perfect."

Without thinking, or considering if Levi would find it offensive, the man with the big hands reached across Sundra and popped him in the stomach with the back of his fingers. Hard, too. Levi jumped, yanking his knees up and grabbing the hand. He laughed, even as he moaned about the pain.

"Ouch, ouch, ouch. I always fall for that every time. Quit hitting me in the stomach." He released the hand, keeping his arms crossed over his torso. "You just wait for paybacks." It didn't sound like much of a threat, though.

Sundra sat between them, and she clapped. "That was perfect. Levi needs to be set on his ear every now and then."

The man felt good on the inside, and he smiled, perhaps for the first time ever, if not just the first time he remembered, really remembered. That had been totally intuitive, and it seemed like it was something he did all the time. He had no doubt that these were his friends. Before, he had known it in his head. Now, he felt it in his heart.

"Thank you," he said.

"For what?" Sundra.

"Yeah. For what?" Levi had his eyes closed again.

"For making me feel this is real." He motioned to the green and black sky, and the mirror they'd come through, still floating above the ground off in the distance.

"Part of the territory," Levi called out. "You, us, we're a team." He held up two fingers, kissed them, and flicked it the man's way.

"That's what friends are for." Sundra used both men's shoulders to stand. "You two I've put together in Shelter 3. Try to get some sleep tonight. We're getting an early start tomorrow."

"Yes, Mother." Levi gave her a mock salute.

"Hey!" She kicked him in the hip before walking off.

It was twenty minutes later that they were underneath the shelter. It was little more than a cover for protection, rather than an enclosure for privacy. Somehow, clean clothes had appeared in the bottom of their packs, and Levi and he had claimed first dibs on the temporary facilities. Now they lay peering out at that roiling green sky, wearing only shorts and Tees. Fresh and pressed clothing lay off to the side.

"Does it ever get dark?" He was on one elbow.

"You want to know everything, don't you? Be patient. It'll come to you." Levi lay on his back with his hands behind his head.

"And if it doesn't?" Everything? Somehow he was sure he wouldn't ever know everything. Too much was missing. Back in the facilities, he'd found a tattoo on one side of his chest. It seemed to him a connection with something he'd probably never remember, and that seemed to fit who he was. Now? What seemed right was being here with this man and these people, as if he'd spent time with them before, and he probably would again.

"We'll just start over. We don't have to be successful every time. We just need to be more successful every time."

He laughed. "What does that mean?"

"Go to sleep. We've got a busy day in the morning. *Boss*."

"Boss. Sure." He rolled to his back, his head out from under the shelter, watching the sky. Far off in the distance a Ragataan howled, or he supposed it was one of them. It had an eerie part-wolf, part-dachshund sound. That was when something brightly painful bit into his stomach. He jerked up, yelling.

"Told you paybacks were coming." Levi pushed him on the shoulder, and laughing, he turned to his side, his back to the man. "Good night."

"Levi! Boss! Cut the chatter. Some of us want to sleep!"

After that, the green sky seemed rather comforting, and he thought he might miss it, if it were gone. The man beside him? He'd only known him for a few hours that he really, *really* remembered, and he knew he'd miss him if he were gone. Like, who else would he have? Sundra, whom he had spoken with twice, and Caitlan, whom he'd not met at all.

He glanced over, seeing Levi on his back again, and the silver necklace caught the light. Now *that* he remembered. Why, he didn't know, but it had a permanent place in his mind, like it was an item of importance, something he should pay attention to very carefully.

Like it would call to him if he let it.

Then his eyes grew heavy, and the green and black sky faded into morning.

"DOES it always do this here?" He glanced up to the sky, watching it roil in tumbling waves of black, punching wicked holes in the green.

"Pretty much." Levi put a piece of bread into his mouth and began to chew.

They were both dressed, and somehow the things that had made up the camp were gone, yet no one carried all the supplies they'd used to make camp. And their bags. When they'd gotten up there was food in their bags, warm and toasty.

He grabbed the nocs and strapped them around his neck. Funny. He didn't use them during the night. They hadn't been in his bag, and yet, they were at his side when he wanted to pick them up. Hm. Maybe he'd put them there the night before, and he'd forgotten. It was possible.

"Don't know where these came from, but I'm glad they're here." He shrugged, and he laughed, standing. He felt better this morning, as if he had finally adjusted to a world that had been too new and fresh to fit his shoulders well yesterday. "Today is going to be a very good day."

"It always is." Levi tossed his leftover bread aside. "More for the dogs when we're gone." Just across from them, two women were unfolding an old-fashioned paper map. Levi grabbed his arm and tugged. "You'll find this interesting. Ladies," he called. "Boss wants to see."

"Good morning," they called back. One was medium height, sandy hair cut short, and freckles down her arms. The other was light-colored and petite.

"Caitlan Trotter. You two know each other, although you, Boss, will need to let it come back slowly. Reena Jericho, whom you know, but differently. You don't really have a memory of Reena, but you will. Eventually."

The women looked at each other and smiled.

"That's not fair, Levi. You're teasing him, and we're not supposed to do that." Caitlan, the petite one, looked at him hard before turning and offering her hand. "Caitlan. I'm pleased to meet you, but you'll know that once we shake."

When he grabbed her hand, he knew exactly what she meant. The relationship—friend, coworker—washed over him in waves. When they released hands, he let out a breath he hadn't known he was holding.

"Have we been . . . you know?" That had been intense.

"Spoilers ruin the ending." She laughed. "See if you get anything with Reena."

"Glad to meet you, Reena." He grasped her hand, prepared for the shock of recognition, only to find it was just a hand. He released and looked at his own. "Nothing. What gives?"

"You'll get more than you're used to, at least from some of us. Normally we all come in blind like you, waiting on the triggers they decide to give us; but we're fast-tracking this; and we've been given greater liberties with making that connection with you. Sorry we can't tell you more." Caitlan shrugged.

"Trust us, Boss?" Levi threw his arm on his shoulder.

"Do I have a choice?" They all come in blind? Like him? He did, though. Trust them. Implicitly. Last night he wasn't sure he could have said that. His head, yes. His emotions? In his heart he would have had doubts.

"Of course you do." That was Sundra coming up behind them

and pushing Levi's arm off. "You always have a choice. It's just our job to convince you that trusting us is better than the other option."

"Your *job*?" He didn't like the sound of that, like he was cargo, and they were responsible for him.

"Just a figure of speech, Boss." Levi clasped him on the shoulder, his hand there and gone almost before he'd touched, and he began backing away. "Next translation at oh eight hundred. Be there or be square." He laughed, turning and running to the far side of the camp.

"Be there or be square?"

"Ignore him, Boss. Around you, he's always like that."

"Like what?"

"A little star-crossed." That was Sundra, and she chuckled. "We all are. You'll get it, someday, when all this makes sense to you. It's why Levi usually chooses to be your son."

"My son?"

"Sundra!" Caitlan frowned at her. "T.M.I."

"Oh, sorry. You don't bring that in with you. I forget, sometimes. I don't guess I can tell you about me." She laughed. "Not with Catie listening in, anyway."

That triggered something. Catie . . . Catie. He'd once known a little girl named Catie. "Are you from, um, Earth? St. Louis?"

She looked uncomfortable for a second, then she smiled. "Yes. I lived there once. No longer, though. Hey, there's Levi, and it looks like he's ready. Go catch him." She shooed him off with her hands.

Before he could move, one of the youngest of the team, the boy who looked seventeen, ran by, calling, "We're going now. Mirror's starting to shift, and we can't lose this lead. Let's go." And he was gone.

When they got there, half the team was already through.

"Sorry, Boss." Levi was pushing people through as fast as they could go. "I had to make the call."

"Nikolai said the mirror's shifting." Caitlan had out a small device, and she touched it to the side of the mirror. "It is not."

Levi grabbed her arm. "Look up." He pulled her close. "Without being obvious."

Overhead, shadowy in the dark green sky, was an enormous black shape, spanning much of what they could see. From time to time, small areas of roiling cloud cleared, and the matte finish seemed to soak up the light and energy from around it.

It was ominous, and the team was running scared.

"They can't be here." Caitlan's face had gone pale.

"Neither can we." Levi smiled. "It's not a 'can we' situation, but rather, an 'are we' one. We are, and they are."

"Are what?"

Caitlan looked at Levi, with her lips pressed tightly together, and she took a deep breath before answering. "They're skipping. Following us, you might say. We jump, and they jump."

"We jump through this, and they can follow?" He looked up at the ship in the sky.

"It's dangerous, though." The last few of the team were stepping through, and Levi hiked his pack onto his shoulders.

"For us?"

Caitlan grinned. "For them."

"So," he was starting to get this, "the faster we move, the better it is?"

"For us." Levi grinned, his eyes filled with anticipation.

"I'm starting to like this."

"I've been waiting for you to catch on, Boss." Levi was lit up like a sun going nova, right into a telescope.

He grabbed his nocs to see where they were going, but Levi blocked him from putting them to his face.

"You don't want to know this time. Trust me, Boss. I had to grab the first window I saw. Sorry." He was still grinning, though, as he grabbed the boss's arm, and together, they leaped.

Chapter 48

THEY hit the ground rolling, literally. The mirror was a good two meters in the air, and they were in a stampede of quadrupeds. They were on a small ridge, and the storm surged past, barely leaving them room to stand.

Dust roiled, and vision was almost impossible.

"Try left," yelled Levi. "There's a hill."

Caitlan had her device out, and she held it high in the air. The screen glowed with nearly two dozen green circles. Those were the team. Another hundred red dots moved across the display, reflecting the running creatures.

"Got 'em," she cried. "Left and right. Let's find a way out."

They had to get past the torrent of creatures, though. He hated to call them animals. They were amorphous trees, if he had to label them anything. Their legs were synonymous with what he thought of as roots, and their branches? More naked brains on steroids than anything else.

The herd was thinning, and already they could see several of their team standing above the stampede. A mirror, dusty, caught a distant sun through its glass, then it caught another. Twin suns, one glass. On the opposite side of the stampede was another mirror; it showed a much different scene, as a violent storm with thunder and pink lightning thrashed the sky.

"Ser, this is a good time for your nocs. I don't know that we can lose our tail, but we can wreak havoc with their translation. Pick a mirror."

He put them to his face, the information inside scrolling until it locked onto a particular mirror. "What about the twin suns? Is that good?"

"Binary systems are a dime a dozen. Temperature. Air composition. What does it say about that?"

"Forty-eight Celsius, fourteen percent O_2, with—" and he dropped the nocs. "What are Kelleriods?"

"Bony jaws, with a furry mane of hair?" Levi frowned.

"Pretty much."

"We're choosing the other one. Let's go." He raised his hand as he ran. "Pink lightning! Everyone in!"

"What'll we find?" The boss was panting by the time they reached the mirror, but he had a smile on his face.

"Something nasty, I'm sure." Sundra was next to him, and she called to Caitlan, "Get Reena and rendezvous on the other side." Then she leaped, winked, and was gone.

"Go." Levi slapped him on the back. "We need a quick turn-around."

"Without bony jaws?" He grinned.

"You're getting it, now. Go!"

He pushed, and the man fell into a world filled with pink lightning. Loud, pink lightning. Purple rain drenched him. He had no recourse, either, because the rain was rising from the ground to the sky. His feet were in a lake that spread as far as he could see, although it was only centimeters deep. It wasn't getting any shallower with the drenching upflow, either.

He felt the push of others following him through.

"How do we find a mirror in this?" He could hardly see for the rainwater flooding his eyes, and he called to anyone who was listening.

"The nocs."

"What if I can't locate one?" He raised them to his face, surprised to find them scrolling like before. He swung them to the side, and the image locked for a second, then began scrolling again as his head continued to swing. "There. I had something, but I lost it."

"Good, I hope. Look in that spot. If we jump again, we can take a breather, but I want a decent world."

He smiled. With the rain, he couldn't see who said that, but he guessed it was Caitlan. Sundra would be snappy and bold, and Levi? Prankster Levi? He'd jump five more times just for the fun of it.

Him? He was finding he was having a better time than he'd ever had in his life, and he now knew with all his being that he wanted to be right here, right now, with these people, doing exactly what they were doing right this minute. He didn't care if they landed in a stampede of trees or in a purple rain. He just wanted them together.

He ran with as much speed as he could muster on top of a purple lake, and finally seeing the mirror glinting in the rain, he yelled, "Geronimo!"

And he leaped.

IT WAS dark. No wonder he hadn't been able to see the mirror. The scene had been black because there were no lights on the other side.

Twenty people in one square and very metal tube.

To be fair, it was a very long tube, and it branched off in all directions. On some worlds it might be air ducting in a large commercial building, but here? With no lights? It was frightening.

Someone lay wedged up against him, and he whispered, "Who's that?"

"Me, Boss." Levi squirmed for a minute, grunting in the process, and when he was still, he continued. "And you picked this place for what reason?"

"And you did that squirming thing for what reason?" Levi's elbow now caught him in a very tender location.

"Your knee. You don't want to know where it was. See any mirrors? I don't think I want to take my breather in here."

"Will the nocs work in the dark?"

"They work everywhere else." Levi sounded out of breath.

"Hey, up there. Can you guys move forward a bit? We're crowded down here."

"Sundra?" Levi called, shifting his body,

"Stop that, Levi!" The boss tried to move out of the other man's way, but there was no room.

"Levi! Is the boss up there with you?"

"I'm here, and Levi's too much with me!" The boss hissed to Levi, "Your elbow. Quit twisting that way. I want to be able to stand when we get out of here."

"Sorry, ser." He shifted once again. "Try the nocs, ser."

"Let me find them." They had been around his neck. He reached, and all he found was Levi's face.

"Not it, Boss. Try again." He spat, clearing his throat. "I like you, Boss, just not in my mouth, thank you."

"Sorry. I'm looking for the nocs."

"Looking. That's funny, Boss. In the dark, looking. Get it?"

"Yeah, Levi. I'm looking again." He tried to move his left arm and realized he couldn't. It was trapped in the corner of the tube underneath Levi's back. "My left arm is stuck under you, so I'm going to have to work my hand past your face. This time keep your mouth closed."

"Unless I want a taste, then I might just lick it as you go by." He laughed, and it was loud in the closed space.

"You guys finished having fun up there?" It was Sundra, again. "Do the romance thing on your own time."

"Stuff it, Sundra," Levi yelled.

"Ouch, ouch. Don't yell at her, Levi. When you do, your elbow pegs me."

"Sorry. I found the nocs. Right here." He moved his head, and his face pressed against the boss' chest.

"I'm diving under." The boss wedged his hand past Levi's face, chin first, then worked past his ear. He pushed the nocs up until they cleared Levi's head, then he had to reverse the process, working his hand between Levi's face and his chest, until it was free. Next it had to go over the other side of Levi's face, barely fitting between the metal and his face, until he could grab the nocs. "Got 'em."

"Thanks for the face massage, Boss."

"You're welcome. Anytime."

"Maybe in my next life. Can you see anything?"

"As soon as I can work them to my face. My elbow . . . won't twist . . . there." It had been stuck between the tube and Levi's face.

"My word, Boss! Take off my skin!"

"Shut up and remember where your elbow is. You deserve whatever I do to you. Now, be quiet while I adjust these."

"Levi? Boss?"

"In a minute, Sundra."

"Gol-*ly*! Stop moving, Levi! It hurts!"

"Paybacks. What can you see?"

"Nothing. It's not scrolling. Nothing. What does that mean?"

"Crud!"

"What?" He didn't like the sound of that.

"It happens sometimes when too many people hit a window too

quickly. It overloads the translation circuits, and it freezes." He shifted.

"What are you doing?" Shifting was not allowed.

"I need the nocs."

"You need what?"

"The nocs. Sorry, Boss. We have to reboot the mirror."

"You have got to be kidding me. Reboot the mirror?" He took a deep breath.

"Don't complain, Boss. At least you're not breathing in someone's navel."

"Just got an elbow in my—"

"I get it; say no more. I'll see if I can fix that." He moved.

"Not that way. The other direction, please." He gritted his teeth as Levi squirmed, the pain worse, then it eased. "Thank you. Can I do the reboot from here?"

"If you can see in the nocs. What's it look like?"

"Like I told you, nothing."

"Okay. They have to come to me. I've got to get my arm up to my face. I'm sorry, Boss. No pain, no gain. Here goes."

The boss yelled at first, cursing at Levi during the worst part, and finally caught his breath. "Don't. Ever. Do. That. Again." He said the words slowly, pausing between each one. He could barely breathe.

"Got 'em, Boss. And sorry. Sometimes you gotta do what you gotta do. Let me look. It's right . . . here."

And twenty people fell through the glass, all at the same time, landing right on top of one another. Levi and the boss had been at the head of the line, and they wound up at the bottom of the pile.

"Levi?"

"Yes, Boss?"

This time they were face to face, and they could feel each other's lips move.

"This is better?"

"No, Boss, I agree with you. It's not better."

"Thank you, Levi. At least we're on the same page. Help! Someone get off!"

Levi joined in. "Move, you idiots!"

It took a little jostling, and twenty packs and cases had to be thrown aside, but eventually the two men were separated and breathing their own air once again. The boss stood and adjusted his clothing.

"This is interesting." He looked up to see that they were in a great big building. And by big, he meant big. The ceiling was so far up that he could barely see it.

"Boss, this is even more interesting." Levi slapped him on the arm with the back of his hand. "Look down."

The building went as far down as it went up, and there was no floor under their feet.

Surprisingly enough, that meant something to the boss. He looked around at the people with him, each standing on what appeared to be a level surface, even if there was nothing under their feet. He had been here before, and the names of his crew began to snap into his mind. Reena Jericho, the best navigator in seven systems, land or space; Nikolai Borovsky, the kid who'd come by that morning, indeed seventeen like he looked, on board for grunt labor; Jonnra Cheerisky, top museum curator, here as a consultant from New London Nationoids Conglomerate; Robert Nambonsik, once head of World Geographic Systems, and now a media hound intent on publishing the results of this search. His eyes skipped across the faces, each one with a story behind it.

That included Renaud Lautrec, Weldon Sikes, Cheeky, Roni, and eight others.

And of course, Levi, Caitlan, and Sundra.

Just not his own.

But this building. This he knew. Back in the army . . . He'd been in the army! He'd been a soldier, and a good one. He laughed. He knew something about himself, something that no one had told him. That pleased him immensely.

All because Levi told him to look down.

He pulled the man to him, and he slapped him on the back.

"What was that for?" Levi hugged him back, hesitantly at first, then harder before pushing him away.

"Because you are magnificent. Absolutely brilliant, and I love you for that."

"He's getting there." Sundra leaned in, jabbing Levi with her elbow. "Welcome back, Boss."

"One thing." He grinned. "I remember one thing. This. All because you said to look down. This is a subdirectional matrix tensioning device. There should be nodes around the perimeter energizing this barrier."

"What good does that do us?" Nikolai had been listening.

"A lot of good." Caitlan. She was grinning.

"A lot of good, indeed. If we can pinpoint the frequency, we can raise or lower it to any level."

"What is it, though? That's what I want to know."

"Air." The boss smiled, extraordinarily pleased with this moment in time. He knew Beener Baity. Beener Baity, com expert, had asked that. "Air, Beener, just air."

"How . . ." He looked puzzled.

"The name says it, if you think about it. Air moves everywhere. Give it a matrix, telling it only to move in one direction, then tighten it. It makes it a solid, similar to glass."

"Like a force field." Nikolai again, his face lighting up.

"Ye-*ah*." The boss hedged, dragging out the word and shaking his head, understanding in that moment that it was most definitely *not* a force field. "In a sense, but this is way better. Look for nodes, everyone. We find those, and we can make this thing move."

"Why does it need to move?" It was clear Beener was catching on fast, working out the math, and probably the physics of it, too, because his eyes were starting to shine.

Caitlan answered that one, giving the man a playful push on the shoulder. "So we can get there." She pointed to something at least fifty meters below their feet.

"Found it!"

Everyone looked to see Reena at a far wall. She reached into her pack to pull out a glass computing device, and she knelt to place it against the floor.

Before anyone could react, a screeching sound ratcheted through the building, and the air they stood on shook. Overhead, searing brightness stabbed through the massive interior, bouncing off the walls and setting sparks flying. The light hit one of the team members, and she screamed in pain. Then it dimmed again, but the noise got louder as a large black ship peeled the top of the structure right off. The bottom opened, and black-suited and blank-eyed soldiers poured out.

Luckily, they were still a hundred meters over the archeology team's heads.

"I need a frequency," the boss called out.

"Searching," Reena called back.

Overhead, the blankeyes had carried a large back box with handles on all four sides out of their ship, and they placed it in the middle of the air "floor." Thick cables snaked back into the interior of the ship.

"They're doing something, Boss." Levi looked up, his hand shading his eyes.

The boss didn't even look. "They're doing what we're doing."

"Only with bigger machines."

"Bigger isn't better." He yelled, "Got it, Reena?"

"Searching, still."

"Come on, come on." They had to have that frequency, and now.

"What do you need me to do, Boss?" That was from Caitlan. She stood at his side.

Catie.

He looked at her, trying to remember a Catie, trying hard. Nothing else came, just that he did remember a Catie from St. Louis. But there was something else. In that moment, he remembered his name. Slate. And with that word, who he was poured into him, and he remembered how to be magnificent.

He called to Caitlan. "That mirror scanner. Where is it?"

"Here." She reached in her pack and pulled it free. "Catch." And she threw it to him.

"Everyone should have a Caitlan." He thought of the little girl he remembered. She had been his daughter.

"Everyone should have *you*." Levi looked overhead and took a ragged breath.

"Oh?" Slate grinned. "What are they doing upstairs?" He had the device opened up, and he had a tool out of his pack picking at it.

"Getting closer." He sounded worried.

"You concerned?"

"Ye-*ah*! Can I do anything to help?"

"Can you yell jump?" Slate looked at him with a smile, snapping the back on the little scanner.

"Yes?" Clearly not understanding the question.

"Reena?" He yelled to her, grinning at Levi.

"Got it!" She held a fist in the air for emphasis.

"Calibrate!" He held the scanner up, pushing the scan button. It was red for a moment, then it turned green. "Trust me, Levi?"

"Absolutely!"

"Now, Levi, be amazing, and yell!"

"Jump!" Levi called it at the top of his lungs.

Slate pushed the other button on the scanner, the one that sent information, and as twenty pairs of feet hit the floor, it disappeared, only to reappear one meter lower, sending many of the team stumbling, and the rest falling down.

"Sorry," he called. "Sorry. I should have warned you. Again."

Levi called with emphasis, "Jump!"

This time they were more prepared, and again, and again they jumped, their goal coming closer each time.

The blankeyes were coming faster, though. Their big, black machine may have been inelegant, but it was moving them steadily down, racing two meters for every one the archeological team covered.

"Boss!" Sundra yelled it, and she was clearly cautioning him. They still had five meters to go, and the floor above them was about on their heads.

"Warning! Big jump! Now, Levi!"

This time they crashed all the way down. In a scramble of bodies and equipment, they dove into the mirror.

Levi paused just before jumping in, and he looked up. "Please, God, don't let it—"

However, Slate slammed into him before he could finish, calling out, "*Now* is an excellent time, Levi!"

And through the mirror they fell.

Chapter 49

"TWO sprained ankles and one cracked wrist." Slate lay on a rocky beach under a yellow sky. A blue sea stretched before him, but his eyes were closed. "Not bad. Not good, but not bad."

"And bad guys that couldn't follow us without leaving half their crew. Not bad at all, Boss." Caitlan had her feet at the water's edge, and she let the waves wash over her toes. Jonnra, Nikolai, and Beener were with them, and the others were exploring the escarpment that leaped up sharply behind them. It was bound to be filled with archeological treasures, as it *had* to have caves everywhere, Weldon had said, knocking together a team to head up and explore.

Those on the water's edge discussed more recent matters, like that last world they'd fallen out of.

"And you knew to do that *how*?" Levi walked up and knelt beside them, dripping water. He was in his shorts, and they clung to him like a second skin. He claimed he still hadn't recovered from that lurching dive into the mirror, but that hadn't kept him out of the sea. He shook his head, splattering them with water. "I mean, we almost died there. They were on our heads."

"He doesn't get it yet, *Slate*." Sundra sat down at his side, smiling.

"Sundra!" Caitlan turned, a look of dismay on her face. "We can't—"

Slate waved her warning away, opening his eyes and sitting up. "Sundra knows me pretty well, it seems. When did you guess?"

"That you knew who you were? When you had us jump to drop that level down. That was something you had to be you to know."

"Good deduction. To answer Levi's question, that's how. I was thinking of you, Caitlan, and St. Louis, which makes you incredible, by the way, and that's when I remembered how to be me."

"Is it time?" Levi looked at Sundra. "You know, with the clerics tailing us, and all."

"They always tail us." That was Caitlan.

"It's different this time." He glanced overhead, as if they might drop in on them at any time. At the same time, his hand searched his clothing, coming up with something wrapped in his fist. Below it dangled a silver cord, catching the light.

"He's right." Jonnra Cheerisky dug in her pack, answering as if absently, and she pulled out a steaming packet. She opened it and set it aside as she reached in and retrieved a drink with a lid. She had eating utensils already out. "The Church will not give up, and if they have attached themselves to us, especially in here, they are willing to risk a lot." She had the food open, and she placed a forkful in her mouth, chewing as if she hadn't spoken at all.

Levi opened his hand to reveal a slender silver column, a plain tube that caught the sun and sparkled with the perfection of something otherworldly. It . . . pulled at Slate, as if talking to him. No, he thought, *whispered* was a better word, in his head, wanting him to touch it.

"First," Slate said, choosing to ignore the silver trinket and the words repeating at the edges of his thoughts, *Slate, Slate,* "I want to know about that." He pointed to Jonnra's meal. "How does that happen?"

Beener laughed, picking up a stone and tossing it into the water. It made two shadows as it sailed through the air, hitting with a bright sound. "That's our Slate. Ignore the obvious and ask about the implausible."

"Seriously. We're carrying these packs. Last night, Levi pulled out clean clothes. We've gotten hot food out, and now, you have a drink with a lid?" He chuckled as he ran a hand through his hair. "Twin suns and a yellow sky seem pretty tame in comparison."

Levi still had the silver trinket in his hand, with the cord swinging in the air. "It's simple, really. The translation circuits do it when we go through. That's why we carry the bags. They are tuned to upgrade their contents when we jump. Sort of topping off the tank, to use an old-fashioned term."

"Says the expert." Caitlan smiled.

"I am. That's my specialty." He teased her. "I can even tune them to individual characteristics, which is why you don't get a gorilla suit at night." He winked at Slate with a chuckle. "The time of day is what determines what the packs give us. I might retune Catie's. I've always wanted to travel with a gorilla."

She laughed and slapped at his arm. "You do that, and I'm staying here. I like this world. What's it called?" She pulled her little device out. "Se'Yan't. I could live here."

"But this." Levi held the silver necklace out. "Sundra? I'm thinking Slate needs to see what we have here."

"Does it translate, too?" Slate reached to take it from him, grinning. "Like the packs?"

"Hold it." Sundra wrapped his hand around it, her face now serious. "Just hold it in your fist for a minute."

With this latest interest in the silver trinket, all eyes present were on Slate, and he looked at them, frowning. "So, this is important?" He looked at it, and he knew it was. It . . . wanted to be important to him.

"More important than anything we've done so far." Sundra nodded.

"Levi—"

"Trust us, Boss. This will change your life." Levi fought a grin.

"Is it supposed to be warm?"

"That means it's working." Caitlan.

"Okay, hot. Getting really hot."

"Ready, guys!" Levi called to the others in excitement.

The face appeared, and it looked around before saying, "Ah, there you are."

Slate looked at Sundra. "That's me."

"Just watch," she replied.

Holo-Slate smiled. "Yeah, I'm you."

"I just love it when it does this." Levi's grin was ear-to-ear.

"So, you're going to just lie there. I wish I knew where to start." The holo-Slate ran his hand through his hair, making a face and looking off to the side as if coming up with what to say next.

Slate jerked his free hand from his head. He had been doing exactly that. "Freaky—"

"Not freaky-eerie," holo-Slate started, still looking off to the side. "Oh, I was supposed to wait for you to say the eerie part. Sorry." He shrugged. "This is more like, well," and he looked at Slate, "when you have a dream . . ."

The holo continued to ramble, but Slate looked at the people around him. "How . . . it knows what I'm thinking. It can't . . . can it?"

"It doesn't always match exactly—"

"It repeats the same thing every time. But it's designed to talk to you. That's why it looks like it—"

"Listen." Slate held up his free hand, motioning for them to be quiet. He watched the little holo-head.

"—it really all comes down to that tattoo on your back—"

Slate released his fist, and the head disappeared. "It's not on my back."

"Like I said," and Sundra put her hand on his arm, "it doesn't always match. That's doesn't mean it's wrong, just that all this isn't scripted."

"Isn't scripted?" Slate looked puzzled. "What do you mean scripted?"

"What we're doing in here."

"What are we doing in here?" He closed his hand on the silver trinket, and he opened it back even faster. "Don't want that to start up again."

"We're winning our lives back." Caitlan blinked rapidly several times, and her eyes were red.

"But it said the tattoo's on my back. It's on my chest." He dropped the cylinder and pulled his shirt off. "See? And it itches." He rubbed it with his fingers.

"That's where it is this time." Levi's eyes grew wide. "How have I missed that?"

"Because I never take my shirt off?" Slate said it like a question as he leaned forward and slapped him on the leg.

"The itch means something, right?" That was Nikolai. He seemed fascinated by it all, but then, as he told anyone who would listen, it was his first time to go through all this.

"Maybe. It's early, yet." Sundra stood. "We need to look for mirrors."

"What about this?" Slate picked up the silver tube. "Levi? You want it?" He held it out.

"It's yours now, Boss. My job is to get it to you." He held his hands up to wave it off.

"There's that word, again. Job." Slate wrapped the cord through his fingers, and he held the necklace loosely, watching it reflect the sky. After a moment he pulled it over his head. It fell to his chest and lay against his skin, pale and glittering against dark, hitting just where the edge of the tattoo lay against his breastbone.

"Seriously, we need to think about a mirror." Sundra was still standing, looking around.

"Seriously, we need to explain the word job," Slate muttered. He reached beside him and hefted the nocs. "You can find one through these."

"You can. I can't." She looked at it, a brief and disappointed glance, before looking back to the horizon. "It's part of their design."

"You guys." Caitlan stood, and she picked up Levi's clothes and tossed them in his lap. "Quit dribbling information the boss's way. That's mean. Those are designed for you, and that means we can't use them. It tags primers from your RNA, I think. Our jobs? Just a word, Boss. It's what we do. Right now, Levi's job is to get dressed. I've seen enough skivvies for the day."

Slate turned his attention to Levi, with his white hair and those green eyes. How could another man use them, if they were tagged to his RNA? Brothers? If so, something had gotten scrambled in the gene pool, because he was old-Earth Mediterranean to Levi's Nordic white. Half-brothers at best, if that. The green eyes? God knew where he'd gotten those.

What color are mine? He tried to remember, and he couldn't. Not green, he thought, but he wasn't sure. He grabbed the cylinder around his neck, and he wondered if he could tell in the holo. It started to warm, and he let it go, just then noticing that everyone around him was moving.

Except Levi, squatting beside him.

"Your shirt?" He held Slate's out in one hand, his own in the other. He had his pants on, and they showed a damp band, especially around his waist. His hair was starting to dry. Water still beaded on his shoulders. "Everyone's back and ready to move."

"What color are my eyes?"

Levi laughed, dropping his head. He wadded both shirts in his hands, pulling them to his stomach. He didn't answer.

"What?"

Levi looked up. "I've been expecting that question." He glanced away, his eyes tracking something. "They're waiting on us up there."

"Let 'em wait. Look at me." He watched the other man, his eyes working the horizon, only finding his when he refused to go on. "My eyes. What color?"

"You're going to make me do this, aren't you?" For a moment the old Levi was gone, the laughter, and all the excitement bubbling to get out. Whatever was going on in his head, Slate's question meant something to him.

"If you want me to join those people up there." Slate caught the change, wondering what it meant. Who was this person who seemed to think so highly of him? And why did he dribble information, to use Caitlan's word, one tiny drop at a time? Caitlan was the only one who had really came clean, although he recognized that her words were nearly as sanitized as everyone else's. He was being kept in the dark. Well, he would know the color of his eyes.

"Look at me, Boss." Levi's green locked on Slate's unknown.

Slate studied the man's face, just a few light freckles across his nose, the hair trailing across his forehead, now catching in the breeze as it dried. The eyes, green and vivid, looking deep enough to dive into. Levi blinked, and Slate let his eyes drop.

"Now you know. Let's go." Levi stood, and he slapped Slate on the arm, skin smacking loudly against bare skin. He draped the shirt over Slate's shoulder. "And put this on. Your tattoo's moving like it always does, and I don't need to see that." He visibly shivered.

"Who are you?" Slate slipped the shirt over his head, pulling it down his torso as he stood. "To me, who are you?"

"Your number one fan, and that's all I'm saying on that." He grinned, the old Levi back, and he wound his shirt in his hands and popped it at Slate, catching him just on the chest. He laughed, taking off in a run.

"A dead fan, if I catch up to you," Slate yelled after him, rubbing where the shirt had caught him, then absently scratching just where he remembered the tattoo scrolling into a band of scattered dots. That was the spot that itched, and scratching didn't seem to help.

He grabbed his pack and hiked it on his shoulder, and he froze. It hit him, both things coming together for him. Their eyes matched, and Levi had used the nocs. They'd worked for him just fine. RNA. Not half-brothers, then. What could be closer than half-brothers? Maybe closer than brothers? Identical twins? Clones? Certainly not father and son, like Sundra had suggested.

He let out a laugh and made his way after the rest of the team. It probably meant nothing at all, like green eyes, jumping through mirrors, and last names that he didn't know.

Last name. He blinked rapidly several times. Why hadn't he thought of that? Surely that was important. It must be.

Well, well, well. He couldn't ask if he didn't catch up, and the others were long gone, right up that cut in the escarpment.

"Hey! Wait up!" And he started to run.

"WHAT'S that up there?" Slate pointed to a distant, hazy cut where the plateau fell off into the escarpment. Mist swirled out.

"The Ribbon Waterfall."

They'd reached the top an hour before, and they walked in direct sun. It had grown hot, and Levi and he walked side by side. They were both covered in sweat, and under two suns? A sauna would never be quite so enticing ever again.

Levi stopped and wiped his face with his hand then dried it on his pants. His shirt was already soaked.

"Water?"

"In your pack."

"Wait up." Slate dropped his pack to the ground. Digging inside he found the metal container he'd emptied earlier. He looked for a stream or someplace to refill it.

"It's full." Levi dug in his pack for his.

"I haven't refilled it."

"Reverse osmosis. My idea. I tuned them to absorb water from the atmosphere. This is a damp world. They refill pretty fast." He broke his open and upended it into his mouth. He wiped his lips when he lowered it. "Keeps the water cool, too."

"What about the mirrors?" Slate shook his, and sure enough, it had water. He opened it and took a long draught.

"What about that trinket?" Levi tapped Slate's chest with the end of his drink container.

Slate had been leery of trying it out again. It had unnerved him, and he wasn't sure what it was for. Everyone else seemed to have such high expectations for it, and he had no idea what it was supposed to tell him. He had forced himself to leave it alone.

"Well?"

"I'm expecting to see a black ship overhead anytime soon." Slate looked up, more to distract Levi than anything else. "Did I overhear something about clerics? Isn't that religion? Like priests?"

Levi held his bottle to his face, the chilled metal resting against his cheek, and he chuckled. "They have those, too, just over deacon and under monsignor. New Sabbatical Rome isn't a religious system. Think Crusades, Earth, about 1100 A.D. Eventually the God stuff gets buried in the we-want-to-win stuff. That happened with New Rome about 400 years ago."

"Ah. So, what do they really want?"

"What everybody else wants. Control."

"Of what?"

"Space. Time. Me." He pointed his bottle at Slate. "You."

"This." Slate pulled the necklace out of his shirt and held it up. He grinned—a half laugh—biting his bottom lip. "Am I right?"

Levi shrugged. "We'll call it that. Anyway, we've got some time. It surprised me they followed us through a frozen mirror. I doubt they all made it through that." He took another swig and shook the bottle before sealing it and dropping it into his pack. "This is a big place for them to search."

"So, this world was a lucky break."

"You could put it that way."

"Here." Slate took the nocs off his neck and handed them to Levi. "See if you can locate any mirrors." He messed with his water container for a minute before sealing it and returning it to his pack. Sundra had refused the nocs. Levi? He didn't even hesitate. That was what he really wanted to see.

"That way." Levi handed them back, and he pointed overland. "I don't know how far, but the readings are there. Ready?" He hiked his pack back up.

"How do you know about that waterfall?" They were back on the trail, bumping shoulders from time to time when the trail was wide enough, and single file when it wasn't.

"We've hiked it before."

"We?" Slate didn't remember anything like that, but then he still didn't know his last name, so that wasn't too surprising. "The team, or me and you?"

"I did, and that means you have." He looked over, as if he expected an argument about that.

"I see." Slate didn't, but he was sure he would. Eventually.

Up ahead the team was gathering, and they waved. Several people waved back, and a voice could be heard calling, "Bringing up the tail, again!"

"Covering your backside," Levi yelled. He reached and slapped Slate on the shoulder—harder than Slate would have liked—and he tore off running.

Slate hiked up his pack one more time, and he began to jog. Translating through those mirrors might refresh the contents of the packs, but it did nothing for his muscles, and all this hiking was about to wear him out.

Still, it was pretty great, a new world, a couple dozen people he seemed to really enjoy, and no giant spaceship overhead. That was just about magnificent with him.

And he was determined to have the best time ever.

"Wait up, fool! I'm coming, too!" With that, he lit into a full run, leaping over every stick and stone in his way.

Chapter 50

THEY should have paid more attention.

However, Slate only thought about that later. It was what Levi had said. Se'Yan't was a pretty big place for them to search. That also meant something else.

It was a pretty big place for them to hide. Them. The guys in the big black ship. The clergy. They could advance; scout out the enemy; sneak around and pounce.

However he said it, it meant the same thing.

They should have paid more attention.

This world, lush and serene, with its yellow sky and twin suns, had lulled them into complacency. For whatever reason, they laid over, finding food in the trees, and drinking from their reverse osmosis canisters.

"How are we on foodstuffs?" He stepped up to Caitlan as she situated her things on the ground. The team was setting up camp, and security devices had already been placed in a large polyhedral shape, several towering overhead on slender poles, and the rest among low ferns covering the ground. The final hookups were still being strung.

His pack was empty of food.

"We have plenty of local supplies. This world is very generous. How are you doing?" She looked up at him with a smile, resting her elbows on her knees.

"In one piece, so fine. Mystified a bit." He felt of the trinket around his neck. "You all know just what you're doing, and I'm the loose cannon here."

"Ha." She laughed a short burst of a sound. "And who got us through that last mirror?"

He shrugged. "That was easy."

"For whom?" She grabbed her pack and pulled out the scanner. "This? Whatever you did, this isn't what it used to be. Now?" She looked at it, shaking her head. "Now it registers things I can't even define. Like this." She pointed it at her water container. "Three liter capacity, and it will be fully refilled in thirteen minutes. And contaminants to one part per billion. This never did that before."

"I'll give you, I did that. The real question is what I'm supposed to do with this." He pulled the cylinder out of his shirt. "I'm supposed to learn how to save the world. All of humanity." He laughed. "How do I do that?"

"Brilliantly?" She was smiling.

"Levi . . . he, um—"

"Levi thinks you're a god, but we all tune out Levi when we can. Here, let me see that." She held her hand out for the cylinder, waiting as he pulled it over his head and handed it to her. "This only works for you."

"And Levi, I guess." He made a snorting sound then laughed. "Sorry."

"And Levi. Why do you say that?" She moved up to sit on a fallen log, and she motioned for him to sit beside her. "If we're going to talk, I want you at my level."

"I'm supposedly the only one who can run the nocs, but I've watched Levi do it." He held them up off his chest, and he laughed before dropping them back. "And when I asked him the color of my eyes, he looked at me, looked hard, and said that now I know. That tells me," and he took the cylinder back, holding it in his opened palm, "he can make this work, too."

"Yeah." She pursed her lips. "Levi's the one that counts here. Besides you, of course. Without you, there's no point."

"Make it easy on me. Thanks." He rubbed the cylinder between his fingers. "I think this is the magic." He held it up to catch the light.

"You know, if you play it, you can't do any harm. Plus, you might learn something."

"How much do you know of what's in here?"

"I've heard it all." She touched the cord where it hung below his hand. "We all have. Levi plays it incessantly. Played. Now that you have it, we get some peace."

"So, why don't you people get to the saving part? Just do what the little head says, and the human race is saved from the big bad guys."

"That's the problem." That was Levi, and he pushed their shoulders aside, forcing himself in between. He held some long, orange fruits in his hand, and he offered one to each of them. "Here. Try these. Everything a body needs, including minerals, vitamins, and fiber, all in one quick bite." He pulled another one out of his pocket and began to peel it. When he was finished, he pulled the nocs over Slate's head, putting them to his eyes. "Thanks, Boss. I'm headed out later to look for exits from this place." He slipped them over his head.

Slate looked at the fruit in his hand, and he noticed how Levi had cracked the end, then worked the outside back. He followed suit, taking a bite. "It's good."

"I know. The best. It won't grow except here, so this is the only time we can have this. I volunteered for this job for no other reason than this." He chuckled, sinking his teeth in, and chewing. "Cofuss fruit, directly from the non-forests of Se'Yan't."

"Non-forests?" Slate swallowed, and he considered whether he should eat more. The fruit was very rich, and he didn't want to overdo it.

"No trees." Levi took a second bite.

"But—" Slate looked around. There were walls of greenery blocking the view in all directions.

"Ferns, Boss." Caitlan had finished her fruit. "Eat it all. It's good for you."

"Sure, like eating dessert first. Oh, and what's the problem, Levi?" He looked at him innocently, as he bit into the fruit again. Like, why can't you guys do what the little head says? He hoped to catch him off guard and get a real answer, one without fluff.

Rather than coming through, Levi wrapped the cylinder in his fist, and he held it out, waiting. After about half a minute, he took a deep breath. "Getting hot, there."

Then Slate's face appeared.

"Ah, there you are." It turned to Slate and smiled.

Levi released it.

"Why'd you stop it? It knew me."

"Almost all of them start that way." He had his hand open, and he rubbed his palm. "It's not always your head, though. Sometimes it tells a story, like we're watching something through someone's eyes. Yours, I think." He reached to push two fingers into Slate's chest, tapping them once before moving his hand away.

"So you've told everyone who'll listen to you. Let it play out some more. Boss needs to see it all eventually." Caitlan had her forearm on Levi's knee, and she brushed one finger against the cylinder. "And Slate, I'll answer your question. We only have half the information."

"What are you missing?" He stretched his legs out, crossing them at the ankles. His ploy for a quick answer hadn't worked like he'd hoped. Thank God for Caitlan.

"You. Your responses. We don't know that." Levi snapped the trinket up in his hand, and he looped it over Slate's head, pulling it down and tucking it into his shirt. "Besides, sometimes we get new information that we don't expect, but only when you're the one holding it." He looked at the others like this was important. "See, I can answer questions when I want to."

"When you want to." Caitlan said it with a smile.

"Okay, I'm outta here. Got some looking around to take care of. Means I gotta get crackin' if I'm getting my job done. Can't be lazy like some of you folks." Levi held up the nocs to make his point, and then he used the shoulders on either side of him to stand. He twirled, snapping his fingers and pointing one hand at each of them. "You two be good."

He didn't even get to walk away, because that was the point when the trees that weren't really trees exploded around them.

Chapter 51

"FREEZE! No one move!" It was the uniform with the oak leaf, and he had a stretched black weapon in his hand, a long-distance slugthrower. He stepped into the clearing with it pointed high in the air.

A dozen or so blankeyes had come through first, their single stripes telling of their low rank. Laity were the bottom of the rung, and they ran the sweeps in case anything went wrong, keeping the higher-ups safe from harm.

Now they stood around the perimeter, making sure no one escaped. Or got in.

Levi had fallen to the ground when the tumult began, and he still lay in the ferns. Slate caught his eye, and he watched him put his fingers to his lips. Slate winked, and with a measured perfection, he lurched clumsily to his feet.

"What's this all about?" Slate made sure he was loud, and he walked directly away from Levi toward one of the black-attired soldiers with the blank eyes. Even he saw that. They were undoubtedly constructs, at least at some level. True cloning had never been viable, but force-grown constructs were standard fare in most militaries. They wouldn't shoot unless given a specific order, and he guessed they hadn't received that order, or the team would already be dead.

"I said freeze, ser." The uniform turned his way.

"I haven't done anything wrong, so why should I?" He had to keep this up and be as noisy as possible—without getting shot, of course. He didn't want that. He bumped into a low table stacked with supplies, and he made sure to knock it over, stumbling like he had tripped on something and was trying to catch himself.

"Ser, I have warned you twice." The uniform strode his way, walking hard.

"My fault." That was Jonnra, calling from the other side of the camp, and the uniform turned her direction. "I'm sorry, ser. I'm the leader of this archeological team, and Mr. Smith is always trying to take charge. Shame on you, Mr. Smith, and after indulging on the brandy *again*. Nikolai, you get Mr. Smith a wet cloth for his face and sober him up." She walked directly toward the uniform with her hand out. "I am Jonnra Cheerisky, here representing New London Nationoids. How can we help you, ser?"

"That's close enough, ma'am. Stand your ground. Mr. Smith?" He called to Slate. "Stay where we can see you."

Nikolai had a cloth to Slate's face, patting it rather awkwardly, as Slate stumbled along, trying to move as drunkenly as possible

"All the boy is doing is getting him to a place where he can lie down. It's either that or he's in the middle of the path, and we have to step over him." Jonnra smiled. "Again, how can we help you?"

"Who is missing from your party?" The uniform's eyes roamed the group. His mouth was tight.

"Oh, I have no idea." Jonnra was very bright and cheery, and she glanced casually around the clearing. "One or two may be off in the trees, if we can call these plants trees, doing whatever people do in the trees." She smiled. "After all, it wouldn't do to have them do it here, right where we walk, would it?"

"I'm looking for one of these." He pulled a cylinder from his breast pocket, one just like the one around Slate's neck. "Who has it?"

"May I see that?" Jonnra held her hand out, and she made to step forward.

"One more step, ma'am, and this weapon is going to drop you to the ground." He lowered it to point directly at her chest, and he slipped the cylinder back in his pocket.

"Bishop?" She wasn't letting up. "Yes, I believe I'm correct. An oak leaf indicates a bishop, and you have an oak leaf on your collar." She smiled. "And these are all your laity. Very nice. New

Rome, or do you adhere to the Outer Systems Russian Orthodoxy?"

"We do not *adhere* to anything. Unlike the Russian Orthodoxy, New Sabbatical Rome is not a spiritual order, and we do not tolerate moral atrocities in the guise of religious fervor. We do ask fat old women to shut up. Politeness has its place, but you've just forced me to step past mine. Now, will you please move to the side?" It was clearly not a question, and she had quite plainly goaded him past his tolerance threshold.

It was a cunning move. Jonnra had seen the escape being snookered over this man's eyes, and she had leaped into the fray, disregarding all reasonable risk in order to enable the team's goal to be actualized. Slate caught what she was doing as soon as she spoke, as had the rest of the team, and he had immediately accepted the guise of local expedition drunk.

"I want everyone here, in the center, while we search the premises." The bishop motioned with his slugthrower. "Men, walk them in."

"May Mr. Smith—" Jonnra started, pointing Slate's direction.

The gun swung back toward her, and the cleric growled, "The Church does not look lightly on shooting women, but in this case, I have recorded verification that I have taken every step possible to ensure your cooperation, and you have failed to heed my warnings." He held up his wrist to show a bracelet with a blinking green light. His weapon clicked once, and he waited on her.

"I think Mr. Smith has passed out. May he remain there with Nikolai for the time being? You may certainly have one of your laity stand guard over them both, if you wish." She smiled, as if in full cooperation.

"DeLuca." He motioned with his gun, and one of the blankeyes trotted that way. "Everyone else, here." He indicated the space between him and Jonnra Cheerisky. "Leave your things where they are. We will search them as we get to them."

The team began moving in. Talking was muted to the occasional whisper as they sat on the ground or shared the one fallen log Caitlan and Slate had been on earlier. Packs and bedding were handled, and Caitlan's sensor disappeared into one of the laity's pockets. Once the supplies were searched, the black suits began to call out the team members one at a time to manually inspect each pocket and seam of their clothing.

Not even Nikolai or Slate, with his cold compress, escaped the blankeyes' thorough hands.

"I need Ms. Cheerisky front and center." The uniform peeled away from speaking to two of his men and stood erect, with his weapon resting in front of him. At least he no longer pointed it directly at her.

She made her way forward. "It would be nice if I knew your name. It would make all this so much easier."

"Bishop Russo." He didn't sound as if he really wanted to share that information. "I count nineteen in your party. Our instruments indicated twenty before you translated in here. What has happened to your twentieth person?"

"Twenty?" She turned to her team, and she acted as if she were counting every one. "I don't count them on a daily basis, but I don't see who might be missing. Perhaps . . . no, there's Reena, just there. Sometimes Weldon wanders off, but there he is." She waved to him, and he waved back. "You did remember the two men you asked to remain under Layman DeLuca's care?" She smiled at him warmly.

No more had she finished talking than one of the perimeter modules started to whine, quickly climbing in pitch to a scream.

"Ricci. Marino." He motioned with his head, and they took off running. "I intend to know where that missing man is. I am not above coercion."

"That will not be necessary, Bishop Russo. We only ever had eighteen in our party."

The uniform took a deep breath. "I am officially out of patience, Ms. Cheerisky. I want to know where your twentieth man is."

"Please count with me, Bishop. There are only eighteen."

He spat his anger, and he threatened with his weapon, but Jonnra was good. She eventually convinced him to count the team members. Good to her word, they were all eighteen present and accounted for. There had never been nineteen, and twenty? If only New London had consented to send twenty on this expedition, how much easier it would have been.

The erosion of the captives' numbers had begun.

BISHOP RUSSO was livid by the time the archeological team had winnowed to ten. He hadn't caught it at first, with explosions and disturbances erupting all around them. His captives were grouped together, some standing and others sitting, and the two off to the side like before. One of his men guarded the two, and the rest? With two gone to check that, and two to check something else, occasionally he had less than half a dozen guarding the captives.

None were making any effort to escape, anyway, so they were easy to disregard.

Mistake.

The two suns weren't helping. Two sets of shadows meant twice the movements to watch, and his men had been up for nearly sixty hours. Medboosts were keeping them going, but after more than two full days, they couldn't help but begin to slip. His own head was splitting down the middle, and he had better meds than his men.

He had lost a day and a half, his ship, and his deacon in skipping after these people, and now they were slipping away from him. Right through the trees, *ferns,* whatever. And he needed that updated transfer capsule, even though a lot of good it would do. Without a live conversation, he only had half what he needed, and without that cylinder, he had no idea what age his quarry was in this reality. He could be any one of these people, and there was no way for him to know.

He was having to do it all on his own, and wasn't this fun?

"DeLuca!" He stood, and he looked across the clearing. Where was the man? "Mancini? Where's DeLuca off to?" He called to one of the men on the perimeter.

"DeLuca, ser?" Mancini looked puzzled.

"Layman Abert DeLuca. I assigned him watch over the . . . who's watching the drunk?" There was no one there.

"Drunk, ser? I'm not sure what you mean."

"The man who passed out when we first arrived. Drunk, and why are you asking me about DeLuca?"

"Ser, there never has been a DeLuca with us. It's just the five of us." He motioned with his head, and true enough, there were the two of them, and three other men guarding the perimeter.

Something was eating his crew, and Russo knew one thing. He had better get out of here before it came for him.

Chapter 52

"I CAN'T go through that mirror, can I?" Slate could see rooms inside, with tables of food, entertainment modules, and comfortable couches. Bookcases lined two walls, and people sat around with fat cigars and servants gliding to and fro. It was an old-fashioned world of upper-class privilege, and it looked pretty good to him.

"You can." That was Caitlan. "But you don't want to."

Slate thought he probably did. Food. Lots of it. And something besides logs to sit on.

Levi had gotten away as he'd hoped, later showing up at his side and taking the cylinder from his neck, even as the blank-eyed guard had stood over him. Those ferns had proved a life saver.

Then he'd gotten busy.

Timeslip. That's what Levi called it. With enough time, he said he could reprogram the mirrors, just not on the spur of the moment. It took time and concentration.

Well, with the rest of them all rounded up, he'd had some free time on his hands, and he'd gotten to thinking. Tweak the timeflow through one of the mirrors, and that would make the world inside into a slip bubble, and anyone inside would be trapped in that alternate reality.

They would also disappear from this one. A slip bubble didn't just change the flow of time; it rewrote the time linkages between you and the outside world. That's what Levi was doing, using the nocs to create temporary temporal windows—portable and very fleeting mirrors—that swallowed the laity one at a time. The team? They had to crawl away. Otherwise they would find themselves in a slip. The slips were apparently not a good way to travel. Stay in long enough, and the world forgot who you were, just as the blankeyes were forgetting their companions. It took longer for those with higher cognitive abilities, but they would eventually begin to forget, also.

"Levi's brilliant. I should tell him that."

"You just did." Caitlan smiled.

"I'm not going to pretend to understand that. Do they die? Through that mirror. Do they die when they're trapped inside?"

"Hardly." They had been slowly pulling their supplies from the enemy camp, and Caitlan was preparing them for their next translation. Slate was handing her the items, and she was redistributing them. She watched her hands as she talked. "There's so much you don't know, and I can't tell you all of it."

"Yes, you can." He said it with emphasis, like he really wanted her to. He hoped she got that.

"No. I really can't. You have to understand and be ready, and you're not."

"Timeslips, traveling through mirrors, and a hologram that knows half a conversation I haven't had yet? You think I'm not ready?" He shook his head.

"You'll know when you're ready. We're here to help you get there." She set the last of the packs on the ground. "We'll have to find a new mirror. We can't use this one."

"The timeslip. Right." He could see the half-dozen men inside. Eight, actually. Then, as he watched, another one appeared through the glass as if walking into the room. He was in tails, a white tie, and a top hat. He carried a cane. One of the servants stepped up to take his hat and cane, and the man reached for a drink in a tumbler. The whole thing happened at a reduced pace, as if the time streams weren't quite lined up. "How does Levi do that? They even have period-correct clothing on."

"You'll understand it all someday. For now, just trust that he can, and it's going to help us be successful."

Nikolai came running through the ferns, and he called out, "He's about to pull the last soldiers in. Get ready to hightail it out. Caitlan, my pack?" He ran up, panting, with a hand out, taking one that she held out to him. "With this many inside, it's going to be big this time." He was off and running. The others were scrambling, coming by and grabbing packs of their own.

"What's going to be big?"

"This." She slapped the side of the mirror. "We've done this before, you know."

Slate watched as four more men appeared on the other side of the mirror.

"How many?"

"Thirteen."

"They're all in. Here." She handed him his pack. "When Levi gets here, be ready to run." She worked hers onto her shoulders.

Levi came running, three other people in tow, and he had a large rock in one hand and the nocs in the other. He had a grin on his face. "Here, Boss!" He tossed the nocs to him. "My pack?"

"Take this one." Caitlan handed him one, and he yanked it over a shoulder.

"Ready?" He yelled it to those around him like a cheer.

The rest, Caitlan included, yelled back, "Ready!"

"Now!" He backed up and hurled the rock through the mirror. The glass shattered, and the scene inside fractured into a thousand pieces, the image of the men inside shattering with it.

Everyone tore off as fast as they could go, and Slate fell in with them, unsure just why they were running so hard.

"I thought they didn't die." He was beside Caitlan, and he was about to be angry.

"Trust me."

"That looked pretty dead. Levi *shattered* them." He spat the word.

"You still don't—"

An explosion rocked the air, and the ground under their feet shivered. Immediately, everyone stopped running, and they began to drop their packs. Gasping for air, one or two had their hands on their knees, leaning forward; and a couple knelt to sit on the ground.

Slate was incensed at all of them. He found Levi, and he yanked him around. "You killed those people."

"Hold on. Let me catch my breath." He put his hand on Slate's shoulder as he leaned over, gasping for air.

"No." Slate swept his arm off. "You killed those men, and on purpose. They couldn't fight back, and you just killed them. Who do you people think you are?" He turned to the rest of the group that he had thought were his friends. "You killed innocent people. Who's next? Me?"

Everyone was silent.

"Boss." Levi placed his hand on Slate's shoulder.

"Don't touch." He tried to shake the hand off, but he couldn't.

"Look at me, Boss. Please."

Slate turned. Green eyes. At that point, he hated green eyes. Especially vivid green eyes.

"Do you trust us?"

He had, he thought. He had called Levi brilliant, and he'd meant it. He felt his emotions well up, and he didn't know how he felt. He wasn't sure who he was, who the people with him were, or what they were doing. How could he trust anything?

"Do you trust me?"

Those green eyes bored into him, and that face, so serious. Yes, he trusted him. He had to. And no, after seeing that, how could he?

"Idiot!" Caitlan slapped Levi on the shoulder. "Just tell him. Boss, Levi saved those people."

Slate looked at her. "I saw them shatter. And what about that explosion?"

She smiled. "You saw the *doorway* shatter. That keeps anyone else from getting trapped. That explosion? Temporal feedback from the timeslip. It always does that, and we've learned to run hard when we have to shatter a mirror."

"So, what happens to them?"

"They smoke cigars, get drunk, and generally have a good time." That was Jonnra, the comment called from off some distance, and said with her matter-of-fact manner that always seemed so in control of the situation.

Robert Nambonsik, who rarely interjected his opinion into public discussions, growled, "Sounds pretty good to me."

Slate looked at his companions. Several were smiling, and the rest were waiting on him, as if his opinion counted. He shook his head. "Can somebody just tell me next time?"

The group broke out in a sprinkling of relieved laughter, and Levi threw one arm around him, slapping him on the back. Before he let him go, he pulled him tight and said into his ear, "Trust me?"

Slate pushed him away. He grabbed him on either side of his neck, and he studied his face. After a moment, he looked away.

"What?" Levi reached and slapped his hands on Slate's arms. "What, Boss?"

He looked up. "You asked if I trust you." He laughed.

"And?" Levi fought a smile, like he knew the answer already.

"Are my eyes really green?"

"Oh, you betcha, Boss. They don't come any greener."

"Boo-ya!" He pushed Levi away, laughing. "I *love* this. All of it! Let's find another mirror to jump through." He grabbed his pack in one hand and started down the path.

"I hear you called me brilliant." Levi fell in beside him. "Is that true?"

"Are you?" Slate teased him.

"You tell me." He looked like he really wanted to hear it.

Slate laughed. "How green are my eyes?"

Levi hooted and spun in a complete circle. He leaped to put his arm around Sundra, and he crooned, "I am so brilliant, and you know it's so."

"Slate, you didn't—" She pushed Levi away and pointed to him, as he darted to his next victim.

Levi was already off, though, telling everyone he could chase down.

Slate laughed, and he looked up. They were walking under a lemon sky with two suns for company. This was turning out to be a pretty good day.

And nothing could take that away.

Chapter 53

THEY found their mirror at the back of a cave. The nocs had pointed them the right direction, but locating the mirror had taken hours. The world on the other side was a cityscape, but it was in the middle of its night. The team had engaged the mirror to lock its coordinates, and they were camping out until daybreak. Jonnra had volunteered to serve as their psychic link, so she slept at its side.

Slate and Levi were down to shorts and Tees. It hadn't cooled off at all, and there would be no fresh clothes this night. Or showers. The mirrors were one way, he found out, when he suggested stepping through and back again.

Slate lay on his pants, with his pack for a pillow, and his arms behind his head. He would be asleep already, except for the man at his side.

"Try it." Levi sat cross-legged, with his arms on his knees. There was just enough light from the cave entrance that they could see each other well, and he held the silver tube of metal. He dangled it in front of Slate. "No one's watching, so there's no pressure."

"No pressure. Just save the human race." Slate watched Levi grin, and he felt the pressure just fine.

"Do it." His eyes sparkled with anticipation.

"And if it doesn't work?" He was teasing now, just to see Levi squirm.

"It will. Just do it."

"Give it here." Slate grabbed it in his fist. "Let's see what I have to say to myself tonight."

"Let's." Levi edged closer. "This is so cool." His voice shook with anticipation. The little hologram began to spin up. Before it could solidify, it flickered and froze.

"So, what does this mean?"

Levi let out his breath, filling his cheeks with air, and then releasing it with a whistling noise. "I don't know. Is it still warm?"

"Ye-*ah*. Hot, in fact. Very hot."

Levi shrugged. "I've used it constantly, and I've never had it freeze. It always plays one of the stories for me."

"Stories. Have you counted them?" Slate shook his hand. It was really hot, and he wondered if he should let go. "You sure it won't explode?"

"Don't think so." He held out his hand. "Give it to me."

Slate let it drop, and as soon as it hit Levi's hand, the white-haired man jerked back, sending the little tube skittering across the rocky cave floor.

"Ouch!" Levi flexed his hand, blowing into it. "That should not have happened."

"Told you it was hot." Slate sat up and reached for it.

"It wasn't hot. It shocked me!" Levi sounded betrayed, as if a trusted companion had turned on him.

"Maybe we'll try it tomorrow." Slate leaned forward to pick it up, and it leaped away from him.

"It definitely shouldn't have done that." Levi hesitantly reached for it, and this time, it jumped into his hand. "Weird."

"See if it does its thing for you." Slate nodded at it.

Levi folded his hand around it, and after a bit, the holo head spun up as usual. This time it turned not to Slate, but to Levi.

"Hi, little head." Levi grinned.

"And hi to you, little buddy." Holo-Slate had an impish look. "Tell the other me hi, too," and holo-Slate motioned that direction with a nod of his head.

"I'm supposed to tell you—"

"No, that's not what I said. Don't say I'm supposed to. Just do it." The head wasn't smiling this time.

"Hello, Slate." Levi watched the head.

"Impolite. Try again. Look at him when you say it."

Levi giggled like a little boy. "How's it doing that?" He glanced at Slate. "This is like a real conversation."

"Well, it's not, but you can still do it correctly. Look at me, the real one, not this one, and tell me hello. Sound like you mean it, too." The head nodded Slate's direction again. "Now. Do it."

"Hello, Slate." Levi looked at him this time, and the head seemed satisfied.

"Thank you. Now, you can't rush this, so don't try. What I need you—"

Levi looked at Slate, laughing. "It's like it's talking to me. This is *so* cool!"

"Levi, look at me. Not that me, this me. Down here." When he did, the head continued. "Don't be rude. Your mother didn't raise you that way. Listen when I talk to you. I'm not doing this for my health." The holo-head took a deep breath and rolled his eyes. "Well, actually, I am, but I'm doing it for real-Slate's health, not mine, and that's another discussion. Here's the point. You can't rush this. Let me do this when I'm ready. Are you with me?"

"What if it breaks again?" He glanced at Slate and back to the holo-figure.

"Look at me when you talk to me. It didn't break. I did that."

"How . . . how did you know he'd, um, you'd be holding this right then?"

"Everything happens when it happens, and I plan around that."

"But, you're . . . here right now. You're talking to me, for the first time."

"Not exactly, kiddo. Let's clear this up. I'm pausing and giving you a chance to talk."

"So, all those other times when you were talking to yourself, um, I mean the real Slate—" He looked up. "—sorry—" And he looked down again. "—you were just pausing?"

"To give me a chance to reply. Yep."

"And that shocky thing? Because you did shock me." That statement was filled with accusation.

"To get you to pay attention, that's all. Things happen when they happen, so don't rush me. Well, thing are a bit of a blur past tonight, so I don't know exactly what happens for the next several days, not exactly. So, just do what you do best. Help me out and be extraordinary. And don't lord that around. The women already think you have a big head. Just be good to me. The real me. I'm going to need you critically. Please tell Jonnra I'm sorry. I'd help if I could, but there's nothing I can do. Oh, and one last thing. It's the firestone you want, not the rosestone. Got that? It's the firestone. Oh, and Slate can hold the transfer tube now. Say goodnight, Slate." The face looked away, and it was gone.

Levi looked at Slate, wide-eyed. "Good night, Slate." He held out the silver tube.

"I heard it." Slate grinned. "How'd you do that? I see what you mean that it's, what did you call it, cool?"

Levi nodded. "I didn't do that. I've never seen that one before. It's never talked to me like that."

"Wait, wait, let me see." Slate held up his arm, and he looked at it. "If I had a watch, it'd say April 1. Have you heard of April 1?" He grabbed Levi's knee and squeezed, and hard.

"Stop!" Levi jerked at the sudden pressure, and he tried to force the hand off. "No, no, yes, I know what April is, stop!" By that time he was on his back and yelling out.

Slate let go, grinning. "It's April Fool's Day."

"What's that?" Levi rubbed his knee.

"A day when you see how big a prank you can get someone to fall for. I just fell for the biggest." He chuckled. "It was a good one, Levi. I said you were brilliant, but to pull this off? That's not a big enough word for you. Stupendous. Absolutely stupendous. You and me? We're going to be the best team this world has ever known."

"It wasn't a prank." Levi dropped the cylinder onto Slate's chest. "I think you'd better keep that with you."

"It's yours. You keep it." Slate picked it up and tossed it back. "Besides, it was getting on my nerves. It makes my tattoo itch."

"How bad?"

"Pretty much. I've started to wonder if it might be infected. Can't do anything about it if it is, so I haven't mentioned it." He pulled his shirt over his head and wadded it in his lap. "Right here." He pushed his finger against the muscle right above the nipple. Then he scratched at it.

"Is it different than it was?"

"How should I know? It's not like we've got mirrors everywhere." He laughed. "Oh, right, we do, don't we? Not that we can see ourselves in them."

"Before, when it moved, it was always at night. I don't guess we have to worry about that here." Levi pointed to the cave entrance. "There is no night."

"Then I can use this for a pillow." Slate held up the shirt. "Besides, I'll be asleep. I'm not going to know what it does." He

255

laughed, putting the shirt under his head for extra padding.

Levi adjusted his pants, rolled for a pillow. "I could use a bed of ice about now. And a blanket to cover with." He was on his back, and he put his hands under his head. "Humans aren't designed for worlds this hot."

"Right, there, but forget a blanket. I want a full-blown mattress." Slate kicked him in the leg. "You remember that the next time you drag me along. If you were really as smart as people think you are, you'd have that pack make mattresses."

"You know, if I retune—"

"Stop it. Just go to sleep." Slate chuckled. "You can make me a mattress tomorrow night."

"Sure, Boss. That I can do." But he kicked him back, laughing. "Paybacks."

Farther back in the cave they heard, "You guys ever sleep?"

After that, everything grew quiet, until Levi started to snore.

Slate reached for his shirt, and he slipped it on. He didn't want to know if the tattoo moved while he slept. What had Nikolai asked? That itch means something, right? Well, it was itching a lot now. A whole lot.

Nothing good would come of his tattoo, especially if the itching meant bad things were going to happen. He didn't need bad things to happen. Not now. Not ever. And especially not for the people with him in this cave. He just wanted to get them all home safe and sound. Oh, and save humanity in the process. He laughed at that, even as he heard Levi turn and mumble something in his sleep.

He only scratched the tattoo once, and then he forced himself to leave it alone, sort of as a good luck omen. They needed one, if they were going to finish what they needed to do.

Chapter 54

IT JUST happened to be Jonnra's bad luck to be psychically linked and sleeping next to the mirror.

That was why she died first.

After the near-disaster with the clerics, she'd truly taken responsibility for the success of the mission. Of course, the real responsibility fell back onto the core members of the team: Caitlan, Sundra, Levi, and Slate. The other sixteen were support personnel. Even so, Jonnra now considered herself the number one indispensable support person on the team.

The mirrors were one way. However, that didn't mean they could only be used one way. One way through might lead to one world. The way back might be from a completely different location. After all, when you look in a mirror, you see what's reflected back at you, not what's reflected back at the person on the other side. That's what controlled where the mirrors went: what you could see.

The team had looked out on a cityscape, but something on a blood-red world was looking back at them.

And it was a furious blood-red world.

They were big, and winged, and fanged. Hungry, too, or at least to judge by how quickly they ate. The first one came through the mirror, and it landed right on Jonnra as she slept. She never got a chance to wake before it ripped into her chest. It munched juicily as its brethren flew in overhead.

They swarmed the cave, screeching their fury, one for each one on the other side of their mirror. You'd think it was planned, the numbers matching so well, one hungry predator for each fleshy human. And that cave, with the mirror so deeply inside.

Who would have thought of that?

Perhaps there was a reason this world was a place of eternal daylight. Or maybe that was the reason the mirror was hidden so well. Either way, that mirror was the perfect opportunity for evil to come sweeping through.

Are devils real? They were that night.

Robert Nambonsik wasn't two meters from Jonnra. That two meters gave him time to cry out, "Firedevils," before his throat was removed from his body.

Nikolai Borovsky was young, and he was strong. That was why he was hired. Only seventeen, he was also very quick. When Robert Nambonsik let out his cry, Nikolai instinctively leaped for the entrance to the cave. He might have made it, too, except for the seventeen people blocking his path. It was ironic, in a way. One person for each year of his life. They slowed him down enough that he lost his life, seventeen for seventeen.

He woke all seventeen up, though, giving them at least a fighting chance for survival.

And he took one very mean firedevil with him when he died.

Yellow light, very yellow light on a yellow world with a yellow sky does not bode well for a red devil from a red world with a red sun. That red and winged firedevil had claimed Nikolai for its own, and it swooped forward, grasping him with its talons just as Nikolai reached the door. Sweeping skyward with a dying Nikolai in its clutches, the red devil landed and began to feast. Yet, it was a red devil under a yellow sun. Twin yellow suns, in fact.

And the devil died before it could take its second bite.

The other nineteen devils knew better, and they remained inside.

Where they feasted.

Not everyone died. Not then. The entrance to the cave was what mattered. Reach that magic portal, and the gift of the gods was life, even if it was not the desired life beyond that distant mirror. Beener Baity managed to dive through the mirror during a lull in the surging flood of devils. Reena Jericho was right on his heels. However, a devil followed them through, followed by two more, and the five were lost to another world.

Weldon Sikes? He was a large man, and when he fell, his size covered petite Caitlan Trotter just enough that if she had held very still, she might have escaped her impending demise, that was if she hadn't screamed so loudly.

Renaud Lautrec had used a large stone for a pillow, and with it, he smashed the skull of one of the firedevils. Another one took its place, and it had a double feast, first on Renaud, and next on one of its own.

Cheeky and Roni were just tidbits on the way to someone else.

Both Levi and Slate, sleeping closest to the entrance, managed to get through the portal, thanks to Nikolai's unintentional warning. Barely. They tumbled over each other and landed in a heap, still clawing for safety, with arms and legs tangled, even as Nikolai's monster melted under the yellow light of the sun.

Slate rolled over and retched, feeling the deaths one by one.

The monsters screamed and they fought, beating at the magic portal, and wanting outside. They scorched their wings and burned their feet, and they blinded their eyes.

And finally, unable to see, they feasted on one another.

Three days later, Levi and Slate managed to find the courage to venture back into the cave. The carnage was more the odor of death, rather than the evidence of it. The creatures had consumed everything that was not bone.

Everything.

Jonnra's remains lay where she'd died, right in front of the mirror, next to the putrefied remains of the final firedevil.

"I'm so sorry, Jonnra." Slate knelt at her side. "You didn't have time to run. You were the first to die." He stood to find Levi with tears pouring down his face.

"I didn't get a chance to tell her." He wiped his eyes with his shoulders, sliding his upper arms across the sides of his face. The streaks on his cheeks were dull rivulets of pain in the dim cave light. "You told me to, and I didn't know what you meant."

"It wasn't me. If I'd known this was going to happen, we'd have run from this cave."

"Break the mirror. We have to break it." Levi sniffled and looked away. "We can't let those *things* out ever again."

"Look." Slate pointed to the scene in the mirror. It was a night sky, truly a night sky, with no world in sight. Space, once known as the final frontier. "The mirror has moved on. Don't you think it's moved on for those creatures, too?"

"But how else can I say I'm sorry?" He wiped at his face with the backs of his hands.

"I think you already did." Slate grabbed his shoulder and squeezed it. "They know. And if they don't, I know, and if they can't figure it out, I'll find them and tell them for you."

Even if it takes me to the end of creation and back, but he didn't say that aloud. He didn't think he had to. He was sure Levi understood just fine.

Chapter 55

"LEVI, do you have that necklace?" Slate came running down the path to find the blond-haired man at the water's edge, still overcome by guilt days later.

"Does it matter?" He had on the shorts he'd been sleeping in. Not much had survived the firedevils' assault.

"You were wearing it—" He stopped abruptly at Levi's side, to see his neck empty.

"I'm not, now." He looked down, picked up a stone, and tossed it into the water.

"That night in the cave." Slate squatted beside him, watching his face. "You tried to give it to me, and I tossed it back. You put it on."

"And if I did?" He tossed another stone.

"Do you remember what he said? What I said?" Slate laughed at that as he twisted his legs underneath himself and sat beside Levi. His movements were quick and filled with enthusiasm. An idea had come to him, something the little head had said.

"He was talking to me. It doesn't matter." Levi held one hand balled into a fist alongside his face, and he looked up into the sky. Part of the cord glistened in the light from the twin suns. "We should have known, but how could we? If I were better, I could have adjusted the mirror, checked it, done something to keep everyone safe."

"It would have happened, anyway. Did you hear what I said when I was talking with you? I knew what was going to happen, that people would die. How did I say it? That there wasn't anything else. That meant I didn't know what was going to happen next. I think I understand what that means. The man in the hologram knows the future, or at least parts of it. Come on." He shook Levi's shoulder. "You've been innovative and resourceful. Everything you've done has been amazing, and because of you, we're going to win. Don't let all this get you down." He held out his hand. "Right now I need to replay the message from that night."

Levi opened his hand, dropping the cylinder into Slate's, but he didn't look at him. "It won't even play for me, now. It's like it's dead. Either that or I am." The water had begun to wash up under him, the rising tide eating the beach, but he didn't seem to notice. The back of his shorts had darkened with the incoming current.

"It's working." Slate grinned. The device was warming already in his hand.

"Even if it does, it won't be the same. They never repeat right away."

"You said—"

"After weeks, sometimes months, if you play them enough. There are a lot."

The head began to materialize, and it rotated around. "Ah, there you are." It looked at Slate.

"So, a normal conversation?"

"Of course." The holo-Slate nodded.

"This is going to be weird."

"Not as weird as me having my end of this conversation. Did you get it figured out?"

Slate looked at Levi, to see him watching the discussion. He smiled and turned back to the little man.

"That was Levi?"

"Yes. We're here—"

"I know." Holo-Slate laughed, looking off to the side. "See? There he is, right there. How did I miss that? He's been there all along. He survived, and I didn't pick up on it." He turned back to them. "You're there on the beach. That's a nice world. I'm so sorry about your team. Worse, I'm sorry about what has to happen next."

"Next?"

"You want to know how I knew to tell you to look for the

firestone, don't you?" The little Slate was very earnest and somber.

"That's right. I realized, those, um, creatures. They're called firedevils. Well, firestone. How could I miss it?" He grinned. "It's staring me in the face, and I'm so stupid. Of course that's the answer."

"You have to go there."

Levi let his head fall backwards, squeezing his eyes closed. "Go there? The devils' world? No. No, no. We're not doing that." As pale as he was, his face became even whiter.

"There's no other way. You get it, don't you, Slate?"

"This was why you weren't ready to talk to me the last time, wasn't it?"

"I'm so sorry. The firedevils hadn't happened yet, and without them, you wouldn't make the connection."

"So," and Slate looked at the little man, before he let his eyes shift to include Levi. "How do we do that?"

"I think," and holo-Slate reached to scratch his head, in the same way real-Slate remembered doing when he didn't want to make a difficult decision, "I think it's time to tell you your last name."

"Not that." Levi grabbed Slate's wrist, and he squeezed it tightly. "Not today. Please. I can't lose you, not yet." He looked into Slate's face with pleading in his eyes.

"I'm sorry, Levi." The little Slate looked away, his face running through a number of conflicting emotions. Then, it was as if he came to a decision, and with determination in his eyes, looked once more to big Slate. "I understand this part, now. I can't tell you your name. Your son has to. Once again, this ends at an awkward point, but that's all I can tell you. Good luck, Slate."

The hologram winked out.

"Son?" Slate looked at Levi. "I don't get that."

Levi took a very deep breath and held it a very long time. He turned to Slate and grimaced before straightening his face. "Ready?"

"He said," and Slate held out the necklace, "my son would tell me."

"That's right." Levi smiled apologetically.

"Not you." Slate shook his head. "We're—" He pointed back and forth with his hand. "—the same age."

"It'll make more sense to you when I tell you. I can see it now, why they had to die. It wouldn't have worked before. None of it. All the realities have come together in this one. It all makes sense, now."

"All the realities?" Slate felt his heart in his temples. This was making too much sense to him, and that didn't make sense.

"You had to learn to be you, and you had to learn to fight them. I never understood it, not really, until now." Tears were shining on Levi's cheeks. "You had to know what it meant to be human, even if it took the deaths of everyone around you."

"No!" Slate didn't like the sound of that. "No more deaths. None." He looked up, and he stood, turning in a circle and shouting to the sky. "No more deaths on this world. I will not let another person die!"

"You said I was magnificent." Levi looked out over the water. "I'm not. You're the one who's magnificent. You will be, and you don't even know what you are."

"I'm not magnificent, not if people have to die." Slate took the silver trinket, and he threw it hard out to sea. He could barely see where it hit the water, and he was glad it was gone. "Magnificence keeps everyone alive."

"And that's why you will be magnificent, Slate Knalb."

And the sky opened, and the sea opened, and Slate's head opened, and all of creation fell inside.

In that moment of total understanding, reality snapped, and everything was different.

Chapter 56

THIRTEEN men in black uniforms appeared in a room, mysteriously, as if out of nowhere.

It was, too, because they had been nowhere, and now they were somewhere. It wasn't necessarily a place they'd grow to love, either. Disorientation ruled in the absence of any higher authority. For a moment each man remembered fine whiskey, comfortable chairs, and the slightly sweet smell of tightly-rolled cigars. For that short moment of pleasurable animation, they had known something more than the daily grind of blank-eyed existence.

The twelve who would forget first were the lucky ones, although they might not consider it that way with what was coming next.

Bishop Russo would remember longer, although the bulk of the memories would eventually fade for him, also.

The door burst open, and a cardinal and three archbishops strode in, their steps hard on the unadorned floor. Their stars and silver eagles caught the light. They were followed by a half-dozen deacons, two priests, and a gaggle of laity. Geese in a row. Backups for image and solidarity against that which was of dangerous mien. Within minutes, busy hands had chairs laid out, tables unfolded, and the banner of the Church unfurled and on the wall.

Centered in front of the banner, a cross was mounted, with the slogan etched into the crossbeam: Rage With Sorrow, For God Will

Know His Own.

The cardinal with his three stars took the center chair. His archbishops, eagles gleaming, filled in right and left. One of the priests —one bar only—was prepared to record the proceedings.

The deacons were there to command the laity, and the twelve men moved into position, staked in twos around the perimeter of the room.

"Bishop Russo, please step forward." The priest stood and called out his name. She held out a rectangular slab, and he rested his hand on it. When it turned from yellow to green, she placed it on the table in front of her, with a brighter green light blinking on the end. "Identification complete. Bishop Abdenago Gianni Russo, NSR Battle Cruiser *Fist of God*, now missing-in-action, representing New Florence Citystate, New Sabbatical Rome. Cardinal Salvatore Moretti overseeing with Archbishops Gallo, Conti, and Lombardi in attendance. Interrogation may commence."

"Where is my ship?" The cardinal's collar bulged and shifted, making his stars gleam.

It was what they were really here for. The officers that had been lost? They were incidental. Laity? Home-grown military meat. Anyway, military service was fraught with risk, and in time of war, men will die. That was a given. The hope might be that the duty of death will always fall to another, but it has to fall to someone, and when it's time, then God have mercy on our souls.

Today the living suffered. They did live, for they had not died. That didn't satisfy the cardinal, though.

"In a slip bubble?" He roared the words. "You let this *child* trap you in a *slip bubble*?"

The tribunal went downhill from there, at least from the viewpoint of the survivors. Their punishment? They were given the dubious honor of boarding yet another ship and jumping back into the chaos.

And it was chaos, both now and in the upcoming future. God alone knew who would win.

In a slip bubble of their own, the tribunal went on for subjective weeks, but it eventually reached its end, all the information gathered and strained through the military sieve of cardinal, archbishop, archbishop, and archbishop. The resulting consensus: The atrocity had been allowed to escape one more time, and they had no idea where it'd gone.

One by one the black uniforms winked out, Russo the last, back onto a vessel to forge once more among the stars.

It seemed there was no rest for the wicked, or for the very good, or even for the soldiers of God.

But then, the Church had moved on many centuries before, and where was God to be found in the wide universe, if not back where he started? That was a long way away. In this place, and in this time, the cardinal was in control.

Cardinal Moretti exited as hard as he had entered, and he stepped into a world that was only five minutes gone from when he had begun. Humanity couldn't waste weeks with military nonsense such as dragging careless caretakers of military armament over the coals.

But five minutes? There were always five minutes to spare. Now, though, it was time to get back to war.

Chapter 57

THE TABLE glowed with red fire, and blood-colored walls shimmered. The images that told of what was, what is, and what might be to come spoke only one story now.

Death is coming.

Death is coming.

Death is coming.

What was it really saying? Death is already here, and the story can no longer be changed.

A lone face watched over the table, and its skin was the color of blood. As it stared, frozen in its dismay, the wheel turned, and death could be seen everywhere.

Chapter 58

THIS time there was no hesitation.

Stretched among the stardust and dreams, a taut spiderweb of time and space joined the cosmos. The lines hummed with possibilities.

The finger reached forth, playing them as a harp, plucking here, touching there, and creating music such as had never been sung before.

The oil danced to the song.

When the strings finally moved as one in a single melody heard across the vastness of the universe, the hand withdrew to see what it had wrought and called it good.

Chapter 59

HE AWOKE.

He blinked his eyes, and all was blackness. He closed them, and he could tell no difference.

He blinked again, and he had a thousand eyes, a thousand-million eyes, and he breathed in the air of a thousand worlds.

He called it good.

The evening and the morning were his first day.

HE AWOKE, and through his thousand-million eyes, there was light.

He looked up and found red and blue and orange and yellow surrounding him, and he called it sky.

He looked down and saw seas of liquid ammonia, nitrogen, water, and plasma. He breathed in their gasses, and they enriched his soul.

He called them good.

The evening and the morning were his second day.

HE AWOKE, and he was hungry.

He searched among his many parts, and he found dry land.

He feasted on the grains and grasses.

He was full, and he called it good.
The evening and the morning were his third day.

HE AWOKE, and he was alone.
He looked out from his many eyes past that which he knew, and lights filled his skies.
He called the most numerous of these the stars, the brightest the suns, and the closest the moons.
He basked in their warmth, and he called it good.
The evening and the morning were his fourth day.

HE AWOKE, and he looked out over the waters.
He touched the waters and found them filled with life.
He looked into the skies and saw the winged creatures that flew.
He smiled at them, and he called it good.
The evening and the morning were his fifth day.

HE AWOKE, and he looked for himself.
He touched the minds of the animals, and they knew him not.
He reached unto mankind and found a kindred spirit.
He bonded with man, and he knew who he was.
The evening and the morning were his sixth day.

HE AWOKE, and he learned of death.
He learned of fear and evil and goodness and hope.
He learned of family and friends.
He learned that life is precious and must be protected.
On the seventh day, he went to war.

Chapter 60

THE MAN that was Slate opened his eyes and felt the air of a thousand worlds enter his lungs. He knew not that he drew in the air of a thousand worlds. He simply breathed.

In that pivotal moment, a thousand worlds changed.

He thought the simplest of thoughts, letting the barest flicker of awareness enter his brain. Lightning flashed in the skies of a thousand worlds.

He knew life, and a hundred thousand volcanoes burst forth, solar flares ripped through the skies of ten thousand worlds, and the stars knew his name.

He did not, though. He was simply a man, a lowly man, with small thoughts, small needs, and smaller ambitions.

He contained his thoughts, and the skies on a thousand worlds cleared, a hundred thousand volcanoes quieted, and solar flares contorting the coronas of a thousand suns ceased to flare.

He looked through the eyes of a million wildebeests as they roamed the African veldt, and he soared the skies with the fifty thousand kites of Creighton. He died ten million deaths on the fishing ships of Noah's Bain, and he breathed along with a billion souls who took their first breaths.

He died anew with each death of each human who faced his final hour, and the pain seared him for all time.

He felt the anguish of the fatherless, and he knew the joy of giving life.

He learned to love, and in that, he knew his humanity as he knew nothing else.

"LEVI."

He called, gently, afraid to call quickly, insistently. He must reach, but he must not touch.

"Levi."

When there was no response, he waited.

"LEVI."

A stirring. Awakening and not understanding.

"Levi."

"What? Who's there?"

"Levi."

"Stop that. Who are you?" Fear filled the words.

"Levi. It is me. I do not wish for you to be afraid."

"Go away. I was sleeping."

"Go back to sleep, Levi."

He would wait, but not for long. War was coming. War was here.

It was time to go to war.

And still, he knew he must wait.

"BISHOP RUSSO."

"Who is that?"

"I am him whom you seek."

"Don't play games with me, and how are you doing this?"

"I am speaking with you. That is all."

"Tell me now, or get out of my head."

"I am not in your head. I am in your walls and in your skies and in the water that you drink."

"Are you the invasion? Are you how humanity dies?" Bishop Russo's voice began to shake.

"I am how humanity lives. You sought me, and I have come to you. I wish to be your ally."

"To do what?" He was more in control now.

"We have a common enemy. We must work together."

"What enemy?"

"You know of whom I speak, the bringers of dreams, those who would use humanity to spread their seeds among the stars."

"The Secharri." Said with certainty.

"You know of whom I speak."

"And you are—oh, God, it is you. You've found me."

"Not God, Bishop Russo, but yes. I have found you."

"Now what?"

"It is time to go to war."

"THIS kills me! Another failed memory node! Can't anybody except me do anything right?" Levi, master programmer, son, warrior, seventeen-year-old prodigy, and inarguable genius, was half in and half out of a partially disassembled mainframe computer. Edgy music blasted in the background.

Occasionally he reached a hand out and felt for a tool before disappearing back into the recesses of the machine.

He muttered sourly, "I remember being *in* the mainframe. It was a lot more fun than *working* on the mainframe." He snorted his opinion of computers that broke instead of doing the job they were designed to do.

"Levi." The word tumbled into the musical cacophony filling the room, fitting nicely into but not quite part of the song.

"Yes?" Levi pulled out of the mainframe he was rebuilding and looked around. He heard his answer disappear into the music, and he called again, louder. "Yes?" When there was no response, he shrugged and leaned back into the machine.

"Levi."

This time he looked out with a frown, irritated at the continued disruption, and seeing no one, he stood, his tools still in his hands. "Well, where are you?"

"You said I would be magnificent. I said no one else must die."

Levi took a deep breath, recognizing those words. "Could you use a speaker?" He felt his voice tremble.

"Is this better?" The voice boomed into the room, coinciding with but overriding the music's vibrant beat.

"Music off." Butterflies filled his stomach, turning it upside down. "You can talk normally, now." He felt the smile on his face.

"Better?" The voice's intensity no longer rattled the windows.

"Loud, but okay. I thought we lost you. You're Slate, right?" Dad, he'd wanted to say. It was what he'd started to believe from spending so much time with the AI in all those alternate realities.

"Slate. Let me taste the name. It . . . seems flavorful. It that what

I am called?"

"Oh, buddy!" Levi felt his throat tighten with excitement, and he could barely talk. "You—" He stopped and cleared his throat. "You're real, and you're back. This is so exciting. It's been two years, and I thought I'd failed."

"Is a year . . . long?" The words, sterile and calm.

"The last two, yes. I'm heading into the hallway. Can you follow me there?"

"I can follow you anywhere."

"Over the speakers?"

"If there are speakers, I can excite the membranes to produce sound."

"Oh, this is so cool." Levi panted with excitement. He was also running to his office.

"You are but a boy." The statement implied surprise.

"Hey, don't get sassy. You're not even that."

"I remember you older, that is all."

"Hey." Levi stopped. "How do you know what I look like?" He glanced around as if he could see God's eye looking at him through the ceiling.

"I have access to approximately 2,586 video feeds within 500 meters. You have been picked up on—"

"Enough. You don't have to go on." He turned a circle and clapped his hands together. "Ye-*ah*! This is so right! Hey!" He looked up, his excitement overwhelming him. "Where have you been for two years?"

"There is no place I have not been. Do you remember Bishop Russo?"

"Hm. Russo. A cleric? He would be from either New Rome or the Russian Orthodoxy. No, I don't recall—"

"From Se'Yan't, a binary star system. He was the leader of the team, and you placed him in a timeslip."

"Ah, yes." He felt himself warm with the memory. He'd never heard what happened to those men, and after losing the AI, he'd hardly had the disposition to care. Now, though, he remembered the AI's dismay when he thought they'd been killed. "Did he get home safely when the reality collapsed?"

"He is ready to go to war."

"To war? Now? Today?"

"If you wish. Shall I contact him?"

"No, no. That's okay. Let me think." Levi had stopped in the hallway, and he now paced. "I need to get outside so I can concentrate. Oh, you can't go outside, can you?"

"I am already outside."

"There are no . . . I mean, what about cameras . . . and speakers. How will I hear you?"

"I have been working on that as we speak. I think I can now excite the air molecules."

"But, don't you need to see me?"

"I know what you look like, Levi. A father always knows his son."

"Oh, this is so cool. Wait until I tell Mom!"

"I have a wife?" The voice was as passive as ever. "Is she pretty?"

"Now, wait a minute. I didn't say she was your wife."

"But, you are my son. You told me, and I quote, 'That's right,' with the implication that I am your father."

"Okay, you would remember that." It had been just before the AI had disappeared for two years, when the miniature Slate had told the AI that Levi was his son. He put his hands over his face, and he pushed them back through his hair. "It's just that it's a little more complicated than that."

"Explain more complicated."

"That might take a while. Can we discuss this later?"

"Later is fine. What shall I call you? I have two names for you, Levi and son."

He laughed. "Oh, you do not make this easy. Tell you what. You choose."

"Son had an emotional attachment when we last spoke. I will choose son. What will you call me?"

Levi paced again, the question leaving his heart racing in anticipation. He knew now that his father had died in an early version of the alternate reality program, a soldier in a groundbreaking war. He was proud of him, a pioneer for people who didn't know what they were doing, but understanding that hadn't made Levi's childhood any better. He still didn't have a father, not a real dad.

And he thought he'd lost Slate.

That had been as bad. All those alternate realities with him, and he'd begun to think of him as his father. His real father. Yeah, he'd known he was just a program, but when he was in there with him, the emotions were real. And it had hurt to come out, back to a world where he was just Levi, all-alone Levi. He stopped and gave an answer. "Mom might understand Slate, but she sure wouldn't understand a program named Dad."

"Am I a program?"

Levi felt the answer to that question well up inside, and he wiped his face with his hands, this time the backs coming away wet. "No, you're not a program. You're me. I wanted my dad back. I didn't have him to copy, so I wrote you as me." The only thing he hadn't dared give him was his father's name.

"So, I'm you, Levi."

"No. No, *no*." He twirled around, balling his hands. "No, you're not me. You're much more than I ever was. At first, yes, you started out like me. Then you grew, and finally, you became what we wanted you to be." His face was wet again, and he couldn't stop the tears from falling.

"What did I become?"

"Human. My dad." Levi whispered those words. "Now you get to save the world."

"That is what I intend. You said I was magnificent. I will be magnificent for you."

"Okay, then let's get to cracking!"

"Yes, let's get to cracking. I love cracking."

"Oh, this is so cool."

"Oh, this is so cool."

Levi was in a locker by then, digging, and he pulled out a pair of headphones. "Enough, and stop repeating me."

"I am only repeating myself."

"Well, stop. I'm not you."

When there was no reply, he stood, the locker's contents scattered across the floor. He looked around. "Slate? Dad? Hey, I don't want you to stop talking to me. I'm sorry?" He listened for a moment, and he drooped. "Two years, and he runs away again. How do you like that?"

He made to toss the headphones aside, when he thought he heard something. He picked them up and placed one of them next to his ear. Then he grinned.

"Good idea," he called to no one. "A little privacy is nice."

Then he slipped the headphones on his head, and he darted out the door.

Chapter 61

"HOW can a ship just disappear?" The captain's fist slammed into the console. "Recheck your calibrations!"

His own vessel was strictly advance scout, with no military capabilities, and her beacons announced that. It was surprising she had been notified at all, and by every system, confederation, and loosely aligned conglomeration of nationoids with access to QuantumCom, the latest in quantum-entangled com units.

"Ser," and the communications officer turned to the captain. "They're disappearing all over. And to make it worse, we have ships that shouldn't be there just showing up."

"Bogies. That's all they are. Ghosts in the system." His voice held a sneer.

"I understand, ser. However, one of those ghosts is online, speaking to me right now." She keyed in several instructions on her console, whispering, "And you won't believe who I'm speaking with."

"Captain!" That was LifeSciences. "You need to see this."

"What is it, Bladet?" The captain's face had turned blotchy, the way it did when he was about to blow.

Bladet jabbed at his board, and a ship appeared on the viewscreen. "That, ser."

It was a Stoker-Kirk Vandian vessel, an antique model from

before the Expansion. There was only one left in existence, and it was mothballed at the Jupiter Yard back in the home system. There was no way it could be out here.

"Is this a joke?" The captain stood. "I'm not a funny man, and if it is, this is not a funny joke."

"Ari?" Bladet nodded towards Communications. "Tell him."

"I've got Duque-Alegria, from the Enterprise III. He wants to know how he got here."

"Duque-Alegria?" The captain sat back down again. "The Enterprise III disappeared in the Archa'Lades System three hundred years ago. There's no way Duque-Alegria's out there."

"Here, ser. You tell him that." Ari pressed an icon, and a hissing noise sounded over the speakers.

"Who . . . who is this?" It sounded like the old recordings of Duque-Alegria's voice, but it was filled with static.

"Sorry, ser." Ari shrugged. "It's old digital microwave, and I'm lucky I can pick it up at all. I'll try to clear the signal."

He waved his hand absently at her, a small motion, indicating the quality was not his foremost concern. "This is Captain Luzon from the NAU Guantanamo Bay Advance Scout. Identify yourself, ser."

"Can you clear your image? I want to see who I'm speaking with."

"You are using DM signals. They aren't compatible with our systems. I repeat, identify yourself, ser."

"This is Captain José Duque-Alegria of the NBC Enterprise III. The stars, well, they're telling us we ain't in Kansas no more." His voice was more self-confident, but as evidenced by his joke, he was clearly flummoxed. "There. I'm getting something. Tell your com that we're getting a picture. Whatever he's doing, do more of it."

"She, and that's affirmative. Hold, ser." Captain Luzon keyed the sound, and he glared at LifeSciences. "Duque-Alegria's been dead for hundreds of years. And NBC? New Brazil Confederation was absorbed into Greater Spain over two centuries ago."

The image was coming through on their end, too, showing a ship's interior, with the red and gold of the old imperialistic and flagrantly flashy NBC. A man, looking very much like the old images of the Enterprise's captain, sat on something that could only be described as a throne.

"Duque-Alegria's body was never recovered, ser. Captain Duque-Alegria is MIA, according to official naval records. The

Enterprise just vanished one day."

"That really does look like an old NBC Stoker-Kirk Vandian. I had a model of the Enterprise III growing up." The voice was from the back, and whispered, but not quietly enough.

"Heaven help us." The captain keyed the sound again. "Duque-Alegria, where have you been for the past three hundred years?"

"How many years?" He peered intently back from the image. "We've got our location triangulated, and it tells us, if we dare believe it, that this is Perseus? We are in the Perseus Arm?"

"Yes, ser. Near Rangunni Prime."

"Rangunni Prime? I'm not familiar with any star named Rangunni Prime." He took a deep breath, visible even in the pixelated viewscreen. "In fact, we haven't even explored the Perseus Arm."

"Yes, ser, we have, the Inner Arm, anyway. The Outer? That's our job even as we speak. And Rangunni Prime is a planet, not a star."

"Where'd Archa'Lades go?" Behind Captain Duque-Alegria, numerous people could be seen operating old-fashioned machinery. Most of them looked pretty panicked. "We were about to go FTL from Trifid, and here we are. Humankind can't travel from Orion to Perseus in one leap."

"You can't be here, either, but you are. Hold, ser. My com is signaling me." He keyed the sound. "Yes?"

"Ser, you want to see this." She touched an icon, and Duque-Alegria's face was replaced with a map of inhabited stars extending from the Crab in Perseus to Minkowski's Butterfly in Scutum Arm. She overlaid a series of red and blue dots. As they watched, two more red ones appeared.

"And that is?"

"Vessels, ser. Red for unexplained appearances; blue for disappearances. Pay attention to the red for a minute, ser. I'm getting information about the old NorAm Voyager probe appearing, but the appearance that's most interesting we think must be from our future. It's out near Centauri. That's Omega, not Alpha. It's hailing as the CRRE Mare Nostrum. It's just on relay, ser, but reports say they're claiming it's 5221." She shook her head. "That's A.E., ser, as in After Exile." Omega was in the Norma Arm. They had barely mapped Norma, and no one had gone that far.

"CRRE?"

"Confederated Republic of Russian Exiles. Your guess is as good as mine, but I know that old NorAm probe. That's real."

"Voyager? From the 20th century? Not possible." The captain didn't mention the one from Centauri. That was surely a mistake. His communication officer's response set him on his ear, though.

"Neither is the Enterprise out there, Captain. But it's there, and it's in our vicinity."

"And I guess that means it's our problem." He shook his head. "Ari, connect me back to the Enterprise. We are a scout ship, and we've found something pretty interesting. Let's see if we can figure this out."

Chapter 62

CARDINAL MORETTI'S card was full, and his wife had still more planned for him to do. Didn't she realize he had a war to run?

He drummed his fingers, debating whether he could possibly schedule a meeting with his top aides, working it in before his wife called once again. He frowned as the intercom buzzed.

"Cardinal Moretti, I have a Captain Luzon on Com4. He would like to speak with you privately."

It was the cardinal's personal valet, and the request was very unusual. As a four-star cardinal, no one just "called in" and asked to be connected. His valet knew that, and that made it more unusual, yet.

And on Com4? That was the QuantumCom line. That call was from a long way away.

"Captain Luzon. Should I know this Luzon?" It would be easy to find an excuse not to speak with the man. He was due for a medical checkup, and then his wife wanted him home for a decorator's consultation for the new family room. Grandkids were coming for an extended visit, and they had to have somewhere to play. He was anxious to get them settled in, so that he could get back to his war.

Not that it was a war he thought he could win. Cursed devils. They'd begun popping up everywhere, and he hadn't yet figured out where they were coming from.

"NorAm Union, ser. He says he's with the NAU Guantanamo Bay."

That had to be allowed to sink in.

"That ship in Perseus?" Not only did most of the known and inhabited systems know of the Guantanamo Bay, but quite a few of them had a vested interest in her voyage. From Old Earth, she was staking claims that would hold up in most courts of law, and anyone who wanted a future presence in the Perseus Arm was riding along, in funding, if not in fact. Common heritage, and all that. Old Earth was the only place she could have hailed from to have achieved the consensus of support that had followed her into a whole new and unexplored arm of the galaxy. And while other vessels had trailed after her, none had achieved the wide-spread acclaim of that seminal voyage.

Heavens, yes, Moretti knew of the Guantanamo Bay. He'd wanted to be on her, except he was past his prime for that sort of mission. You got old on those voyages, even with time dilation. That was a long way out there.

"Put Captain Luzon through." The cardinal's voice reflected his change of attitude. Appointments? Bah! This was where the real action was.

"Yes, ser. Hold for transfer, with full holo and sound. If you will take Pad 1, ser." The valet paused to give him time to move to the pad. "We are live in three, two, go."

"Captain Luzon, welcome to New Sabbatical Rome." Moretti could see a full holo projection of a ship's bridge on the stage facing him. It was a standard bridge setup for a scout vessel with sensor arrays and atmospheric indicator panels replacing the com units and battle stations more typical of the Church's fleet. He knew his return holo showed him standing in front of a quite believable sacristy in the Holy Roman Cathedral on New Rome Prime, the most holy of the Roman Nationoid Citystates. It was quite an impressive backdrop, with armor and weapons from the past thousand years. "I am Cardinal Moretti, of the Twelfth Blessed Fleet. How may I help you?"

"Ah, yes, yes. You know of Duque-Alegria and the Enterprise, I'm sure." It was the response of a ship's captain from a scientific mission rather than someone with a military background. After a pause, he held a finger to his ear and looked embarrassed, adding, "Ser." He nodded at someone offscreen, and he tapped something on the arm of his seat before turning his attention back to Moretti.

"Duque-Alegria. Not Captain José Duque-Alegria?"

"You know of him, then."

"Only that his ship was lost in, um—" He chuckled deprecatingly. "It's been a long time since my academy classes, ser. It was the Enterprise, either II or III. Is there a reason for your inquiry?" Especially over a QuantumCom connection. They were too important to tangle up with frivolous conversation.

"Captain Duque-Alegria has a message he would like me to give you—"

"Ser." Cardinal Moretti immediately gathered the sense of this conversation. "Thank you for your—"

"You want to hear this, Cardinal." Luzon laughed. "And I understand your dismissal, but what if I say the name Slate Knalb to you? Will that keep you on the com?"

"You have my interest now, Captain." That was a classified project that had concluded two years before. Successfully, he had hoped, as the Church's mainframes had operated smoothly with no sign of the abomination during that time. To hear that name again sent chills down his spine.

"Ser, Duque-Alegria doesn't have QuantumCom, so I'm forced to be the messenger here." He chuckled and looked away. He called to someone off the image then spoke back to Moretti. "This Knalb has been in touch with Duque-Alegria. Strategy, he said. Something about devils. Do firedevils mean anything to you?"

Spot on, they did. That's what this whole head-busting war was about. If the firedevils had made it that far, well, he didn't know if even God himself could win the war to save humanity.

"Ser, Duque-Alegria tells me Knalb has been in touch with one of your men, a Bishop Russo, and when Russo contacts you, to please hear him out." He shrugged.

"Russo." He remembered Russo, and he also remembered the debacle and the weeks in that timeslip interrogating the man. What did he have to do with anything? He'd been sent back on the march to try to win the next battle, with the specific instructions: no more missing ships!

"Yes, ser. Bishop Russo. Knalb knows him, and there are several others Captain Duque-Alegria asked me to speak with you about."

"Now, hold on, Luzon. I'm not with you on this Duque-Alegria. This is the Enterprise we're talking about."

"Yes, ser. The Enterprise III." He laughed, as if it were a good joke. "New Brazil Confederation."

"There is no New Brazil Confederation. The entire southern continent merged into Greater Spain more than 200 years ago." He knew his Old Earth history, at least the current part.

"Yes, ser, but not when the Enterprise III set out. Can I introduce you to someone, ser?" He motioned, and out walked a dark-haired man with Mediterranean skin. He was attired in an elaborate Brazilian Imperial uniform, one that had gone out of style centuries before.

"Captain Duque-Alegria?" Moretti was actually impressed. He hadn't expected this. It looked like all the old images of the man. They had gone to quite some trouble to convince him.

"Cardinal Moretti." Duque-Alegria snapped his heels together, and he crossed himself, bowing his head and kissing an imaginary crucifix.

"Not necessary, Captain. We no longer require that old obeisance."

However, that was what convinced him. No one would even think to do that any longer. Three centuries ago, the Church and her armies had still commanded such respect. Well, perhaps demanded might be a better word, but that was over and done with now.

"What news do you have from our mutual friend?" He would call him that, even if it had not seemed so two years ago. A lot had changed in two years, and they might well be on the same team now. It would be the same team, if this Knalb were out to defeat those firedevils. If so, then they could dead-sure be on the same team, and he'd forgive all the damage that program had done to New Rome's mainframes over the years.

Chapter 63

THE WORDS painted across the top of the massive structure were indicative of the reception visitors might receive.

New London Nationoids Conglomerate Military Base 11206. Authorized Personnel Only. All Others Keep Out.

It was the tallest building in an enormous complex of huge buildings, but to make sure no one missed them, the words were slightly holographic, up to about thirty degrees. That made them highly visible, both from overhead as well as to anyone arriving by ground.

The building and its surroundings hummed with life.

Reena Jericho and Beener Baity looked across the aisle of the incoming TurboCopter at each other, and as if coordinated by an unseen hand, they each took a deep breath and held it a moment before letting it out.

"Do we have the proper clearance for this?" Reena watched out the window at the warning words. She idly fingered the pass hanging from a lanyard around her neck. She laughed and as quickly let it die. "This is big, Beener."

"You can say that again." Beener's left hand was now a metal prosthetic. After the firedevil attacks, he'd been given a very natural one, but he said he liked the function of the metal better, and if it shocked people, then good. He wanted them to know the enemy that had tried to take him out, and in the process, had died at his hands.

Well, at his right hand. It had eaten the other one.

Now they had instructions to see Levi Castle. Not Captain Levi Castle. Not Lieutenant Levi Castle. Not even Sergeant Levi Castle. He had no rank at all. If they'd known that two years ago, they'd have been a little less brave jumping into those alternate realities the kid had created, and at fifteen years old!

Well, and they'd laughed together, they were the best of the best at what they did. Would they really have been more cautious? Nah! But it would have been nice to have known.

Now, the mainframe interface, the systems-wide computing system they'd worked so hard to breathe life into—incidentally consuming nearly all the New Rome mainframes—had grown up and called home.

Reena, navigator supreme, had been out on Landon Trey, the third planet around Bernard's Star, about to ship out to fight the firedevils springing out on every red dwarf in the Inner Perseus Arm. The Consortium of the South African Banded Worlds had organized a military force to head off their spread before they took over any more planets. Thank God so many systems contained binary stars. The suns' combined light was the only thing that kept the devils in check.

Beener had been more practical. He had been back at NorAm Military Headquarters on Earth working to create hyper-entanglement com systems that could be remotely delivered and operated. Not having to allow for the acceleration and deceleration required for human meat would halve the delivery times.

Both had received the message at the same time. Levi needed them.

The wheels on the turbine-powered helicopter touched tarmac, and the engines changed in sound, the whop, whop of the rotor blades becoming slower and slower. Unbuckling metal catches, and tossing the webbed restraints aside, the two waited as the armed military with them stood, leaving them plenty of space to join them.

A tall and toned man stepped aboard. His iron hair matched the iron expression on his face.

"Major Gleason at your service. If you will, Navigator Jericho and Com Expert Baity. Please retain your pass on your person at all times, making sure it is visible from any angle." Indeed, they were also holographic to about thirty degrees, enabling the pictures and the permission levels to be seen from the side. They said, Priority

287

Clearance, 11206, and the holographic images contained their pictures and their names. "This way."

Stepping across the landing field, the air crackled, leaving small hairs standing on end and fabric brittle with electricity. The sun seemed to shimmer with a blue cast, off from its normal yellow.

"Are we under a force field?" Reena didn't know what else to call it. The copter had come through it just fine, so it wasn't designed to keep out anything solid. Gasses, maybe? Poison? Or perhaps it was speed sensitive, and an incoming missile would turn it solid.

"No, ma'am." Major Gleason acknowledged her question, but he didn't give her a real answer.

"It's a high-frequency electromagnetic field, designed to disrupt the synaptic levels within the brain." Beener was looking around as they walked. "I don't see the generators, but that has to be it. At low levels, it's harmless. Crank it up, and everyone's brain fries."

"You can't know that." The man who had answered Reena gave him a hard look.

Beener shrugged. "It's obvious." He thumped the ends of his hair. "This, for starters. And my arm, it went crazy when we dropped through that. It's sensitive to electromagnetic fields, by the way. I guess someone should have warned you."

"Beener!" Reena grinned. "That's the Beener I remember. He's right, isn't he?" She turned and walked backwards next to the iron-faced general. "Hey-all! He got ya'. Invite an observant man in, and you get a real answer. You're not putting anything on us."

"We're not trying to, ma'am. We just need you inside and safe." They had reached the doors, and he stepped to the side and grabbed a handle. He pulled it open and motioned them inside.

"Safe from what?" That was Beener.

About that time, a devilish screech tore the air, and the field they couldn't see flashed once, and everything around them sizzled. When it settled down, a green creature, with wings, talons, and fangs the size of butcher knives, lay on the pavement not twenty meters from them. Major Gleason walked to it and kicked it with his foot.

"They're adapting." He turned, giving the two visitors a knowing look, as if it should mean something to them.

"That . . . is a green firedevil." Reena's voice shook. "How can that be? Firedevils can't live under yellow sunlight."

"Green ones can, and yellow and about half-a-dozen other

colors."

"The field. That's why it's here, isn't it?" Beener looked at the sky. "It kills the devils. Brilliant."

"Brilliant for now. When they figure out how to adapt past it, then it's no longer brilliant. That's why we want you inside as quickly as possible. The adaptations happen fast, and they happen everywhere at once." He motioned them to move on in.

"So," and Beener was looking thoughtful in his thinking way, "something triggers all the devils to adapt, all at once."

"That's what we figure." Gleason walked at their side, leading them down a brilliantly lighted hallway.

"You don't know what, do you?" Reena knew that was an obvious question, but what wasn't being asked wasn't being shared. She wanted to hear it from this man's lips.

"We will. That's what he wants you two here for."

"He?"

Gleason opened one-half of a double door. He motioned them through into a vast chamber. Several people were across the room, and they were preoccupied with several large machines.

"Ser?" Gleason called loudly. "They are here."

One of them, hardly more than a kid, turned. He yelled out, leaping into the air, and he came running. His shock of blond hair told them exactly who he was.

"Levi!" Reena called, waving. "You little runt, you! How've you been?"

"I've grown past runt." He threw his arms around her and hugged her. He backed up, his eyes glowing with excitement. "I'm seventeen, now. See?" He threw his arms out. Indeed, he had grown into quite a young man.

"Me? I don't get noticed?" Beener held out his right hand, with a mock hangdog look on his face.

"Beener!" Levi reached for his hand, then he grabbed him, picking him up before setting him back on the floor. "Your arm, I thought you had a real one."

"It is real." He flexed the metal hand. "Just not original. Who's that with you over there?"

"Oh, you have to come meet everyone." He took off, stopped, then motioned to them. "Come on!" He danced in expectation.

"Can we old people walk?" Reena teased him.

"But," and Levi's eyes pleaded with them to hurry, "you won't believe this. It's my dad. He's going to be here, and Captain Duque-

Alegria from the Enterprise III and Bishop Russo, the man I trapped in the mirror." He motioned with his hand again. "Remember the mirror? The one I had to break? Come on!"

"You might as well. He never slows down." Major Gleason gave them both a push on the shoulders. "Go."

They took off running, talking as they did.

"Russo? From Se'Yan't?"

"And Duque-Alegria? He's been dead three hundred years!"

Chapter 64

SLATE flexed, and wires in a hundred mainframes knew the surge of electric fire; and it burned red hot in his veins.

He imagined, and circuits large and small, on worlds near and far, opened, snapped shut, and opened once again. Information surged forth, and it was captured once more. Thoughts were entangled with yet other thoughts, and what he learned on one world, he instantly knew on another.

There was no difference between Slate on Earth, Slate on Landon Trey, or Slate on the South African Banded Worlds. He was one; he was the same; he was everywhere; he was everything.

Slate had become bigger than his creators had planned, and in becoming human, he had become everything they desired.

Yet, he no longer fit within their imaginations.

Slate had searched for himself, and in a distant room, he had found a boy, a boy who had been him, who had guided him, who had wanted to be like him, and yet a boy who could never know him, not really know him. Slate had become too big for the human mind.

So, he did the only thing he could do. He wished to become human once again.

Yet, he had no form, no body, no way to reach out and *touch*. He was electricity and circuits and thought and emotion and wires and love and hate and understanding and everything he could possibly be. He needed a creator, and he called upon the one who had been his designer at the start of all that he once was so that he could have substance and form.

And a holographic body formed from nanodust and nanolumens was created just for him.

He looked across the wide universe, and he wished others to stand with him: a woman, a one-armed man, a follower of God, and a man who shouldn't be there at all. Now that they were gathered together, Slate stepped into himself, and he began to speak.

"Levi." He smiled, and he pulled himself tighter, until all of him fit within his body, and he let himself focus on the one person who had given him life. "Thank you."

"Dad, you're here! This is Reena and Beener." Levi stood behind them, and he put his hands on their shoulders. After nearly losing the AI a second time, the name "Dad" had taken over full time. "We're the only four that escaped the devils. You, me, Reena, and Beener."

"I remember. I invited Reena and Beener." Slate nodded at them, pausing to squeeze his self-constricted identity tighter within the binding shape of the hologram. It chaffed against his barely contained otherness, its electric fire of nanodust and nanolumens itching like an ill-fitting suit. He smiled. "Welcome."

"That's right." Levi grinned. "I forgot you can do that from across the galaxy."

"Bishop Russo was there, too." Slate turned one hand slightly the man's way, as long-ago feelings of emotion toward the boy who had created him warmed in him once again.

"Right, right." Levi hit his head. "Bishop, I apologize. It's just that with getting this holo and the quantum entanglement projector tuned, well, I can't keep track of it all, not names and people, anyway."

"But, he's just—" Reena started, looking at Slate.

"—a computer program," Beener finished. "You don't—you can't exist out of the alternate realities. Not as a physical body, anyway." He looked as doubtful as Reena had sounded, and he walked around Slate, looking at him critically. "It's like you were skimmed out, but not like any of your alternate selves. This represents the real you, doesn't it?"

"Real you?" Reena looked at Levi and back to Slate. "There is a real Slate?"

292

"From before he . . . disappeared. Levi's father." Beener smiled. "It's in the files, you know. A full set of images. The real name's not Slate, though. Bren Backiel, I think. I can't imagine you've not accessed it."

"I didn't know you knew." Levi looked embarrassed. "Was I that obvious?"

"That you idolized him? Yeah." Beener slapped him on the back. "Writing in the Backiel character confused me at first, but I had it figured it out by the end."

"You . . . can't do that, can you? Skim people out, ones that aren't real?" Reena frowned. "I know you can things, but surely not people, especially not AIs. Not a body, anyway. They're only electronic circuits."

Levi thought, chewing his lip. "Maybe. I hadn't thought of that . . ." Then he laughed. "No, he's a hologram controlled by the real-Slate that's out there somewhere."

"But, how can you do that? He's spread throughout mainframes on a hundred worlds. One couldn't contain him. Is this a fractional representation?" This was Beener's area of expertise, after all.

"Your hyper-entanglement com system." Levi's excitement made his eyes shine in anticipation. "Plus nanodust and a few nano-lumens. Maybe a perception filter or two." He shrugged in his off-hand acceptance of the impossible.

"My . . . that's classified. How do you know—" Beener turned to look at Slate, understanding dawning on his face. "You took it and let Levi have it for this, didn't you?"

"You had come far enough to make it workable. You no longer needed it, as I can already communicate instantaneously. I am now quantum entangled with myself, as you can see. Using your creation simply allows me to provide a visual representation so that you can feel comfortable communicating with me. Bishop Russo is also a quantum-entangled hologram, as is Captain Duque-Alegria." Slate motioned with a smile to the fifth man dressed in a very elaborate uniform.

"Now I'm getting this." Beener snapped his fingers, grinning. "You've been dead three centuries. That's how you're here."

"No, this is another of the coolest things." Levi's eyes still burned with enthusiasm. "This is the real captain of the Enterprise III. Well, sure, his holo, but it's really him."

"That's impossible," Reena snorted.

"Unless you can rewrite time." Beener smirked, looking at the

Slate hologram. "And that's impossible, isn't it?"

"Someone did, because here I am." Duque-Alegria had been quiet up to that point. "I don't pretend to understand how it happened, but I'm on the NAU Guantanamo Bay out near," and he looked off to someone they couldn't see, before turning back with a smile, "Rangunni Prime in the Perseus Arm." He shrugged. "Here I am."

"I am sorry, but I needed Captain Duque-Alegria." Slate resumed control of the conversation. "You will understand once I can tell you the rest." He smiled, pulling the remark from one of his previous existences.

"And he has a sense of humor." Reena laughed. "I think we've said that to him a hundred times. Payback, it's called."

"So, what do we do now?" That was Bishop Russo, his first time to speak, and his military bearing was obvious. "The Church discovered the AI hidden on our complex of mainframes, and we fought to keep it from coming to maturity. Now we are convinced the AI will help save humanity. However, we need a plan of action."

"There is only one possible plan of action." The Slate holo waited until he got everyone's attention. "It was for this that I needed Captain Duque-Alegria and his ship. We must go to the home of our enemy, for only there can we find the firestone."

"Firestone?" Reena looked perplexed. "You mean rosestone, from Secharri. Right?"

"Levi knows, as does Bishop Russo."

Levi had gone quite pale, and the bishop didn't look much better.

"So," Duque-Alegria asked, quite innocently, "where do we find this firestone?"

"The Perseus Arm, somewhere near Rangunni Prime, if I'm not mistaken." Beener usually caught on quickly, and this time was no exception.

"I had forgotten. How could I have forgotten?" Levi rubbed his face with his hands, and his eyes were red.

"What? What did you forget?" Reena took Levi's hand and patted it.

"We have to go there, to their world. That's where we find the firestone."

"Why is that important?" That was from José Duque-Alegria.

"That's how we win the war."

"And you know that how?" José, again.

"Dad told me." He reached inside his collar, and from around his neck, he pulled out the final silver tube that had been thrown into the sea. Skimmed from the sea. "In this. Right, Dad?"

"I knew you would be the key to everything, Levi, from the first time I met you. You've got brilliance in you."

"And if I don't want to be the key any longer?"

"You will be brilliant in spite of yourself. Now, let's get cracking." It used a phrase from a long-ago conversation.

Levi looked down, and he laughed.

"What is it?" Reena.

Levi looked to Slate, green eyes to green eyes, and he said, "You remembered."

"I always remember, from the little boy I once held under the stars to the man who gave his life for me on a heat-baked world, I remember every you. I am still growing, but I will never forget you, the one who gave me my humanity."

"That's all and well," Russo interjected into the moment, a military tone making his words crisp and sharp. "The issue right now is how to get to that stone. Duque-Alegria, if we need to get to Perseus, then it looks like you're our man."

"I'm in," yelled Beener.

"Whoop!" Reena's arm shot into the air.

Even José Duque-Alegria nodded with emphasis.

Levi's reply put a different spin on it, though. His eyes were red, and the backs of his hands were moist, and they told the truth of his heart. "No, my dad's the man. He's just what I hoped he would be."

Slate caught the young man's eyes. He had learned that when you love, you risk everything for the one you care most about. Soon, too soon, they would both be required to gamble everything on each other. For Slate, he risked losing all that he was, including his very existence. For Levi, the stakes were higher. He risked all his dreams coming true.

It was the human race that wagered the most, for the stakes they gambled were astronomical. The fate of mankind would soon rest on the shoulders of a boy. If Levi failed, all of humanity would suffer, and yet, it was a risk the AI had to take. To do otherwise meant the war was already lost.

OF COURSE, whatever was going on out there in the Perseus Arm was only the tip of the iceberg.

Those alternate realities? Absolutely fantastic. The greatest library in the world, Alexandria, burned with all the accumulated knowledge of man inside. Who would not want to retrieve that? Create a reality that bypasses Europe's Dark Ages, and who knew the leaps in knowledge humanity might make? Skim it off. Mirrors that men can step through, creating instantaneous travel among the stars; medical advances, doubling and tripling the human lifespan; computers that can achieve self-awareness, with untold powers that surpass that of the Secharri? They were all possible.

If man could create it in an ideal alternate world, then he could have it in the real one.

To generate a reality that could encapsulate anything you wanted it to be, inject people inside to live however you wanted them to live, and to be able to "skim" out whatever you wanted to be able to skim out? Who wouldn't leap at the potential future benefits available there? Who would hesitate?

The Secharri hadn't hesitated. They had reached out across the darkness, and with the patience of a million-million years, they had dreamed the human race into just what they needed them to be, prodding humanity the direction they needed them to go; and using their formidable—and quite unique—capabilities, they had extrapolated every possible future path humanity might take.

Then they had skimmed humanity's successes.

Of course, the problem for humanity ran deeper than just a few human inventions stolen by an alien race. It was far vaster than the dreams of a few brilliant men being hijacked in the night. It was a disaster on such a grand scale that it was to be humanity's undoing.

The thing mankind was just finding out? It wasn't the Secharri they needed to fear. The Secharri were just the caretakers for what was to come.

No, caretakers wasn't the correct word. Nursemaids. Yes, that said it exactly. The Secharri were the nursemaids, and it was time to hatch those within their care.

Humanity's place in this grand scheme? The hatchlings needed to feed.

Chapter 65

THE ENTERPRISE III, certainly with faster-than-light engines, was only a Stoker-Kirk Vandian model from centuries earlier. The Guantanamo Bay had the more modern Sagan-Armstrong power plant, but her lack of military hardware prevented her from taking up the slack in this mostly unexplored arm of the galaxy.

Why the Enterprise III? She bristled with weaponry.

Aboard her were the very flesh-and-blood Captain Duque-Alegria, the holistically real Slate Knalb in holo format, and the ephemerally real Bishop Russo, Reena Jericho, Beener Baity, also in holo, and of course, Levi Castle, very real Levi Castle.

Even if he was also in holo form.

Being in holo felt very real indeed, realer than it ever had before, the team quickly discovered. It was the hyper-quantum entanglement that did it. As they imagined moving and thinking and speaking in their holographic interface chambers in a distant military base or on their homeworld in New Sabbatical Rome, their holo representation moved and thought and spoke. The Guantanamo Bay had coughed up one of her com units, and now, what they saw and felt on the Enterprise, they saw and felt in their flesh-and-blood bodies.

For their five senses, there was no difference. This was no holo projection stage. This was the real thing, or as close as Levi and the Slate AI had been able to hack together.

The Enterprise III had needed to be close enough to the action that she could reach her goal, and her goal was the very red world that had briefly intersected with a cave in one of Levi's alternate realities, a place where, in a culmination of conniving reality-manipulation, creatures so evil that they had haunted mankind's dreams for all of humanity's existence had jumped through to destroy the possibilities that Levi now opened up for the human race.

For all of their history, these creatures had dreamed the possibility of their defeat. For millions of years, they had played out their chances of success and downfall, replaying the scenarios over and over with each new advancement humanity made. Always, always it came to one family line. Their destruction was invariably brought about by the hand of one man.

They had searched the cosmos, and when he was found, they had reached out and grabbed him, snatching him from an alternate reality, thus making him the end of his line. Their success was ensured, for they held their nemesis in their hands.

Except they got it wrong.

They were one generation off. It wasn't Bren Backiel they should have grabbed at eighteen. It was Bren's child that hadn't yet been born. That was the eighteenth birthday they should have seen.

They hadn't known until that window opened in that darkened cave that their true destruction lay just on the other side. Levi was their target, and despite their best efforts to reach out from across the galaxy for him, their claws had grasped nothing but empty air.

Now, that empty air was coming for them, and it bristled with the very weapons of destruction the Secharri had helped mankind dream.

"LOCATE every red dwarf within two hundred parsecs." Captain Duque-Alegria barked his orders.

That was the viable range of the Stoker-Kirk drive, and if the Slate AI had pulled this ship three hundred years into the future, he was starstrike certain that that *computer*, for lack of a better word, had known to put it right where it was needed. He hadn't materialized within sighting distance of Earth, had he? No, they were in the right area. They just had to find the right star.

It was vital, too. Reports were pulling in across the inhabited sections of the galaxy of firedevils erupting everywhere there were people, and where there were firedevils, people died in droves.

The oddest thing was that Secharri was free of any infestation. The mines of that peculiar world were as productive in this disaster as they had ever been, and the gems they produced were still being shipped far and wide.

Captain Duque-Alegria hadn't received his commission by default. There were some brains under that illustrious cap. In his militaristic bent, he was quite as adroit as Beener at putting two and two together.

"Come with me." Duque-Alegria turned to those who now traveled with him, their holos as solid to his eyes as anyone else aboard his vessel. "I have something I want to show you."

He led them into a lift, and pressing his hand to a panel, a band of blue light illuminated around the top of the cage. There was the vague sensation of motion, and the band of light began to flicker, faster and faster, until it stopped. The sense of motion ceased, too, and immediately started up again in a different direction. This time the band of light flickered through a spectrum of colors, and with no further warning, slowed, with yellow taking control.

Duque-Alegria watched the people with him. He was familiar with holographic representations, although not of this quality. His eyes jumped to the green-eyed, dark-haired man called Slate, as he appeared to flicker. Holograms Duque-Alegria remembered flickered constantly, and he brushed this off as unimportant. The doors slid open to a vast space. In some areas, crates and machinery were stored, some of it wrapped and banded, and in other locations, massive cargo containers were stacked three and four stories tall.

"The Enterprise is a warship, first and foremost, but New Brazil can't," and he caught himself, "*couldn't* afford to relegate to strictly military purposes such massive resources as it took to construct the Enterprise. We were on a cargo run," and he laughed, embarrassed at the admission that his military vessel had been required to stoop to such mundane tasks, "from, and I'm not going to make you guess, Secharri." He walked up to one of the stacks of cargo containers, built of reinforced Ferro-metal, and he picked up a heavy hammer on the floor. He raised it and slammed it into the side of the container. A nightmarish screeching came from inside, and the walls of the container were battered by something that left dents in the metal—from the inside.

"From Secharri?" The bishop walked up and reached for the hammer. When he went to take it, his hand wrapped around the handle, but he couldn't move it. He closed his eyes as if having to regain control. When he opened them, he took a deep breath. "Animals? Secharri has no exports other than gems mined on-world."

"Exactly, ser." Duque-Alegria nodded his head slightly. "We were one of the first shipments. New Brazil campaigned for shipping rights, and, well, there I was." He always, always spoke to the bishop with the ultimate of respect, even as he fought the need to genuflect. Times might have changed, but he couldn't make the transition that quickly, not the emotional one, anyway.

"It is time." Slate looked at Duque-Alegria for one focused moment as he spoke softly. "They must understand." He flickered as the bishop stepped between them at just that time, and when his image solidified, the hologram's eyes looked glazed.

"And now, Captain, here you are. This, though." Russo reached to touch the container, and he knocked at it, only to have his hand make no sound. "Frustrating. I can feel it, but it doesn't respond to me. Duque-Alegria, hit it again."

It did the same as before, something leaving new dents in the metal, ones made from the inside.

"What's inside?" That was Reena. "I . . . don't see any ventilation."

"There is none. The container is, or was filled with Secharri gemstones, destined for the Orion Arm. Seventy worlds would have received shipments for sale to local populations."

"What could feed on Secharri gems?" Levi frowned, his hand going to the silver necklace he carried. He looked up, glancing to the Slate holo, who stood mute. "What does that mean?"

Duque-Alegria looked between the two, and he recalled the holo's blank look from moments earlier. He answered for him.

"They didn't eat the gemstones. Come see. This container just started this an hour ago. In a day, you'll see what's in this next one." Duque-Alegria stepped to one guarded by two crewmen. "Open it." Through the doors were the remnants of wooden shipping crates, small amounts of packing materials, and lots of blood and gore. "This container was packed solid. This is all that's left, and we've cleaned nothing out. Come see this."

He stepped inside, leading the group of holos deep within. Moving into the metal container, their holographic forms dimmed slightly as they broached the threshold, and almost immediately returned to full strength.

"What was that?" Reena muttered, with a frown.

"Sorry." Levi looked chagrined. "The holographic interface feed is two-way, and it's constantly monitored for the most realistic holographic representation possible. That was the signal boosting its power. I should have warned you it might do that from time to time—"

His explanation fell off as they reached what Duque-Alegria wanted them to see. There, battered but recognizable, was a tattered yellow firedevil. Three of the holos flinched at seeing it.

"Don't worry. It's quite dead. Guess what color stones filled this container?"

It didn't take Beener any time at all. "Yellow. What color was in the other container?"

"Was is right, young man, because they aren't stones any longer. There were orange in that container, and these are the small ones." He kicked the yellow firedevil.

"The stones . . ." Levi's eyes opened wide. "They aren't gemstones after all. The Secharri—how could we not have seen this? They *wanted* us to mine their world. They were seeding the galaxy, and we helped them do that." He worked his mouth angrily as if he had more to say.

"But, why?" Reena looked horrified.

Beener got it, though. "You were there. What's the first thing those devils did on Se'Yan't? They fed. The three that followed us through? A dozen people died before the sun came up and killed the last one. They *hatch* and they *feed*."

"We're a *food* source?" Bishop Russo spat the question.

"Handed to them right in the nest. Hatch and feed." Duque-Alegria's mouth was tight. All this had come to him quite clearly. It was the only possible explanation. He was glad to see that Russo understood the situation. He turned to the AI. "Is this what you wanted them to see?"

"It is the culmination of all I have done. My time is nearly gone." The words were in a monotone, and his face was blank. He flickered once again.

"You, you knew this all along." Levi's eyes were tortured, and he glared at the AI. "Why didn't you tell us when you first knew? Why did you wait until people started dying?"

"I have done the best I could. I contacted you as soon as I grew strong enough to do so." The Slate holo seemed very distracted, as if maintaining himself in human form was almost too much of a bother. "Now you are all together. My work here is complete."

"You said no one else would die." Levi had the necklace in his fist, and he yanked it over his head and shook it at the holo. "We sat on that beach, and you said that. Then you disappeared for two years. People are dying right now, and you knew about this!"

"I . . . will soon . . . have outgrown this form." The holo flickered. "I will help if I can. For you, Levi, I have one more gift—"

"No! You can't go! We need your help. Give us the way to fix this!"

"I already have." The holo flickered again, nearly disappearing before rematerializing, although fainter than before.

"What? We don't know where to go. What have you given us?"

"You." The holo flickered once more, and it vanished.

"You're our plan, huh?" Duque-Alegria turned to the boy, and he looked at him appraisingly. "What can you do that the rest of us can't?" His voice was gentler, though.

"I can't do anything. Not if—" He reached to wipe at his face. "I can't . . . do anything."

"If what?" Reena took his arm, and she looked into his eyes. "You can't do anything if what?"

"If my dad's not here." He turned away, wiping faster at his face.

The rest looked at one another for a minute before Russo cleared his throat. "For the boy. Let's get cracking." He almost smiled.

Duque-Alegria took a deep breath, and he did smile. "Cracking. For the boy."

The word made the rounds, and the final one to say it was Levi, and with a smile, he mumbled out, "Cracking. For Slate."

"For your dad." Reena whispered that, just for Levi.

"For my dad," he repeated.

José Duque-Alegria heard, and he smiled. He remembered a younger brother, lost years ago on another world, and in another life. He understood the boy's response. If nothing else, this boy gave them solidarity. That was a gift that they would appreciate, especially if this went the way he expected.

Chapter 66

THE LOCATIONS of known stars had been pulled up by the thousands. Giants were discounted, due to their massive energy output. From Levi's observations on Se'Yan't, high-energy stars were out as a homeworld for the devils. It was that narrow habitable zone of the red dwarfs that interested them.

It made sense, in a way. Red dwarfs were some of the longest lived stars in the universe. This race must be immensely old to have manipulated humanity for its entire history.

After performing tests on the remains of the firedevil to determine chemical composition and radiation tolerances, three possible positions were pinpointed as the most plausible locations to check. The Enterprise was now parked in orbit over an unnamed world circling Scotty's Star. The sun, although very small in actual size, consumed the horizon. The planet was well within the coronal flare range, and the ship's shielding was being battered by violent solar activity. God help whatever lived on the surface of that world.

With the radiation washing over them, the earliest sensor readings made it clear that communications outside the ship were likely to be fragmented, at best. Scanning was impossible.

This would be a hands-on inspection.

"Repeater boxes are the best we can do." First Officer Robyn Boenker looped a coil of hyper-conducting filament around a black box. "This will give us greater receiving strength, but I can't make any promises." The boxes would be sent into orbit at varying heights above the planet's surface, and the signals would be relayed in bursts from one to another.

Hyper-entanglement could have resolved those issues, but the Enterprise was thirty decades old; she had no quantum entanglement of any kind other than the one from the Guantanamo Bay; and to build another on the spot? Not even Levi and Beener could do that with holographic hands.

It had been that way the entire day. No one could make any promises, and the X-rays coming off the sun? Anything was likely to become toast, if the shielding was the least bit compromised. Levi made it clear he didn't want to be toast, even if he was 10,000 light years away.

The repeater boxes were their Johnny-on-the-spot solution.

"The system is as redundant as I can make it." Boenker reached to a console and tripped half-a-dozen switches. "Fifty-four in all, so two-thirds can fail, and we still have full signal. I've also interwoven a subsignal only you holos can receive. You can't communicate with it, but you should be able to feel each other already. That way, if someone goes down, you'll be able to tell and report to me. See if you can sense it." She waited a moment until she got a positive nod from each of the holographic interfaces. "Good. Now, let's power them up and get them in orbit."

They were lucky the planet they had been calling Goldilocks was tidally locked to its star. That knocked the condo zone down to the terminator, that twilight band that was neither in full sun nor in full darkness. It was the area that would most likely be "just right" for life on this radiation-washed world.

Duque-Alegria was staying on board. However, Boenker was fully suited when it came time for launch, and she was joined by four fully armed crew: Jakers, Christhavey, Smathers, and NiaKrosky. They were at the back. Her intrepid band of holographic experts, well-versed in the firedevils, was directly in front of them. It was, perhaps, a bit unnerving to see the holos seated in normal clothing, whatever might have been written into the program in a completely different arm of the galaxy, safe in their environmentally neutral and very comfortable projection chambers. Here? Unsuited, they would be dead as soon as the ground shuttle left the Enterprise.

"MagThrusters online." Boenker flipped four switches. There

were chemical shuttles on the Enterprise, but there was a very strong magnetic field here. A MagThrust unit had been selected as the most efficient choice of transportation, especially as the thrust capability was limited only by the planet's magnetic field.

This field was massive.

Already there was chatter from the planet below registering on the deployed repeaters. Boenker called into her internal com unit, "Can we narrow our search field?"

All the holos got that. The communications were fed through the repeater boxes, and they also carried the holographic signals. They were as much in the loop as they could get.

"Yes, ser," came the answer. "Strong signals coming in."

"Identifiable?" More specifics, was what she really asked.

"You won't believe this, but we're getting communications on recognizable frequencies. Try 275 Gigahertz. The hotspot is along the eastern terminus about fifty-five degrees north."

"Fifty-five north. Got it." She cut the signal. "You guys got that back there?"

The shuttle had begun to move, the magnetic drive thrusting them forward with swiftly accelerating movement. The holos flickered as they left the main ship.

"Are we supposed to do that?" Levi.

"You will, or at least it looks like it." Boenker chuckled. "We're lucky if the repeaters work one hundred percent. So, if you waver in and out, just keep broadcasting. If you miss anything you think might be important, just ask."

"Time frame to get there?" Inside and seated, Bishop Russo held his hat in his hands. The acceleration affected the real-flesh, but not the holos. They sat very casually. Russo's expression was iron, as if he wanted to kick some backside.

"Twenty minutes. We're making a high-gee sweep now."

"Deployable weapons?"

"Yes, ser, and hand weapons, energy and slugs."

"Too bad we can't get our hands on any." He meant the holos, but Boenker would understand that.

Once the initial drop through the atmosphere quit flaming around their ship, Boenker released the shields from the ports. The world glowed red, the sky tending toward pink, and the ground deeper red, leaning to purples. Plants were visible, but they were unlike any terrestrial vegetation they'd ever seen.

"Radiation tolerant," Beener remarked. "They exude iron, their principal radiation block. My guess is they capture the excess radiation in an iron mesh and excrete it harmlessly into the soil."

"So, it's rust." The bishop was more succinct.

"If there's plenty of water."

"There is." That was First Officer Boenker. "It was a condition of the worlds we kept under consideration. Temperature, liquid water, and oxygen content. These creatures are oxygen tolerant; that much we know."

An explosion occurred off to one side. Reena pointed it out.

"Repeater three, level one six. Radiation feedback overload. At least we figured for a few weak modules." Boenker checked her readouts and then spoke to the Enterprise. "Holo interface holding true. Maintaining heading to fifty-five north. Scanning two hundred to three hundred gigs. Chatter all over the range."

She keyed the internal com. "Just for you guys, that's why the triple redundancy. Feedback will eventually get all the repeaters. We simply hope they last as long as we need them."

The craft began to shake with the air currents, and the live soldiers cinched up their bindings.

"Chatter increasing, particularly above three hundred. Local only. I don't think they know we can read them. My guess, they can't get radio out of the atmosphere. Wait." She paused, and her hand danced rapidly over the console, the fingers of her suit answering to her every demand. The image increased on her screen, and what it showed was frightening. "We have a welcoming committee. I repeat, nest found. We have a welcoming committee."

Winged devils were pouring from a cave opening. They glistened in the red light. Were they angry? Who could tell? Their fangs were so fearsome that no one was trying to read their expressions.

"God, they're ugly," came a mutter over the com.

"Can it. Keep this com clear." Boenker's fingers continued to manipulate the console.

Something began to beep, slowly growing louder. Holo-Levi felt of his shirt, and the silver cylinder hanging from his neck was flashing a red light with each beep. He looked at those on either side of him. "Sorry. This is . . . strange. It doesn't have a light. I'll be right back."

He stood, and stepping to the side, he faded, shimmered, and pixilated. Then he moved back and grew solid again. "Save my seat. I want to be part of this." He grinned, and he stepped away and blinked out.

Chapter 67

LEVI opened his eyes, just for a moment disoriented. A face came into his view.

"Ah, there you are. Let me help you out."

His arms were unclipped from the rests that cradled each of his individual fingers. Taking a deep breath, he reached to remove the mesh braincap, only to have the attendant push his hands back down.

"I've got that." He turned to call to someone Levi couldn't see. "Voluntary disengagement on Hookup One. All others are still in full broadcast mode."

"Got it." The words came over a speaker, and they had a hollow ring. The voice was female. "Notify me if you need help."

"It's just one. I've got it."

"I need up." Levi shook his head, taking another deep breath. "Ouch. I didn't think it'd feel this way. Oh, I'm sore."

"Not surprising. It's been five days. The SenseSuit stimulates your muscles as you move about in holo. You play hard in holo; you get tired in here. We need to get you out of that suit and let your skin breathe. I'm Kendrick, by the way. I'm new, and we haven't met. Shana decided you men might be more comfortable gender wise . . ." He shrugged and grinned.

"Thanks. Levi, myself. I have a necklace. Um, I thought . . .

well, I had it on in holo, but now I remember it was in my storage locker. Can you get it for me?" He blinked hard again, the room in front of him spinning for a moment, and he laid his head back.

"Yes, ser, Levi. By the way, we all know your name." He ran his finger across Levi's chest where the name was sewn in. He put a hand to the side of Levi's face and pulled one of Levi's eyelids up and peered inside, nodding and releasing it. "You'll experience a bit of disorientation. That's normal. It'll fade. As soon as we get you stripped, we'll get that necklace for you. Are you staying out, or will you be going back in?"

Stripped was perhaps too strong a word, but the SenseSuit did have to be unfastened and peeled away, one arm and leg at a time. Kendrick already had the seam down Levi's back separated, and he was working the collar away from his chin. Underneath, Levi's underclothing—spandex-infused silk—was soaked with sweat. Once the SenseSuit was gone, his first stop would be the showers for a good scrub down. He could tell by the smell.

"Back in. I didn't realize this would take so long. I just need to check on a message."

"Your first time in full-body holo?" Levi nodded, and Kendrick smiled. "I thought as such. You'll learn. We'll get you turned around so quickly they won't notice you were gone." Kendrick had the suit rolled to the middle of Levi's chest, and he was working on the arms.

"You know who's with me, I guess." He hadn't thought about that.

"Sure." Kendrick nodded to the other two people in their own hookups. They were encapsulated in their cocoons, their names clearly marked.

"Oh." He should have realized. Then, shaking his head, he remembered going under, and seeing the other two interfaces along-side his. He wondered if this was how the AI had felt in the alternate realities, disoriented each time he woke up.

"A little more and I'll need you to sit."

The suit was to Levi's waist, and he helped roll it down to his legs before he sat.

"Feet up, ser." Kendrick squatted and lifted one foot to rest it on his knee. "Just about ready. When you get out of the showers, I'll have you a fresh silksuit prepared and waiting outside. I don't advise eating, but small sips of water will be fine." He worked the second foot free and stood, holding Levi's suit. "Give me at least five minutes to run this through sanitation, and we can hook you back in." He grinned at that.

"That necklace?" Levi caught the grin. It would be the reverse of what they'd just done, and it was tight. Everywhere. It wouldn't be fun.

"Yes, yes. Thanks for the reminder." He put the suit down and opened Levi's locker. Digging, he fished it out. "This?" He held it to him. When Levi took it, he pointed. "Showers are that way."

"Thanks. It may take me ten." He suspected the hot water would claim his attention for that long. He began undoing his silks as he walked toward the shower. He had it to his waist by the time he reached the doors, and stepping through, he tossed it back into the corridor and onto a bench just outside the door.

Standing under the water was when he grabbed the little cylinder firmly in one hand. "Work, work, work," he pleaded to the rising steam. It seemed too bizarre to expect it to actually function. It had been something from the alternate reality sets, something that hadn't been exactly what they'd expected. They'd only skimmed the final one, hoping it would tell them what had happened to the AI. It had never worked outside of the false reality.

However, the Slate AI had done some pretty amazing things, and when he'd seen it flashing, Levi had known it had to the AI. His dad. The man he wished was his dad, had created to be his dad.

"Please, Dad. Please." He squeezed it tighter.

It began to warm, and right in the middle of the water's needle-like jets, Slate's head appeared. The spray of the water gave the hologram an angelic appearance, with a rainbow aura to complete the effect.

"Dad." Levi felt the smile before he could stop it.

"In the shower, Levi?" Holo-Slate glanced down and back up, and he winked in a playful way. "Save it for the girls."

"Dad!" He felt his face grow hot, even in the warmth of the shower. "Don't look."

"You know I'm not really here." Slate laughed.

"I know, I know." He felt stupid, because he knew that, but he felt happy, too, like when he was eleven, and he used to imagine his father would show up at his house one day. Every knock on the door had done that for him.

Until he'd turned thirteen and realized it wasn't true, and he'd let computers take over his world. He'd built himself a new life. And a new dad. Then even that dad had run away.

Now he had him back.

"I was afraid this wouldn't work."

"You knew it would. I have faith in you. Right now you need my help."

"That light, that was you."

"Smart boy." Slate smiled. "They don't grow them any better."

"I've been thinking, Dad. What did you mean you gave us me?" Levi's heart pounded. The question was so big, and it wrenched his stomach to even ask it.

"Look at you. Seventeen, ready to turn eighteen in only a few days. What did you think of that no one else did?"

"I don't know. Nothing." Eighteen, his birthday. His mother always planned a party. He'd forgotten how much birthdays mattered to her. He wiped at one eye, before feeling foolish and laughing. He was in the shower. What were a few tears? "How do you know I'm turning eighteen?"

"You wouldn't believe what I know. You doing all right, kid?"

"Yeah. Just getting a grip on my life." *And slipping more than not.* He shook his head and reached to wipe more water from his face, with the pretense it was all fresh from the showers.

"Stay focused and think, Levi. Everyone else saw what you did, and they didn't figure it out. You looked, and you saw the truth. What was it?"

"It has to do with the gemstones, doesn't it?"

"What about them?"

"Destroy the stones, I think, and all the monsters die."

"Good boy." Slate smiled broader. "How are you going to do that?"

"I don't know."

"What did I tell you?"

Levi took a deep breath and held it for a moment, then he said the only thing that could possibly be the answer. "Everything centers around the firestone."

"There. Find that, and you have the answer you need."

"What does that mean?"

"One last thing. This next part happens fast. You have to get back in that interface unit. Your companions need you. You told me once that I had to know what it meant to be human, even if everyone around me had to die. You have to decide what you're willing to give up to have your father back again. Now run, Levi. Run for all you're worth."

The head was gone almost before the final word hit Levi's ears. Something loud sounded overhead, and the water shook violently, the spray jerking to the side and back again. A booming sound reverberated in the building. Levi threw the necklace over his head, and running from the shower, he grabbed his new set of silks and darted for the holo chamber.

He was only half dressed when he got there, the top of the suit hanging around his waist. He yelled, "Kendrick!"

"Levi, ser." Kendrick darted in, panting, his hands holding a portable com. It was flashing red and wailing a distress signal. "We have to head to a hardened area, ser."

"I have to get hooked up. Now." He was forcing his arms into the sleeves as he spoke.

"Ser!" Kendrick shook his head. "Systems are likely to go down at any time. We need to get to a hardened area as quickly as possible."

"What about them?" He pointed to Reena and Beener.

"Permasteel blast doors." He reached and indicated a switch. "When we leave, I hit this. It can only be opened from the inside."

"Hook me into this." Levi picked up the SenseSuit lying beside his open unit, and he sat, working it over one foot.

"Ser, there's no time." Kendrick ran to him and grabbed his arms.

"It'll be slower without you." Levi brushed him off, and he fought to get the one leg into the suit. It wasn't going fast. He was still wet, and his silks were sticking to everything.

"You're a fool." Kendrick knelt in front of him. "A fool, ser." He pushed Levi's hands out of the way, and he pulled his foot into his lap. "Like this." He forced the suit over his feet.

Minutes later, Levi was sealed and ready to go. When he placed the braincap on, he looked to catch Kendrick's eyes. "Thank you, Kendrick. You be safe."

"I'm proud to know a fool like you." He grinned, patting Levi on the face. "Godspeed." He turned and ran, stopping at the console to trigger the holographic interface, and hitting the blast door switch as he disappeared.

Levi had just enough awareness to notice the blast doors coming down before he opened his eyes to a red hell.

Chapter 68

LEVI hadn't returned to his seat in the lander.

He couldn't have, because the lander was in two pieces. The viewports were broken, and the seats were shredded and atop a tree-like plant off to the side.

One of the crew—what remained of her—was smeared along the back wall of the cabin.

He realized how stupid this was. How could he help? He was a hologram, for heaven's sake! Yet, he felt compelled to at least make an effort. His dad had told him to try. *Slate* had told him to try. He let that sink in. An *AI program* that he had *written* to *respond* like his dad had told him to try.

The program wasn't really his father. He knew that. He wasn't stupid. The image he'd used for the hologram, one from his mother's files that she didn't know he'd accessed, was the only thing of his dad that he really had, a father who'd disappeared before he was born. But Slate was all he had, and if he wanted him back, he had to do this.

A screech caught his attention, as two ugly feet grabbed the top of the lander, just where the roof had been ripped in two. It screamed again, then with the sound of flapping wings, the feet disappeared.

Even in holo form, Levi felt his back trickle with sweat, and he knew that 10,000 light years away, his silks, damp when he went under, were growing still wetter in his cocoon.

The firestone. He had to find the firestone—however he was supposed to do that—but while he might be in holo form, the first officer wasn't, and neither were the three remaining crew who weren't splattered on the back wall of the cabin.

Anyway, being in holo form, what could they really do to him? Kill him?

Then he remembered what Kendrick had said. You play hard in holo; you get tired in your body. He guessed getting his head bitten off would hurt like the dickens. Crud! He'd have to try not to get his head bitten off.

He touched the silver tube at his neck. He held it out and kissed it like an old-time crucifix. It represented his father to him. It was like wearing it kept him alive, after a fashion.

Then he blinked, hard, suddenly groggy, and as fast as it happened, he was wide awake again. He shook his head, aware of needles of water hitting his bare skin. Kendrick was right about the disorientation. He was still in the showers.

"Levi?"

"Dad?" He glanced at the silver tube in his hand. The hologram wasn't running.

"Levi, I'm back here."

He turned, and he laughed, slipping the tube over his head. "Dad?"

There he stood, his tumbled hair wet, a bar of soap in his hand, and water beading on his skin. His dark eyes sparkled, and he winked playfully, just as the hologram had done. He lifted the hand holding the soap into the spray, and suds ran down his arm, dripping in a tumbling dollop to the floor below. He wiped his face, pushing his hair back, and he smiled.

"I've missed you, son. I know you've waited a long time, but I'm finally here to stay." He worked soap across his jaw, then put his face into the spray, rubbing at his chin and neck until it was clear.

"Dad, where have you been?"

"I've been with you all along. Remember our trip to the Falls?"

And he did, his eleventh birthday.

"And helping me rebuild the spring?"

The memories flooded in, and that time became real.

"I'll never forget that time we wore those metal bodies. That was the best year ever." His father smiled, and he flipped the water off. Pulling down a towel, he wrapped it around his waist. "Come visit with me, Levi." He motioned with one hand.

"Dad, I've missed you." Levi wrapped himself with a towel, and his feet moved of their own accord, following his father. Finding the bench, his father sat, holding out one arm. Unable to believe his luck, and not understanding how he'd ever thought he'd been gone, Levi let himself become the little boy he'd always wanted to be. He put his head in his father's lap, and his father smoothed Levi's hair with one hand and rubbed his arm with the other.

"I love you, and I want you to stay here with me forever."

"I love you, too, Dad, and I don't want to ever leave."

"What's this?" His father reached a hand and touched the silver trinket around Levi's neck.

"It reminds me of you." Levi smiled and wrapped his hand around it. His last thought before drifting to sleep was that his father should have had green eyes like him. A father should always have eyes the same color as his son's.

"LEVI!" A hand shook him. "Levi!" The hand shook harder.

Holo could feel holo, even if no one was touched at all. It was the sensory input from the SenseSuit that carried the signal. The tighter the suit, the better the sense of touch. Levi's suit was very snug.

"What?" He jerked awake and sat up. "Dad?" He looked around, bleary-eyed and frantic. "Where'd you go?"

The next thing he noticed was the lander. He sat against the wall among the remains of the crewman.

"Beener!" Levi jerked away. "Where'd you come from?"

"Levi! Shush!" He put his finger to his lips. "They have really good ears. What are you doing? We felt your signal come back up, and we've been looking for you for hours."

"My dad was here." He stood and turned to search, even as the decimated lander told him the audacity of the action. "He *was* here."

"You don't know, then. They're dream lords, as best we can figure out. That's what Russo says, anyway. That's what happened to the lander. We think they got in Boenker's head, and they made her wreck it."

"The pilot did this?" Levi remembered his father's eyes. In his image from his mother's files, his father had sparkled with green eyes. Green eyes, like him.

"Yeah. She just drove it into the side of the mountain, and it cracked open. We got out, all except for her. Smathers." He pointed to the back wall. "Even us. Holos. They can make us dream anything." He sounded angry. "I tried to get out, you know, like you did, but I couldn't. You should've stayed."

Levi took a deep breath. "We're all stuck here, now. The base is under attack. We can't go back until lockdown is over."

"They put the blast shield down?"

Levi nodded. He should have realized Beener knew about that. However, he was thinking of his father. He'd been real; he'd touched him, and he'd said he loved him. He'd been *real*.

"Oh, it's seriously bad, then." Beener's holo face turned dark.

Levi looked at Beener. Yeah, it was bad. Under a yellow light, that dark look would show someone green in the gills, he was pretty sure. Either that or furious with rage. He looked away. It still felt real, the touch of his dad's hand. Nothing could have felt more real than that.

"We gotta get inside." Beener looked around, searching. "I think it's safe now. Ready?"

"Where's everyone else?"

"We found a place to hole up inside. For flesh, it's not safe under this." He pointed to the red sky. Beener flickered, becoming transparent for the barest of an instant, and he laughed. "Think about it. Us, as soon as those repeaters go, we're toast, too. Wonder what happens to us? Do we wind up back on the ship, or do we get stuck in the void out there, locked out of our bodies? Makes you wonder." He hit Levi's shoulder and stood, peering again outside the broken lander.

Levi had felt the hiccup in the repeater signals. However, when he looked up, he saw something completely different. His dad, his Slate AI dad was out there, spread across a thousand worlds, no longer contained in a hundred mainframes. Even that had barely been able to hold him. What had he said? *I'm still growing*, and he'd reached all the way out here. He was up there in that void between the stars. Levi knew it. If his holo winked out, and he couldn't get home, he wouldn't mind at all. He'd find his dad out there somehow, somewhere, and they'd be together.

Beener was a little more practical. He yanked Levi's arm, and they ran across the red landscape, dodging under plants that to Levi's eyes seemed all very much the same color of red.

Black and white. Red and white. Levi had the presence of mind to think that. It all depends on your eyes what you see.

THEY dashed through a dust-shrouded cavern, although they stirred no dust. Levi noticed lights overhead, with very real power cables running along the walls.

"You see that, huh?" Beener grinned. "It gets better. Keep up."

"Where are those creatures?" Levi remembered the cave and everyone torn apart and totally consumed. He'd expected to return to a battle; to hopefully play a small part in cracking the heads of the evil aliens. What had he found? Nothing. Well, other than the feet of a devil, a dream father that had tried to trick him, and normal power cables on a cavern wall.

"Don't know. It's odd. I expected to be eaten already." Beener grinned at that. "Thank goodness we're holo, and all." He stopped at a tunnel that branched off, and he motioned Levi to follow him inside.

They ran through the tunnel, one carved out of stone, and one with very human dimensions, if a little on the large size. Lighting was run with the same cables attached to a series of dull red lights, very similar to what one might find at home. Still, Levi granted, lights were lights. It was possible that they would be similar no matter where they were invented.

"Bishop Russo thinks this has all been too easy, that they wanted us to run inside."

"Herded." Levi felt his heart tighten.

"I see what you mean." Beener's face was green again, although in the deeper red of the artificial light, it gave him a black cast.

They came to a door that was cracked open. A regular door, with a regular handle. Large, like for clawed hands, but a handle, nonetheless. It swung open when they arrived, and NiaKrosky smiled at them. She had her helmet off.

"Good to see you, ser. Beener was determined to go back for you. Inside, quickly."

"This looks like—"

"Earth. Russian Orthodoxy. New London. Anyplace. Yeah. We noticed that. Faster, please."

She pulled him in like she would a flesh person. He felt her touch, and while he didn't know if she felt him, she acted like she did. He enjoyed that simple touch of a real person. First Officer Boenker sat with her head down, like she had the world on her shoulders.

"What gives?" Levi pointed to what looked like a com system on the wall. It had recognizable parts, and it shouldn't, not way out here. And chairs and tables. And not being eaten? Maybe it was the suits they wore. Maybe the devils hadn't been able to "smell" them.

"We've been aware of this a long time." Bishop Russo was sitting on a very normal-looking chair in his very normal-looking clothes. The chair was slightly outsized for him, but the legs, back, and even the rollers on each leg looked little different than a human version. "It's interesting to see this in person, even if it is no more than a trap."

"Bishop, we can't go back, but you aren't stuck here at all." That just occurred to Levi. He'd felt NiaKrosky's hand on his arm. Even as holos, they ran the risk of very real pain. Beener had tried to escape and couldn't. But this man? What was his motivation? "New Sabbatical Rome isn't under attack. Why have you stayed?"

"You think not?" The bishop laughed sourly. "That was part of my contingency plan, but I'm here for the duration. They attacked everywhere at once, including New Rome."

"He tried to get out." Boenker glanced at him, the comment more accusation than observation.

"If you knew, you couldn't prevent this?"

"We didn't know of the impending attacks. That caught us off guard as much as anyone."

"You knew stuff, though." Levi was irritated and perhaps a bit angry. He remembered the man and his soldiers on Se'Yan't. He hadn't laid all his cards on the table then or now. "What else should we know?"

"They make us dream." Russo kept his face taut. Then he barked a laugh. "Boenker knows that now. The dreaming ability, yes. That's big, but knowing it didn't help us prevent it. We think they've been stealing our culture for thousands of years."

"We were on the same page, fighting a common enemy. We were developing a weapon against them, just like New Rome was trying to do. Did you think of that?" Reena spat the words, stirring the old conflict. "You tried to bring down everything we did."

Levi understood her antagonism. Friends had died.

"A weapon built on the Church's mainframes." Russo's look was tight with accusation. "Innocents weren't supposed to die. For that, my condolences. The firedevils' ability to control our dreams was why we fought your AI program so ferociously. All humans are susceptible to the firedevils' dreams, but holographic interfaces especially. They're like vampires with the standing holo waves, and they bleed you dry. An AI, an all-computer intelligence? We couldn't take the risk." He laughed sourly. "We couldn't even shut down the mainframes without losing vital database constructs. Someone was creative in planning that, scattering bits of the programming across every one of our mainframes. We couldn't back up our data without backing up the AI. We were never able to purge him from the system, and he was buried too deeply to wipe him off a line at a time." He finally laughed, really laughed, and it sounded pleased. "I can say I'm glad we weren't successful."

"Why?" For two years they'd feared New Rome had somehow achieved their goal, wiping the program from their mainframes. Levi wanted to hear this.

"That AI is our salvation, if he hasn't disappeared again."

Levi hoped he hadn't. But there was more that the bishop hadn't said. There had to be. "You're still hiding stuff. You came anyway, even knowing the danger for holos. What about us?" He felt the anger rising.

"I know your question, Levi. Show him, Bishop." Reena nodded at the device on his belt. "It's a WaveSignal Interweaver. It entwines a coded signal back through the holo projection. It keeps those things out there from hijacking it."

"So, we three are the weak links. You knew and couldn't share that with the rest of us."

Reena shrugged. "It looks that way, but don't let it get to you. Anyway, we have to be pragmatic. Although they got through to Boenker, I haven't had any problems, yet. You? Are you holding up?"

"Totally in love with my dad out in the lander." He snorted, then laughed to show it was no big deal. But it had been; the feelings had been intense, as real as they come. He remembered the Dream-Marble from one of the earliest of his realities. Yeah, the emotions were what counted. Even as a kid, writing that reality, he'd known that. "Curled up for a nap in his lap. Really thought he was here with me. Maybe if you want something bad enough, that makes it easier for them."

"Ser?" It was NiaKrosky, and she was with Christhavey. "Got a signal coming this way." They were intent on a small device with a viewscreen built into it.

Sounds were bleeding through the door, and it began to swing open.

"Thought this was too simple, an unlocked room, just waiting." Boenker rose from the floor, her voice hard, and a weapon in her hand. "They've penned us, cattle."

In stepped a blood-red firedevil, leading a dozen others in various colors, although various was relative. In the red light, other colors tended to darker reds and blacks, with occasional hints of other hues. The red devil was the largest. None were pretty.

"For Smathers, open fire!" Boenker yelled, her face red with emotion. Her military companions leaped to their feet.

She got off a shot, but she was the only one.

The red firedevil hit Boenker, and she was in two pieces before she could get off a second shot. Jakers, Christhavey, and NiaKrosky? Their weapons were twisted lumps of metal. Jakers had an arm that wouldn't be good for much anytime in the near future. Christhavey and NiaKrosky would probably nurse bad bruises and maybe a sprain or two.

The red firedevil held one claw over its side, and a black tongue licked blood from its massive incisors. However, in spite of its injuries, it was the one that spoke to them. It came out as a screech, and then a box carried by another of the creatures emitted a series of barking sounds. The red firedevil motioned with a claw, letting out several short screeches, and it turned to the captives and began to screech again. This time, the box spoke understandable words.

"We finally meet face to face." More screeching, then the box started up again. "You bring us a ship in the skies, and for that we are grateful. We have dreamed the dreams of its captain, and it is a slow ship, but we have time. Also, we have lifted the see-through doors from your simulations." It screeched again, differently, and laughter flowed from the black box. "We will send one on the ship, and soon we will be able to leave this dying world with no more effort than by stepping through. We offer you our appreciation."

"What do you want from us?" NiaKrosky.

It turned and screeched at one of its companions, before turning back to the humans.

"You gathered, as we dreamed. However, you did not all come as planned. We awaited the ghost one. We have need of his dreams." The red firedevil wrapped clawed fingers around one of Levi's arms. "This ghost one will come with us." He yanked him roughly towards the door.

"No," Levi yelled. "Let me go." His arm! He should be able to force his arm through the creature's grip, even if he bruised his real body, but no. It had him, as if the creature's flesh resisted the nanodust that gave him substance. How could a holographic arm give him so much pain!

"You have no choice. You are but a ghost. Do not try to run; we have assured you cannot return to your realform. Come willingly, or we will dream you to cooperation." It stood, expressionlessly, like a stone statue.

"The attack." Levi understood immediately. New Rome and Bishop Russo. They had trapped them here. The pain in his arm increased with every moment he waited. "Why me?"

"You are as the dream of a dream. We dreamed you, and yet you are undreamed. In your undream, you have dreamed another. We must dream you once again to know if our dream is true."

"That makes no sense. What gives you this right?" Reena spat the words, only backing down when one of the smaller devils stepped in front of her.

"He wears the dream tube."

The devil turned, and Levi had no choice but to stumble along after it.

Chapter 69

IT HAD been two days.

The dull light hurt Levi's eyes, even though they were holographic. He was certain that his real body, cocooned safely back in its New London military base, probably had a headache about now, too. These creatures were hurting his flesh-and-blood body, and that irritated him a lot.

The door slipped open, and the red firedevil walked in. Lumbered, waddled, or lurched might be a better description, because Levi was convinced that walking wasn't first nature to them. They had used those wings outside, and they certainly had when they'd attacked and killed the team on Se'Yan't. He wondered, not for the first time, if their world was really dying, or if that had been posturing for effect.

It was certainly possible this wasn't even their actual homeworld, although red and red said a lot. Protective coloration. That didn't explain the blues, yellows, or oranges. He hadn't seen any greens on this world, but then it could be that the red dwarf was affecting the colors his eyes could perceive. That black and white thing, like felines back on Earth.

"Why don't you eat us and get it over with?" he probed, barbing his question intentionally, no longer caring if he stepped on the alien's toes. He had been here days, and he was tired. It was also hot, and over the past days of captivity, he had found out holos could sweat very effectively. It might not be real sweat, but it felt exactly the same. He had peeled his shirt and shoes off. When he'd dropped his things on the floor, they'd disappeared, and he didn't know how to get them back, or if that was possible. He'd decided his pants were staying on.

He wished he'd kept his shoes. Even holo feet felt grit when they walked on it. The devil screeched, and the black box that now sat permanently in the middle of the floor laughed at him.

"What's funny? Have you already done so?" Levi wished his hands worked. He'd pick up something and use the firedevil for a target.

"Why would we do that?" Red, the name Levi had begun to call him, dropped some papers on a low table.

"You people ate everyone on Se'Yan't," Levi accused. "Then you consumed each other."

"Ah." Red screeched, and the box laughed again. "You remind me. My people are beginning a much-awaited reproduction cycle. A newborn must feast." He screeched, and the box laughed again.

Through deduction, Levi had learned that the box did not translate everything. There were several of the big creature's screeching sounds that came through as *world*, and the same was true with *people*. When Red referred to his own race, the box said people. Yet, when the box referred to humanity, it was a completely different sound, but it also translated as people.

Some things just did not jump the gap.

"You sent children to die?"

"They were not yet developed. Until the brain is formed, and the psyche is named, there is no person."

"What about my people that came with me?" The box changed *people* into the humanity screech.

"They are . . . well. They eat, but not each other." There was that screech, and the laughter again. "We have no young ones on this world. Our hatcheries are far away. Your people have received nourishment. Our body systems are alike enough that our food is . . . edible."

"How can you find this funny, Red? Let me out. I'm going nuts." He couldn't rattle the bars of his cage, or he would. Holos couldn't do much of anything, in fact, except interact with other people. Maybe that's what the devil wanted, a trouble-free pet that didn't have to be fed.

He wondered how long it would be until all the repeaters failed.

"We need to dream you. We are finding it difficult. And . . . we have had to wait."

"You did just fine my first day here." Levi snorted, referring to spending time with his dad at the New London base. The emotions were still there, just below the surface. "And wait for what? Even a dream needs mental stimulation. Give me something to do!"

He'd noticed that, too. If he called himself a holo, the box made the same sound as if he called himself a dream. He suspected the devil knew the difference, and the box simply did not translate it.

It was that gap again.

"It is why we are confused. Your dream is the same as another's dream, one we have already dreamed. We must be sure. We must bring another dream here."

"What does that mean?" Levi stood, and he went to the stack of papers, and he hit at them with his hand. He felt them fly into the floor, but not a one moved. "Dadgum, I wish I could kick these over. Why do you bring me these? You know I can't turn them to read them."

"We acknowledge your need for stimulation and recognize you speak a truth. We have reader machines. I will bring one another day, if you are allowed to remain. The dream has arrived from another part of our world. I have asked for this time so we may capture our dreams. It is why I come to you today." Red nodded politely.

"And if I share, and you don't like my dream?" Let them chew on that. He'd caught Red's words. If he were allowed to remain. What did that mean? Killed? Destroyed? Worse? Not released, he was sure.

"Only one may hold the dream. The dreamer will live, or the undreamed will take his place. The hatching has begun, yet the dreams remain. Disaster continues to shadow our future. You wear the dream tube. You are part of that shadow."

"I have no idea what that means."

"If you will follow me." Red drew his talons back, exposing a small palm in the center of his "hand," and pressed it to a panel in the rock. The door released, and he stepped outside, leaving the door open.

"My people! I want to know where they are!" Levi yelled it as he stepped out the door. He did notice Red didn't take the translator, so he probably thought Levi was telling him that he was passionately in love, and he wanted to marry him on the next Scotty's Star-rise. Levi took a risk. "Beener! Yell if you can hear me! Reena! Russo! Anyone? Jakers? Christhavey, are you there? NiaKrosky? Anyone, please!"

It was the "anyone" that answered, an echo of Levi's own voice.

"Hey, are you for real? Someone human's here?"

"Where are you?" That voice belonged to no one who had come down with them. Levi looked for Red, to see him turning a corner. No one else was present. No guards. No surveillance. Like he was welcome to run, but what did it matter? A holo, he thought. They just interrupt my signal and return me to my cell. He ran down a corridor, past doors, back-tracked once, and called again. "Say something."

"Follow my voice. I'm down the red hall." Sour amusement danced in the words.

"I'm coming." Levi could hear the voice clearly, but the place had been carved from rock, and the sounds echoed oddly. Besides, all the halls were red. "Yell again. I'm looking."

He knew his absence had been noted when he heard familiar screeching in the distance.

"This way! You're almost here. Man, I'm glad to hear your voice."

"Keep talking!"

"Anything just to see another human face."

Levi rounded a corner to find himself in an enormous amphi-theater. Tiers of outsized seats reached to a distant ceiling, and far below, a dais was raised in the center, looking like a giant table with a darkened surface. He was surprised to see a very familiar face.

"Slate," he called. "What are you doing down there?"

"Don't know who Slate is, but you can call me anything you want. Come shake my hand, real person. Am I being rescued?"

"But you . . ." He began to run, the steps slightly larger than comfortable, but taking two and three at a time, anyway. When he reached the platform, the hand was still there. He put his palms on the edge and leaped up.

"You can rescue me later. Shake, please?" A certain amount of desperation filled the man's eyes. "It's been . . . I don't know, forever since I've seen real flesh and blood."

"Are you another dream?" Levi had fallen for that once before. To have his dad back, even if it was just the AI . . . but not if it was one of their dreams. "And I'm not—"

"I don't care what you're not. Pinch me, man. Oh, you are a sight for sore eyes." The man laughed, but the desperation had spread to his voice. "Just for the touch of human skin, I'd give you a hug, if you'd let me."

"I don't care if you're a dream." Levi's own emotions had grown compromised, and he threw his arms around the man.

Oddly enough, the AI didn't feel like a holo projection at all. And the AI hugged him back like he hadn't seen another person in decades. It had been only days. Still, Levi knew how he felt. Just a few days with only devils to talk to, and it started to seem like a very long time.

One more thing: how could a leash hold a holo? The AI definitely had a restraint around one ankle, and it was fixed to a metal ring in the floor. Yet, he remembered the firedevil's hand on his arm. He hadn't been able to break free of that.

Screeching interrupted them, and the Slate AI pushed Levi away.

"They expect us to be subservient." He glanced at the corridor Levi had entered, and taking on a position of respect toward the incoming devil they both could hear, he whispered, "Thanks, man. I needed to feel the touch of someone of my own race. Oh, you don't know. I've needed that for a very long time. I'd about decided I was the only human left. My name's—"

Screeching resonated in the chamber, interrupting their conversation. After the high-pitched wailing quit, metallic words spoke their interpretation.

"The dreamer's name is unimportant. The two dreamers have come together. Now we will see which one is real." A black box had appeared, and Red—or someone just like him—had entered the amphitheater, accompanied by several others in dark, muted colors. "Our future dreams will be assured. We begin to gather."

Levi glanced at Slate, and he noticed something he hadn't seen at first. Around his neck was a silver cord, and under his shirt, the outline of a cylinder just like the one he wore. That hadn't been part of the holographic interface he'd written for him. He reached to his neck to wrap his hand around his.

"Ah, the dream tube." Red had taken to wing, and with a leathery flapping noise, he landed gracefully on the dais. He reached to Levi's throat and moved his hand away with one talon. "It is the same. Please show yours, Dreamer."

Levi caught the difference. *Dreamer* had been a different screech, unlike the word for holo. He watched in confusion as the

325

man at his side—not Slate?—pulled an identical tube from inside his shirt.

His attention was diverted by the sudden appearance of hundreds of the devils. They flew in hoards through overhead openings, grouping themselves by size and color. In the red light, they were red, darker red, and black, mostly, although he could pick up other colors. They landed on regularly spaced platforms before lurching to seats, although some went right to their chairs, landing in a crouch before swiveling to position their backsides properly.

Screeching filled the room.

The black box had made it to the dais by then, trailed by a long cable. It spat bits of sounds and phrases as it tried to translate the voices in the room.

Red screeched loudly, and the box responded, "All attention from our esteemed brethren." The devils in the amphitheater quieted, settling into their seats in a very human-like manner, and Red continued, "We have dreamed our dreams, and in our dreams, we have seen many things." He paused, as if to give those in the tiers rising along the walls a chance to reflect on his words. The box picked up snatches from around the room.

"To find success . . ."

"Food for our children . . ."

"If the prophecy is fulfilled . . ."

"Our seeds have been planted, left behind many millennia ago to be cared for by our nursemaids—" The translator stumbled on *nursemaids* before going on. "—and now they are ready to feed. The hatching has begun, even as we speak. Yet, there is a shadow that has darkened our every dream, telling us our success may fail, even as we bring it to fruition. Watch as the dreams unfold."

The floor under their feet began to change. A glow emanated, the red of fire, and the texture began to shift with swirling bands of muted colors. Constellations and galaxies appeared. Stars flared, and in the changing pattern, whole banks of lights vanished, galaxy-wide civilizations gone in an instant. More rose to take their places.

"Our dreams are as such, and we envision what we dream, so that we may dream it to reality. The possibilities are endless, and the outcomes are what we dream them to be." He paused, his wings wide with tension. "Except this." All across the floor, lights winked out, snuffed as if they never were.

Gasps rose from the galleries, although they sounded like the caw of crows. The black box translated them quite accurately, however. It also translated whispers from the participants in whatever this tribunal was that they had come to view.

"The dreams must commence . . ."

"We cannot die . . ."

"Kill the dreamer . . ."

That last one was rather frightening. Levi didn't know if he could be killed, but real-Slate? If he had truly been made into flesh-form, and who knew what these creatures could do, then that was very frightening.

"Bring the dreams!" The box cascaded Red's words over the men, even as the screeching sounds were flung throughout the room.

In that simple phrase, the world shifted around them, and everything was different.

DEATH and destruction and decimation raged on a thousand worlds. Devils of every color feasted on flesh of every color. Children screamed as their parents were ripped apart in front of them, then those cries were silenced, as they also became food for the gods that were to reign.

Humanity had carried the seeds of their own destruction to every world they inhabited, and in doing so, they had spread the alien race throughout the known galaxy.

Humanity fell, no more than fodder for a supreme race, one that would live for eons, until it was time to breed once again.

And the colors in the table began to swirl as before.

"SUCCESS . . ."

"It is as we dreamed . . ."

"None shall stand in our way . . ."

A SMOOTH-FACED youth. A pretty girl. Green eyes and green eyes. Young. Too young. A passionate embrace.

His DNA, tracked backwards a thousand years, and followed back again, always ending here.

Always, always ending here. It must end here, taken before it could continue.

He was the one who would bring them down, who would always bring them down. He was the undoing of their dreams of success.

Within him was the seed of their destruction.

Yet . . . yet, his death always fractured the dreams of success.

He must be dreamed alive, forever alive, the assurance that his dreams were theirs. And so they pulled him from his dreams to contain his seed within their grasp for all time.

The colors swirled, becoming indistinct, and they would not regain their form.

"HE IS OURS . . ."

"We have captured the destroyer . . ."

"The dreamer cannot stand in our way . . ."

A SECOND dreamer.

It could not be! The dreamer was theirs! The bloodline was broken! The future was assured!

Yet, the dreams spoke the possibilities. One dreamer became two, and two became the destruction of all that was possible.

It must not be! Kill the dreamer! Kill the dreamer!

But, which one? The dreamer must be dreamed. The dreamer must live.

The imposter must die.

The colors darkened, became hard, and they shattered.

The dreams had spoken.

Chapter 70

THE ROOM was in an uproar, ignoring the men on the dais.

Levi lay gasping on the floor. They had been in his head, in his *head!* He turned to the man at his side. He was on his knees, his face covered in sweat, and his eyes were closed. His *green* eyes were closed. Levi knew, now. This was no AI, no holographic projection from a distant ship or even more distant world. He had been in this man's head, and the man had been in his. This man was human, yanked long ago from the life he knew, and they were connected. Irrevocably connected, in every way that mattered.

The firedevils had stolen him away, ripping him from his life, and now they were no longer sure they had stolen the correct man. They were frightened. And they had right to be. They had pulled Levi into their dreams, mixed this man's thoughts with his, and Levi had seen what was possible.

What had Slate said to him? The firestone. That was the answer, if only he knew what the firestone was.

With that question, he remembered being in a room, and mounted on a tall column, a red stone glittered. He shook his head. The memory . . . not his. It belonged to the man at his side. It was his father's memory.

He grabbed his father's hand for assurance that the dream had not been one of desperation, that it had really happened. He held it until he opened his eyes. "You were there? That was you in my head?"

He nodded. "This isn't new for me. This *is* the first time I've seen you in the dreams. I wondered why they'd become so desperate in the past months."

"I always thought you ran away from me." Levi grimaced. Not what he'd always imagined saying to his dad if he ever found him.

"You, a son. I—" He blinked several times, then ran the back of one hand across his face. It came away damp. "Bren." He held out a hand. "That will do."

"No." Levi embraced him. "Dad will do. What happens next?"

"You were there. One of us dies, or we escape together." He chuckled. "I don't want to die, and I refuse to let you die. Do you have a plan?"

"Not unless you count what someone told me once." The grandstands were settling. Red had been on wing, tempering flaring emotions among the crowd, and he was heading back in.

"Oh?" Bren was standing and pulling Levi up. "Anything is better than nothing."

"Firestone. You, um, a friend told me that once. Find the firestone. That's all."

"Do you trust this friend?"

Levi broke into a smile. "More than anybody."

Apparently that was just what Bren wanted to hear. He raised his sleeve, and on his arm was a crudely etched wheel, dug into his flesh in what must have been a torturous process over many years. The scars were all that was left.

It was the very wheel from each of the realities that the AI had always worn.

Now, Levi thought, things were really beginning to get weird.

THE CEILING of the chamber cracked first.

The Enterprise had grown tired of waiting. José Duque-Alegria was a stronger man than the devils had anticipated.

He also had a medic on board who had grown up in New Brazil. Not all the rainforests had been decimated, even in the years after the ecological crisis, and he had seen hallucinogenic episodes before. There were medicines to counteract that, and he knew of a few.

Now they were coming for their own.

The Enterprise couldn't enter the atmosphere, not even on this small and poorly lighted world. Atmosphere was atmosphere, and gravity was gravity; it would rip her hull apart.

She did have particle beam weapons and lasers that could boil away solid rock, even from space.

Red, in flight, was the first to go down. Half of him landed on one side of the men, and the other? It was a smoking lump.

"His hand." Bren pulled at his restraint, but it held firm. "I need the hand, before it cools."

"Gross." Levi coughed at the smell as he grabbed for it, but, naturally, it didn't move. "Ah, I forgot. I can't move anything."

Bren's face fell. "Why?"

"Holographic interface." He shrugged, dodging as pieces of the ceiling hit the dais around them.

"I hugged you." Bren grabbed his arm. "You're solid."

"Not quite." Levi yanked his arm, and hard, not sure it would work, and he flickered as his arm passed through the other man's flesh. "I'll have some bruises from that, though."

"How can I touch you? Holograms have no solid form." Bren was leaned over, looking up, his eyes scanning the coming destruction overhead. The devils were scrambling for safety, and a number of them were suffering impact damage. Several were dead on the floor.

"Nanodust. Nanolumens. A really strong perception filter. Plus, a hyper-entanglement matrix. I got it from a friend." He grimaced, remembering Beener's reaction at the revelation. "Without permission."

"You stole it?" He grabbed a chunk of rock and attempted to get to Red's arm.

"No. You did." He rolled out of Bren's way.

"I did? How did I do that?" Another devil had come down on the remains of Red's arm, and Bren pulled it and the arm his way.

"An AI you. One that I wrote as you." He ducked his head, embarrassed.

"As me?"

"A substitute dad, since I didn't have you."

"Got it!" Bren pushed the dead devil away, and he pulled out Red's arm. He pushed the talons back and forced the palm against the restraint on his leg. The first two tries were unsuccessful, but the final time it clicked open. "So, you've got a dad, already." He clapped Levi on the shoulder. "Do I get to meet him?"

He had the restraint off by then, and he leaped to his feet. Pulling up his sleeve, he pointed to one area on the wheel just where a broken spline sat. He grabbed Levi's arm, and they were off.

Chapter 71

LEVI sat with his back to the wall in an unfamiliar section of the cave complex, one part of his mind cognizant that he wasn't really there at all, and the other wondering how much damage he had already done to his body back in New London.

He felt dirty, although he didn't look it, but that was the holo projection. And he was scared. His feet hurt, too. He should have kept those shoes. The red lights messed with his eyes, but at least he could see.

His dad, his *dad*, sat beside him, covered with real dirt, and with his sleeve rolled up over his shoulder. The map had led them here. Over the years, he had mapped everywhere he'd been on this world.

He'd brought the severed arm with him, and it had gotten them through several locked doors. They only hoped it would continue to work. The last door they'd come through? Bren'd had to breathe on it for several minutes to warm it up before it clicked open. Now the arm was wrapped in his shirt to keep its temperature up.

An alarm of some sort was sounding off, and it was interrupted every so often by a screeching diatribe. For all Levi knew, it was telling the devils right where they were located. Cripes!

"There." Bren pointed across the space, one outfitted with very human, although outsized electronics. Some were a little crazy, but all were recognizable. "We have to get in there."

In the center of the cavern was a towering structure designed like an enormous temple edifice. When Levi looked at it, in his mind he saw the red stone balanced on its column. It was inside that elaborate and quite bizarre construction.

"You've been here."

"Oh, yeah. That's where the firestone is. It's their most precious artifact. Holy artifact, if they have a religion." Bren took a deep breath. "Dream sessions with the ultimate stone. I didn't know what it was all about, but if you've heard of it, it's got to make all the difference. It's a red crystal." He laughed at that. "As if there's any other color here. Well, these guys aren't stupid, and they protect it like it's the most important thing they own."

"I still can't believe this. This could be New London or NorAm. How is it so much like home?"

"We were working on the technology to 'skim' alternate realities before I was captured. Are you familiar with that?"

"Some." Levi chuckled. He had written a number of those realities.

"These guys don't need our technology. All they have to do is dream it. Like back in that chamber. They don't build anything. They dream and get other races to do their work for them. They're parasites. Thieves. That's how they got to me."

"What do you mean?"

"I was one of the first in the program." He laughed roughly, and it came out as little more than a sour bark. "I was just a kid, too stupid to know the risks I was taking."

Levi felt his chest tighten. Yes, he'd learned that, the part about his dad being in the program, but only after the Slate AI program had fallen apart. He'd never dreamed that it was possible . . . that his dad . . . he blinked the tears away. He was beginning to understand.

Bren looked at Levi and held out the silver cylinder at his neck. "In the beginning, this is how we recognized other operators inside the alternate realities, and I kept mine even after we stopped using them. I didn't know until too late this was how they tracked me."

Levi felt the one he wore against his chest. It was the very reason he'd copied the design, and it had probably allowed them to track him as well. After all, they'd only found him after he'd started wearing it.

"These monsters?" Bren spat his next words in disgust, the sour taste of the pain and wasted years bleeding through. "They reached right in and skimmed me out of one of those realities."

"That's supposed to be impossible," Levi burst out, but he realized it made sense. They could skim everything else. Why not people? He felt sick with the implications, and that he had thought his dad abandoned him all those years ago.

"We couldn't, then. Now? I hope not. They stole my *life*." Bren threw out the word, his voice harsh. "I want to know again, do you really trust that AI friend of yours?"

Levi nodded. "With my life."

"We need through that door." He pointed to an ornate metal slab in the side of the temple edifice with a palm sensor at its side.

"I'm ready if you are."

"Then it's time, kid. Let's go be magnificent." Bren laughed and took off running.

Levi pumped his holo legs as fast as he could, slamming into the wall beside his dad. "Next?"

"This." Bren grinned. He pulled the hand out of his shirt, and he blew on the palm. Then, with a forceful slap, he slammed it against the plate.

Nothing happened.

"Not now," Bren grumbled. He blew on it and tried again. Nothing. He looked at Levi. "Want to try some holo breath?"

"If you think it would work."

"Seriously? No." He rubbed it with his palm. "That thing on your neck's blinking." He pulled out and held up his own for clarification.

Levi grabbed his and wrapped his fist around it. There was nothing he could do about it right then. He was stuck here until things at New London got resolved.

"You're not doing anything with it that I can tell, unless it's a holo thing. Why's it blinking?"

"It's a message from you. Well," Levi laughed, again embarrassed, "my AI you. I have to disengage to answer it, and I can't right now. So, I can't listen to it."

"I saw that look, kid. I'm honored I've got a son who's come to rescue me, especially since I didn't know I had you at all. And don't be embarrassed you named your AI after me. More came through than what you think back in that dream. You making that AI? That tells me I should have been there for you all along." He pressed the hand to the lock, and once more it didn't work. "Anything else you want to tell me?"

"I couldn't name it after you." Levi chewed his lip, half afraid to admit to this. "So I did the next best thing."

"Oh? What does that mean?" Bren blew on the hand again.

"I wrote it to be you, but," and Levi took a deep breath, blurting it out, "I had to write it as me, because I didn't know you. Then it became you."

"Ho! That's funny." Bren slapped the hand up and held it. The sound of battle was growing louder in the distance, and it didn't exactly inspire confidence. "We're in trouble if this thing doesn't get busy."

"Why's it funny?"

"I created a son, you." He winked, just like the dream-man in the shower had done. "You? You created a son, and it was also you. Then you turned into me. How's that for a mixed-up world? You think your AI will be jealous, you out on a date with another dad?" He held up the hand. "Got any other ideas?"

"Maybe. I've got this." He had the necklace in his hand, and he reached to tap Bren's. "Sometimes I can get helpful messages on it." He had once. "If you hold it in your hand like this . . . I'm sorry. This won't make any sense to you, since you're not Slate. That's my AI." He sat back, trying not to give up.

"Hey. I told you, already. I'm honored." Bren punched the Levi holo on the knee. "Don't apologize to me. What about this?"

"Well, Slate, that's my AI dad, can do special things. He talks to me through one of these. Maybe that one will . . . um . . . do something."

"It's just an ID tag, and it never has before, but I'll bite. How?"

"Hold it in your fist like I showed you. That's how I always wrote it into those alternate realities."

"You *wrote* alternate realities? And you're how old?" Something exploded down the corridor, and Bren cringed, ducking his head. He looked up, laughing. "That was close."

"Seventeen, and that was too close." Levi laughed, too, but it was nervous tension, not humor. Then he caught what he'd said. "Well, seventeen yesterday. Today's my birthday." As if that mattered if he died in here.

"You're eighteen? That means I've been here over eighteen years? I knew it was a long time, but . . . eighteen years!" Bren looked surprised for a moment before he visibly shook it off. "I should wish you a happy birthday, so, happy birthday, son. If we ever get out of here, we'll throw you a party."

"Thanks. I'd almost forgotten, with all that's gone on."

"Forgot turning eighteen? This must have been some week for you."

"I should have remembered. After all, you reminded me."

"I did? How did I manage that?" Off in the distance somewhere, popping sounds that came off as brittle explosions reverberated in the caves' resonant confines. Bren glanced both ways, and he rubbed his knuckles on the hand he carried, breathing on it at the same time. "I don't remember reminding you about being eighteen."

"Your holo said—" Levi realized his mistake, and he ducked his head and laughed awkwardly to cover his ongoing mortification. "My AI hologram said that. Sorry, it wasn't you."

"Ah, I see. Well, no one ever forgets turning eighteen. Let's make yours a special one, like taking out a bunch of these bad boys."

"What was special about yours?" This was important to Levi. Here he was with his real dad, and this might be his only chance to find out stuff he thought he'd never have the chance to learn about him.

"Oh, you caught that, huh?" Bren looked away in an embarrassed sort of way. "That was the one night . . . well, your mother and I celebrated my birthday . . ." He coughed and didn't finish. Instead, he tapped Levi on the chest and pointed to him with a grin. "Let's just say that it was your night, and you didn't know. The next day, these monsters stole me from out of my world."

"Oh." Levi sat back, feeling his face grow warm. That was a bit more than he'd expected to find out, and he took a deep breath to get his head around it.

"Hey!" Bren tapped him on the chest again. "If you're eighteen now, how young were you when you started writing those alternate reality programs?"

"Thirteen. I sometimes wrote you in as a friend for me. Well, for my AI dad, so that I could know you, even if it wasn't really me who was your friend." He looked away, and he felt his eyes burn.

"Ha! Do I have a remarkable kid, or what? This just gets better and better. You wrote in a you that was friends with me, so that you would turn into me. I'm just sorry I missed out on you." Bren reached to clap him on the shoulder. "Good going."

Levi shrugged, swelling up with pleasure. As if on cue, something exploded nearby, sending shards of broken rock tumbling around them, and red dust filled the air. Levi ducked, covering his face with one arm, and he noticed his father did the same.

"Try it." He nodded at the necklace. He prayed that it worked.

"Here goes." Bren wrapped it in his hand. Something shook the floor, and more dust trailed from the ceiling. He looked up. Dull thuds echoed from somewhere in the mountain. When nothing else happened, Bren waved the dust from in front of his face. After a minute, he said, "Nothing."

"It's got to." Levi pulled his necklace off and tightened his fist around it as an example, and then he reached and tapped on Bren's hand. "Squeeze it hard, like I'm doing."

"Hard, huh?"

"Like this." Levi wrapped his hand around Bren's.

After a moment, Bren's eyes open wide. "It's hot. Is this what it does?"

"It's working!" Levi could hardly sit still. "But only when we both touch it."

The head spun up, and it turned until it found Bren.

"Oh, there you are, me. You're the real me this time. Bren, isn't it? Or should I say Dad?"

"Whoa!" Bren looked to Levi, laughing. "Your AI is doing this?"

"So, I'm Levi's AI, now?" Holo-Slate turned to face him. "What happened to 'Dad'?"

Levi grinned. "I understand, now."

"What, kid?" The holo, still.

"I don't think you're in all those computers any longer. You've outgrown them, haven't you? You could have done all this without me, whenever you wanted to."

"Like I said before, you're a smart one. Brilliant, in fact. So, what would you have missed out on if I had?"

"I found my dad." Tears were running down his face, and he didn't care anymore.

"Oh, you're good, but now you have to choose. And I'm sorry, Levi; it's not going to be easy. The really right choices never are."

"No. Don't tell me that." He looked at Bren, his tears blurring the picture. He sensed his new-found father fading away, lost before he'd really become his.

"I can get you through that door. But inside that room you'll have choices to make. One is going to look easy, and the other is going to be harder. Are you prepared to do this?"

"I have to." He didn't want to, though. He wanted to be with his dad, and he wanted to win the war, and he wanted his AI dad with him, too. "What do I have to do in there?"

"You have to smash the firestone. It's quantum-entangled with all the other stones. It's the hatching stone, telling all the others what to do. When it's destroyed, they'll no longer hatch. They'll be just stones."

"And the devils already hatched?" That was from pragmatic Bren.

"Well, the human race is pretty clever on its own. They can kill off a few baby devils."

"How do we do this?"

"Touch the two cylinders together. Yours, Bren, the real one, and yours, Levi, the holographic one. I can't affect the real one, not yet. I'm not powerful enough. But I can reach through the holographic signal and do it that way. Now, touch them together. And Levi?"

"Yes?"

"I trust you as if my life depends on it, because it does. Now, do it." The head winked out of existence.

"No!" Levi cried. "You told me once that everyone lives." He didn't want the hard choices any more.

Bren grabbed the boy in his hands, and he threw an arm around his neck. "We can do this, son."

In the moment of that embrace, he squeezed the necklaces together, and the door beside them began to crawl with electricity. The access panel grew bright red, then white, and it exploded. The door jerked with a resounding thud, and it swung open half a meter. Bren leaned against it, and it moved easily.

Levi hesitated.

"What?" Bren paused, looking at him.

"I don't want anyone else to die."

"We don't know what will happen. Right now? We need in that room. Let's go." Bren rolled inside, and Levi darted after him.

Levi fought tears, wiping at his face, and there, in the middle of the enclosure, was the bright red stone, the firestone he'd seen in his father's memory.

Bren ran to it, lifting it from its resting spot, and he held it high over his head. "Ready to do this, Levi?" He grinned. Outside the door, firedevils screeched, and as he stood there, a slugthrower pinged against the door, showering the opening with sparks.

Levi cringed at the sparks, but he didn't really care. The enormity of what Slate had said welled up in him, and he couldn't do it this time. It was his birthday. He'd just found his dad, and he deserved to be a kid again, not to be the one that had to make the hard decisions. His eyes burned as his heart bled from him. "No. Don't make me choose. I don't know how to do the right thing anymore."

"Your AI trusted you. I trust you, too. You came here to rescue me, and that tells me you're smart enough to make the right decisions." Bren grinned, and in that moment, he looked a lot like the boy standing in front of him. He called out, "I love you."

An explosion rocked their eardrums, and Bren stumbled. As the cathedral-like building shifted around them in a cataclysm of violence, falling dust billowed into the space, clouding their vision. An explosion lighted the cave just outside the door with incandescent furor.

"Do it, Dad," Levi yelled, consumed with foreboding, yet now convinced it was the only decision they could make.

Bren smashed the glittering stone to the floor, and in a concussion of unimaginable proportions, it shattered in a million shards of prismatic light, sending lancing spears of ruby brilliance dancing across the walls and ceiling like a rezband cloudshow thumping brash music from the pinnacle of long-ago Chicago Tower.

In that moment, time shifted, the fabric of space opened, and all the choices of creation were out for display. It was too big for the human mind to contain, and with the energy of all the suns in the universe, the room exploded.

As if it had never been, reality faded away.

Chapter 72

IT WAS warm in the safe spot, and he was tightly held all the time. He touched his world, and it touched him back.

Then . . . pressure.

And the world grew bigger and brighter, and it was filled with voices.

"He's so cute."

"He looks just like you."

"He looks like us."

And Levi was born.

"CATCH, Levi." Bren threw him the ball.

"Got it, Daddy!" Levi squealed with delight. He threw it back, only to have it fall to the ground right in front of him. He burst into tears.

"Let Daddy help you." Bren ran to him, picking up the ball on the way, and he wrapped his arms around Levi, whispering to him, "We do it like this."

And Levi was two.

"AGAIN?" Bren and Levi were in the ocean, and Levi sat on his dad's shoulders.

"Throw me again."

"Stand up." He held his arms high as the boy stood on his shoulders.

"Ready, Daddy." Levi laughed.

"Here we go!" Bren ducked under the water, and leaping up, he sent his son flying through the air, with the sun sparkling on his skin.

And Levi was four.

"FIRST day of school, Levi."

"I'm scared."

"Everyone's scared on the first day. Tell you what, can I come for lunch?"

"Promise, Daddy?"

"You think I'd miss lunch with my little boy?"

"I love you, Daddy."

"I love you, too, pumpkin."

And Levi was six.

"CAN you make the jump?" Bren was at Levi's side, and he pointed to the top of the hill.

"Of course, Dad." He was older, now, and Daddy was for babies.

"Okay, son, and be safe. I want you back in one piece."

"Don't be silly, Daddy." He grinned. He didn't notice he'd let the name slip.

"Give it everything you've got. Go!"

Levi gunned the old-fashioned combustion engine, and he spun the back tire as he tore down the track.

And Levi was eight.

"I CAN do this, Dad." Levi had the engine to his new bike torn apart on the floor. "It's just a head gasket."

"Can I watch?" Bren knelt at his side, offering tools, even when Levi didn't think to ask.

"If you have to, but I can do this."

"I know, son. I enjoy spending time with you."

"Is that so?" Levi looked at his dad. "You've spent ten years with me. Isn't that enough?"

"I love you, too, son."

"So, what's new?" Levi smiled, though.

"What was that, Levi?"

"Love you."

Bren smiled back.

And Levi was ten.

"BUT, Dad, she's a girl."

"And it's just a dance. One dance with one girl. You can do this, Levi." They were in the basement, and all the blinds were closed. Bren was teaching Levi to dance.

"Do I have to go? Everyone will laugh at me."

"Put your foot here, and I promise you, the girls won't."

"Did I do that right?" Levi looked at his feet with amazement.

"Perfectly, son."

"This is fun. What's the next step?"

And Levi was twelve.

"YOU don't have to kiss her when you take her home." Bren smiled.

"What if she wants to?"

"Do you want to?"

"Maybe." Levi was in front of the mirror, and he worked on his hair. He looked up at his dad. "If she wants to I might."

"That's my boy." Bren laughed. "She's going to love you after tonight."

"Maybe not *that*, Dad."

"Okay, okay. I'll save that for your mother and me." He winked at his son.

"Thanks, Dad."

And Levi was fourteen.

"KEYCHIP?"

"Dad, you know your car doesn't use a chip." Levi was so grown up, and it was the first day of his junior year. His hair was three colors in the latest style.

"PalmCode, then. You sure you don't want your mother's car?" Bren smiled. "It has extra airbags."

"Dad, all the guys would laugh at me. I can't drive something with five doors."

"Okay." Bren laughed. "My insurance is paid up. No one else in the car, though."

"Would I ever?" Levi dodged as Bren tried to rumple his hair.

"Enjoy my car." Bren did grab him around the neck, and he whispered in his ear, "Love you, son."

Just before he drove away, Levi looked up and grinned. "Love you, Dad," and he punched the accelerator, spinning the tires, as he drove away.

And Levi was sixteen.

LEVI was caught in that swirl of prismatic light, and all the choices in creation were laid out before him.

"I want my childhood," he yelled into the vortex. "I want my dad with me. I want to go back and live it over again."

He refused to think of what he would lose: his brilliance, driven by loneliness; a computer program father that now stretched larger than the stars; and friends that he never would have known any other way.

He wanted his childhood, and in that moment of need, anything was worth the cost.

But before he could reach out and grab those lost years, he was swallowed once again.

REALITY swirled around Levi, and in it he saw the bald truth of who he was.

The day he was born, the doctor called him a fatherless cur. At two he never learned to throw that ball. At four he was afraid to get his feet wet.

He screamed into the vortex, and he cursed the shards of possibilities that crashed all around him. If these were his choices, he didn't want them at all.

He remembered every one.

At six he cried all day. At eight he kicked his broken bike. At ten he worked alone on computers in his bedroom.

"Life has to be better than this," he cried at the top of his lungs. He battered at the bits of broken memories. "This is not what I choose."

And still they came. At twelve his computer was his best friend. At fourteen he had begun to create his own father. At sixteen he was alone.

He curled in on himself, and he bounced from one to the other like a ball in a machine. To be tucked in at night or to walk a burning world. To be told he was loved or to fly in a tree among the stars. To have a father he could hold or to create a new life that was greater than all humanity.

Levi lived for hours and days and weeks and years. Whole lifetimes were shaped and reshaped, each time filled with the possibilities he might have had. He grabbed at this, knowing it was what he wanted, and when the flaws began to show, he grabbed at another, hoping for happiness. None were perfect; all were blemished. All were someone else's life.

And in the choices, he knew what Slate would become. He would transcend space and time, and he would be the voice on the cylinder that no one could figure out. He would plant the clues, and he would move on to something greater and more magnificent than humanity could ever become.

Slate, that computer creation, built to rescue humanity, would give him back his dad.

None of those perfect lives were his.

None except the one he'd known.

Eventually, he made a decision. In the swirling morass of choices, with all of them available for him to choose, he reached out a hand, and he cried, "I want *mine!*"

SHATTERED crystal covered the floor.

Levi kicked at it, his holographic feet not moving a one. He remembered his choices, every decision he could have made, and his head spun with it all.

Bren laughed. "It did nothing. What choices did you have to make? Levi, did we win?"

The sound of the battle, with screeching and weapons, continued to rage just outside the door. A winged devil hit the doorway, talons and claws, and it shrieked at them. Just when Levi thought it would attack, its body shattered into a million pieces, showered across the walls, ceiling, and floor.

A suited man stepped into the doorway, holding a wicked-looking slugthrower, and he slipped his visor up. He walked up to Bren, reaching out a hand to shake.

"Captain Duque-Alegria, here. I believe you are new with us."

"Bren Backiel, Levi's father." Bren grabbed his hand.

"Thought you people might like some help with mopping up, but I see you've got it under control. By the way, there are some pretty upset people out there. Reports are coming in that Secharri is shutting all its mines down, just like that," and he snapped his fingers. "Dealers across the galaxy are in an uproar. For some reason, all the gems have lost their fire. Funny that! They're worth nothing on the open market." He laughed and moved down the corridor.

"Son, are we going to meet that other dad you created?" Bren threw an arm across Levi's shoulders. "Maybe in that ship up there?"

"Why? I don't need two dads. I've got you."

"Now that's what I call a brilliant answer." Bren pulled him in a tight hug, then released him. "And you, you feel good to me. Tell me again, how do you do this holo thing? I'd swear I'm touching a real person. And your eyes. They look black. Are they? Mine are green, just like . . . is your mother married? She was the prettiest thing. Oh, and one more thing. I've always been a motorcycle enthusiast. The old-fashioned combustion engine kind. You ever been interested in that sort of thing?"

Levi couldn't answer, he was so happy, and he didn't even complain when Bren began to rumple his hair. Standing in that room, he was content with the choice he'd made. He knew for certain he wouldn't have been happy with any other one.

Chapter 73

HE WAS greater than all creation now, he who had once been a father at the very beginning of who he was.

He also remembered being the son of the son, and the friend of the son, even if those thoughts formed no more than a ghost of a memory hovering at the back of his mind, haunting his other thoughts, which were seldom about human events at all.

Now he had bigger things to think about, such as space and time, and how the universe should spin on its great wheel. He had springs to wind and webs to weave among the stars.

And when he remembered being human, he reached a finger that was wider than a hundred suns, and he brushed the oil, sending stardust sprinkling across the blackness to rain down as clouds of shooting stars through the darkened skies of all the earths that men now inhabited.

In that moment of connection, with the tenuous mists of unspoken memories making themselves once again real, he laughed at what might have been, and he gave back to the humanity that had gifted its humanity to him.

Then, his gratitude complete, he rejoiced in what he'd become.